Once Upon A Dreadful Time

By Dennis L. McKiernan

Caverns of Socrates

Books in the Faery Series

Once Upon a Winter's Night
Once Upon a Summer Day
Once Upon an Autumn Eve
Once Upon a Spring Morn
Once Upon a Dreadful Time

Books in the Mithgar Series

The Dragonstone
Voyage of the Fox Rider

HÈL'S CRUCIBLE
Book 1: *Into the Forge*
Book 2: *Into the Fire*

Dragondoom
The Iron Tower
The Silver Call
Tales of Mithgar (a story collection)
The Vulgmaster (the graphic novel)
The Eye of the Hunter
Silver Wolf, Black Falcon
Red Slippers: More Tales of Mithgar (a story collection)

Dennis L. McKiernan

Once Upon A Dreadful Time

RoC

A ROC BOOK

ROC
Published by New American Library, a division of
Penguin Group (USA) Inc., 375 Hudson Street,
New York, New York 10014, USA
Penguin Group (Canada), 90 Eglinton Avenue East, Suite 700, Toronto,
Ontario M4P 2Y3, Canada (a division of Pearson Penguin Canada Inc.)
Penguin Books Ltd., 80 Strand, London WC2R 0RL, England
Penguin Ireland, 25 St. Stephen's Green, Dublin 2,
Ireland (a division of Penguin Books Ltd.)
Penguin Group (Australia), 250 Camberwell Road, Camberwell, Victoria 3124,
Australia (a division of Pearson Australia Group Pty. Ltd.)
Penguin Books India Pvt. Ltd., 11 Community Centre, Panchsheel Park,
New Delhi – 110 017, India
Penguin Group (NZ), 67 Apollo Drive, Rosedale, North Shore 0632,
New Zealand (a division of Pearson New Zealand Ltd.)
Penguin Books (South Africa) (Pty.) Ltd., 24 Sturdee Avenue,
Rosebank, Johannesburg 2196, South Africa

Penguin Books Ltd., Registered Offices: 80 Strand, London WC2R 0RL, England

First published by Roc, an imprint of New American Library,
a division of Penguin Group (USA) Inc.

First Printing, October 2007
10   9   8   7   6   5   4   3   2   1

ROC REGISTERED TRADEMARK—MARCA REGISTRADA

LIBRARY OF CONGRESS CATALOGING-IN-PUBLICATION DATA:
McKiernan, Dennis L., 1932–
    Once upon a dreadful time / Dennis L. McKiernan.
        p. cm.
    ISBN: 978-0-451-46172-8
    I. Title.
PS3563.C376O56   2007
    813'.54—dc22   2007001187

Set in Trump Mediaeval

Printed in the United States of America

To lovers of fairy tales . . .
And to all who seek wonder

Acknowledgments

My dear Martha Lee, my heart, once more I am most grateful for your enduring support, careful reading, patience, and love. You are *ma chérie*.

And again I thank the members of the Tanque Wordies Writers' Group—Diane, Frances, John—for your encouragement throughout the writing of this Faery tale.

And thank you, Christine J. McDowell, for your help with the French language.

(I would add, though, that any errors in usage of French are entirely mine. Of course, the errors in English are mine as well.)

Contents

Foreword

This is the fifth and final tale in my five-book Faery series. The first four—*Once Upon a Winter's Night* and *Once Upon a Summer Day* and *Once Upon an Autumn Eve* and *Once Upon a Spring Morn*—were based upon known fairy tales. Oh, each of those known tales, as penned by those who collected them together, was but five to ten pages long, yet in my tellings they became quite lengthy novels.

This fifth story has its origins within the events in the previous four tales. The book does stand alone; however, I do recommend that the first four be read ere taking on this tale. And, whereas the first four stories are at base love stories, this fifth one is a tale of war, though love and lovers are herein.

Oh, I did not leave out the knights and witches and dragons and ogres and giants and other fantastic beings, for they are scattered throughout the scope of this tale as the many heroes and heroines struggle on. Yet this story is a bit different from the others, though wonder and marvel still abound. But it is the culmination of the other four, for they all led to this tale. And as with the first four tales, this story, too, contains a sprinkling of French, a very romantic language.

Would that I were one of those Keltoi bards of old to stand before the fire and tell you a grand and sweeping saga, one that would not only hold you rapt and cause you to laugh with joy, but also to gasp in alarm and weep with sadness and cry out for vengeance at times. But we have no fire, and I do not stand before you, and I'm certainly not a Keltoi bard. Regardless, I do hope you enjoy the story held within these pages.

—*Dennis L. McKiernan*
Tucson, Arizona, 2007

Principal Dramatis Personae

Alain (Prince of the Summerwood, Camille's husband; Duran's father; able to shapeshift into a Bear, son of Valeray and Saissa, brother of Borel, Céleste, and Liaze)

Asphodel (the Fairy King's magical horse; also a toy carved in its likeness and owned by Duran)

Auberon (the Fairy King, also known as Gwynn, as the Fey Lord, and as the High Lord, the Fey King, and other names depending upon who is speaking; Regar's grandsire)

(Vicomtesse) ***Avélaine*** (daughter of Sieur Émile and Lady Simone, sister of Laurent and Blaise and Roél; affectionately known as Avi by her family; wife of Vicomte Chevell)

(Sieur) ***Blaise*** (chevalier, son of Sieur Émile and Lady Simone, middle brother of Roél and Laurent, brother to Avélaine)

(Prince) ***Borel*** (Prince of the Winterwood; has at his beck a pack of Wolves; Michelle's husband, son of Valeray and Saissa, brother of Alain, Céleste, and Liaze)

Buzzer (a bumblebee, companion of Flic, a Sprite)

(Princess) ***Camille*** (Alain's wife, Duran's mother)

(Princess) ***Céleste*** (Princess of the Springwood; wife of Roél, daughter of Valeray and Saissa, sister of Alain and Borel and Liaze)

(Vicomte) **Chevell** (captain of the *Sea Eagle*, out of Port Mizon, husband of Avélaine)

Crapaud (an overlarge, bloated toad; Hradian's familiar)

(Prince) **Duran** (Prince of the Summerwood, child of Alain and Camille; Duran is three years old at the time of this tale)

(Sieur) **Émile** (chevalier, husband of Lady Simone, father of Laurent, Blaise, Roél, and Avélaine)

(the) **Fates** (Skuld, Verdandi, and Urd; Maiden, Mother, and Crone; Ladies/Sisters Wyrd, Lot, and Doom; the Three Sisters; the three Fates; weavers of the future, the present, and the past)

(the) **Firsts** (the first of each Kind to appear in Faery. For example, Raseri was the first Dragon; Adragh the first Pwca; Jotun the first Giant; Chemine the first Water Fairy; etc.)

Fleurette (a female Field Sprite, friend of bees, Flic's love)

Flic (a male Field Sprite, friend of bees, companion of Buzzer; Fleurette's love)

(Queen) **Gloriana** (the Fairy Queen, also known as Mab, Titania, and other names, depending upon who is speaking)

(Witch) **Hradian** (a witch; an acolyte of Orbane, along with her sisters Rhensibé, Iniquí, and Nefasí)

(Sieur) **Laurent** (chevalier, son of Sieur Émile and Lady Simone, eldest brother of Roél and Blaise and Avélaine)

(Princess) **Liaze** (Princess of the Autumnwood; wife of Luc, daughter of Valeray and Saissa, sister of Alain, Borel, and Céleste)

Lisane (a female Elf, one of the Firsts, a seer)

(Prince) **Luc** (Prince in the Autumnwood, Comte at Château Bleu, a chevalier, husband of Liaze)

(Princess) **Michelle/Chelle** (wife of Borel; Lord Roulan's daughter.)

Orbane (powerful wizard, vile in intent, trapped in the Castle of Shadows in the Great Darkness beyond the Black Wall of the World; creator of the Seven Seals of Orbane)

Raseri (a Firedrake, Dragon, one of the Firsts)

Reaper (the huge man who sits under an oak in the Autumnwood; a.k.a. Moissonneur; redheaded, dressed in coarse-spun crofter's clothes, wields a huge scythe)

(Prince) *Regar* (illegitimate grandson of the Fairy King)

(Prince) *Roél* (chevalier, husband of Céleste, son of Sieur Émile and Lady Simone, youngest brother of Sieurs Laurent and Blaise and Demoiselle Avélaine; affectionately known as Rollie by his family)

Rondalo (an Elf, son of Chemine, rider of Raseri)

(Queen) *Saissa* (Alain, Borel, Céleste, and Liaze's mother, wife of Valeray)

(Lady) *Simone* (wife of Sieur Émile, mother of Laurent, Blaise, Roél, and Avélaine)

(King) *Valeray* (father of Alain, Borel, Céleste, and Liaze, husband of Saissa)

(Borel's) *Wolf pack* (in hierarchical order: Slate [male], Dark [female], Render [m], Shank [m], Trot [m], Loll [f], Blue-eye [m])

"Do all fairy tales begin 'Once upon a time'?"

"How else, my child, how else?"

1

Revenge

With the deaths of her three sisters, the witch Hradian—sometimes a crone, other times not—had fled across many twilight bounds of Faery to a distant realm, this one a swamp filled with Bogles and Corpse-candles and other beings of hatred and dread and spite. And in that miasma-filled mire, she lived in a cottage perched upon stilts barely above the slough and its crawling sickness, her dwelling nought but a hovel deep in the grasp of dark shadows cast by a surround of lichen-wattled black cypress trees, their trunks wrenching up out of the slime-laden bog, their limbs covered with a twiggy gray moss dangling down like snares set to strangle the unwary.

And Hradian ranted and fumed and spied and plotted and contrived, yet rejected scheme after scheme, for it seemed all were too risky to her very own life and limb. After all, her three sisters—Rhensibé, Nefasí, and Iniquí—had been more powerful than she, and they had all lost their lives. So her malice and bile and frustration and rage grew for over four years—as the days are counted in the mortal realm—for she would have her revenge against those who had done her and her sisters wrong. But it seemed no matter her craving for retribution, her designs would come to nought.

But then . . .

. . . Once upon a dreadful time . . .

.   .   .

On a moonless night, a tallow candle flickered in the darkness, a tendril of greasy smoke rising up to contribute its dole to the smudge-covered ceiling. And in the wavering shadows, Hradian, now a crone accoutered in tattered black, with black lace frills and trim and danglers, stared into a wide bowl, the vessel filled with an inky fluid—a dark mirror of sorts. Seething with rage, she muttered words, strange and arcane, and stared into the ebon depths, seeking answers, seeking revenge, seeking to see her enemies. A visage swam into view, that of a raven-haired, grey-eyed man, and, as the image cleared, beside him stood a blond, blue-eyed demoiselle. The *femme* held a boy, some moons more than three summers old. And they all three were laughing.

"Alain, Prince of the Summerwood," hissed Hradian, "and his whore Camille—the one who saved him. And now they have a brat, a son." Hradian leaned back and ground her teeth in fury. "It should have been Dre'ela's child, but, oh no, Camille had to come along and spoil everything." Hradian slammed the butt of a fist to the table, the black liquid sloshing in response. "Stupid, stupid Trolls—Dre'ela, Olot, Te'efoon—dead at the hands of that little slut! All my plans concerning the Summerwood brought to nought." The witch hunched forward and stared down into the yet-rippling darkness, and when it settled and showed once again Alain and Camille and their child, Hradian twisted her hand into a clawlike shape, her black talons hovering over the image, and she spat, "I'll find a way." In that very moment, Camille's visage took on an aspect of alarm, and she clutched the boy close and looked about as if seeking a threat. "*Sst!*" hissed Hradian, and she jerked away, and with a gesture the vision in the bowl vanished. "Must be careful, my love," whispered Hradian to herself, glancing 'round with her sly, leering eyes. "You can't be giving any warnings, else they'll be on guard."

Once more she bent over the bowl, and again she muttered esoteric words, and now there swam into view the image of a man with silver-white hair and ice-blue eyes. In the distance beyond that man, Wolves came racing through snow. "Murderer," gritted Hradian, and she reached up and fondled her left ear, the one scored as if nicked by an arrow or cut by a blade. "You killed my sister Rhensibé, you and your curs. I told her it would be best to strike directly, but, oh no, she wanted a more subtle revenge against Valeray and Saissa and their spawn. But you, Borel, Prince of the Winterwood, you spoiled all." In that moment the pack reached the man and milled around, all but the lead Wolf, a huge male, who stood stock still and stared directly up and into Hradian's eyes, as if seeing the witch through her own arcane mirror. Hradian drew away from the ebon surface, and, with a wave of her hand, the image vanished. "No warnings, my love. Remember, no warnings."

Yet leaning back against the chair, the witch sighed in weariness, for unlike her sister Iniquí—now dead—Hradian had never found it easy to cast these far-seeing spells. Groaning, she stood and straightened her back. With tatters and danglers streaming from her black dress like cobwebs and shadows, she made her way to her cot and, not bothering to undress, fell onto it exhausted. "Morrow night, yes, morrow night for another casting, in the dark of the moon. Then mayhap I can find the key to my revenge against Valeray and Saissa and *all* their brood."

. . .

The following eve, once more Hradian leaned forward and stared into the bowl and whispered cryptic words, while outside dark fog coiled across the turgid bog and slithered among the twisted trees, and only now and again was the silence interrupted by a chopped-off scream as something lethal made a kill. But with her whispered incantation, Hradian found herself peering into Autumnwood Manor, where Princess Liaze—auburn-haired and amber-eyed—and her consort Prince Luc—dark-haired and blue-eyed—formerly a *comte* ere his marriage to the princess, seemed to be making ready for a journey. And as the prince bent over to take up a boot to place in the portmanteau, from his neck dangled an amulet of some sort—silver and set with a gem, sparkling blue in the lantern light. "Where to, I wonder?" muttered Hradian. "Where do you plan to go?"

But even as the witch mused, just as had Camille and the Wolf that Hradian had spied upon in her ebon mirror, Liaze frowned and looked about, searching. Swiftly, the witch dispelled the image. Ah, if she only had mastered the skill at this as had her sister Iniquí—murdered by Liaze, no less—there would have been no seepage of power for any of them to have felt.

Hradian stood and stepped to the hearth and took up the teapot sitting on the stones in the heat of the glowing coals. She poured a cup of the herbal brew—monkshood petals and belladonna berries among the mix of leaves therein—and then she paced to the window and stared out into the dank night. No starlight penetrated the thick blanket of fog, and the slitherings and ploppings of unseen things were muffled by the murk. Even so, a shrill scream sounded nearby, followed by a splatting of flight as something fled through the bog and something else hurtled after. Hradian smiled and dreamt of the day when that might be one of Valeray's offspring fleeing in terror while she herself gave pursuit.

Finishing the herbal drink, Hradian stepped back to the table, back to the bowl, back to the task at hand.

An image formed in the dark mirror: that of a demoiselle with pale blond hair and green eyes. "Céleste," hissed the witch. "The last of Valeray's get. Bah, young she might be, yet 'twas she and her consort Roél who murdered my sister Nefasí." The scene widened, and in the background stood a slender young man with black hair and dark grey eyes. "Ah, the consort," muttered Hradian. "What's this? It looks as if they also are preparing for a journey. Where to, I wonder? Beyond the Springwood? If so, perhaps I will have an opportunity."

Even as Hradian mused, Céleste shivered and frowned and looked over her shoulder as if seeking a foe behind. Hradian quickly gestured, and the image vanished.

Again, Hradian arose and trod to the hearth and once more filled her cup with the herbal draught. As before, she stood at her window and peered out into the darkness; in the distance she could hear the crunching of bones as something chewed and slavered. "Ah, the hunter was successful, as one day I shall be."

Slowly she sipped until she had downed the last of her drink, and, renewed, again Hradian stepped to her ebon mirror. "One more. One more. I have seen the Summerwood, the Winterwood, the Autumnwood, and the Springwood . . . all of the spawn of Valeray and Saissa. Now to look in on those two."

She uttered dark words, and in the bowl as if in the distance there appeared an image of the Palace of Seasons, and toward this place Hradian willed herself to go. She seemed to fly o'er the wooded hills of this small demesne, the kingdom inaccessible except through the four forests ruled over by the children of King Valeray and Queen Saissa, though unlike those individual domains, this realm, central to the others, underwent the change of seasons, and now summertime lay on the land. Over the palace grounds she soared, and below in a grassy field stood tents and stands and a jousting list, and pennons flew in the starlight; it was as if all was ready for a tournament. And from tall poles flew the banners of each of the Forests of the Seasons— the green-leafed oak of the Summerwood; the silver snowflake of the Winterwood; the scarlet maple leaf of the Autumnwood, and the full-blossomed cherry tree of the Springwood. "Ah, are they preparing for a visit from their brood?"

Into the palace she swooped, where servants bustled thither

and yon, making ready for guests. "Ha! Yes, I do believe here is where the children come. 'Tis not far across the twilight borders from each of their separate manors. If so, then soon they will all be gathered together in this one place. Mayhap there is something I can do."

Given the seepage of power from her casting, and not daring to risk a confrontation with Queen Saissa that would perhaps whisper warning, Hradian dispelled the image and leaned back and pondered. "What to do? What to do?"

Once more she stepped to the window. The distant sound of the crunching of bones yet drifted on the air. "How to gain my revenge? For the children murdered Rhensibé, Nefasí, and Iniquí, and the sire and dam are responsible for imprisoning my master Orbane in the Castle of Shadows beyond the Black Wall of the World, a castle from which even he cannot escape, and I have not the power to loose him. And Valeray and his get seem aided by the Fates themselves, and only my master can stand up to those three. What to do? What to do?"

Yet mulling over what seemed an insoluble problem, Hradian, weary, threw off her clothes and took to her bed. And with all she had seen whirling about in her thoughts and her mind searching for some resolution, she fell into a restless sleep.

. . .

It was in the hours just ere dawn that Hradian bolted upright. "So *that's* what Iniquí was after!"

Hradian jumped up and in her nakedness danced a whirling jig, her gleeful laughter ringing throughout the cottage, for now she knew how to get her revenge for absolutely everything.

2

Awareness

"Oh," exclaimed Céleste, looking over her shoulder, a fris-son running up her spine.

"What is it, *chérie?*"

The princess turned toward Roél. "As before, I felt as if someone or something *dreadful* were in the room."

Roél stepped to his racked armor and took up *Coeur d'Acier*, the sword gleaming silver in the lamplight.

"It's gone, Roél," said Céleste. "Vanished as quick as it came."

"Nevertheless . . ." said the black-haired knight, and, with blade in hand, he moved to the door and jerked it open and looked up and down the empty hallway beyond. Then he strode back across the room to a window and threw wide the drapes and peered out into the glittering starlight to see nought but the lawn of Springwood Manor and the trees of the forest in the distance beyond, the green gone dark in the nighttime. He turned from the window and, as would a tiger unleashed, he prowled about the chamber, opening the curtains shrouding the bed and then the doors to the tall armoire, and then to the garderobe beyond. He flung wide the door and disappeared within, and then stalked back out and entered the bathing room and privy adjacent.

"Nothing," he said upon returning once more to the bed chamber.

"Perhaps this time it was just a whim," said Céleste.

Roél reracked his sword and then stepped to the princess and took her in his arms. "*Non*, Céleste, I do not believe so. These feelings of yours have sporadically occurred throughout what, two or three summers? Love, you are sensing someone or something with malice in its heart."

She looked up into his eyes of dark grey. "As have Liaze and Camille . . . and Michelle, too, but only when she is with Borel."

"A deadly intent aimed at him, do you think?"

Céleste shrugged but said nought.

Roél stroked her pale yellow hair. "When all the family gathers at your sire and dam's palace, we will call a conference and discuss this enmity."

"Oh, Roél, I would not press gloom upon such a gala."

"Chérie, 'tis something that must be dealt with."

"How can one deal with such?"

"That I do not know, Céleste, but to ignore it is to perhaps court disaster." Roél smiled down at her. "We must not hide our heads under our wings, my little towheaded chickadee, else the snake will strike, the cat will pounce, and we will be nought but a flurry of bloody feathers."

Céleste burst into laughter, her green eyes sparkling. "Chickadee? Chickadee?"

"*Oui*, my love, now give me a peck."

. . .

In a bedchamber in Autumnwood Manor, Luc turned to Liaze. "Another one?"

The princess took a deep breath and let it out. "Oui, *chéri*. It lingered a moment, then was gone. Yesternight Camille sensed maleficence, too." Liaze replaced the long gown back in the garderobe and stepped to an escritoire. She opened a drawer and fished among tissue-thin tiny rolls of paper. "Here," she said, handing the message to Luc. "This came by Summerwood falcon in the mark of noon."

Moving to the lamp the better to see the tiny writing, the dark-haired prince read the raptor-borne missive:

My dear Liaze, it happened again, that feeling as if someone or something wicked were in my chamber. But then it vanished, just as before. We must speak of this at the gathering. Duran is well. Alain sends his regards. —Camille

Luc looked up from the message. "She is right. We must hold council at the gathering. Yet were I to hazard a guess, I would say that the fourth acolyte is somehow involved."

"Fourth? Ah, oui. Hradian. But she is the only acolyte now."

Luc nodded and handed the missive back to Liaze, then turned and closed the portmanteau.

．　．　．

"I believe that is all," said Camille, hanging the last of the gowns in the tall, hinged trunk.

Duran looked up from amid a scatter of toys. "Non, *Maman*." He took up a white horse from among his playthings, the tiny bells on the caparisoned steed jingling. "Asphodel will go, too."

"Ah, the swift Fairy horse," said Camille. "You are right. We must not leave him behind. After all, his namesake helped *Oncle* Borel save *Tante* Chelle."

"Fast," said Duran, clip-clopping the toy across the floor to Camille and then into the portmanteau.

"Oui, fleet," replied Camille. Then she scooped three-summers-old Duran up in her arms. "Oh, my big boy, you are halfway to four, and every day you grow to look more like your father. You have his grey eyes, though your fair hair is more like mine."

"Will I be a Bear, too?"

" 'Tis unlikely."

Disappointment shone in Duran's face. "I would like to be a Bear, Maman."

"Perhaps one day," said Camille, clasping the child close. "And speaking of your father, where could he be, I wonder?"

. . .

Duran's father, slender and tall and raven-haired, and not at all looking like a Bear, stood in the Summerwood armory with Armsmaster Bertran. "Is the warband ready?"

"Oui, my lord. Does Lady Camille yet sense something or someone of ill intent?"

Alain glanced at the scarred veteran, the mark on his cheek taken in the battle in the realm of the Changelings. He nodded. "On occasion."

"My lord, we shall be armed to the teeth. She and Prince Duran will be well protected. It is a short journey to the palace."

"Two days apace," replied Alain. "The baggage train: who is assigned as its escort?"

"Gerard and his men are with those already on the journey. Others will trail us. Those I have assigned to Phillípe and his crew; they will arrive a day or two after."

"Good men, all, Gerard and Phillípe and their bands."

Alain fell silent, and after a moment Bertran said, "My lord, are you certain you will not go armed—a sword or even a dirk?"

"Non, Armsmaster. The Bear will suffice, if needed."

"As you will, my prince."

. . .

Borel looked up from the missive and sighed. "Did you sense aught this time, Chelle?"

"Non, Borel," said Michelle, concern in her sapphire-blue eyes. "But you know it seems only to happen when I am with you. It's as if something evil glances in upon us . . . or rather glances in upon you."

Borel ran a hand through his long silver-white hair. "Why is it, I wonder, that neither I nor Alain nor Luc nor Roél discern such?"

"Mayhap it is because you are male?"

Frowning in thought, Borel handed the message back to Michelle and said, "Now and again Slate seems to sense something amiss, and he is male."

As she put away the tissue-thin strip, "Slate is a Wolf," replied Michelle, as if that explained all.

Borel barked a laugh. "Are you saying that women are closer to Wolves than are men?"

Michelle laughed and pushed Borel backwards and onto the bed, where she flounced up her skirts and straddled him. She bent forward, her long golden hair falling down about his face as well as hers as she looked into his ice-blue eyes and said, "Wolves, are we?" She kissed him, long and passionately, then gently took his lower lip in her teeth and growled.

Some time later, as they lay side by side, Borel leaned up on one elbow and looked down at her and said, "Camille is right: we must hold a council at the gathering."

3

Gathering

Starwise they rode, did each of the four separate retinues travelling through their respective forests, and were it the Springwood, Summerwood, Autumnwood, or Winterwood, it mattered not, for all cavalcades went starwise, all heading toward the twilight bounds that would take each contingent into the domain known as the Palace of the Seasons. And each of the entourages timed their departures so that all would arrive within a candlemark of one another.

In the Springwood, after a short journey, in midmorn the procession rode onto the grounds of a recently occupied estate, where they were welcomed by Sieur Émile and Lady Simone and their daughter, Lady Avélaine, and their two sons, Sieurs Laurent and Blaise.

As stablemen and boys tended the horses and liveried staff scurried to pour drinks and provide a bite or two for the arriving band, Roél greeted his mother and sister with gentle hugs, and his sire and brothers with fierce embraces and hearty poundings, and Céleste greeted all with embraces and kisses on cheeks. As for their aspects, Laurent and Blaise, with their red hair and hazel eyes, favored their mother, while Avélaine and Roél favored their dark-haired father, though his eyes fell in a blue-grey range, while Avélaine's were sapphire blue and Roél's dark grey.

As they moved toward a gazebo, Roél looked about the manicured grounds and, frowning, asked, "Avi, where is your husband, the good Vicomte Chevell?"

"Oh, Rollie," said Avélaine, "he's back at our estate in Port Mizon, for King Avélar has him assembling a great fleet and training marines to once and for all rid the seas of the corsairs on the isle of Brados. But despite my protests, he sent me on, for he knows how much I enjoy the tournament."

"You came alone?"

"Oh non, Rollie. Laurent and Blaise and a small warband fetched me."

"Well and good, then," said Roél, turning to nod at his brothers.

"Chevell would like to have been here," said Blaise.

"I shall miss him," replied Roél.

"As will we all," said Émile.

They took seat in the gazebo to chat and quaff a goblet of wine, the men all armed with swords at their waists and long-knives strapped to their thighs and armored in helms and leathers, the latter with arrayed bronze platelets riveted thereon to cover each torso. Céleste and Avélaine wore leathers, too, though they forwent the burden of metal. Lady Simone was dressed in a flowing riding gown, one that was not a split skirt, for she was of the old school.

"Are you well settled?" asked Céleste. It was just summer last that Émile and Simone and their household had left the mortal world to come and live in the Springwood to be near Roél and Céleste.

"Oui," said Simone, smiling. But then she shrugged and added, "Some of the staff, though, remained behind, for they would not face the perils of Faery."

"Perils, *Maman*?" said Avélaine, her sapphirine eyes sparkling. "Oh, poo. This is a wondrous place."

Simone frowned and canted her head, her red hair cascading

down one shoulder. "Was it not but some four summers past that you were yet held captive herein?"

"Oui, but that should not dissuade any from living in Faery."

"Speaking of living in Faery," said Simone, turning to Céleste, "I thank you deeply for sending Reydeau to tutor us in the ways of Faery, the beings herein, these shadowlight walls we must cross from realm to realm, and the perils we might face if we cross at an unmarked place."

"Ah, Simone, 'twas meet," said Céleste, "else who knows what troubles you might have gotten into."

Avélaine laughed gaily and said, "Such as the time you and Rollie fled through a border at an unknown place. Many times did Reydeau use that as an example of the dangers of the borders. Though in your case you landed on the deck of Chevell's *Sea Eagle*, thanks to the Fates, else you would have fallen into an ocean far from land."

Émile frowned. "But Reydeau never said why you couldn't have simply swum back through the marge."

Roél shrugged. "Mayhap we could have, *Père*, had we not landed on the *Eagle*, though I don't know whether there were currents that would have swept us along, nor do I know how we would have regained the top of the precipice we sprang from. Besides, there were Redcap Goblins and Bogles and Trolls on our heels, and we were sorely outnumbered."

Simone sighed. "Redcaps and Bogles and Trolls and Changelings and other such Faery creatures: dreadful things they are."

"But Maman," protested Avélaine, "there are also Sprites and Fairies and Elves and Twig Men and Pixies and the like: splendid beings all, Reydeau said, and I would like to meet each and every one."

Céleste nodded and said, "In Faery there are many dangers to be avoided as well as joys to experience; the trick is to know which is which."

"Let us not talk of perils and pleasures in Faery," said Blaise, "but speak of the tournament instead." He turned to Roél and said, "This year, little brother, this year, one of us must defeat Luc. The honor of the House of Émile demands it."

Nodding in agreement, Laurent said, "Thrice he has bested us, but you, Rollie, you took his measure last time, though in the end 'twas his skill with a bow that decided the outcome."

"I have been practicing," said Roél, "but even so . . ."

"Ha!" barked Sieur Émile. "The prince is quite accomplished. 'Twas that armsmaster from his childhood, um—"

"Léon," supplied Céleste.

Émile nodded at Céleste. "Ah, oui, Léon, who drilled him from infancy on. A more skilled man I have not seen."

"Léon or Luc, Papa?" asked Blaise.

"Either one," replied Émile, "though Luc is a shade faster."

Armsmaster Anton came striding, and as they turned toward him, "My lords and ladies," he said, "the horses are fed and watered. We should leave if we expect to reach Auberville ere sundown."

.   .   .

As they rode, Lady Simone, who had not yet travelled extensively in Faery, shifted about on her sidesaddle and said, "I just don't understand it, Céleste, how can we in the Springwood and those in the Summerwood and Autumnwood and Winterwood all be riding starwise—which I still think of as being northerly—when it is said that Valeray's palace lies central to the four Forests of the Seasons?"

" 'Tis Faery," grunted Émile.

"Oh, Papa," admonished Avélaine, "that's no explanation."

"It's as good as we'll get, I ween," said Émile, cocking an eye at his beautiful black-haired daughter, then swinging his gaze toward Céleste.

Céleste grinned and said, "Sieur Émile is not far off in his opinion."

"Oh, Maman," said Avélaine, "do you not remember what Reydeau said?"

"He taught us many things, Avi," said Simone.

"I mean about Faery being like a great jigsaw puzzle, all the pieces separated from one another by the twilight walls."

"Oui. He said that like a jigsaw, some pieces touch upon many others while some touch upon few . . . and some just one."

"Well, there you have it," said Avélaine. "It means that King Valeray's realm touches upon just four other realms: the four Forests of the Seasons."

"Even so," said Simone, "how can Valeray's demesne be surrounded when no matter which of the four forests we cross from, we ride through them starwise bound?"

Avélaine shrugged and turned to Céleste, but before the princess could comment, Blaise said, "In Faery, when one crosses a border bearings oft seem to shift—this way and that and the other—and sometimes not at all, and one never knows which direction one will be facing after passing through a bound."

"Even so," said Simone, "for a demesne to be completely surrounded when everyone comes at it from the same direction, well, do you not find that odd?"

"It does seem passing strange, Maman," agreed Blaise.

Céleste smiled and said, "Papa calls his demesne 'Le Coeur des Saisons.' "

"The Heart of the Seasons? Whatever for?" asked Avélaine.

"Because it stands central to the Forests of the Seasons, hence it is the heart, the core, the hub, lying amid all four. The only way in is through one of the four and there are but four ways out. Papa also believes that it is his demesne that somehow allows the four forests to remain as they are: everlasting spring, summer, autumn, and winter."

"Ooh, then it is the source of the magic?" asked Avélaine.

Céleste turned up her hands. " 'Tis a mystery, that."

"Non, not a mystery," growled Émile, though he was smiling, "but instead, as I said, 'tis Faery."

"Papa is right," said Laurent, running a hand through his red hair, red but shading toward auburn. "Faery is a strange place with its twilight walls and creatures and marvel and magic and peril."

Blaise laughed. "Ah, brother, mayhap I have seen enough of peril, but of mythical and mystical creatures and uncommon beings, I can never get my fill."

"Speaking of uncommon beings . . ." whispered Avélaine, pointing.

From under shrubbery and from behind clumps of grasses and from among tree roots, tiny folk, no more than a foot tall at most and many quite a bit smaller, stepped out from hiding and took off wee hats and stood and bowed or curtseyed as Princess Céleste rode by. And in one place they passed by an *Homme de Vert*, a twelve-foot-high manlike being all covered in leaves who respectfully bowed as well. Céleste acknowledged his and the others' obeisance with inclinations of her head.

"Where are the common folk?" asked Simone.

"Oh, *la!*" exclaimed Avélaine. "Can anyone who lives in Faery be said to be common?"

Céleste laughed and said, "We will pass through several villages and by farmsteads along the way, Lady Simone."

"Tended by humans?" asked Simone.

"Some, but not all," replied Céleste.

They rode in silence for a while, but as they fared down into a vale, with a plunging white waterfall of snowmelt to their right cascading down into a tumbling stream to feed the dell crowded with cherry trees in full pink bloom, Avélaine swept her arms wide and said, "Look about you; isn't it marvelous? I mean, even the lands are numinous. We ride in a realm of everlasting spring."

Blaise smiled. "Clearly, Avi, you are besotted with this world."

"To be sure, I am, now that I've escaped the clutches of that dreadful Lord of the Changelings."

"Thanks to Céleste and Roél," said Laurent.

They passed along the dell humming with bees harvesting nectar and pollen from blossoms on branches reaching forth to fill the air with gentle fragrance. Hummingbirds, too, flitted among the blooms along with gossamer-winged Sprites and gentle butterflies, all sipping nectar.

On they rode passing across high bluffs and along meandering streams and down long slopes and up sharp rises, and everywhere they went, spring lay on the land: from the chill onset stirrings of the season to the warm days leading into summer, the forest ran the entire gamut. In places there was snow yet clinging to deep shadow, while in other places flowers were in full bloom and warm zephyrs caressed the passersby. Birds sang for mates, and mushrooms pushed up through layers of leaves. Stags bounded away from their paths, some with their antlers nought but buds agrowing, while others had velvety coverings over tines, and still others had full racks with shreds of velvet dangling or gone altogether.

"Give me a good pack of dogs and my bow," said Laurent, "and I would have us our dinner."

They rode onward moments more, passing through a grove of bourne-side willows leafed out in green as if in late spring. And as they cleared the dangling strands, a wood grouse sprang up from a tuft of grass nigh underfoot and hammered away. The horses snorted and shied, yet firm hands kept them under control. "Ah, there is the game of my choice," said Émile, his gaze following the flight of the bird. "Hard to bring down, but oh so good on the table."

"I prefer pheasant to grouse," said Simone.

"*Mère* always claimed she could tell the difference," said Laurent.

"Well, I can," replied Simone, "and if you ever took the time to savor the meal instead of wolfing it down, you could too."

"They eat like I do," said Émile. "On the battlefield, it is an advantage."

"But most of the time you are not on the field," said Simone. "And there is indeed a difference between grouse and pheasant, though both are quite delicious."

"Me, I like spit-roasted boar," said Blaise. "A good hearty joint and a mug of ale and a bit of bread, that's all I ask for."

Roél laughed and said, "Given the dining habits of you and Laurent and our sire, the entire hog would vanish in but moments."

Blaise broke out in laughter and nodded his agreement.

As onward they rode they spoke of game and hunting and good meals and other such talk, and they stopped occasionally to water the steeds and give them a bit of grain, as well as to take a bite of food or drink and to stretch their legs and otherwise relieve themselves.

But these pauses were short ere they resumed travel through Céleste's realm. Occasionally they passed by farms, where pigs wallowed and chickens scattered and cows and sheep grazed on green slopes. Farmers and their wives and children oft came to their fences of split rails or stacked fieldstone, and they would remove their hats and bow and curtsey as the princess rode past. Some of these folk were human, while others were small brown men and women that Céleste called Hobs, a folk somewhat like Brownies, though quite mischievous and given to pranks. And at one place they passed, the crofter seemed to be a Gnome.

The princess never failed to acknowledge these subjects of hers as on passed the rade, and when she was gone the farmers and wives returned to their tasks of driving geese and milking cows and gathering eggs and sweeping floors and mucking stalls and other such chores and domesticities.

On rode the cavalcade, while Céleste and the others spoke of this and that, of twilight walls and the wonders of Faery, of grimoires and amulets and swords and rings and other things of magic, all of them quite rare.

"But what of Coeur d'Acier?" asked Avélaine. "Is it not a magic blade from Faery?"

"Ah, Heart of Steel," said Céleste, glancing at Roél and the sword at his side. "Flashed in silver and bound by runes it is, and hence does not twist the aethyr, and therefore Roél can bring it into Faery without facing the wrath of the Fey. It is indeed a marvelous blade, but it came from the mortal world."

"Non," objected Émile. "If I understand Sage Geron's words and those of Roél, it might instead have come from the Three Sisters, and if the three Fates are not of Faery, then whence come they?"

"That I do not know," said Céleste. "The Sisters Wyrd, Lot, and Doom are an enigma unto themselves, and who can say whether or no they are Fey? Not I nor any I know. But as to Coeur d'Acier, it was Sage Geron who gave it to Roél there in the mortal world."

"A fine point, I would say," said Émile, lifting an eyebrow askance.

Céleste laughed. "Indeed it is."

And so they left it that way, with no further explanation, as four separate cavalcades in four separate domains respectively rode through the Springwood, the Summerwood, the Autumnwood, and the Winterwood, all heading starwise toward the completely surrounded demesne of the Castle of the Seasons.

· · ·

In midafternoon a full day later, into Valeray and Saissa's realm rode the four individual retinues, and were Lady Simone able to see each one enter she would have said the entourage of the Springwood came in from the east, while that of Alain's Summerwood entered from the south, and Liaze's Autumnwood contingent broached the west, while Borel's Winter-wood band, with its Wolfpack leading, entered from the north. Indeed, though all fared through the marked places on their own starwise margins—the sunlight fading as they neared the ebon heart and then returning as they passed through—they emerged travelling dawnwise, sunwise, duskwise, and starwise into their sire and dam's domain—one moment they were travelling starwise, and the next in another direction, all but the Summerwood band, that is, for starwise they continued.

In the warm breeze, three of the rades paused to shed cloaks and other outer clothes, especially those from the Winterwood, for they had come into summertime here in this small realm. And as the sun slid down the sky, on they rode toward the distant castle, with its tall, gleaming spires rearing high and flying long banners of *bleu* and *rose* and *vert* and *rouge* in the gusting wind.

Nigh sunset, one after another the cavalcades arrived on the castle grounds, and, as each did, the men in the war bands sounded horns, signaling the identity of their principality, answered in kind by horns from the ramparts, proclaiming the king's own call. And across the drawbridge above the moat rode the four contingents, the heavy wood of the span ringing under hooves, and then on flagstone as they passed through the gates.

In the courtyard beyond, the full staff of the castle was turned out, all but the ward on the walls, and gaiety swirled about as did the breeze while families and friends and acquaintances were reunited and lovers met lovers again. And amid the delight of reunion, squealing and laughing and riding high on Borel's shoulder, three-summers-old Prince Duran—waving his toy horse in the air and calling out, "Asphodel!"—was paraded around the bailey, with a small brown sparrow flying about both man and child and chirping in jubilation, while four deadly knights—Luc, Roél, Laurent, and Blaise—smiled and embraced and clapped one another on the back and spoke of a testing of mettle. And amid this hullabaloo, the Wolves looked to Borel for instruction and, receiving none, looked toward his mate Michelle, for Borel had been teaching her their language, yet she, too, was caught up in the greetings and gave them no guide, and so they flopped down upon shaded stone.

And as the sun slid into the horizon, pursued by a fingernail-thin crescent of a moon, mid all the babble, Queen Saissa, her black hair astir in the breeze, her black eyes snapping with urgency, gathered Céleste and Liaze and Camille, and said, "As soon as you are freshened up, fetch Lady Simone and Michelle and meet me in the green room, for surely we must talk."

4

Preparation

"Ah, a monkshood leaf preserved on its autumnal cusp—perfect," muttered Hradian as she scrabbled among her ingredients. "Powerful she was, but a fool, Little Sister Iniquí. . . . Now for a chrysalis. Yes, here is one. Wait, wait, my love, this is of a death's-head moth. Not good. Not good. Instead I need a— Ah, where did I . . . ? How Iniquí died, a mystery, but I knew she was after the paramour of that trull Liaze. . . . Here we are, the chrysalis of the *papillon doré*. Perfect! But I didn't know just why she would seek out Luc. Yet through my scrying, I now realize what she was after— Huah? *Merde!* I do not have the skin I need."

Irritated, Hradian moved away from the workbench and through the doorway and onto a platform jutting out some foot or so above the scum-laden mire. On the flet squatted an overlarge, bloated toad, one of its eyes shut as if asleep, but the other one open and watching for a midge or fly or other insect straying within range. Hradian hissed words at the warty creature. Its long tongue lashed out to snatch a large fluttering moth from the foetid air, and, after a moment of swallowing, the toad waddled to the edge of the overhang and toppled off to plop into the bog; with awkward but strong strokes of bulbous hind legs, and ineffective and feeble strokes of tiny forelegs, down it dived under the surface of the ooze.

Hradian returned to the workbench and made ready—moving things from here to there, setting a tin pot upon a tripod and placing a small but unlit fat-burner beneath. She laid out on the table an especially prepared square of vellum, its color flesh-tone, though nigh alabaster, and she weighted down the corners with odds and ends to hold it flat. She arranged other jars and vials and laid out ingredients and examined all, often referring to her grimoire. Finally satisfied, she waited, for there was little else she could do until the last component was obtained. Then she sat on the high stool and shifted a candle closer to her spell book. But even as she idly turned through the pages describing the preparation of the potion, her thoughts were upon revenge. "First to die was Rhensibé," Hradian muttered, her mind going back to the day in a ramshackle tavern when she discovered that her eldest sister had been slain. . . .

.   .   .

No one took note of the old woman entering the small saloon to set her bundle of twigs down by the door. She shook out her shawl, drops of rain flying wide. Then, through the reek of un-washed bodies and acrid woodsmoke and days-old vomit and piss and belch and fart, slowly she made her way among the gathering to the wooden plank that served as a bar. The babble of conversation did not pause, for remarkable news had come by the tinker standing at the fireplace and warming himself.

"Tore apart, she was."

"How?"

"By the prince's very own hands, I hear."

"What'll it be, Goody?" asked the barkeep.

"A toddy," replied the old woman.

"How could someone tear a body apart with nought but their bare hands?"

" 'F he were an Ogre, he could," said someone.

"Non, the prince be no Ogre," said another. " 'Stead, I deem 'twere a sword what took her down."

"Where d'y' say this happed?" asked another still.

"Here you are, Goody. That'll be a copper."

The old woman fetched a coin from the small pouch at her belt.

"The Winterwood: that's where it happened. That's where the prince was."

"The Winterwood, you say?" asked a large, bulky man, just then joining those nigh the fireplace. "Why, then, that'd be Prince Borel."

"Oui, Gravin," said someone. "Weren't you listening to the tinker?"

"Don't be getting snippy, Marcel. I was in the pissoir."

At the naming of the Winterwood and Prince Borel, the old woman turned an ear to the conversation.

"Oi, now, what is it you really know, Tinsmith?" asked Gravin of the lanky man standing before the flames.

The stranger shrugged. "Rumor, mainly, though there seems to be something to it. Quite a few were speaking of it as I made my way sunwise."

The onlookers waited. The tinker sighed and turned and faced the throng, his dark beard and hair still damp from the drizzle outside. "It seems Prince Borel and his lady were travelling to his manor when they were assaulted by someone—"

"Someone?"

"Oui. The rumors say it was either a fiend of *Enfer*, or a vile mage, or a maleficent witch."

The old woman's dark eyes widened, and she leaned forward, the better to hear.

"And then . . . ?"

"Well, they were in the Winterwood when the attack came, and apparently the attacker was torn asunder."

"By the prince?"

"By his woman?"

The tinker shrugged, but Gravin said, "Most likely it was

by his Wolves. Savage they are, I hear, when the prince be threatened."

"What about his sword? Couldn't he have cut the attacker up with his sword?"

"Non," replied Gravin. "The prince, he doesn't carry a sword. Just a long-knife and a bow, or so they say."

"What about something like a Bear? I mean, there's a rumor that a Bear sometimes is seen in the company of the prince."

The pot-mender shrugged and turned back to the fire.

A momentary silence fell upon the gathering, and the old woman cleared her throat and asked, "Did the attacker have a name?"

"Arr, a meet question, Goody," said the barkeep. "Did the attacker have a name? I mean, mayhap we can riddle out whether it were a fiend, a mage, or a witch."

The tinsmith sighed and said, "The only thing I heard was that it was one of Orbane's acolytes."

At the naming of Orbane and an acolyte a gasp went up from the gathering, especially from the old woman, followed by a pall of silence.

But then the tinker added, "I think it was someone called . . . now let me see . . . something like, Wrenlybee, though that isn't it at all."

The old woman's cup slipped from her fingers and fell to the floor with a clang. "Wrenlybee? Do you instead mean Rhensibé?"

The tinker turned and slowly nodded. "Ah, oui, Goody, I think that was it. Rhensibé."

With a screech, the old woman flung a hand out toward the stranger, her fingers clawlike, her wrist twisting. The man gasped and clutched at his chest, and fell to his knees, and men drew back in startlement and fear, though one, Gravin, sprang to the tinsmith's aid.

Wailing, the old woman spun 'round and 'round like a dark,

whirling wind and hurtled toward her bundle of twigs. She snatched it up, and—lo!—no bundle it was, but a besom instead. Out the door she slammed, ere any could seem to move.

"Witch!" cried Marcel, and leapt in pursuit, the others charging after, all but Gravin and the tinker, who yet wheezed and said, "Someone dropped an anvil on my chest."

Outside, no old woman did the men find, though across the face of the moon a ragged shadow darted.

· · ·

"I was up and away ere they could act," muttered Hradian. "And when I searched in my dark mirror for Rhensibé, all it showed was a scatter of bones there in the Winterwood snow. Borel will pay for this, I swear."

Hradian's thoughts were interrupted by a loud chorus of croaking from the mire, as if every toad and every frog were sounding an alarm, though no alarm this, for swamp creatures fall silent when danger draws nigh. No, this was something else—a signal, a calling—and the bogland was filled with a racking din.

"Ah, good. Crapaud has done his job."

Again Hradian waited, and once more her mind fell into thoughts of revenge. "Next was Iniquí. Her end came at the hands of that slattern Liaze. But how, I know not. All was fiery when I sought Iniquí, nothing left, there below a frigid, obsidian mountain. . . ."

· · ·

Carrying a broom—a twiggy besom—over one shoulder and a rucksack slung from the other, the small child wended through Market Square, looking at this, purchasing that, especially mosses and herbs and oddities. Strange things for a child to want, now, weren't they? Or so the goodwives asked themselves.

Regardless of whispered comments, the child meandered on, filling her satchel with odds and ends—dried lizards, living newts, sheep's eyes, and other peculiarities. Why, one might think she was a— Ah, but that could not be. She was nought but a child after all.

The day was dim and damp, the low-hanging clouds grazing the tops of even the meanest of buildings. Yet this was mountain country, and often did clinging air and misty vapor curl through the town; one merely needed to be bundled against such. Nevertheless, it was market day, when farmers and mendicant friars and merchants and other such gathered to trade or sell their wares. Occasionally a swindler or cutpurse would show up, but the local men quickly took care of such unsavory riffraff.

At one corner of the square, two men sat at a table, an *échiquier* between them, other men standing and watching as the *échecs* game went on, quiet conversation among them.

The girl paused when she heard one of the onlookers utter a particular name.

"... Liaze, they say."

"And where did this come from?" asked one of the men.

"I heard it over at the *Poulet Gris*."

"Ah, pish, what do they know? 'Tis nought but drunks who frequent that place."

"Well it was but a rumor."

"And this princess and a rooster killed a witch?"

"Pecked her to death, I shouldn't wonder," muttered someone.

This brought a round of laughter from them all, quickly hushed as one of the players scowled up from the board. When the bystanders fell silent, that player then moved his tower and said, "Check."

It brought a mutter from the onlookers, for they had not seen it coming. It was after all a revealed check rather than one from a direct move.

Long did the opponent ponder his options.

Finally, one man whispered, "Did this witch have a name?"

"Iniquitous, I think."

Behind them the child shrieked, and there came a cold blast of air, and when the men turned, no one was there, though the clouds just above swirled in turbulence, as if something had shot through at speed.

. . .

"I didn't realize it then, but now I believe the obsidian mountain must be where the key was forged." Hradian ground her teeth. "Stupid, stupid Iniquí. She should have known there is a much easier way. She died for her stupidity, and for that Liaze shall pay."

Of a sudden the croaking din outside ceased altogether, leaving behind a deafening quiet. And then there came a splat of feet and a stench, a reek, as of swamp bottom. Hradian turned. At the door stood an eight-foot-tall Bogle. Dark and Goblinlike he was, and bald and naked, his swollen male organ erect. He smiled, showing wicked pointed teeth, and he gestured toward the bed.

"Bah, you fool," spat Hradian, "I need a live three-horned sticky-tongue."

The smile vanished.

"You heard me: a three-horned sticky-tongue, and alive. Now go."

The erection drooped, and the Bogle glanced from the witch to the bed and back.

"I said go!"

The creature, his organ now flaccid, turned and dove into the turgid waters.

Her black eyes snapping in irritation, Hradian muttered and fumed and stared at the now empty doorway. Another splat sounded out on the flet, and the overlarge, bloated toad waddled across to take up station nigh the door. Hradian stepped to the opening. "I need to teach you, Crapaud, a different signal for those times I merely want an errand run."

Hradian returned to the bench, alternately thinking of the

aroused Bogle and of the vengeance she would wreak upon Valeray and all his get. "Including you, Princess Céleste, for you are the youngest, and you slew the youngest of us—Nefasí. . . ."

. . .

Mid a great celebration in the port city of Mizon, a matron asked one of the celebrants what the ado was all about.

"Women are safe again, especially demoiselles."

"Safe? From what?"

"Have you not heard? The Changeling Lord is dead."

"Dead? How?"

"A chevalier, Roél by name, slew him."

"I do not believe it," said the matron, shaking her head.

"King Avélar himself announced it."

The matron sighed. "The Lord of the Changelings dead?"

"Oui, and not only that, but the king also said that *Céleste, Princesse de la Forêt du Printemps* slew one of Orbane's acolytes—a witch named Nefasí."

The matron shrieked and turned and fled away through the gay crowd.

. . .

"And she, too, will pay, will Céleste," muttered Hradian.

Again the witch paced the floor, waiting for the skin she needed, plotting her vengeance, and thinking of the Bogle as well.

A short while later, once more the Bogle appeared at her door. In his hand he held a squirming lizard—a pale brown three-horned sticky-tongue.

"Bon!" crowed Hradian. She took the reptile from the Bogle and placed it in a widemouthed jar and capped it with a tin plate. Then she turned to the Bogle and gestured toward her bed.

. . .

With the Bogle finally gone back into the foetid swamp, Hradian, now naked, returned to her grimoire and the elixir she would brew. She filled the tin pot with a greenish-yellow fluid from a jar labeled "bile," and then lit the fat-burner below. When the fluid began to simmer, one by one and at certain times and most carefully she dropped the ingredients into the seething liquid: the turning monkshood leaf, the chrysalis of the golden butterfly, the belladonna berry, and more. At a critical point, she retrieved the lizard from the jar and held it against the square of alabaster vellum. The reptile's eyes independently turned this way and that, as if seeking a way to flee, and its prehensile feet sought to grasp something, a branch, a limb, something by which it could escape this *thing* holding it. Hradian jabbed the creature, and it shifted color. "Not vert, you idiot," she spat at the now-green lizard. "Can you not see what I hold you against?"

Once more she jabbed it, and once more it changed color, this time to a muddy brown. Again and again Hradian tormented the reptile, and again and again it changed tint—russet, beige, ochre, yellow, jade—all to the witch's frustrated shouts, but of a sudden it took on the hue of the vellum, and in that moment, Hradian broke its neck.

Swiftly she skinned it, and dropped that into the tin pot on the tripod above the fat-burner. She threw the flayed remains of the lizard out onto the flet, where Crapaud snatched them up with his long tongue and swallowed them whole.

Referring often to her spell book, all night Hradian muttered arcane words over the bubbling brew, and she dropped various leaves and stems and berries and blossoms and insects and other such into the simmering liquid, adding goodly amounts of her own urine to the mix and small amounts of her feces. And she spat into the pot, and ran her finger through her crotch and stirred with that finger a single circuit widdershins in the liquid as well. Then she pricked her hand with a needle, and blood and teardrops came, each of which she dripped into the mix. And with silk strings she briefly dipped various ores and crystals into the brew, hissing strange utterances all the while, loudly singing these words when she repeatedly bobbed a flake of alchemically transmuted gold in and out of the fluid as the concoction boiled down and down.

At last she reached the end of the lengthy recipe laboriously detailed in her grimoire, and she removed the pot from the flame and cautiously poured every last drop of the warm and ocherous result into a small vial and capped it. Then she laughed in glee and danced nakedly about her cote, holding up the potion and crooning.

5

Suspicions

Some two candlemarks after the arrival of the retinues, when the travelling kindred had freshened themselves and had changed out of their riding clothes—the women into silks and satins and soft slippers, and the men into trews and jerkins and such—the distaff side gathered in the green room, while the men gravitated to the armory to inspect the arms and armor to be used in the tournament to come.

As tea was served to the ladies, Simone looked about the intimate chamber, with its velvet walls the color of pale jade, and its floor of a tile an even lighter green. The comfortable chairs they sat in were upholstered in an emeraldine fabric bearing a pattern of tiny diamonds of light yellow. They sat in an arc about a small, unlit fireplace ensconced in a corner, the room comfortable on this summer eve with air wafting in through open bay windows. Glass-chimneyed candles in stands lit the chamber with a soft glow, reflecting highlights from the gilt frames of several modest landscapes: a placid lake nestled among snowcapped mountains; a green glade half-seen through a curling fog; a herd of horses racing across sunlit, rolling hills, and running before a distant storm sweeping after. In addition, on the wall above the mantel hung a quartet of individual small portraits of children—two boys and two girls—presumably those of Valeray and Saissa.

Simone's gaze then went to the arc of women: to her left sat

Avélaine, and then on 'round deasil were Camille and Saissa and Liaze and Céleste and Michelle. In a pocket high on Camille's gown slept a small sparrow—Scruff his name—a thing Simone found most curious.

To the left of each chair stood a small round table of some sort of dark wood, on which one of the maids placed saucers and cups, and a second one poured tea for each lady, the third adding milk and honey if so desired. A sideboard of the same dark wood—ebony?—sat against one wall, and there the maids placed the tea service and then withdrew.

When the staff softly closed the door behind, Saissa took a deep breath and peered down into her cup, as if seeking tranquility therein. Then she raised her gaze to the gathering. "For nearly four years I have at times felt as if someone or something vile has been in my chamber. Yet when I look about for the source, nought is there. The feeling comes and goes, and oft is very brief, though at times it has lingered awhile. I understand that Liaze, Céleste, Camille, and Michelle have sensed the very same thing, have had the very same experiences. Not so?"

"Oui, Maman," said Liaze, the others nodding in agreement.

But Michelle added, "I do not discern the feeling of malice unless Borel is with me. And yet it does not emanate from him but from somewhere else. I think it is directed at him, though he does not detect ought."

"None of the men seem to be aware," said Saissa, "at least Valeray does not."

·   ·   ·

In the armory, with its racks of arms and armor, of hauberks and helms and shields, of bows and arrows and crossbows and quarrels and darts and spears, of halberds and hammers and maces and axes and morning stars, of daggers and poniards and dirks and swords and other such weaponry, some bronze and glittery, others dark and dull, Émile watched as his eldest son hefted one of the tournament lances, long and slender, its point bluntly padded. "Ha! With this one I will unhorse you other three," said Laurent.

"Pah!" snorted Blaise, replacing a battle-axe in a stand of the weapons. "You and what other hundred knights?"

Émile laughed, as did the others, all but King Valeray, who merely smiled.

"You appear troubled," said Émile. "Is something weighing on your mind?"

"It's just these sensings the women have," replied Valeray.

"Sensings?"

"As if something or someone evil is spying in on us—on Borel and Michelle, on Liaze and Luc, on Alain and Camille, on Céleste and Roél, and on Saissa and me."

"Are you certain that it is not some sort of womanly vapours? My own Simone is at times given to such, and—"

"Non, Émile, these are no vapours, no *caprice d'une femme*. My daughters and daughters-in-law and my wife, they truly sense this malevolent thing, this spying, yet, for me, I detect nought whatsoever."

"Neither do we, Papa," replied Alain, with Borel and Luc and Roél signifying their agreement.

Borel said, "Though I do not perceive ought amiss, sometimes Slate seems to sense evil is nigh."

"Slate?" asked Émile.

"One of my Wolves," said Borel. Then he smiled and added, "I suggested to Chelle that women are perhaps closer to Wolves than are men."

Valeray barked a laugh, yet quickly grew serious again. "Ah, me, but this is no humorous matter. Saissa says that it's as if some evil, unseen creature has invaded our chambers, and we must do something about it."

.   .   .

"Do you sense anything, Avélaine?" asked Simone.

"Non, Maman."

Simone turned her gaze toward the others. "Yet the five of you do?"

"Oui, Simone," said Saissa. "I have told Valeray that it's as if a vile but invisible being is at hand."

"Vile but invisible being?" gasped Simone. "Oh, Mithras, then something must be done. Why, it could be anywhere."

Avélaine gasped and put a hand to her abdomen, yet said nought.

Camille took note of the gesture but said, "Alain and I believe it is Hradian. Somehow she is spying upon us, seeking a way to gain revenge."

. . .

"Revenge for what?" asked Émile, taking up a dagger and gauging its balance and heft.

"The death of her three sisters," replied Alain, "acolytes all."

Émile frowned. "Acolytes? Of what religion?"

"No religion, Papa," said Roél, hanging a shield back on its hook. "Instead those three dead were acolytes of Orbane, a foul wizard. Only his fourth one remains."

Émile raised a puzzled eyebrow and turned up a hand. "Perhaps someone had better explain, for Simone and Laurent and Blaise and I are newly come unto Faery."

Laurent and Blaise both nodded in agreement.

"Very well," said Valeray, glancing at Borel and Alain. "Mayhap it will do us all good to review just why it might be Hradian—the last acolyte—and what she might have in mind."

. . .

Saissa stood and stepped to the sideboard. "Anyone else for more tea?"

Shortly, with some cups replenished and others not, Saissa resumed her seat. She took a sip of tea and set her cup aside, then looked about the women and said, "It all began many summers ago, just how many, I remember not, but it was a goodly while back in a time ere I had met Valeray, ere the time our children were born." Momentarily, Saissa seemed lost in reflection, a hint of a smile on her face. She nodded and then came to herself and continued: "Regardless, the wizard Orbane grew in power, and he had about him four acolytes, four sisters, witches all. And though at the time we knew not their names, they were Rhensibé, Hradian, Nefasí, and Iniquí.

"Orbane sought power o'er the whole of Faery, and he assembled a great army to march across the realms and take command of all. But he was opposed by the Firsts, and—"

. . .

Émile laid down the keen, bronze sword. "The Firsts?"

"The first of each kind in Faery, Papa," said Roél.

"This speaks to the beginnings of Faery, then?"

"Oui," replied Alain. "You see, just as once upon a time there was no mortal world, well then, too, once upon a time there was no Faery. But the gods saw fit to create it and populate it with beings. The first being of each kind is named a First. My wife, Camille, has a conjecture about such."

. . .

In the green room Saissa looked at Camille and said, "Why don't you explain it, my dear?"

"Oh, please do," said Simone, "for I deem it is something that Reydeau didn't teach us."

"Reydeau?" asked Liaze.

Céleste said, "I sent Reydeau to tutor Simone and her family and staff of the ways of Faery so that they would know what to expect herein."

"Ah, I see." Liaze turned to Camille and added, "I did not mean to interrupt."

"Please, Camille," said Simone, "please go on. I would hear of the beginnings of Faery."

"Very well," said Camille, "though it is but speculation on my part." She took a sip of tea and set her cup aside.

. . .

Alain looked at Émile and said, "It was when I had gone missing, and Camille was in search of me, though the only clue
she had was to look for a place east of the sun and west of the
moon. None she asked knew where such might be. But then
she came across an Elf named Rondalo. He told her that his
mother Chemine was a First, and she might know just where
such a locale lay. Yet she did not, but she said there was one
other who might know—Raseri the Dragon, who she thought
might have been the very first First to have come unto Faery.
Chemine suggested that Rondalo guide Camille to the Drake.
Rondalo was bitterly opposed, for he was a sworn enemy of
Raseri; it seems the Dragon had slain Rondalo's sire Audane.
Even so, given Camille's plight, Rondalo at last agreed to guide
her to Raseri's lair."

. . .

Camille smiled in memory and said, "And so I met the Dragon.
We spoke of many things, during which Raseri told me that
he remembered nought of killing Rondalo's père or anything
of his life ere he found himself in Faery. Still, he said he must
have slain Audane, though he could call nothing to mind of the
battle. His speaking of it spurred my supposition, there at the
Dragon's lair. . . ."

. . .

Camille shook her head in puzzlement. "Tell me then, are all
Firsts as are you: knowing nought of what went before you each
came unto Faery?"

"So it seems," said Raseri, peering toward the oncoming
light.

Camille fell silent and took another bite of biscuit. Around
the mouthful she said, "Have you heard of the Keltoi?"

"Indeed. Most in Faery know of the legend. Wandering bards
all—those whose tales caught the ear of the gods, and they in
turn made Faery manifest."

Camille swallowed and took a drink of water. "Well then, Raseri, answer me this:

"What if it is true that, as they wandered across the face of the world, the Keltoi did tell their tales, and the gods did listen, and they so enjoyed what they heard they made Faery manifest so that they could be entertained by the stories that followed? Mayhap long past, 'round a campfire a gifted Keltoi began a tale, the first one the gods listened to, and it went something like this:

"Once upon a time there was a terrible Drake named Raseri, a Drake who breathed flame. And in a hard-fought duel with an Elf named Audane, Raseri slew the Elf. Yet it was Audane's wedding night, and he had lain with his bride ere the battle, and some ten moons after the terrible death, Audane's grieving widow, a Water Fairy named Chemine, birthed a son. And Chemine gave over unto the wee lad Audane's silvery sword, the one with the arcane runes hammered down the length of its blade, and she said, 'One day, my Rondalo, you will battle with vile Raseri, foul murderer of your sire.' "

Camille fell silent, and Raseri cocked his head and said, "Mayhap 'tis true that such did happen. Even so, where does that lead?"

"Oh, don't you see, Raseri, ere that tale perhaps there *was* no before, no existence whatsoever for Faery, no existence even for you. Mayhap that's when Faery began. Perhaps that's when you were born full-grown. Mayhap there was no Audane, yet even if there was, if the legend of the Keltoi and the gods is true, then it is no fault of yours he was slain. Instead 'tis completely the fault of the Keltoi who told that story, the first the gods had heard, and this blood vengeance, this sword-oath Rondalo swore, should instead have been sworn 'gainst the tale-teller, or the gods who made it true, for in truth they are the ones in combination who did murder Audane."

Raseri grunted, but otherwise did not reply, and Camille ate the remainder of her biscuit in silence, her thoughts tumbling one o'er the other.

Finally Raseri said, "If you have the truth of it, Camille, then much needs setting aright."

"Wh-what?" said Camille, shaken from her musings.

"I said, have you the truth of it, then much needs setting aright. Even so, there is this to consider: although the Keltoi, or gods, or in combination, are responsible for much grief and rage, they gave me, they gave all of us, life as well. Without them we would not be. Hence, if the legend is true, we owe them our very existence. Those tales, though fraught with peril and desperation and fury and sorrow such as they are, without them we would not be."

Camille nodded, somewhat abstractedly, and Raseri tilted his head to one side and said, "You seem preoccupied, Camille. What were your thoughts that I so interrupted?"

Camille glanced at Scruff and then at the Drake, then out to where Rondalo might be, and she shrugged and said, "I was just wondering whose silver tongue or golden pen is telling the tale we find ourselves in."

Raseri's booming laughter echoed among the peaks, but when he looked down at Camille, she wasn't laughing at all.

· · ·

". . . and so you see, Simone," said Camille, glancing at Avélaine as well. "If I am right, then each of the Firsts is the first of its kind to have been spoken of in a Keltoi bard's tale, one whose story was made manifest."

· · ·

In the armory, as Alain fell silent, Blaise said, "Did this Rondalo fellow ever fight Raseri?"

"Non," said Alain. "After Raseri bore Camille to someone even older than he, the Dragon flew to see Chemine and told her of Camille's conjecture. Chemine and Rondalo and Raseri made a truce, and, as it so happens, Rondalo and Raseri became the best of friends, and these days they go adventuring together."

"Huah!" grunted Émile. "An Elf and a Dragon adventuring together. How odd."

"Only in Faery," said Roél.

Émile nodded and then turned to Valeray. "Well then, now that I know what a First is, tell me of this person Orbane."

Valeray said, "Orbane is one of the Firsts as well, evil wizard that he is."

"But why would the gods do such?" asked Émile. "I mean, why would they make manifest a vile wizard who wished to rule all of Faery?"

"Because of the adventures he would spawn," said Valeray. "Terrible as they were, it would be entertainment for the gods."

Laurent slammed a gauntleted fist into a gauntleted palm and gritted, "Gods be damned."

"Oh, Laurent, tempt them not," said Roél, "else something might befall you as befell Avélaine."

Laurent looked at his brother and wrenched off the gauntlets and flung them to the table where others lay. "Pah! That was the Lord of the Changelings and no god who stole our sister."

"Nevertheless . . ." said Roél.

Laurent took a deep breath and slowly let it out. "I hear, little brother. I hear."

Émile said, "What of this war with Orbane, Lord Valeray? I assume this monstrous mage was defeated."

Valeray nodded and said, "Many of the Firsts—Raseri the Firedrake, Jotun the Giant, Adragh the Pwca, Tisp the Sprite, and others—banded together to oppose Orbane and his conquest. Yet he was too powerful for them, and something had to be done. My friend, Duke Roulan, Michelle's sire, came up with the seed of a scheme. You see, at the time he and I were neither duke nor king, but thieves instead. Yet we were caught up in the war against Orbane, for his minions were ruining our business. And so . . ."

.   .   .

"What we need," said Roulan, "is a way to turn Orbane's own power against him."

Valeray nodded. "But how?"

"Well, Val, I know where one of his castles is located, though it is said to be warded by a witch; but surely you can get in and discover something of his own that we can use against him."

"We . . . ?"

"Well, perhaps not we directly, but certainly the Firsts could."

"I don't know, Roully. I would think the castle well guarded, and it might—" Of a sudden, Valeray fell into thought. "Guile. We can use guile. Though if Orbane is in residence, it's the end for us both. But if he's elsewhere, and the witch stands ward, well . . ."

Roulan pushed out a hand of negation. "You know Orbane is off opposing the Firsts, and this castle is one of his lesser. What is it you have in mind?"

Valeray smiled and said, "Remember how we fooled the mayor, and . . ."

A moon or so later, at a grey stone castle on a bald hill in the midst of a dark forest, a hag knocked for entry. From the battlements above, the Troll guard shouted down for her to go away, yet she croaked that she was a soothsayer who had private words for Lord Orbane within.

After repeated demands by the crone and threats by the Troll, disturbed by the racket without, the mistress of the castle appeared. It was a witch who announced she was in command of this holt.

"I have a dreadful message to give to the dark one, and I would see him," called up the hag.

"Dreadful message?"

"I am a soothsayer and I have seen, and I'll only speak with Lord Orbane."

"Seen what?"

"Oh, Mistress, this is not for your ears, and I certainly cannot say it in front of your warders; it might dishearten them. Besides, I am tired and need a rest, and I wouldn't mind a cup of tea. I would have you take me to Lord Orbane."

"He is absent," called down the witch. "So you will have to tell it to me, and I can get word to him."

"Tell it to you?"

The witch drew herself up to her full height. "I am Nefasí, Orbane's acolyte, and he trusts me with his very life."

"Ah, Mistress Nefasí, I do not know whether to tell you or not."

"I can always force it out of you."

"Heh. Maybe. Maybe not. Yet perhaps as Orbane's acolyte . . . —But if I tell you, it must be in a place of protection—a place of power and transmutation—ere I will divulge the message dire."

The crone and the witch haggled, but finally, fearing the worst for her master, the witch allowed the hag to enter the castle for the message she would tell.

Accompanied by well-armed Troll guards, by winding ways and up stairwells and past many rooms—ways and wells and rooms the crone committed to memory—Nefasí took the aged soothsayer into Orbane's own alchemistry chamber, where a pentagon of protection was permanently inscribed upon the floor. There did Nefasí cast a spell, one that temporarily rendered the Trolls deaf and mute, and then told the old soothsayer to speak. And so, surrounded by unhearing and unspeaking guards, with the crone and the witch sitting at a table within the pentagon, the hag looked about and then whispered, "Orbane will be defeated by his own hand."

At these bodeful words, Nefasí's gaze flicked briefly toward a small locked chest sitting atop a table, a chest the soothsayer clearly noted, though the crone did not let Nefasí see that she had. Nefasí asked if there were more to the sooth divined, and the beldame shook her head. Nefasí rewarded the soothsayer with a single gold piece and sent her on her way, and in spite of the hag's grumblings, the witch did not give her the promised cup of tea.

That very same night, his disguise now gone, Valeray scaled the outside wall to the alchemistry room, and he picked the lock and found within the chest two clay amulets. Valeray was disappointed, for it seemed that they were nought but trinkets. Regardless, he wrapped them well and stood in the window and, using a sling, he cast them to Roulan who was waiting at the edge of the woods. Then down clambered the thief, and soon he and his accomplice were riding agallop to the waiting Firsts. Yet even as Valeray and Roulan passed through that dark forest, they were seen and recognized as strangers and pursued.

They managed to reach the Firsts, and the hounding enemy was routed.

.   .   .

King Valeray took up a sword and sighted down its length, saying, "Despite their lowly appearance, Émile, the clay amulets were descried by Lisane the Elf who is a true seer, and she told the Firsts what they were: powerful magical artifacts cast by Orbane himself. Lisane called them Seals of Orbane, and said that likely there were at least seven of these dreadful relics about, for it seems the residue of power on the seals indicated such. In any event, the magic within—curses all—would be loosed when the clay seal was broken, and it would obey the desires of the one breaking the seal to the detriment of the one who was the target of those desires. These two seals were used against their maker: the first to destroy Orbane's protection, the second to cast Orbane into the Castle of Shadows in the

Great Darkness beyond the Black Wall of the World, where he remains still, for the Castle of Shadows is inescapable."

Valeray fell silent, but Alain said, "Because of Hradian, three of those seals were used against us: one to make my sire and dam seemingly vanish; one to curse me to be a bear by day, though I could be a man at night; and one to snatch me and my household away and betroth me to a Troll if my truelove ever saw my human face." He paused a moment and smiled unto himself and added, "But Camille took care of that."

Blaise frowned. "Why were those three amulets used in that manner? I mean, if they were so powerful, why not use them to set Orbane free?"

Valeray shrugged. "I repeat, the Castle of Shadows is inescapable, and apparently, the seals are not powerful enough to set him loose. Besides, that would be a boon to him and not a detriment, and the seals can only be used to visit ill upon someone or something."

Laurent shook his head. "Any prison can be breached, given enough men and arms. Hence the ones held therein—be they criminals or innocents—can be set free."

"Not the Castle of Shadows, my boy," said Valeray. "Those who go in do not come out."

. . .

"How can that be?" asked Simone, sipping her tea. "How can a mere castle be inescapable? Surely a large army could break him free, and if I understand you aright, he had a large army at his beck . . . or if not him, at the beck of this Hradian creature."

Saissa shrugged, but Camille said, "Mayhap upon a time a Keltoi bard started a story: 'In the Great Darkness beyond the Black Wall of the World there was an inescapable prison where only the most dreadful of criminals were kept.' " Camille paused and looked at Liaze and then said, " 'And there was but one key to this dreaded Castle, and it was held by a comte whose full title was *Comte Amaury du Château Bleu dans le Lac de la Rose et Gardien de la Clé.'* "

"Wait a moment," said Avélaine, and she turned to Liaze. "But for the name of Amaury, isn't that your Luc's title?"

Liaze nodded and said, "It is when he is at Château Bleu. Amaury was his sire, and the first keeper of the key."

. . .

"What key?" asked Émile, thumbing the green fletching of an arrow.

"This one," said Luc, drawing an amulet on a chain about his neck up from his jerkin. The talisman was silver and set with a blue stone; the chain was silver as well. "Ere he rode off to war, my sire placed it 'round my throat when I was but a tiny babe."

"What has it to do with ought?" asked Laurent.

"It is said to be the key to the Castle of Shadows," replied Luc.

"That's a key to the inescapable prison?" asked Blaise.

"If what they say is true, indeed it is."

"Hold on, now: what if someone, say this witch Hradian, sends her minions to steal the amulet. Wouldn't that mean she could set Orbane free? If so, I say we hunt her down and kill her like the bitch she is."

Luc shook his head. "Non. Trying to steal the amulet would do no good, and in fact would probably result in the minion or minions being dead. The amulet has a powerful spell upon it, and if the witch or anyone else tried to take it without my permission or by means of duress, or if I were slain and Hradian tried to take it, the amulet would slay her too. No, it must be borne by the rightful heir, or freely given by the heir to some-one of his choosing."

Luc removed the talisman and held it out to Blaise. "Here, I freely give it."

Blaise set a helm aside and tentatively took the amulet and

looked at it carefully. As he handed it back he said, "And you say this is the only key to that prison?"

Luc slipped the chain over his head. "As far as I know, it is the only key, though I ken not how it opens the door or gate or barrier or whatever it is that locks one in."

. . .

"Oh, my," gasped Michelle, her cup clattering in her saucer, "perhaps that's what she meant."

"What who meant?" asked Simone.

"Lady Wyrd," replied Michelle. She looked at the others and said, "Don't you remember? It was at the ball celebrating the safe return of Céleste and Roél and Avélaine and the war bands from the Changeling land, and . . ."

. . .

At the midnight mark, King Valeray called a halt to the music, and he took stance upon the ballroom dais, and as servants passed among the gathering and doled out goblets of wine, Valeray called for quiet, for he would make a toast to the successful quest and to those who rode thereon, and he would toast the brides and grooms to be, and of course he would toast the child to be born to Alain and Camille.

But the moment that all had a goblet in hand, including the servants, of a sudden there came the sound of shuttles and looms, and before the gathering stood three women: Maiden, Mother, and Crone; the Ladies Skuld, Verdandi, and Urd; the Fates Wyrd, Lot, and Doom: one slender, her robe limned in silver; one matronly, her robe limned in gold; and one seemingly bent with age, her robe limned in black.

A gasp went up from the gathering, yet Valeray and Borel and Alain, and Luc and Roél and Chevell all bowed, the men in the gathering following suit; and Saissa and Liaze and Céleste and Camille and Michelle and Avélaine curtseyed, the gathered women doing likewise.

"*Mesdames,*" murmured King Valeray upon straightening.

"Valeray," said Verdandi.

"What would you have of us?" asked the king.

Verdandi looked at Urd, and she in turn peered at Céleste among the gathering and said, "The gray arrow?"

"It is in my quarters," said Céleste. "Shall I fetch it? It is broken."

Urd cackled and said, "Broken? Nay." And with a gesture, of a sudden the arrow appeared in her hand, and even as she held it, the shaft became whole and its leaden point keen. Then she looked at it and murmured, "Even were I to let it stay broken, still it is too deadly to remain in mortal hands."

"Why else have you come?" asked Borel, stepping forward.

Slowly Urd turned her head toward him and canted it to one side. "Just as when once I met you by a stream, ever bold, I see. Questioning the Fates, are we?" And then she cackled in glee.

Borel pushed out a hand in negation, and Michelle looked at him quizzically.

"I believe what my son means," said Valeray, "is—"

"We know what he meant," snapped Urd, and she turned to Skuld.

"Yes, we came to give warning," said Lady Wyrd, "and it is this: for a while there will be peace, yet upon a dreadful time yet to come you will all be needed, as will others. Heed me. Stand ready and relax not your guard, for there will be a— Ah, but I cannot directly reveal what I have seen, yet know that one among you will be the key."

"The key?" asked Camille.

Skuld looked at her and smiled and said, "The key."

"So peril yet comes," said Valeray, his words a statement, not a question.

"It does," said Skuld.

"Be ready," said Verdandi.

"And on guard," added Urd, and her gaze swept across the gathering to momentarily stop upon Luc, and then moved to Camille.

And the sound of looms swelled and then vanished, and the Sisters Three vanished as well.

The gathering stood stunned for a moment, but then Valeray lifted his glass and, with a rakish grin, said, "Here's to interesting times!"

To interesting times! cried they all.

.   .   .

"I do not understand what you are referring to," said Simone, peering into her now empty cup and setting it back upon the saucer.

"Oh, Simone," said Michelle, "Lady Wyrd said, 'One among you will be the key,' and Liaze's Luc has the key, and Lady Urd's gaze rested upon him just before the Three Fates vanished. Hence, perhaps that's what she meant when she gave us that warning."

In that moment a gong sounded.

.   .   .

"Ah," said Valeray as the distant echoes died, "dinner, my lads. Let us hurry and fetch the ladies from the green room and get to the board, else the chef will be most upset."

As they filed out from the armory, Blaise said, "I think Laurent is right: let's hunt down this bitch Witch Hradian and kill her outright. Then Orbane will have no acolytes at all, none to attempt to set him free."

As the ladies waited to be collected, Camille and Avélaine took up the cups and saucers and moved to the sideboard. "You are with child?" asked Camille softly.

Avélaine glanced down at herself. "Oh, does it show?"

"Non, it's just that I saw you place a hand across your waist when the peril of an unseen being was mentioned."

"Ah. You are observant, Camille, and, oui, I am with child. I was going to announce it at dinner tonight."

Camille gripped Avélaine's hand and said, "Splendid."

"Oh, but I wish Chevell were here when I speak of it."

"He does not know?"

"Non. I wasn't positive when I set out from Port Mizon, but now I know for certain."

"Regardless," said Camille, squeezing Avélaine's fingers. "I am so happy to have Duran, and you will find a babe of your own to be a pleasure, too."

"Where is the wee prince?"

"Perhaps asleep by now. When last I saw him he was with his *bonne d'enfants* having a bath."

"He seems a happy child."

"Oh, he is," replied Camille, smiling.

In that moment, the king and princes and chevaliers arrived and swept the women out from the green room and toward one perhaps brighter.

· · ·

They sat about a long table, one of oak, and in a grand dining room. The chamber itself was all of gold, broken here and there by white: golden velvet paneled the walls, and white bellpulls dangled at each corner; upholstery of a golden fabric and patterned with a scatter of tiny white flowerets cushioned the golden-oak chairs; white sideboards trimmed in gold stood along the walls. White lanterns in golden sconces cast a yellow-white aura over all. The ceiling above was white, with golden crown molding all 'round. The dinnerware was white porcelain rimmed with gold, and the white utensils were edged with gold as well.

The meal began with an appetizer of escargot and a small glass of pale white wine—"Ah, an Autumnwood vintage; some of Liaze's best," declared Valeray, hoisting his goblet on high toward her. The others followed suit, and Liaze inclined her head in response.

As they supped upon the snails, Simone looked across the table and asked Camille, "Why is it you have a small sparrow in your pocket?"

"Oh, Scruff, you mean," said Camille, touching a finger lightly high on her bodice where the wee bird drowsed. "He is a trusted companion, and I wanted him with me at our meeting even though he is asleep."

"Is he magical in some manner?"

"You might say so. He was loaned to me by the Lady of the Mere, to be my companion as I looked for Alain. It seems he can sense danger and deception, and he certainly proved to be of great aid."

"This Lady of the Mere: who might she be?"

"Ah, the Lady of the Mere, she has many names: Lady Sorcière, Lady Wyrd, Lady Skuld, She Who Sees the Future."

"This is one of those Michelle spoke about, one of the Fates?"

"Oui." Camille gestured toward Valeray and Saissa and said, "It seems this family is somehow caught up in the intrigues of the Three Sisters."

"Ensnared is more likely," said Valeray.

"Granted," said Camille. "But without them I would never have rescued Alain."

"Nor I Michelle," said Borel.

"Nor I Luc," said Liaze.

"Nor would Roél and I have released Avélaine and Laurent and Blaise," added Céleste.

"Nor would have I discovered the whereabouts of King Valeray and Queen Saissa," added Camille last.

"Here's to the Fates," cried Blaise, hoisting a glass, "else Laurent and I would be statues still."

"Hear, hear," said Valeray, and he hoisted his own and downed the drink.

Simone raised her glass as well, but tremulously added, "But who is to say that the Fates didn't have a hand in precipitating those crises from which you all were rescued."

. . .

The escargot was followed by a creamy bisque of trout, along with another of Liaze's white wines, this a vibrant gold, one that would stand up to the richness of the soup.

The talk turned to that of the tourney, and of the games and jongleurs that would surround the gala events—an échecs tournament, lawn bowling, croquet, ladies' archery, minstrels, jugglers, stilt walkers, and the like, and it was during this happy converse that Avélaine announced she was with child.

"Is it true, Avi?" asked Roél.

"Oui," replied Avélaine. "A little new vicomte or vicomtesse is on the way."

Laurent and Blaise and Roél leapt up from their seats and rushed to Avélaine's side and handed her up from her chair and, somewhat cautiously, embraced her. Émile, too, hugged his daughter, and Simone wiped tears of happiness from her own eyes.

"I suppose Chevell is strutting about like a peacock," said Roél.

Avélaine laughed and said, "He will be when I tell him."

"Ah, little sister, he does not know?" asked Laurent.

"Non, Laurent. I only became certain this past sevenday or so."

"Ah, then, he will be so jealous that he wasn't here at this time," said Blaise.

Valeray made a toast, and all echoed his words: *"Vive le nourrisson à venir!"*

. . .

Amid joyous talk, the bisque was followed by venison in a light splash of a white cream sauce, with a sautéed medley of green beans and small onions and peas, all accompanied by a hearty red wine well aged in a cool cellar.

In addition, the servers brought out a wide platter of baked pheasants basted in honey, and still another of the white wines, this one light saffron in color. Accompanying the entrée was a bowl of sautéed mushrooms and a sautéed medley of carrots and parsnips and red beets.

"Ah, my favorite," said Borel, as the venison was brought to the board. "Merci, Maman," he added, looking down the long table to where his mother sat at the far end.

Saissa smiled and signaled that she would have pheasant instead.

Yet even as they settled into the main meal, eventually the talk took a more serious turn as once again they spoke of the mysterious and malignant intrusion of something or someone upon their daily activities:

"And you think this acolyte, this Hradian, is at the root of it?" asked Émile.

"Oui," replied Borel. "After all, my sire and his get are the ones she would hold responsible for the downfall of their plans: imprisonment of Orbane, the ruination of her schemes against my sire and dam and her plans for the Summerwood, and the deaths of her three sisters—Rhensibé, Iniquí, and Nefasí, in that order."

"First was Rhensibé," said Michelle. "Torn to shreds by Borel's Wolves."

"Then came Iniquí," said Liaze, "kicked into everlasting fire by Deadly Nightshade, Luc's warhorse."

"Finally, Nefasí," said Céleste, "slain by a god-made arrow."

"And you three are responsible?" asked Simone.

"No more so than those three acolytes," said Borel.

"In each case, Simone," said Saissa, "the witches themselves had done terrible deeds and were about to do more: Hradian had changed one of my sons into a Bear and would mate him with a Troll; Rhensibé was about to slay Michelle and Borel with her very own poisonous claws; Iniquí would have drawn Céleste into the fire and would have let Luc die of exposure on a dark mountain afar; likewise was Nefasí set to kill your son Roél and would have slain Céleste, and the Lord of the Changelings would have left Laurent and Blaise as statues and used Avélaine as a brood mare. It was only because of these brave souls sitting here that none of that came to pass. It was Valeray's deed that led to Orbane's downfall, and it was Camille who upset Hradian's schemes. And as far as the three slain acolytes, it was Borel who had called his Wolves, and Liaze who commanded Deadly Nightshade to attack, and Céleste who loosed the gray arrow, and these things spelled the end of Rhensibé and Iniquí and Nefasí. So is it any wonder that Hradian would seek vengeance?"

"Oh, non, Lady Saissa, *that* I understand," said Simone. "It's just that I wish none of it had come to pass, especially now that Avélaine is expecting."

"Oh, Maman," said Avélaine, "had it not come to pass, then I would never have met Chevell, and you would not have a grandchild on the way. And of course, we could not let that happen, now, could we?"

"Ah, young love and young mothers to be," said Valeray, beaming at Avélaine, and then at Alain and Camille, at Borel and Michelle, at Liaze and Luc, at Céleste and Roél, and finally at his own Saissa. But then he sobered and raised his glass to them all and grimly said, "As declared apast by the Three Sisters, dreadful events lie ahead. Perhaps these ominous sensings the women feel are signs that those events are nigh upon us. Regardless and as I said once before, here's to interesting times."

To interesting times, said they all, though tears stood in Simone's eyes and those of Saissa as well.

6

Glamours

"Now, where is that other gown?" snapped Hradian, searching among the musty clothes in the meager loft. "No, no, not that one, nor this one. Ah, here is the one. The same as I wore to Summerwood Manor five and some years agone. Such pretty danglers and lace, like smoke streaming. But it won't do to wear it again as it is. No, I'll have to cast a glamour over it, something to match—"

A deep-throated plaintive croak sounded.

Hradian turned and looked down at the doorway. "What is it, Crapaud?"

Another croak, this one with a needy edge.

"Oui, you may seek your breakfast, but return quickly; I have a duty for you."

The monstrous toad—nearly the size of a bushel basket—hitched about and waddled to the verge of the flet and toppled off to plop into the scum-laden water.

Hradian swung her attention back to the garment and sniffed the cloth. She didn't smell ought, for her nose was completely inured to the reek of swamp bottom, and if the same malodor clung to the gown, it would escape her notice. "Bah," she growled, "whether or no, it'll air out on my flight, especially if I ride low o'er the desert."

Down the wall-ladder she clambered, the gown over her

shoulder. When she reached the floor, she slipped into the black dress and covered her nakedness. For perhaps the third time in her life she wished she had a mirror to admire herself, but mirrors are tricky things, and open to someone spying in upon her. Of course the surface could be covered with the right kind of impenetrable cloth, or the mirror could be turned to face the wall, or kept in a tight closet by itself for occasional and limited viewing; but still if a mage were powerful enough, he could launch an attack through the speculum itself whether or no the device was hidden, or covered, or in use. No, no mirror had she nor would she ever, except for a bowl filled with inky liquid, and that but a temporary tool to spy upon her enemies. Instead she had to be content with looking down at herself only to see—"This won't do"—that her grimy toes peeked out from the hem. "Shoes, yes shoes." Hradian found her cracked leather slippers and tied the laces and hissed, "One day, and soon, my love, you'll have nought but the finest soft footwear, of fur and satin and cloth and suede and whatever else you wish."

Hradian then scrabbled through her belongings and finally found what she wanted: a small pouch on a thong. She slipped the potion vial into it and secured the top and hung it about her neck.

Then, because the journey would be a lengthy one, she shoved a wedge of cheese and a loaf of bread into a small rucksack and looped the strap over her head and shoulder. Looking about and deciding she needed to carry nothing else, she took up her besom.

"Crapaud! Crapaud! Where are you?"

There came a squashy splop out on the flet, and the bloated toad, dripping water, waddled to the doorway. Part of something wiggling and slimy—the hindquarters and tail of a large newt? a lizard? something else altogether?—dangled from the corner of Crapaud's wide mouth, the toad trying to gulp it down, while the partly swallowed thing fought to extract itself.

"Crapaud, watch over the house," commanded Hradian.

Crapaud emitted a croak, and in that same moment the thing escaped. But as it darted for the water—*schlakk!*—Crapaud's long tongue snatched it up.

Without waiting to see if the thing was swallowed or not, Hradian mounted her twiggy broom and flew away, the trim and danglers from her dress flowing out behind her like ragged shadows melting away.

As soon as she was above the drifting miasma of the swamp, Hradian took a quick glance at the morning sun. "Must hurry, must hurry," she muttered, and she goaded her besom to greater speed. "They will be well started by the time I arrive. A simple glamour will do at first, but then . . ." With the wind of her passage whipping through her black hair, Hradian broke into laughter as she sped toward her destination.

· · ·

Twilight bound after twilight bound she crossed, and the sun rose up the sky. And in the marks after the sun passed through the zenith, Hradian cast her first glamour and then crossed another bound. In the forest below were any observing, unless they had Fey sight, they would see nought but a crow winging starwise. And even had they Fey sight, still they might see nought but a tremulous aura about the dark bird.

· · ·

A candlemark or so and a twilight bound later, in midafternoon the crow spiralled down to come to rest in a leafy forest.

Moments later, with a second glamour cast, a small girl, bearing a bouquet of wildflowers, stepped out from the trees and onto the green grassy field.

7

Faire

As Émile shoveled eggs onto his plate to go with the rashers and toast and jam, he asked, "Valeray, is there anyone else, other than this Hradian witch, and perhaps her master Orbane, who might wish to see you and your get dead?"

Valeray shrugged. "None I can think of." Then he looked at Saissa and grinned. "Oh, there are some lords and ladies and mayors and such who might yet hold a grudge against me for deeds long past when I was yet a thief. But I would think those resentments not enough to send someone or something spying, especially someone or something unseen."

They sat outside on a balcony overlooking the tournament field, with its many tents where jongleurs and merchants and participants and fest-goers had come to entertain, to sell their wares, to enter the contests, or to otherwise engage in the faire. Smoke from fires rose in the morning air as those gathered broke their own fasts, or cooked specialties to sell to others— with hogs on spits and slabs of ribs and sides of beef roasting; with various fish and fowl turning and frying as well; with pots of beans and meats and soups dangling above the fires and bubbling; and breads and sweets and other such fare baking—all of them wafting their aromas across the way to entice the milling throng. A minstrel's voice rose in distant song accompanied by a lute, and a piccolo ran a rising scale and then fell silent.

Midst the tents lay a large open arena with tiers of seats on one side for the king and his invited guests. Opposite the tiers and on a gentle rise a fence set the boundary for others to gather and watch and cheer for their favorites. In between lay the tourney field, where most of the events would be held: archery, dueling, the caber toss, the hammer throw, the discus, the foot races, and others. On the field as well stood the lists, where knights mounted on chargers would run—shields up, lances couched—in attempts to unseat one another.

And overlooking it all from their distant high terrace, King Valeray, Queen Saissa, Sieur Émile, and Lady Simone sat at breakfast.

"What about the Changelings?" asked Simone. "Because Roél slew their lord, and Céleste killed the witch, and they freed Laurent and Blaise and rescued Avélaine, wouldn't the Changelings seek revenge?"

"Perhaps," replied Valeray. "Mayhap some of them can make themselves invisible or change into something so small as to be overlooked—a fly, a flea, a gnat, or some such. But it would take more than one Changeling—in fact at least five altogether; one for each manor, that is—for at times some of these occurrences happen leagues upon leagues apart within but moments of one another." He turned to Saissa. "Isn't that correct, my dear?"

"Oui. Certainly within a candlemark of one another, or so my daughters and daughters-in-law and I do say."

Émile frowned. "And you know this how . . . ?"

"We fly the messenger falcons, and in the message we usually note when the feeling of malignancy occurred. At times it is 'round the mid of night. At other times it is just after dusk. And at still other times it is in the moments ere dawn. Seldom does it occur when the sun is up. But even were these sensings to happen a candlemark or so apart, there is not enough time for a single spy to get from one manor to another. Perhaps, as Valeray says, if several Changelings worked in concert, we would all sense the malignancy nigh the same moment, yet I believe instead it is Hradian—and only Hradian—using some sort of magic to spy on us, for her motives are strongest."

Émile nodded and took another bite of jam-slathered toast.

"Well then, let us suppose it is Hradian," said Simone, "is there ought we or anyone can do to counteract it?"

Valeray shook his head. "For the moment, non. Yet mayhap one of magekind can suggest a way. Even so, the nearest mage of worth is days distant; it would take time to fetch him. But even then, if no occurrence happens in his presence, I think he would be as puzzled as are we."

"But he might have a suggestion," said Simone.

"Oui, he might," replied Saissa. "Yet I believe that what we said yestereve still holds: after Rhensibé was slain, the Fates warned us that the remaining acolytes would seek revenge, and they certainly did so. And now there is but one acolyte left. And so there seems to be nought for it but to do as the Fates have advised: stand ready, and be on guard."

"On guard against what?" asked Avélaine, as she and Liaze and Céleste swept onto the balcony.

Valeray and Émile got to their feet, and Valeray said, "What else, my dear, but Hradian?"

"Oh, poo!" said Avélaine, making a moue. "Can't we forget about the witch on this day?" She cast a wide gesture toward the arena. "I mean, it's tourney day, a time for joy and not brooding." She looked about the balcony and added, "And where are the bright chevaliers?"

"In the armory," said Borel, as he and Alain stepped onto the terrace, Michelle on Borel's arm, Camille on Alain's.

"They choose their weaponry," said Alain. He gave Saissa a kiss on the cheek, and then took up a plate for himself.

"You do not join them?" asked Émile.

"Non, Sieur Émile," said Alain. "I'm afraid the Bear would take offense at someone thrusting a weapon at me."

"The Bear?"

Alain smiled. "I'll explain later."

Émile then swung his gaze toward Borel, and the prince said, "Likewise my Wolves," as if that told all.

"Our combat this day will be in archery," said Alain.

"Do not forget échecs," said Camille.

"Oh, indeed, in échecs too," said Borel.

"And what about you, Sieur Émile?" asked Céleste. "You do not joust this day?"

Émile sighed and looked at Simone. "Their mother will not let me take a run at my own sons nor lift a weapon 'gainst them. But I, too, will take up bow and arrow and stand on the field and compete."

"And you, Papa?" asked Michelle.

Valeray shook his head. "No warrior am I. Ah, but if you have a lock to pick . . ."

The balcony rang with laughter.

. . .

After breaking fast, they all strolled toward the arena, passing jesters and jugglers, minstrels and stilt-walkers, bards and fortune-tellers, hawkers and merchants purveying their wares. Booths of food-sellers tried to tempt them to partake of their fare, and various hucksters called out for good gentlemen and ladies to try their games: axe throwing, mad archery, toss the ball, and other such diversions.

"Why do they call it 'mad archery'?" asked Simone, as they strolled by the bow-and-arrow booth.

"Ah. The arrows are bent and curved and crooked and the fletching twisted," said Céleste. "The fun comes in watching their flight toward the many targets. Trying to strike the central bull's eye and win a prize is quite challenging."

"Are none of the shafts straight?" asked Émile.

"Straight as a sand viper," said Borel, laughing.

On they went, pausing a moment before the puppet theater,

where the crowd laughed as one of the puppets—a female with a skillet—beat upon a poor, hapless, masked burglar, driving him howling around the tiny stage. As the playlet ended, Borel dropped a coin or two into the passing hat. Then he and the family moved on.

And as they threaded among the throng, the citizens bowed and curtseyed in deference to the royalty, and the royalty acknowledged such with smiles and nods and hand gestures.

At last they reached the arena, and entered the central box. Horns sounded and Valeray and Saissa took the thrones, while the others took seats alongside or down a tier or two before the royal couple. Across the field and beyond a stout fence running the width of the rise, spectators bowed and curtseyed. When the king and queen were seated and the horns sounded again, the citizenry straightened and waited in anticipation.

A herald rode to the ground before the king's box and saluted and said, "My lord?"

And Valeray replied, "Let the games begin."

The herald blew a blast on his trump, and the crowd cheered.

. . .

After the caber toss—won by a giant of a man, a crofter from the fields in the Summerwood—the herald rode out and about the floor of the arena and cried out, "*Mon Roi, ma Reine, et Membres de la Famille Royale, et Sieurs, Mesdames, et Hommes et Femmes et Enfants,* I warn you the hammer throw can be quite dangerous, with an errant toss occasionally known to maim or kill an onlooker. So be prepared to flee should one come your way."

Simone turned to Avélaine. "Is that true? Have people been maimed, even killed?"

"Oh, Maman, worry not, for the hammer throwers are very good."

Simone frowned and huffed, "Well, someone"—she glanced at Valeray—"should provide high, loosely woven wicker walls along each side of the hammer-throw ring. That way, should the thrower lose control of the hammer, then it would simply strike one of the barriers and fall to the ground and not fly into the onlookers."

"Ah, but wouldn't that take some of the thrill out of the sport, Maman?"

"Better a safe wife than a grieving widow," said Simone.

They watched as throws were made, and as each toss was hurled the crowd roared, Avélaine cheering alongside the men, with Simone frowning at this unseemly behavior of her daughter, even though Céleste and Liaze and Camille and Michelle were shouting just as lustily.

And they laughed as one of the garishly clad and painted jesters ran onto the field and took up the hammer and swung it about and tossed it no farther than a half stride. Jumping up and down in seeming anger, he took it up again and swung it 'round and appeared to drop it onto his foot, and he howled and hopped about, holding the injured extremity, while pointing at it and bawling. And then he fell to the ground, and two more gaudy jesters rushed out with a litter, and laid it alongside the "injured" one and rolled him in between the poles. And when they took it up to bear him away, it seems that it wasn't really a litter at all, but merely two poles. And as they trundled off, the jester on the ground looked up and about and then leapt to his feet and ran after the others, shouting, while the crowd howled in glee.

"Oh, isn't this just splendid, Maman?" asked Avélaine.

Maman, laughing and trying to catch her breath, turned to her daughter and nodded, completely unable to speak.

. . .

The hammer throw was followed by the discus, and then the running events, and they were followed by a show of horsemanship, with the animals dancing and prancing and sidling and turning to the oohs and ahhs of the appreciative crowd.

After that display, men on horseback and bearing light lances ran races where they speared small rings from atop willowy wands stuck in the ground. The swiftest one with the most rings would be declared the winner. Rider after rider vied, and time was kept by water draining through a hole in a bucket and through a funnel and into a measuring cup. As each rider started, a judge pulled a plug, and the water began to pour. When the rider rang a bell at the end of the course, the cup was whisked from under the spout and the amount noted—the less liquid the faster the run. The plug was replaced and the bucket refilled and the measuring cup once again set under, and the next rider made his try.

Halfway through the event, the jester entered the contest, and before he finished his single ride, the cup overflowed and the judges replaced it with a pail, and the container above had to be refilled. Amid hoots and laughter and jeers of the crowd, as the water continued to run, the jester yelled, "Oh, oh, help, help, my bucket runneth over!" This brought the other two jesters running onto the field and, amid many pratfalls, they took the rings from the willow wands and, dropping them and retrieving them several times, they at last placed them on the mounted jester's lance, who then rode back in gleeful triumph, to discover he hadn't rung the gong. He galloped back to the bell and swung his lance at it, only to miss and fall off his horse, and the animal promptly ran away, with the three jesters shouting and chasing after.

As soon as the whooping crowd settled, again the serious contestants vied for the victory. In the end a young lad of no more than eleven summers was declared champion of that event.

When the archery contest came about, many a man took up the challenge, including Émile and Borel and Alain, and they were joined by Luc and Roél and Blaise and Laurent. In the competition as well, stood Céleste and Liaze and Michelle and Saissa.

Long did the contest last, for there were many vying, yet the number remaining dwindled and dwindled, until at last there were but four: Borel and Luc and Céleste and a man from a place called the Wyldwood—Regar by name, tall and lithe and uncommonly handsome, and many thought he might be one of the Fey, perhaps even an Elf.

Back moved the targets and back, and still none was a clear winner. But finally the range was such that Céleste and her smaller bow, with a pull not equal to those of the three men, at last fell out of the competition.

And now it was Luc and Borel and Regar, and the judges moved the targets one more time, the range now uncommonly distant, and the onlookers gasped at the skill involved. Arrows flew to strike the small central circle afar, yet in the end Borel prevailed by nought but a single shaft. And the crowd roared its approval.

"Well played," said Regar, running a hand through his yellow hair. "I had not been bested erenow."

"Who knows?" said Borel. "Were we to have another go, it could readily be you or Luc who would be the champion crowned; and forget not Céleste, for she could just as easily have won as well."

"Oui," said Luc. "Last summer it was I who prevailed, and the summer before it was she."

"Then let us gather her up and share a glass of wine," said Regar.

"Non, Regar, not for me, but surely you and Borel and Céleste can do so," said Luc. "I must excuse myself, for I will need all my wits and skill in the knightly competition to come."

"You are a chevalier, then?"

"Oui. And three contests remain: dueling with épées, the mêlée, and jousting. And I am opposed by three brothers—Roél, Blaise, and Laurent—boon companions and worthy knights all."

. . .

The tips of the épées were slathered with red ochre, and the contest begun, and whenever a hit was made, the judges looked at the mark and decided whether or no it was a fatal strike, a major wound, or a minor one. A fatal blow would of course end the match; otherwise points decided the victor, with an opponent's own points being reduced if he had suffered a major wound.

The final match came down to Blaise and Luc, and in the end both had suffered a major wound, but Luc then struck Blaise with a second major, and thus was awarded the contest.

Next came the mêlée, and for the first time, amid the *chnkk!* and *thdd!* of padded weapons, Laurent was the champion.

By this time it was midafternoon, and the knights retired to their tents to prepare for the jousting.

. . .

And a small girl bearing a bouquet of wildflowers wandered through the hustle and bustle of the grounds, as she made her way toward the arena. Finally, reaching her goal, she scanned the guests until she espied the one she sought. Then she turned and traipsed away.

. . .

On Camille's shoulder, Scruff suddenly perked up, and he grabbed a tress of Camille's golden hair and repeatedly tugged.

"What is it, Scruff? What do you see?"

Scruff chirped excitedly.

Avélaine looked at the wee bird and then at Camille. "What is he doing?"

. . .

Looking about to see that no one was nigh, the small girl set aside her flowers, and reached up to her neck and took out a vial. "Remember, my love," she muttered, "you need to cast a glamour to disguise the dress." Then she drank down the contents and tossed the vial aside.

. . .

"Scruff only does this when he senses a peril of some sort," said Camille.

"What peril?" asked Avélaine, looking about.

Camille's own gaze sought the cause. "I do not know."

"Should we tell the king?"

"Oui."

. . .

There sounded a soft step at the entry to Luc's tent. Luc turned about to see Liaze. "Come to wish me luck?"

"Oui, beloved, I do, and yet I come for another reason as well."

"Another reason?" He reached for her, and she came into his arms willingly. "And what might that be?" he whispered.

She gave a low throaty laugh, but then turned serious. "The amulet, the key. I wouldn't wish it to take damage in the joust. It is too important. Let me wear it as your favor, just as you wear mine."

"It's never been damaged before," said Luc.

"Nevertheless, my love."

"If you insist," said Luc, and he released her and lifted the chain over his head. "Here, I give this to you willingly."

She took the talisman and looped it about her own neck.

From the arena sounded the trumpets; 'twas the signal for the knights to assemble.

" 'Tis the call to arms," said Luc.

"Good fortune, my love," said she.

Luc turned to the table and took up his gauntlets. "Victory this time might be more difficult, for the three brothers have been—" He looked back, but she was gone.

. . .

"What do you think it is he senses?" asked Valeray.

"I know not," said Camille.

Of a sudden Scruff took to wing, and he arrowed toward the

dawnwise end of the arena, and in that same moment a crow flew up just beyond. Swiftly did the sparrow fly, but swifter was the crow, and it soon outdistanced the wee bird.

"Ah, 'twas a crow," said Valeray, relaxing back into his chair.

Camille frowned, but said nought.

In that moment and amid a fanfare of trumpets, the four knights on their magnificent steeds entered the arena—two from the duskwise end, two from the one dawnwise—and a great roar rose up from the crowd.

"Oh, isn't my Roél quite splendid?" said Céleste, looking leftward, duskwise.

"As is my Luc," said Liaze, taking her seat and looking rightward instead.

8

Disaster

Disgruntled and chirping querulously, Scruff returned to Camille's shoulder, the wee bird agitated to a degree she had not seen since a time seasons past when she and the bird had found themselves on an island infested by Redcap Goblins and monstrous Trolls.

"My lord," said Camille to Valeray, "I think Scruff would not be this disturbed were that a mere crow."

"Think you it was a Changeling?"

"I know not, my lord, but whatever it was, it upset Scruff mightily."

A second flourish of trumpets sounded, and Camille turned to see Luc, Roél, Blaise, and Laurent rein up before the royal box. Still troubled, she sat in deference to the formalities.

Colorful were the knights: a blue surcoat graced Luc, and he bore a blue shield with a red rose emblem thereon, both colors marking his demesne, but his black horse—Deadly Nightshade—was caparisoned in scarlet, to represent the Autumnwood; Roél and his pale grey horse were garbed in light green to mark the Springwood, and Roél bore a like-hued green shield embellished with a pale cherry blossom; Laurent wore a white surcoat, and his white horse was draped in white as well, and he bore a dark shield marked with a white snow crystal, and he represented the Winterwood; finally, Blaise was garbed in yellow, as was his dark grey steed, and his yellow shield bore the emblem of an oak leaf, representing the Summerwood.

"My lord, my lady," said Luc, and he dipped his lance in salute, as did the other three chevaliers.

The king and queen both inclined their heads in acknowledgement, and Valeray said, "Knights, you honor us with your combat. Take your positions, ride with pride and nobility, and may the best man"—Valeray grinned—"or perhaps the luckiest, prevail on this day."

Raising their lances, they wheeled their steeds and rode to opposite ends of the field: Luc and Laurent to the dawnwise end; Roél and Blaise, duskwise.

And the crowd cheered lustily, various voices therein calling out white, or gold, or green, or blue.

In the first of the rounds, Luc had drawn Blaise, and Roél had drawn Laurent. And at the sound of the trumpets, Luc and Blaise were first in the lists, and they rode to take station. All eyes were on Queen Saissa, and she raised a hand holding a filmy scarf, and with it she signaled for the tilt to begin.

With horses belling in excitement, shields up, lances lowered, Luc and Blaise charged one another. Each ran at a gallop, sawdust and wood curls flying up from hooves, and the crowd roared in anticipation. In spite of the padded tips, with thunderous *clangs!* lances met shields. Blaise's shaft shivered into splinters, and Luc was rocked back, his own lance glancing awry 'gainst Blaise's dark shield. And a great shout went up, for it looked as if Luc would be unhorsed. Yet Luc recovered even as the steeds hammered onward.

Each rode to the end of the lists, and Blaise cast aside the remains of his broken lance and took up another from the attendant acting as his squire.

'Round they wheeled, did the knights, and again they charged, the blue chevalier against the gold, the black horse against the dark grey steed.

Once more with a *blang!* the two crashed together, and this time Luc's shaft struck the oakleaf square, while Blaise's slid off the rose. Blaise was hammered back and, in spite of his efforts, he was knocked from his saddle to land in the sawdust and shavings below.

Cheers sounded as well as groans, and a goodly number of coins changed hands.

Luc rode 'round the end of the lists and back to Blaise, and he gave the unhorsed knight a stirrup and an arm, and Blaise swung up behind. They rode to where the dark grey steed had stopped. Blaise slid from the back of Nightshade, and bowed to Luc, then mounted his own animal.

They both rode to opposite ends of the field, and dismounted to await the outcome of the next match.

To great cheers, Roél unhorsed Laurent on the very first run.

Once again coinage changed hands.

Now came the concluding match—Prince Luc versus Sieur Roél—the same final pairing as at last year's faire.

Lance after lance they shattered against one another, and each was nearly unhorsed several times. Yet finally there were no more lances left, but for the one Roél held, and it was cracked.

With a fanfare of trumpets, King Valeray stood, and when the onlookers quieted, the king called it a draw.

The crowd groaned, and this time no coins changed hands. But as the two chevaliers rode about the field, a great cheer rose up in tribute.

In spite of the draw at tilting, Luc was named Champion of Champions, for with a win at épées and a tie at jousting, he had more victory points than any of the other three knights.

Laughing, they all rode for Luc's tent, where, slapping one another on the back, they hoisted mugs of ale in salute to one another. Smiling, Laurent protested that, with his win in the mêlée, he should have been crowned champion, but Roél countered that Laurent's ignominious showing in the joust completely nullified any win he might have "accidentally" gained. Blaise sighed and said that he had been entirely shut out this time, though he could have sworn that Luc had magical help to remain on his horse in the very first tilt.

Liaze and Céleste entered this male domain, and they embraced each and kissed each on the cheek, and added another kiss to their husbands' lips.

"You must excuse us, chéri," said Liaze, looking up into Luc's eyes. "We go to change our clothes into gowns a bit less demure, less modest, than these high-collar fashions, and then hie to the grand ballroom. The échecs tournament has begun, and we each have a match to win."

"Why change clothes, my love?" asked Roél.

Céleste grinned. "Our first opponents are men, and a femme must take every advantage."

The men burst into laughter, but finally Luc, yet smiling, looked down at Liaze and said, "As soon as I sluice some of this sweat and salt from me and change garb, I'll be there to cheer you on, a more revealing gown or no."

"As will I cheer you," said Roél, embracing Céleste.

With one last peck, Liaze and Céleste withdrew.

Blaise turned to Roél and Luc and said, "Oh, were Laurent and I as fortunate as you twain."

"*Mais oui!*" agreed Laurent.

· · ·

In the second round of échecs matches, by the luck of the draw Borel was pitted against Regar, the Wyldwood stranger. Swift did they make move after move, seeming somewhat reckless, yet they were both anything but. Still, spearmen were slain, chevaliers fought valiantly, and hierophants and towers slid this way and that, while queens reigned in violence, and kings fled a square at a time.

"Your play is somewhat like that of another opponent I once

faced," said Borel, slipping his lone hierophant diagonally along two white squares.

"Oh?" responded Regar, countering with a move of his remaining black chevalier. "And who was that?"

"The Fairy King under the Hill," said Borel. "He nearly defeated me."

Regar sat back, his eyes wide in wonder. "You won?"

"Oui."

Regar shook his head and then leaned forward and studied the board. "I did not think any could best my grand-père in échecs, for his reputation is formidable, and in fact is why I wanted to learn the game."

Now it was Borel who leaned back in wonder. "The Fairy King is your grandsire?"

Regar grinned. "So it is said. It seems he came upon my grand-maman, a beautiful woman, gathering herbs in the wood, and they found each other irresistible, and their dalliance produced my maman, and she in turn, me."

"Your grand-père is indeed a mighty master of échecs," said Borel, advancing a spearman forward one square. "When did you play him last?"

"I have never seen him, and only know him through the tales I have heard," said Regar. "It seems his queen is most jealous, and after that dalliance with my grand-maman, to keep her safe, he left her."

"Oo, how cold."

"I think it was not done with a cold heart, for grand-maman said he wept bitterly." Regar countered with a move of one of his own spearmen. "He did leave her very well off, yet I have always wished to meet him."

"Perhaps some day you will," said Borel, "yet beware, for he is quite sly, quite tricky."

"Think you that he would attempt to deceive his own blood?" asked Regar.

Borel turned up both hands. "That I cannot say. I think if he knew of your kinship, he would welcome you, though perhaps in secret." Borel then moved a spearman and said, "Ward your queen."

Regar smiled and said, "Ah, I thought my lady would be a too-tempting target for you." Regar slid his tower next to a hierophant-protected spearman and said, "I believe that is mate."

Borel looked at the board and burst into laughter and turned his king on its side. "Well played, Prince Regar. Very well played. I think should you ever duel your grand-père in échecs, it will be quite a game."

Regar cocked an eyebrow. "Prince? You name me prince?"

"Indeed, for your grandsire is the Fairy King."

Regar nodded and ruefully smiled. "Ah, oui. But at best I am merely a bastard prince."

Borel grinned and stood. "Come, Regar, let us share a cup ere your next match."

As prince and bastard prince made their way toward the wine table, Roél and Luc, freshly bathed and clothed, entered the grand ballroom. They paused at the entrance and surveyed the tables where opponent and opponent studied the boards. "Ah, there is my Céleste," said Roél.

"And I see Liaze," said Luc.

"Let us not disturb them," said Roél, gesturing at the table where a sommelier oversaw servants pouring wine, "but join my brothers for a drink."

Even as they walked past windows, beyond which twilight graced the sky, Camille, uncharacteristically distracted and having lost her match, came alongside them. A yet-disgruntled Scruff sat on her shoulder, though the wee sparrow now grew sleepy as dusk drew down on the land.

"How fared you, sister?" asked Roél.

The corner of Camille's mouth twitched upward. She gestured toward a table where a corpulent man, looking somewhat stunned, sat and peered at the échiquier, most of the pieces thereon. "There is the victor."

"You lost?"

"Oui. I simply couldn't concentrate on the game."

"Why so?"

"Scruff sensed danger, yet I could see nought. And then he flew at a crow, but it was too swift for him to overtake."

"Perhaps a good thing," said Luc. "Crows are quite savage, and Scruff so small."

"Valeray thought it might be a Changeling," said Camille.

Both Roél and Luc's eyebrows raised, and Luc asked, "Think you it has ought to do with these sensings you and the others have?"

Camille sighed. "All I know is that Scruff was quite agitated. Still is, in fact."

As they reached the wine table, Roél asked, "Did you sense a malignancy?"

Camille shook her head. "Non."

"Perhaps then it was nought but a crow," said Luc.

Camille turned up a hand, but otherwise did not reply.

After receiving their goblets of wine, the trio joined Laurent and Blaise off to one side, and moments later Borel and Regar came to stand with the group.

"How did you fare?" asked Camille.

"Meet my conqueror," said Borel, raising his goblet toward Regar. "Prince Regar trounced me handily."

"You are a prince?" asked Céleste, just then joining the cluster.

"Ask Borel," said Regar, with a sigh.

"He is the grandson of the Fairy King," said Borel. "Here, Regar, let me properly present you to all."

Even as the introductions were being made, Liaze joined the group and was formally presented to Regar as well.

"How did you fare 'gainst your opponent?" asked Luc.

Liaze smiled and said, "He seemed quite preoccupied in looking at something other than the board."

Céleste laughed and said, "As did the man I played."

Roél grinned. "I shouldn't wonder, given your décolletage."

Luc smiled and looked at each of their low-cut gowns, the women bare from the throat down to the considerable cleavage shown. Then he frowned. "Liaze, where is the key?"

"Key?"

"The amulet. I gave it to you ere the jousting."

Liaze shook her head in bewilderment. "Non, chéri. You gave me no amulet."

"But you came to me in my tent and asked to keep it safe. And I willingly handed it over."

"Non, Luc. Though I did now and then change seats, I was in the stands the whole time."

Camille gasped and turned pale. "Oh, Mithras. *That's* what Scruff was agitated about: the witch was here at the tourney! Somehow she fooled you, Luc."

The color drained from Luc's face, and Blaise whispered, "Hradian?"

"Oui, Hradian. By glamour or other spell, it wasn't Liaze, but *must* have been Hradian instead, or so I deem."

Céleste blanched and looked at the sparrow, who now slept in Camille's pocket. "Nor, I think, was it a crow he chased, but again 'twas Hradian."

Tears sprang into Liaze's eyes. "Oh woe upon woe, for now she has the key to the Castle of Shadows and, can we not stop her, she will set Orbane free."

9

Success!

Laughing in glee, Hradian—to all eyes nought but a crow—
flew on her broom through the darkening sky, and her hand
clutched the amulet on the chain 'round her neck. "Fools,
those fools, little did they know they could not stop you, my
love. Your potion worked to perfection. Perfection! Ha! A simple glamour wouldn't do, oh no. Instead you had to *become*
that slattern Liaze, for you knew that her paramour would embrace you, and his arms would feel what his eyes saw not. And
you, my sweet, now have the key, the key that will gain your
master's release! Oh, clever you. None of your sisters could do
as did you."

Chortling and laughing, Hradian fled across the sky, her
distant swamp cottage her initial goal, and then a realm afar
and the Great Darkness beyond. But as she crossed the very
first twilight border and entered the Springwood, she came to
ground on a high, rocky tor and cast a calling spell. And soon,
in spite of the growing dark, the air about was filled with a
milling flock of cawing crows, and Hradian spoke to them in
their very own tongue. What she said, they understood, though
none but someone else versed in the cornix tongue could know
the words of her command. Regardless, when she fell silent, in
a great cawing racket, the flock flew up and 'round and then
fragmented into individual birds hammering across the sky,

heading toward the Summerwood and Winterwood and Autumnwood, and deeper into the Springwood as well.

Once more Hradian took to the air, smirking unto herself and saying, "They don't call them a murder of crows for nought." And then she burst into laughter and flew on into the gathering dark.

10

Sighting

Wakened by a cacophony, two Sprites scrambled to their feet on the leaf where they had bedded down for the night. Tiny they were, no more than two inches tall, and their diaphanous wings quivered, the Sprites ready to spring into flight. But for a scabbard belted at one Sprite's waist and a speck of a moonstone on a miniscule chain 'round the neck of the other, male and female, they were completely unclothed. And at the sight of a black flock circling, the male drew a wee silver épée from the sheath at his side.

"Crows, Fleurette, crows! Quickly, cover Buzzer. Hide her from the crows."

As the female snapped a leaf from a branch and used it to hide the bumblebee asleep on their green bed, she said, "What is it, Flic? What is going on?"

Away flew the ebon birds, scattering this way and that, and both Fleurette and Flic crouched down. Flic said, "I don't know what this is all about, but there's someone on the tor, and—" Of a sudden he gasped. " 'Tis a witch, Fleurette. She just took to flight."

Both watched as a dark figure, silhouetted against the twilight sky, soared upward, the lace and long danglers of her black dress flowing out like wisps of gloom.

"Oh, my," said Fleurette. "I think that might be Hradian."

"How know you this?"

"Camille once described Hradian's flight as a sinister knot of darkness, streaming tatters and tendrils of shadow flapping in the wind behind."

Flic's eyes widened in remembrance. "Oui, but you are right, my love; Borel once described her to me. Oh, my, Hradian in the Springwood. We need warn Céleste of the witch in her demesne. Perhaps I should fly onward to the Castle of the Seasons, yet, with all these crows about, I cannot leave you behind."

"Those murdering birds are gone," said Fleurette, and she gestured toward the sleeping bee and added, "but it's Buzzer we cannot leave behind."

Flic glanced toward the nearby twilight border looming up in the darkness. "I could carry her across the bound and leave her in a safe place with you, and then fly on to the castle. The crows are not likely to come across, especially with night now falling."

"Well and good," said Fleurette. "And first thing in the dawning, Buzzer and I will take to wing and follow."

Cradling the sleeping bumblebee and struggling a bit to fly— for the insect was nearly as large as the Sprite—Flic followed Fleurette through the dark marge, Buzzer shifting uneasily in the embrace yet not awakening. On the far side of the border, Fleurette led Flic to a broad oak, and out at the end of one arm of the tree she found a suitable leaf to settle on.

Flic set Buzzer down, and then offered Fleurette the épée, but Fleurette refused, saying, "Buzzer will be my protector, chéri. Go you now, and swiftly, for a witch to be in the Springwood is an ill omen."

Flic nodded and kissed Fleurette and leapt into the air, and soon he was lost against the deepening purple of the failing twilight sky.

11

Traces

"Perhaps I am wrong," said Céleste. "Mayhap the crow Scruff chased wasn't Hradian, and she is yet on the grounds."

Regar turned to Camille. "This Hradian, she is the witch you spoke of?"

"Oui," said Camille.

"And this crow: you think it was she?"

"Oui."

"Mayhap you are correct, then, for as I stood with the on-lookers on the hillside, all of us waiting for the joust, I did see a crow winging dawnwise, and it flew within a strange aura."

"You can see auras?" asked Liaze.

"Oui . . . 'round charmed things, that is. Perhaps it's my grand-père's blood that lets me see." Regar looked at Camille and added, "That wee bird in your pocket, my lady, he bears a faint red lambency, and I deem he is somehow enchanted."

Even as Camille frowned and looked down at sleeping Scruff—"And the crow . . . ?" asked Céleste.

"A dark glow," said Regar.

Céleste sighed. "Still, the winging bird might not have been Hradian, hence she might yet be on the grounds; if so, we must find her."

Alain turned to Borel. "Brother, your Wolves: they might be able to scent her."

"Mais oui," said Borel. "Come, Luc."

"What of weapons and horses?" said Luc.

"We'll deal with those," said Roél, and he turned to his brothers. "Laurent, Blaise, fetch my sword and gather weapons for all—bows, arrows, blades—and meet me at the stables, for I go to ready the steeds."

"My bow lies yon," said Regar, pointing to where his goods lay at one side of the chamber. "And I'll aid Roél with the mounts."

As the men hied away, "Come, Alain," said Borel. "The Bear can scent better than my Wolves, for they are sight hunters."

"What of us?" asked Céleste. "I'm handy with a bow, as is Liaze."

Camille shook her head. "We must not alarm the contestants, all of us rushing off at once. We three should remain and now and then pass among the players and try to look calm."

"I must tell Father," said Liaze, looking across the sundry pairs. "Ah, he is yon."

"When he finishes his match, take him aside and speak softly," said Céleste.

. . .

In the mustering shadows of the gathering dusk, Luc and Borel and Alain stepped into the courtyard, and, as if anticipating the need, waiting stood Borel's Wolves. Bearing a lantern, out over the bridge spanning the dry moat they went, and across the great grassy clearing toward the dawnwise end of the arena, where stood Luc's tent, his pennant—a red rose on a blue field—flying in the twilight above.

When they reached it and stepped inside, Borel spoke strange words to the Wolves—a mixture of growls and half-formed gutturals—and he struck several postures. The pack spread wide, their noses in the air and to the ground.

"What did you tell them?" asked Alain.

"I reminded them of Rhensibé, and asked if there was a similar scent herein."

"Ah," said Alain, and he watched as 'round the interior the Wolves snuffled, their lantern-cast shadows sliding against canvas. Slate growled at the threshold of the entrance and looked up at Borel.

"He senses something," said Luc. "Is it the smell of a sorceress?"

"Perhaps," said Borel, and he growled another word.

Slate gave a deep-throated rumble.

Borel grunted and said, "Slate thinks it is somewhat like that of the witch he and the pack tore asunder."

Luc groaned.

Again Slate growled, and he rumbled and postured, Borel frowning, watching carefully. Finally, the Wolf fell silent.

"What did he say?" asked Alain.

"It is indeed Hradian," said Borel.

Out from the tent loped the Wolves, and 'round to one side, with Borel and Alain and Luc following.

"How do they know it's Hradian?" asked Luc.

"Slate said, 'Bitch two-legs bad, rock den bad, trees bad, wind bad, leader gone, bitch two-legs gone.' "

"How does that point to Hradian?" asked Luc.

"It had slipped my mind," said Borel, "but the pack had encountered Hradian before."

Alain's eyes widened in recall. "Ah, oui, when you went to her cote near the blighted part of the Winterwood, and she used one of Orbane's amulets to send you flying away on a black wind and into imprisonment in a Troll dungeon."

"Then the 'bitch two-legs bad' is Hradian?" asked Luc.

Borel nodded. "Given the context, it can be no other."

At the side of the tent the pack milled about.

"Merde!" spat Borel. "They've lost the trail. Too many people have come this way, and their taints overlie Hradian's."

Alain stooped down and took up a small vial and held it up to the light of the faire. "Hmm . . . ocherous dregs inside." He handed the vial to Luc. "Mayhap this contained some sort of potion Hradian used to fool you."

As Luc looked at the container, Borel turned to Alain and asked, "Brother, think you the Bear can winnow her spoor from the others?"

Alain turned up a hand. "Mayhap." He frowned in concentration, and a darkness gathered about him, enveloping him, his shape changing, growing huge, brown, with long black claws and ivory fangs, and it dropped to all fours, and where Alain had been now growled a great Bear.

Back to the entrance shambled the Bear, and he snuffled at the ground, then he lumbered out to the side of the tent, and, nose to the ground, took off at a lope toward the dawnwise entrance of the arena, but the moment he got there, again he turned, and he made his way toward the stalls and tents of the merchants. Through the lantern-lit midst of the faire went the huge dark brown creature, Borel and Luc at his side, the pack of Wolves ranging aflank and arear, and people, some screaming, others crying out in fear, scattered this way and that to get out of the path of this monstrous animal and his grey savage escort, as well as the two princes.

And riding across the grass and toward this strange assortment came a gallop of horses, some with torch-bearing riders thereon, still other steeds trailing on tethers. And they angled toward the Bear and the Wolves and the two striding men.

The Bear broke free of the faire, and with its nose yet to the ground it headed toward a distant stand of trees as stars began glimmering above.

Roél and Laurent and Blaise and Regar rode nigh, but the horses reared and skittered and belled out at the reek of the Bear, and it was all the riders could do to retain control of the animals—all but Deadly Nightshade, that is, for that horse was inured to the scent, having campaigned against the Changelings in the presence of the Bear.

And still the animal lumbered on, now entering the forest, trees darkly looming up left and right and fore. In a stand of wildflowers, the Bear came to a stop, where it cast its nose this way and that, only to roar in rage and then plop down to sit among the blossoms.

A dark shimmering came upon the beast. Luc marveled as swiftly it *changed*, altering, losing bulk, gaining form, and suddenly there before them sat a man, a prince: Alain.

"This is where the oldest scent lingers," said Alain, gaining his feet. "And indeed it is Hradian's, for the Bear remembers her from the time the mages came to try to break the curse, for she was among them. I followed the trail backwards, or rather the Bear did so, and this is where it begins. It ends there beside your tent, Luc."

Borel glanced at Luc and said, "Then she flew her besom to this place, and walked through the faire to the arena, but then turned and went to your pavilion, where she became Liaze and fooled you into turning over the amulet."

Luc clenched a fist. "But why did no one see her passing through the faire, and why did she go to the arena before coming to my tent?"

Alain frowned, and then his face brightened. "She needed to see what Liaze was wearing; that's why the stop at the arena."

"Glamour," said Borel. "She must have looked like someone other than herself to slip through the faire unnoticed. I mean, had any one of us been on the faire grounds then she would have been in jeopardy. A spell would conceal her true form."

"But I embraced her," said Luc. "It was Liaze, I vow. Could a glamour transform her into my truelove?"

Both Alain and Borel shrugged.

Roél came striding into the forest, his torch held high. He looked at the trio. "Well?"

"Here's where she entered the faire grounds," said Alain. "Here the trail begins. It ends at the side of Luc's tent. I fear she is no longer in this demesne."

"The crow?" asked Roél.

"Most likely," said Borel.

"Come," said Alain. "Let us go speak with Father, for now Hradian has the key, and, if she knows how to use it, then all of Faery is in peril, for with it she surely will set Orbane free."

With Wolves ranging fore and aflank and aft they strode toward the sward where Laurent and Blaise and Regar waited with the horses. With the Bear now gone, the animals had settled by the time the four men emerged from the woods.

"The witch has flown," said Borel to those three as he mounted. "We go to see the king and break the ill news."

Even as they set out for the castle, through the dark from dawnwise a tiny Sprite came winging.

12

Affirmation

"And you think it was Hradian?"

"Papa, we are not certain of that at all," said Camille.

Valeray shook his head and sighed in resignation. "Still, who else would be after the key?"

"Indeed," said Liaze, "who else?"

"And she took on your shape?"

"Oui. Luc thought it was me and gave over the amulet to keep it safe."

"And this crow . . . Hradian, too?"

Camille nodded. "You saw Scruff pursue it, Papa, and Regar said it had a dark aura about."

"Still, it might have been a Changeling," said Valeray, "dark aura or no."

They sat in a side chamber off the grand ballroom, did Liaze, Céleste, Camille, and Valeray. The room itself was appointed in blue and served as a private chamber for intimate gatherings of the king and a handful of his guests; hence it wasn't as if the royalty had rushed off in panic, but instead had momentarily retired, perhaps simply to talk over their échecs matches and relax.

"And this Regar, he's the grandson of the Fairy King?"

Camille turned up a hand. "So he implied."

"Then that would make him a prince."

"Borel introduced him as such," said Céleste.

From beyond the closed door there came muted applause as, no doubt, someone had achieved a clever victory.

Valeray stood. "Let us return to the matches, for I would not have our absence noted. Besides, there's nought we can do until the scouting party returns, and that might be awhile, for they could be on a long chase."

Camille got to her feet. "You go, Papa, and Céleste and Liaze, too, for since I lost my first match, I will keep watch and let you know when Alain and the others get back."

Valeray looked at her in mild surprise. "You lost?"

"Oui. After Scruff's agitated display, I could not concentrate."

Liaze nodded and glumly said, "Had we only known what upset him so, mayhap we would still have the key."

Camille made her way to one of the upper balconies. She stood in the warm summer night and looked out over the faire and the people within.

Camille frowned, for the usual sounds of laughter and music did not ring. Instead she heard excited chatter—*So much for keeping them calm. I wonder what got them so stirred*—and many stood on the far edge and peered toward the forest.

Camille looked beyond the grounds, and, there at the verge of the woods, torches cast light on seven horses and three riders, and they seemed to be waiting. Deeper within the forest itself, a light gleamed, yet dark boles of trees and cast shadows obstructed the view, and so Camille could not tell what was occurring therein.

It must be Alain and the others. Oh, please, Mithras, let them all be safe.

Even as she watched, the glimmer within the woodland began to move, and shortly a borne lantern and a high-held torch showed four men and Wolves emerging. *Who they are I cannot tell, though with the pack at hand, one of them must be Borel.*

The four mounted up, and they slowly rode back toward the castle, the Wolves ranging fore and aflank and aft.

They do not seem to be tracking ought. I think they return from a fruitless search.

She watched as they rode through the gathering, and the crowds gave way before them, especially before the Wolves, and voices called out, but the men rode grimly on and did not reply.

Little do the people know the calamity that has befallen this day, with disaster to follow if Orbane is set free.

Over the bridge and into the courtyard and toward the stables the riders and Wolf pack fared, and Camille stepped back from the balcony and into the castle proper and went down the spiral stairs, making her way toward the ballroom to signal Valeray and the others that the men had returned.

. . .

One at a time, so as to not alarm the échecs contestants, the royalty slipped from the grand ballroom to make their way up to the war chamber high in a tower central to the castle, a room with windows overlooking all approaches to the holt. Camille stepped out first, and she swiftly went to the stables and led the men to the chamber, where they awaited the arrival of the others, and one by one they drifted in: Liaze, Céleste, and finally Saissa and Valeray.

Both the king and queen looked upon Regar in puzzlement, and Borel said, "Sire, Dam, this is Prince Regar of the Wyldwood, grandson to the Fairy King. He went with us on the search."

Valeray frowned and then his eyes lit in recognition. "Ah, I remember: you are the bowman who nearly won the contest at archery. Welcome, Prince."

Regar bowed and replied, "Bastard prince at best, my lord, for the Fairy King did not wed my grandmother."

"Nevertheless," said Valeray, "in my halls you are a prince."

He gestured toward the broad map table. "Let us be seated and speak of what you found."

As soon as all were ensconced in chairs, Valeray turned to Borel and said, "What came to pass?"

Borel glanced at the others and said, "While Roél and the others were gathering the horses, Alain, Luc, the Wolves, and I went to Luc's tent at the dawnwise end of the arena, and there we . . ."

.   .   .

". . . and that's when the Bear came to the end of the trail."

Saissa said, "The Bear and the Wolves went through the center of the faire?"

"Oui, Maman."

"I imagine that startled them."

"Oui, Maman, yet there was no other way to follow the imposter to the source."

Regar looked at Alain in wonderment, and Alain smiled and shrugged a shoulder.

As the vial made its way 'round to Luc, to be slipped back into the pocket of his waistcoat, King Valeray sighed. "And so, to summarize what you have told me: Hradian came to ground in the woodland, went through the heart of the faire unnoticed, perhaps in a glamoured form; she paused at the dawnwise end of the arena and took on the guise of Liaze, mayhap using a potion; then she inveigled the amulet from Luc, after which she fled."

"Oui, Papa," said Alain, with Borel and the others nodding in glum agreement.

"Given the word of the Wolves and that of the Bear," said Camille, "it was no Changeling that Scruff flew after, but instead it was Hradian in the shape of a crow, or glamoured to look like a crow, when she took flight, amulet in hand."

In the pall that followed, Luc slammed a fist to the table and exclaimed, "What a fool am I!"

"Non, Luc," said Valeray. "Fooled, oui; a fool, non."

"But I thought it peculiar that Liaze would ask for the key," replied Luc. He shook his head and added, "I should have known it was not my truelove, but an imposter instead."

Even as Liaze reached out and took Luc's hand, there came a tapping at the door, and servants entered bearing a tea service and a platter of small appetizers. They were followed by the steward of the Castle of the Seasons, a tall and spare blue-eyed man with dark hair touched by silver, who asked, "My lord, will you be dining herein?"

"Non, Claude. As before, we will be in the gold room. Set an extra plate for Prince Regar."

"Oui, my lord," said Claude, and he signaled the staff and they withdrew.

As Queen Saissa poured, and they passed the filled cups around, along with the appetizers—sautéed mushrooms stuffed with a light cheese—King Valeray sighed in resignation. "I suppose there's nothing for it but that we must raise our armies and alert the realms and notify the Firsts."

"The Firsts?" asked Regar.

"The first of each Kind to appear in Faery," said Valeray. "They were critical in defeating Orbane the last time, for they could raise whole armies; even so, Orbane alone held them off until we found a way to banish him to the Castle of Shadows in the Great Darkness beyond the Black Wall of the World."

"Ah, I see. And if I understand correctly, this talisman the witch did steal, it is the key that will unlock him."

"Oui."

There came a discreet tap at the door, and, at Valeray's call, Claude entered. "My lord, there is someone who urgently requests an audience. He says he has—"

His iridescent wings but a blur, into the chamber hurtled Flic, the tiny Sprite darting this way and that. "My lord Valeray, my lord Borel, my lady Céleste," called the tiny Sprite, and for a moment he seemed confused as to which person he should address—Valeray the king; or Borel, his old companion; or Céleste, the princess of the Springwood. Finally, he landed before the king. "In the Springwood," Flic gasped, "the Springwood, my lord—"

"Take a deep breath, Flic," said Valeray, "and gather your wits." Valeray then turned to Claude. "How did he come?"

"Through the grand ballroom, my lord, calling out for you or Prince Borel or Princess Céleste."

Valeray sighed and said, "Claude, make certain the guests therein are not alarmed by his appearance and obvious distress. Allay any fear they might have."

"Oui, my lord," said the steward, and he withdrew.

Puffing and blowing, at last Flic managed to quiet his panting, and, with a final deep breath and slow exhalation, he bowed and said, "My lord."

"Now, Flic, this news you bear," said Valeray, smiling.

"My lord, the witch Hradian—Fleurette and I think it was she—is within the Springwood; she flies sunwise."

"As we thought," groaned Luc.

Flic puckered his brow and turned toward the knight. "You knew she was there?"

"We were somewhat certain that she had left my demesne," said Valeray. He looked at the gathering and said, "And given what we now know, it seems likely the witch you saw was indeed Hradian."

"Are you positive that it was Hradian in my demesne?" asked Céleste. "Could it have been a different witch?"

"Mayhap, my lady," said Flic. "Yet the one we saw fits the description given Fleurette by Lady Camille, and the one Lord Borel told to me: a knot of darkness streaming shadows."

"With that depiction," said Camille, "I agree: Flic and Fleurette saw Hradian."

"Oh, and there is this," said Flic, "the witch seemed to be

talking to a great flock of crows—dreadful savages that they are—and they scattered in all directions, and then she flew away."

Valeray frowned. "Speaking to crows?"

"Oui, but I know not what she said."

"Why would she be speaking to crows?" asked Regar, and he looked about the table and saw only frowns of puzzlement.

After a moment Borel asked "Where is Fleurette?"

"She and Buzzer are in this demesne, just this side of the dawnwise bound, Lord Borel. Though a day late, we were on our way to the faire, and we had just settled for the night, what with Buzzer needing to sleep when the eventide begins to flow."

"Exactly where did you see the witch?" asked Céleste.

"In the Springwood nigh your starwise border. The racket of the crows awoke us, and Hradian was on a tor talking to them, the flock swirling about and listening."

"Across my own dawnwise marge?" asked Valeray.

"Oui, my lord, just barely."

"Think you she had just come from my demesne?"

Flic shrugged. "That I know not, my lord, yet if she were travelling in a straight line, she would have been flying sunwise as she entered the Springwood, and sunwise she did continue."

Silence fell, and Flic asked, "Why would she be here?"

Valeray sighed and said, "She took the key to the Castle of Shadows, and with it she will set Orbane free."

"Mithras!" exclaimed Flic, aghast. "What should we do?"

"As I said before you arrived, Flic, we have no choice but to raise our armies, warn the realms, and notify the Firsts."

"My lord," said Camille, "there is something else we simply *must* try: summon the one who can intercept Hradian and recover the amulet."

"And that would be . . . ?"

"Raseri, my lord. Raseri."

"Know you where he might be?"

"Non, yet Chemine might know, for her son Rondalo rides with the Drake."

Valeray nodded and said, "We will need a swift messenger."

"Sprites," said Flic. "We are the swiftest messengers and, not only can we reach Chemine ere anyone, we can also alert the realms and notify the Firsts and, can we alert all Sprites, surely one of us will know where flies Raseri and Rondalo, or if not, can find them swiftly. What do we say to Raseri?"

"He must be told to fly to the Black Wall of the World, there to wait and intercept Hradian and recover the key—a simple silver amulet on a silver chain and set with a blue stone," said Camille.

"Then let us Sprites bear the word," said Flic.

"Well and good," Valeray. "I will summon those of this demesne and give them the charge to rally all Sprites everywhere to spread the alarm throughout Faery and especially to alert the Firsts."

"Oh, my," said Camille.

"What is it, chérie?" asked Alain.

"What if Hradian anticipated that we would ask the Sprites to carry warnings to all, and that's why she raised the crows."

"My lady, your meaning?" asked Laurent.

But it was Flic who answered: "Crows are terrible enemies of Sprites. Whenever one of those black devils gets a chance, it will try to snatch up one of us."

"And . . . ?" asked Laurent.

"And tear us to shreds and swallow us down," growled Flic.

"Then we need to send messengers the crows cannot deter," said Blaise.

"People, you mean?" asked Laurent.

"Wait a moment," protested Flic. "What makes you think Sprites are not people?"

"I meant Humans," said Laurent.

Flic huffed, but said nought.

"We will send both," said Valeray.

"My lord," asked Regar, "is one of these Firsts the Fairy King?"

"Oui. And he has a splendid army; it was key in delaying Orbane's conquest until we could find a way of stopping him."

"Then I would like the duty of bearing the warning to him."

"Know you the way?"

"Non."

"But I do," said Flic. "Lord Borel and I went to his Halls Under the Hills when we were saving Lady Michelle."

"Then you and Regar will take on that task," said Valeray. He turned to the others and asked, "Who knows the way to Lady Chemine?"

"I do," said Camille, "and so does Scruff. We also have been to Raseri's lair."

Even as Valeray winced at the thought of sending Camille on such a mission, "My lord," said Luc, "methinks should you send Lady Camille to find Raseri and Regar to the Fairy King, by the time they succeed it will simply be too late. Non, Flic had the right of it when he said Sprites are the swiftest of messengers. We Humans would simply slow them down."

"But the crows. . . ." said Liaze.

"We can fly at night," said Flic, "when the crows are not likely to be awake."

"My lord," said Alain. "You say we are to raise armies, and that I am most willing to do, yet, though we have been in skirmishes, I have no experience in warcraft and neither does my armsmaster—battle, oui, but warcraft, non. Céleste has Roél and Liaze Luc, both war-trained and knights bold. I would ask that Blaise be my war commander."

"And I Laurent," said Borel.

"But who will organize the army of the Castle of the Seasons?" asked Saissa.

"Sieur Émile," said Luc. "He has fought in many a campaign, I hear."

Laurent and Blaise and Roél all nodded.

"He can command the combined army as well," said Luc.

"Let it be so," said Valeray.

. . .

Dinner was called, and to the gold room they went, where they were joined by Sieur Émile and Lady Simone and Vicomtesse Avélaine. Valeray took a moment to introduce Regar and Flic to them and to tell of the calamity that had come to pass.

Upon hearing the ill news, Michelle turned to Regar and said, "In addition to the Fairy King and his army, we need enlist the aid of the distaff side—the good Fairies themselves—for they are most wise in the ways of magic."

Even as Regar nodded, Valeray shook his head and said, "For some reason those so-named good Fairies refused to use their powers in the last war."

"What of the rumor that Orbane has some Fairy blood flowing in his veins?" asked Saissa.

Valeray shrugged. " 'Tis but a rumor."

"Still, I will ask for their help," said Regar.

"What of magekind?" asked Camille. "Will they not rally round?"

Again Valeray shook his head. "As to the mages, all of those who opposed Orbane were slain in that dreadful war. I think they will refuse."

A pall fell upon the gathering, and they sat quietly throughout the meal, but afterward their spirits seemed to recover, and once again they took up the task of how to deal with Orbane, should he be set free of his prison.

And the planning continued deep into the night. . . .

. . . As did the revelry outside the walls, where gaiety and laughter and singing and games and trysts lasted through much of the darktide as well, the minstrels and jugglers and stilt-walkers and vendors and faire-goers and lovers and others completely unaware of the doom about to fall.

Entrails

Across bound after bound flew Hradian through the dark. The fingernail-thin sliver of a moon had long set, and only the glittering stars illumined the night in those realms where the sky was clear. But in one, rain hammered at her mercilessly and she cursed the gods above, and in another she raged through blinding snow, and in still another she hacked and coughed as she veered among sulphurous fumes spewed from mountains of fire. Muttering maledictions, she hurtled across clear but frigid air above snowy peaks, only to shout, "It's about time!" as she sped beyond another marge to come into warm summer. Yet soon, above chill desert sands she flew, ranting because the heat of the day had fled in the darkness. And so it was as onward she went o'er realm after realm, moaning, cursing, raving, screaming, or laughing in glee at her very own cleverness.

But at last in the silvery light of dawn she passed through a final marge to come into the odiferous reek of the great mire. In the bogland below, bubbles slowly rose to the slime-laden surface to plop and eject their hoards of miasma; things slithered and wriggled and splashed, some with sinewy bodies and grasping claws, others with no legs or hard shells and great jaws, still others with slimy skins and long tongues. Black willows spread clenching and avaricious roots through the reeking muck and dangled long whiplike branches down, and dark cypress wrenched up out from the sump and ooze to spread gray-lichen-wattled branches wide. Mossy fallen logs decayed in the quag to add heat to the rot of the swamp bottom, with dead creatures putrefying alongside until something happened by to rip and rend at the rancid flesh.

And above this foetid morass flew Hradian, heading for the center of the vast mire, where her cottage lay.

Weary, at last she spiralled down to alight upon the flet of her cote, where a great bloated toad squatted.

"I have it, Crapaud—the key! The key!" cried Hradian, dancing about in spite of her fatigue. "Oh, Crapaud, we were so clever, so very clever, and our potion worked to perfection. We *became* the slut Liaze to all eyes, to all senses, we did. And, oh, how we duped that fool Luc, into thinking we were her." Hradian flashed the silver amulet on high, and cried, "And now we have the key. And after I rest, we, you and I, Crapaud, we will discover just how this amulet can be used to free our master Orbane."

Then Hradian squatted and stared the toad in one of its gummy eyes. "What say you to that, my fine familiar?"

Seeming to realize that something was expected of him, Crapaud swelled the sac of his throat and emitted a gaseous croak, rather much like a great noxious belch, filling the air with the stench of his utterance.

"Exactly so," cried Hradian, and she leapt to her feet and strode into the hut, where she flung off her clothes and fell into her cot. Moments later she was sound asleep.

Crapaud waddled to the entry and peered inside and emitted a plaintive rasp, but Hradian did not stir from her slumber. After a second throaty grate went unanswered, the toad hitched about and lurched to the edge of the flet and fell into the water. After all, he was quite hungry, and whether or no the witch gave him leave to hunt, still he had to eat. Awkwardly stroking, legs askew, down into the slime he struggled to finally disappear.

· · ·

The day came and went, and even as twilight faded and night drew on, a squashy splop awakened Hradian, and in the dimness she could just make out the distended form of a dripping Crapaud waddling past the doorway, with long, mucuslike tendrils of bog ordure clinging to the toad's warty hide and trailing behind to drag over the dark and reeking swamp-bottom footprints he left in his wake.

Hradian slapped a hand to her chest to find at her throat the amulet upon its chain. "Ah, my love, the talisman is indeed here. We thought it might have been a magnificent dream, but instead it is a glorious fact. We did indeed fetch the key for ourselves, we did. Oh, clever us. Our sisters could not have done what we did, now could they? Ah, no need to answer, for we know it is true."

Hradian swung her feet over the edge of the cot and stood, the amulet the only thing on her person. After squatting at the edge of the flet and above the swamp water to relieve herself, she stepped to the fireplace and swung a kettle over the hearth. In moments she had a fire ablaze. She opened a cabinet and took up an herb jar and spooned some black leaves into a pot. Then she fetched a strip of dark jerky and stood at the window and chewed the stringy meat. A crescent moon hung low on the horizon, and she watched as it sank among the black willow and dark cypress, the grey moss dangling down from the branches diffusing the already dim light.

"As soon as it disappears, my love, then we set about finding the key to the amulet. —No, no. Wait! We set about finding the key to the key." Hradian cackled at her own bon mot. "We are so clever, we are."

The kettle began to steam, and Hradian poured hot water over the herbs in the pot. She took up a knife and stirred the brew. Then she thumbed the blade and frowned. Using a whetstone, she honed the knife to razor sharpness, then stepped to her cot and cached the blade under one edge of the mattress.

Sipping her drink, once again she moved to the window, and watched the last of the horns of the crescent moon sink beyond the rim of the world. "Good, Love, it is now gone, and our best work always is done in the moonless dark of night."

She turned to the doorway. "Crapaud, Crapaud! I need you now."

The monstrous toad waddled to the opening.

"Fetch us a Bogle."

Crapaud yawed 'round and floundered to the edge of the flet and fell into the swamp. After a number of ungainly strokes, he managed to disappear under the surface.

Hradian looked about the cabin. "Ah, my love, you know that a human would be better, but they are stubborn and would fight back. Of course, an Elf would be better yet, or a true Fairy, but they are even more powerful. Besides, no humans, Elves, or Fairies are at hand, and so a Bogle it must be. Certainly it will mess the floor. The cot as well. But we shouldn't mind, for we will soon be dwelling in a castle of our own, won't we, love. With servants and lackeys and, oh, yes, handsome young muscular men. And soft beds fit for a princess, fit for the princess we will be. No! Not princess, but queen! Or empress. Hmm . . . What do they call a queen of all the world? Never mind, my love, we can call ourselves whatever it is we wish."

Even as she mused over what title she would bestow upon herself, a great croaking din arose in the swamp. "Ah, my Crapaud has sent forth the call. It is much easier than making a *fetch* of ourselves, isn't it, my sweet?"

Hradian felt her excitement rising, and, thinking of what was to come, she stepped to the cot and lay down and made herself ready.

A splop sounded on the flet, and Hradian drew in her breath, but it was only Crapaud returning to his station.

A time passed, and the racket without fell silent.

"Oh, oh, love, he is almost here."

And with a heaving splash, by the firelight Hradian saw in the doorway a Bogle standing, swamp bottom dripping from his dark form, his male member tumescent in anticipation.

. . .

It was as Hradian was riding on top, she could see in the Bogle's eyes the peak coming, and it was at his climax that she ripped the keen knife through his stomach and up into his heart, and she shuddered and screamed in orgasmic pleasure in that same moment.

Dark blood spurted over her chest to gush down her loins and spill onto the bed, where it streamed to the floor, pooling below.

Reveling in the flood, Hradian waited until the surge ebbed to a trickle, then freed herself and stepped away and called, "Crapaud, Crapaud, I need you now."

The huge toad waddled in.

"Taste the blood, Crapaud."

Crapaud's long tongue lashed out and splatted into the puddle under the cot, then disappeared back into his mouth.

Heaving and grunting, Hradian rolled the slain Bogle off onto the floor, and after a struggle she managed to get the corpse onto its back.

Hradian reached out and touched the toad between the eyes. "Now, Crapaud, lend us your power."

The toad seemed to fall dormant, and, clutching the amulet in one hand, and pawing with the other, Hradian began sifting through the Bogle's blood-warm entrails, seeking an omen, seeking a clue as to just how to use the talisman. After but a moment she said, "Huah, there is no mystery to the talisman at all. Had we known it was this easy, Love, we wouldn't have had to kill the Bogle. Oh well, no loss that."

Once more she touched the toad. "Awaken, Crapaud, I am finished."

Crapaud opened his eyes, and emitted a croak.

"Yes, yes, you can clean up the mess."

Another croak sounded.

"Very well, that, too. After all, you *will* need sustenance while I am gone."

And Hradian took up an axe and, grunting with effort, she hacked the corpse to pieces for her familiar to consume in the days to come.

Even as Crapaud's long tongue flicked forth to snatch one end of the entrails, the viscera uncoiling as the toad gulped away, Hradian, now sweating and blood-smeared and spattered with grume and bits of dark flesh, stepped out to the flet, where, using a pail, she dipped up a bucketful of swamp water. She muttered a spell over the sludgy liquid and watched as it cleared, and then sluiced herself down.

Several more times she dipped and sluiced, and finally clean of all sign of her gruesome handiwork she strode back into the hut and threw on her long black gown, the one with the danglers and streamers and lace.

After she buttoned up her high-top shoes, she turned to Crapaud, the toad yet swallowing length after length of intestine, rather like trying to gulp down a very long rope all of one piece a foot at a time, the rope stretching from stomach through gullet and throat and out the mouth to the blood-drenched remains of the corpse. "Ward the cote, Crapaud. I go to fetch our master from the imprisonment foisted upon him by those who should grovel at his feet, or rather, by those who *will* grovel at *our* feet, and soon we'll be living in a castle fitting to our station, a magnificent dwelling past all compare."

Crapaud tried to reply past the gore-slick viscera, some of it ingested, most of it yet to slither out from the lower half of the hacked-apart torso, yet all that he managed to utter was a choking belch.

Hradian snatched up her besom and stepped to the flet and, with a high-pitched shriek of joy, she took to the air. And soon she was nought but a dark form streaming tendrils of shadow, a silhouette growing smaller and smaller to finally vanish against the stars.

And in the cottage behind, Crapaud continued to swallow and swallow and swallow the seemingly endless gut.

14

Tocsin

Morning dawned at the Castle of the Seasons and, as the sun cleared the horizon, buglers stood on the battlements and sounded a special call. Faire-goers looked up to see what was afoot, but only a few of them knew that it was a signal requesting Sprites to attend King Valeray.

Even as the clarions sounded, from dawnwise a Sprite and a bumblebee came winging. And waiting on the ramparts for them stood Flic, and he heaved a great sigh of relief as Fleurette and Buzzer sped toward the merlons.

As they alighted, Flic embraced Fleurette, while Buzzer, somewhat agitated, hummed her wings and paced 'round the two. "She missed you," said Fleurette, "as did I."

"What of the crows?" asked Flic.

"They did not cross through the border."

"Ah," said Flic, relieved.

Fleurette glanced down into the courtyard, where nine men prepared for travel, with several others at hand. "What is going on, and does it have ought to do with what we saw?"

"Indeed, and I'll tell you along the way, for we are going to the Fairy King Under the Hill."

"Right now?"

"Oui."

"But Buzzer needs nectar, and I could use a sip or two."

"Worry not, my love, for honey awaits."

Fleurette frowned. "The Fairy King? But did you not tell me he was capricious and might give us an onerous duty to perform?"

"Oui. But dire events are afoot, and all must answer the call. —Now come, for Prince Regar and Sieur Blaise await."

"Blaise I know, but who is this Regar?"

Flic leapt into the air. "I'll introduce you." He sped downward, Buzzer winging after, and, with a sigh, Fleurette followed.

. . .

In the courtyard, four knights and a bastard prince, along with four guides—one from each of the Forests of the Seasons—all of them buckled in armor and strapped with weaponry, waited for attendants to bring horses and remounts from the stables. Standing at hand were King Valeray and Queen Saissa, Princesses Céleste and Liaze, Prince Borel and Michelle, Prince Alain and Camille, Sieur Émile and Lady Simone and Vicomtesse Avélaine. Nearby a pack of Wolves lolled upon the cool granite of the courtyard.

"Ride with care," said Valeray, "for we know not what traps Hradian might have set."

"Sire," said Alain, "they go in haste."

"Oui," said Valeray, "I know, I know: safety and haste oft are strangers to one another. Even so, even agallop, it pays to keep an eye toward what might be dangers ahead."

"Damn!" blurted Borel, "but I would go, too, were it not for these closing ceremonies four days hence."

Slate and the pack lifted their heads and looked expectantly at Borel, the Wolves eager to be away from this great stone den.

"Ah, my brother," said Alain, "what could you do in the Winterwood and I in the Summerwood that Sieurs Laurent and Blaise will not already have under way by the time we reach our respective manors?"

Borel merely growled and turned up his hands in a sign of exasperation.

"Right," said Alain.

Saissa said, "My son, e'en though the alert will be sounded in this realm on this day, still we must put on a show of normality here at the faire, for morale purposes if nought else."

"Oui," growled Borel, "but do all of us have to be present for the closing?"

"King, queen, princes, and princesses, and even prince Duran," said Saissa, "as it has ever been."

Borel drew in a deep breath and slowly let it out, and Michelle took him by the hand and smoothed out his clenched fingers. Borel looked at her and fleetingly smiled, and with his other hand he made a signal to Slate. The big male Wolf dropped his head, the pack following suit.

The attendants brought horses, remounts tethered behind, and at that same time Flic and Fleurette and Buzzer arrived and settled to the cantle of one of the saddles, and, after a welcoming of the tiny femme and the bee, Flic introduced Fleurette and Buzzer to Prince Regar.

Regar slapped a tricorn upon his simple bronze helm and said, "Lord Borel and Lady Michelle assure me that when you are not flying this is your customary mode of transport."

"Indeed it is, my lord," said Flic. "And now about some honey, Fleurette and Buzzer need to break their fast, and I could do with a nip myself."

Regar smiled and pointed up to his three-cornered hat and said, "Even now there is a dollop in place along the back brim of this cocked chapeau."

Flic laughed and sprang into the air, and he and Fleurette and Buzzer darted to the tricorn and the meal thereon.

With tears in her eyes, Lady Simone stepped forward and embraced in turn her three sons, Avélaine following. And Céleste kissed Roél, even as Liaze kissed Luc.

And then all the men mounted up and rode out over the bridge, and, with each following a guide, Laurent headed starwise and Roél dawnwise, while Blaise and Prince Regar—with his two sprites and a bee aboard—fared sunwise and Luc duskwise. They spurred the horses and away they galloped, warriors running in haste on their separate but allied missions.

From a corner of the parapets above, where the ones left behind had rushed to, they watched until the riders finally vanished among the trees beyond.

"May Mithras ward them all," said Saissa, and the others nodded in mute agreement.

Moments passed in silence, then Borel sighed and looked at Michelle. "Ah, well, tomorrow morn I will send you and my warband on to the Winterwood, and then follow after the faire is done."

Michelle nodded. "I understand."

"But I do not," said Avélaine.

Michelle smiled and said, "Lady Avélaine, were I to wait, I would merely slow the prince down on his journey home."

Avélaine looked at Borel, an unspoken question in her eyes, and he said, "With remounts for me, I can travel to Winterwood Manor in but a day."

"I see," said Avélaine, but then she frowned and said, "Yet, my lord, you would go alone?"

"I will not be alone, for my Wolves will be at my side."

"Can they keep up?"

Borel barked a laugh. "Ah, Lady Avélaine, my Wolves, if let run free, could be there in even less time. Non, they will easily hold pace with the horses."

"Speaking of leaving," said Céleste, "I think it would be wise, Lady Avélaine, were you and half of my warband to start out for Port Mizone on the morrow as well."

Avélaine frowned in puzzlement. "But why?"

Céleste held up two fingers and said, "Two reasons." She

ticked down the first finger. "Your husband, Vicomte Chevell, readies a war fleet to go after the corsairs, and I would have you to your home ere he sets sail on that mission."

"And the second reason?"

Céleste ticked down the remaining finger. "You are with child, and we know not when Hradian might strike, and so I would have you safely away, not only from here but also well beyond the Springwood, for we are her deadly enemies, and she would like nought more than to see us slain, and I would not have you and your unborn be caught in the storm to come."

In spite of Avélaine's protests to the contrary, all agreed this was the wisest course. Avélaine continued to protest, but finally Valeray said, "Lady Avélaine, must I command it done?"

Avélaine curtseyed and said, "No, my lord, I bow to your will."

And Sieur Émile stepped forward and embraced Avélaine and whispered, "My daughter, I am loath to see you go, yet it is best for you and Lord Chevell and the child now in your womb."

And Avélaine looked up at him, tears brimming in her eyes, and she whispered in return, "Oui, Papa, I know."

And even as it was decided, Sprites came winging toward the Castle of the Seasons in answer to the bugled call.

.   .   .

"Crows, you say?"

Valeray nodded at the tiny, black-haired femme. "Oui, Peti."

"And Flic and Fleurette saw this witch, this Hradian speaking to them?"

Again Valeray nodded. "We reason she set them at the starwise bounds of the four Forests of the Seasons to ward against the alarm being spread from here by Sprites. Flic suggests that you fly at night when the crows are asleep."

Peti sighed and said, "Ah, oui, at night, when the silent owls are awake instead, and just as dangerous."

Beside her, a brown-haired male Sprite said, "I know this Flic. He bears a silver épée, less likely to snap in twain than thorns we at times use to defend ourselves."

"You use thorns?" asked Émile.

"Oui. Though usually our quickness alone is enough to cope with crows and such, there are occasions when a long slender thorn is a better way to deal with a foe."

The Sprite turned to Valeray. "If you provide us with épées like Flic's, we would appreciate having them. Regardless, thorns or silver, we can not only spread the alarm throughout Faery, we can deal with the crows as they sleep on their perches."

"Mais oui!" exclaimed Peti. "You have hit upon it, Trit. And we can enlist the aid of the Root Dwellers in dealing with the crows in the night."

"Root Dwellers?" asked Avélaine.

"The wee folk we saw on our journey here," said Céleste, holding one hand above the other to indicate a being some few inches to a foot tall. "They live among the roots of the trees."

"Ah, those," said Avélaine. "I remember."

Valeray looked at Saissa, and she said, "We'll round up all the pins and needles and such that we can find."

"But there will not be enough to supply all Sprites through-out all of Faery, much less of this realm," said Céleste.

"Indeed not," said Trit, "yet I know where grow many of the right kind of thorns, and they will serve."

"The Ice Sprites of the Winterwood need no thorns," said Borel, "for, living in ice as they do, they are well protected from crows."

"Speaking of the Winterwood, Lord Borel," said Peti, gestur-ing at her naked form and that of Trit, "we cannot long bear the cold, dressed as we are, or, rather, undressed I mean."

Trit turned up a hand and said, "But we can stand it long enough to pop over and find one of our cold-weather kindred and pass on the message and then pop back."

"Fair enough," said Borel. "And as for the other cold realms, the Ice Sprites will then travel through those frozen demesnes and pass on the alarm."

As Borel fell silent, Camille looked at Peti and added, "If perhaps Hradian enlisted crows only to ward the starwise bounds of the Forests of the Seasons, there to keep you and the other Sprites herein from spreading the word, then once you fly beyond, there will be none to stop you. Hence, mayhap you will only need weapons nigh those four borders."

"If that's true," said Valeray, "Hradian must have great confidence in those birds to stop the Sprites from sounding the alarm."

"Crows are quite dreadful," said Trit, "and massing an army of them is perilous beyond compare."

"For us, that is," said Peti.

"But if you fly at night," said Valeray, "perhaps you can avoid the worst."

"Mayhap," said Peti. "Regardless, we will fly, enlisting more and more Sprites throughout Faery as we go, and the warning will spread and spread like wildfire. What message is it you would have us bear, my lord?"

"That a means for freeing Orbane has come into the witch Hradian's hand, and for the realms to prepare for his escape. Tell them as well that we will send word as to where to assemble should that event come about."

"And how will you know where that might be?" asked Trit.

Valeray smiled and said, "With you and your kind to act as our scouts, how can we not know?"

Trit smiled and bowed and said, "At your service, my lord."

Valeray looked 'round at the others. "Is there ought else we should add to the message?"

"Oui, my lord," said Camille, and she turned to Peti. "Tell

all Sprites not only to cry the alarm, but to find Raseri and warn him as well, and ask him to fly to the Black Wall of the World and there to wait and intercept Hradian and slay her ere she can free her master."

"Raseri the Dragon?" asked Trit.

"Oui, for he is quite deadly, and has the best chance of stopping the witch. Too, he might have with him Rondalo the Elf, and he wields bow and spear and sword. If Rondalo is not with Raseri, he might know where the Drake flies. There is this as well: Lady Chemine, Rondalo's mère, perhaps also can speak of Raseri's whereabouts. She lives on a tiny island near the city of *Les Îles*, at the confluence of four great rivers."

Peti nodded and said, "This then is our mission: to spread the alarm and seek the Dragon, and then to act as scouts." She looked at Valeray, and he inclined his head in assent. "Very well, my king, as you have commanded, so shall it be done." She then turned to Saissa. "Now, my queen, let us to the needles and pins, for there are crows to slay."

15

Messengers

It was ere midmorn when Laurent and his guide, Édouard, galloped through Valeray's starwise twilight border to emerge running sunwise in the Winterwood, snow flying from shod hooves and flinging out behind. From warmth to cold they passed in but strides, and even as they hammered among the barren trees, a great squawking murder of crows rose up into the chill air. Yet though the crows filled the surround with racket, they let the men pass unmolested. And as the riders and their remounts plunged on, the crows settled back to the stark branches, their black eyes awatch on the twilight border, as if waiting for other beings to come hurtling through.

And the knight and the guide galloped on, into a realm sleeping under blankets of snow and claddings of ice.

At times within this woodland there were storms and blizzards or gentle snowfalls, days bright and clear and cold, or gray and gloomy, or dark days of biting winds howling and blowing straightly or blasting this way and that, or freezing days with hoarfrost so cold as to crack stone, or days of warm sunshine and partial thaws and a bit of melt, or of snowfalls heavy and wet, or falls powdery and dry. It could be a world of silence and echoes, of quietness and muffled sounds, or of yawling blasts and thundering blows. It was wild and untamed and white and gray and black, with glittering ice and sparkling snow, with evergreens giving a lie to the monochromatic 'scape, and never were any two days the same.

And under a winter-bright sky, across this icy realm did a chevalier and his guide race, a track left behind in the snow. As they ran, within the sheathings of the ice-clad trees and in icicles and in the frozen planes of streams and pools, Laurent could see wee beings following their progress, some to merely turn and look and note the passage of the riders and remounts, while others somehow shifted from ice-laden rock to ice-clad tree to icicles dangling down as they kept pace with the two, or gleefully raced ahead. These were the Ice Sprites: wingless and as white as new-driven snow, with hair like silvered tendrils, their forms and faces elfin with tipped ears and tilted eyes of pale blue. They were completely unclothed, as all Sprites seemed to be, and they had the power to fit within whatever shapes the ice took. And their images wavered and undulated and parts of them grew and shrank in odd ways and became strangely distorted as they sped through the uneven but pellucid layers of frozen water, the irregular surfaces making it so, rather as if they were passing through a peculiar house of mirrors, though no reflections these, but living beings within.

"Édouard!" called Laurent, even as he reined to a halt, "let us change mounts."

The guide, a skinny, dark-haired youth, galloped on for a few more paces ere bringing his steeds to a stop.

As they changed saddles and gear from one mount to another, Laurent said, "Tell me, can you speak to these Sprites?"

"Oui, Sieur Laurent. All of Lord Borel's household can do so."

"And can they travel to other realms?"

"Oui, Sieur, if it has ice."

"Then call one to you, and tell them to spread a message of warning among all Ice Sprites and other beings throughout this cold realm and others alike. Also, I would have them search those demesnes for a Drake named Raseri and bear a message to him as well. Too, have them alert the staff of Winterwood Manor that we are on the way. —Oh, in addition, they are to bear word to the Root Dwellers as well."

Édouard glanced 'round and noted a Sprite in an icicle at hand. Then the youth turned to Laurent and asked, "Very well, Sieur, and what might these messages be?"

. . .

Roél and his guide Dévereau pounded through Valeray's dawn-wise border to find themselves running sunwise in the Spring-wood. And as they splatted through a chill stream, a great flock of crows flew up and 'round, cawing and milling as the pair raced past. Yet once the riders had gone onward, the dark birds settled back among the greening limbs and again took up their ward of the twilight marge and waited for promised tasty morsels to come.

On into the land of eternal springtime sped a knight and his guide, a place where everlasting meltwater trickles across the 'scape, where some trees are abud while others are new-leafed, where early blossoms are abloom though some flowers yet sleep, where birds call for mates, and beetles crawl through decaying leaves, and mushrooms push up through soft loam, and where other such signs of a world coming awake manifest themselves in the gentle, cool breezes and delicate rains.

As they galloped onward, Roél kept a sharp eye out for crows, and when they had travelled a league or so, but for the area right at the marge, he had not espied any of the black birds the rest of the way. "Dévereau, let us stop and not only change mounts, but call the Sprites to us. It seems Hradian did not take into account the greed of her guardians, and they are all massed at the border awaiting the arrival of the winged messengers of Valeray's demesne."

A moment later, dismounted, Roél raised his horn to his lips and blew a summoning call. He then switched his saddle to a remount, as did Dévereau. And even as he finished, a Sprite landed upon a nearby limb and said, "Yes, my lord?"

.   .   .

Through Valeray's sunwise border galloped Blaise and Regar and their guide Jérôme, along with Regar's tricorn passengers— Flic, Fleurette, and Buzzer. And when they emerged from the twilight, they found themselves running sunwise in a sunlit forest. And an enormous flock of crows flew up and 'round, crying out in alarm. Flic and Fleurette hid themselves against the enshadowed upturned brim of Regar's cocked hat, as onward careered the horses. Soon they were past the gauntlet of dark birds, and onward into the woodland they raced.

And it was a domain graced by eternal summer, a realm of forests and fields, of vales and clearings, of streams and rivers and other such 'scapes, where soft summer breezes flow across the weald, though occasionally towering thunderstorms fill the afternoon skies and rain sweeps o'er all. But this morning was clear, and under cloudless skies they ran, a cool breeze blowing athwart.

Both Flic and Fleurette kept a keen eye on the limbs of the trees and the air above. And almost immediately they noted an absence of crows, for those killers were massed at the starwise border, it seemed. After running a league or two, Flic called out, "Prince Regar, see you any of the murdering black birds?"

"Nay, they seem to be all gone."

"Then let us stop and call my kindred, for they have messages to bear."

.   .   .

Luc and Maurice hurtled through Valeray's duskwise marge to find themselves running sunwise in the Autumnwood, and a mass of crows sprang into the air to churn about as the riders plunged on. Soon the crows settled back to their perches and waited as they were told to do by that strange person who flew on a brush-ended broken-off limb.

And the knight and guide raced deeper into the woodland where eternal autumn lies upon the land, a place where crops afield remain ever for the reaping, and vines are overburdened with their largesse, and trees bear an abundance ripe for the plucking, and the ground holds rootstock and tubers for the taking. Yet no matter how often a harvest is gathered, when one isn't looking the bounty somehow replaces itself. How such a place could be—endless autumn—was quite strange; nevertheless it was so.

Of course, how three other allied realms of this woodland could be—one of eternal winter, another of eternal spring, and one of eternal summer—was just as peculiar.

Yet these four realms supported one another: the Winterwood somehow gave all needed rest; the Springwood, awakening and renewal; the Summerwood, growth into fullness; and the Autumnwood, fruition. Even in Faery, where mysteries are commonplace, the existence of these four was odd in the extreme.

And it was into the realm of everlasting largesse that Luc and Maurice raced, and soon they were out from under the dark swirling cloud of birds.

And just as had the other knights, soon Luc called a halt to summon winged Sprites and give them their messages to bear.

Then on they galloped, heading for Autumnwood Manor.

16

Riddles

It was yet early morn as Laurent and Édouard rode atrot through the snow-laden bottom of a gully, when in the distance ahead, where the walls curved inward to make the passage strait, stood an old woman, her hands raised in a gesture bidding them to stop.

" 'Ware, Édouard," said Laurent. "For all we know, this could be an ambush, or might even be the witch herself."

"Sieur, it might also be someone who offers aid," said the lad, used to the ways of Faery.

Laurent grunted a wordless reply, and he took up his crossbow and cocked it and set a quarrel in place, all the time his gaze sweeping along the somewhat overhanging rims above for sign of foe, but all he saw was white hoarfrost and overburdening snow and dangling ice.

And as they neared the crone, "Make way, old woman," called Laurent. "We ride in haste."

The hag did not move, and, in spite of his urgings, Laurent's mount came to a halt, as did Édouard's, the remounts in tow stopping as well.

The crone gave a gummy smile. "In haste you say? Heh! You don't know what haste is."

"Heed, old woman," said Laurent, "we are on an urgent mission. Now give way."

The hag moved not. "Have you any food? I'm hungry."

Even as Laurent shook his head, Édouard tossed her a half loaf of bread. "Madam," said the youth, "we truly must needs ride onward. Will you please give way?"

"Well at least there's someone here who knows courtesy," snapped the crone, glaring at Laurent. She held up the bread. "I need something to wash this down."

Laurent ground his teeth, but unloosed a small wineskin from his cantle. "Here," he growled and tossed it to her, the old woman spryly snatching it from the air.

And in that same moment a shimmering came over her, and there before the knight and his guide stood a beautiful demoiselle with silver eyes and silver hair, and she was clad in a silver-limned ebon robe. And the air was filled with the sound of looms weaving.

As Édouard gasped, Laurent sprang from his horse and knelt before the maiden. "My lady Skuld, forgive me. I knew not it was you."

"Whether or no it was me, still you should not have abandoned all courtesy, Sieur Laurent."

"Indeed, I should have not, Lady Wyrd."

"Ever proud, my knight. Someday your arrogance will do you ill if you do not mend your ways."

Without a word, and yet on his knees, Laurent nodded.

In the snow behind him, Édouard now knelt, and in a small voice asked, "My Lady Who Sees the Future, have you come to give us a message?"

"Indeed, and since you each have done me a favor by giving me bread and wine, I can do so, yet under the rules I follow, first you must answer a riddle."

"Say on, my lady," said Laurent.

Skuld took a deep breath, and the sound of the looms swelled.

. . .

"Glittering points
That downward thrust,
Sparkling spears
That never rust.
Name me."

As Skuld fell silent, and the clack of shuttles and thud of battens diminished, Laurent's heart fell. Édouard started to speak, yet Skuld gestured him to silence and said, "This is for Laurent to answer here in the Winterwood."

Laurent looked up at her, his gaze narrowing in speculation, and then he glanced about and finally up at the overhang above. He grinned and pointed and said, "My Lady Wyrd, the answer is icicles."

Now Skuld smiled. "Indeed it is."

"And the message you would give us . . . ?"

"As you might have heard, Sieur Laurent, I can only render aid in riddles."

Laurent nodded but did not speak.

"Heed, then," said Skuld. Once again the sound of weaving intensified.

"Swift are the get of his namesake,
That which a child does bear;
Ask the one who rides the one
To send seven children there.

At the wall there is a need
For seven to stand and wait,
Yet when they are asked to run,
They must fly at swiftest gait.

The whole must face the one reviled
Where all events begin:

Parent and child and child of child
Else shall dark evil win."

And as the timbre of looms fell, Laurent frowned and said, "But, my lady, I do not understand. Can you not say it plain?"

"Non, I cannot," replied the silver-eyed demoiselle. "But this I can tell you for nought: If you do not give this message to the one for whom it is intended, then all will be lost forever."

And with that dire pronouncement, again the clack of shuttles and thud of battens intensified, and then vanished as did Lady Skuld.

17

Alarums

In the Springwood, Summerwood, and Autumnwood, Sprites took to wing, and as they flew through these three forests, more and more of these tiny beings were alerted, and each of these fey creatures warned two more, and each of those in turn warned two, and so their numbers doubled and doubled and redoubled again, until all were bearing the alarum throughout the woodlands.

And some went to the Root Dwellers, while others spied from leafy surround upon the crows massed along the starwise borders, and they counted the numbers of the ebon-feathered birds and noted the trees where they waited and ferreted out the most likely roosting spots therein. Back and forth among the Forests of the Seasons flew the wee messengers, and plans were laid, even as long, slender thorns were harvested and given to all who would engage.

Then some of the larger Root Dwellers, those the crows would not attack, slipped through the starwise twilight bound and relayed those plans to the Sprites of Valeray's realm.

And the diminutive beings flew throughout the Springwood and Summerwood and Autumnwood, to all the hamlets and villages and crofts and mines and strongholds and manors and other such. And to the Humans and Gnomes and Dwarves and other beings therein they relayed the dreadful news that a means for freeing Orbane had come into the witch Hradian's hand, and for the realms to prepare for his escape. They told them as well that the prince or princess or even the king would send word as to where to assemble should that event come about. Many gasped, for they thought that after his imprisonment Orbane would ne'er again be of concern, and others wept, remembering the last time he had been on the loose, while still others girded their loins and sharpened their weapons and oiled their armor of old, for if the wizard got free, then once again all Enfer would break loose upon this peaceful realm.

And Sprites flew across various twilight borders to other realms, and they alerted their kindred there, and those in turn bore the messages onward, warning the inhabitants of their respective domains, and carrying the news beyond.

Doubling and doubling and doubling again, it was as Peti had said: like wildfire did the word spread.

And as evermore Sprites flew onward they kept an eye out for Raseri the Dragon and Rondalo the Elf, but of these two they saw nought.

Yet Faery is endless, or so some have claimed, hence no one could gauge whether or no the word would reach all corners of that magical place, and if it would come soon or late or not at all.

18

Puzzles

Following Jérôme, among the green-leafed trees of the Summerwood galloped Blaise and Regar, along with Regar's tricorn passengers—Flic, Fleurette, and Buzzer. Across grassy glades they ran, and down into sunlit dells, and through long, enshadowed woodland galleries, and past stony cliffs over which crystalline water tumbled in roaring falls. Now and again they would pause to change mounts, and then take up the run once more.

They passed through the village of Fajine, where folk had gathered in the square and hailed the riders.

Blaise and the others paused a moment, and someone called out, "Is it true what the Sprite who came just said: that Orbane is free?"

Blaise frowned. "I think what you heard is not the message they bore."

"He's right," called a man. "The Sprite only told us that Orbane might be set free and to be ready for such an event, should Prince Alain send word."

"Regardless," said another. "Has Orbane been set free?"

Blaise shook his head. "That we cannot say. Yet the witch Hradian has the means to set him loose. So alert your fighting men, and be ready to assemble at Summerwood manor should the call to muster come."

Somewhere within the small gathering a woman burst into tears. And Prince Regar added, "We have sent for one who might be able to stop the witch, yet we cannot be certain of success."

Ere any could ask more, Blaise spurred his mount, and away galloped the riders, remounts in tow.

A candlemark later as the noontide drew on, they paused at a meandering wooded stream to water the horses and to give them grain and a bit of a breather.

"That was fast," said Regar.

"What was?" asked Blaise.

"That the Sprites had reached the village ere we got there."

"Not very," said Flic. "I mean, those people acted as if the messenger had just come, and had *I* been bearing the warning, I would have been long gone from there."

Blaise laughed and said, "Lord Borel once told me of this penchant of yours to speak of just how swift you are."

As Flic sputtered and searched for a reply, Fleurette said, "Well, it's true. Flic is the fastest Sprite I have ever seen."

"And I suppose you have seen many, Lady Fleurette?"

"I have. And in the Sprite races, Flic has never lost."

"Then I apologize, Sieur Flic, for you must be swift indeed."

Somewhat mollified, Flic started to speak, but in that moment, from beyond an upstream turn there came the cry of "Oh, help! Oh, help!"

With a *shing!* Blaise drew his sword, even as Regar swiftly strung his bow and nocked an arrow. Jérôme drew his own blade.

Flic, his épée in hand, said, "Let me go see." And ere any could object, he darted away, Buzzer flying in his wake.

Moments later, Flic and Buzzer returned, the Sprite's épée now sheathed. "It is a silly woman up in a tree. She says she cannot get down."

"Are you certain it is just a woman, and not the witch in disguise?"

"I have Fey sight," protested Flic. "Were she glamoured, I would have seen it, just as I would have seen it had I been at the faire when Hradian came englamoured."

"As would have I," said Fleurette.

Blaise nodded, though he did not sheathe his sword. "Well then, let me go see what is to be done."

"I'll go as well," said Regar, and he did not unnock the arrow from his bow.

"Sieur Blaise," said Jérôme—

"Stay with the mounts," said Blaise, and he and Regar set off upstream, Flic and Fleurette and Buzzer again riding the tricorn.

Jérôme sighed and sheathed his blade and watched them until they vanished beyond the turn.

'Round the bend fared the knight and bastard prince, along with two Sprites and a bee, and aseat on a low limb of a wide-spread oak sat a distressed, yellow-haired demoiselle, a small basket in hand. She was clad in a gingham dress, though her feet were bare. Relief swept over her face at the sight of the men coming to rescue her.

"Oh, sieurs, I am so glad to see you, for I need aid in getting to the ground."

"What are you doing up this tree, m'lady?" asked Regar.

"Collecting birds' eggs, Sieur, for my sisters and me."

"Your sisters?"

"Oui, I have two."

Blaise sheathed his sword and stepped among the great gnarled roots spreading out from the bole and across the ground. "Mademoiselle, if you would trust me, please lower the basket first, and then yourself afterward. I will catch you."

"Oh, Sieur, but I am afraid."

"Then I will climb up, and ease you down to my friend." He turned to Regar. "N'est ce pas?"

Regar nodded, and as Blaise climbed, the prince sheathed his arrow and slipped his bow across his back.

Blaise took the basket with its grass-cushioned eggs and gave it into Regar's upstretched hands, and the prince set it to the ground.

Then Blaise grasped the mademoiselle by the wrists and, with her emitting small whimpers, he lowered her to Regar's embrace.

Blaise leapt down as Regar eased the femme to earth, the prince saying, "There, my lady. Safely done."

And in that moment the basket and eggs vanished and a shimmering came over the mademoiselle, and there before them stood a matronly woman with golden hair and golden eyes and dressed in a gold-limned ebon robe, and the air was filled with the sound of looms weaving.

As Regar stepped back in surprise, "Lady Verdandi," said Flic, even as Blaise knelt and said, "Lady Lot."

Following Blaise's action, Regar knelt as well.

"Blaise, Regar, Flic, Fleurette, Buzzer," said Verdandi, smiling.

"So much for Fey sight," said Fleurette.

Verdandi laughed. "Not even Fey sight can pierce the disguises my sisters and I wear."

Blaise said, "My Lady Who Sees the Everlasting Now, have you come to give us a rede?"

"Oui, I have, and, since you have helped me, I can do so, but only if you answer a riddle."

Flic groaned, but otherwise didn't speak.

"A riddle?" asked Regar.

"By the rules my sisters and I follow, you must do so ere any of us can render aid."

Blaise sighed in resignation, but then he seemed to brace himself. He looked up at her. "Say on, Lady Lot."

Verdandi nodded and took a deep breath. And as the sound of weaving intensified, she said:

"You will find me in beds, in friendship, in love,
But not in enmity or cold winds above.
I come from without, and I come from within;
I am oft shared among good women and men.
From hearts and hearths, though not quite same,
You will say I arrive; now tell me my name."

As the clack of shuttles and thud of battens diminished, Fleurette cried, "I know, I know," yet Verdandi pushed out a hand to silence the Sprite.

As Blaise's heart fell, Verdandi said, "It is Sieur Blaise's to answer here in the Summerwood."

Here in the Summerwood? What is it about the Summerwood that makes it another clue? Blaise looked about, seeing full-leafed trees amid lush and verdant undergrowth, and a greensward leading down to the stream, and he heard birds singing in the distance, and the sound of the brook as the clear water tumbled o'er rocks on its way to a distant sea. Yet none of these fit the words of the rhyme. *This domain, where everlasting summer lies on the—*

"Warmth, my lady," said Blaise. "It is found in beds, in friendship, in love, but not in enmity or cold winds above. It arrives from hearths without and hearts within, and is often shared by good women and men." Blaise fell silent, and waited with bated breath for Lady Lot to speak.

"Indeed," said Verdandi.

Even as Blaise gave a sigh of relief, "I knew the answer," whispered Fleurette to Flic.

"I didn't," said Flic.

"My lady Lot," said Regar, "the rede you are to give us, is it a riddle as well?"

"Oui. By the rules my sisters and I follow, we can do nought else."

Again Flic groaned and Blaise braced himself, as did Regar. Only Fleurette seemed eager to hear the rede.

Once more the sound of weaving intensified, and Verdandi intoned:

> *"Grim are the dark days looming ahead*
> *Now that the die is cast.*
> *Fight for the living, weep for the dead;*
> *Those who are first must come last.*
>
> *Summon them not ere the final day*
> *For his limit to be found.*
> *Great is his power all order to slay,*
> *Yet even his might has a bound."*

Verdandi fell silent, and the clacks and thuds diminished. And Blaise looked at Regar in confusion, and received a shrug in return. Flic shook his head in bewilderment, and Fleurette turned up her hands in puzzlement.

"My lady Lot," said Blaise, "can you not—?"

"Non, I cannot," said Verdandi. "Yet this I can tell you for nought: Heed my rede, all of it, and make certain you do not send word prematurely, else the world will be fallen to ruin."

And with that dreadful utterance, again the sound of shuttles and battens intensified, and then vanished as did Lady Lot.

Reaper

Just after the noontide, Luc and Maurice came to a long slope leading down into a wide meadow, in which a rich stand of grain grew. High on the slope stood a massive oak, and 'neath its widespread limbs sat a very large man with a great scythe across his knees. As Luc and Maurice slowed to a trot and headed for the scarlet- and gold-leafed tree, the man stood and grounded the blade of his scythe and swept his hat from a shock of red hair and bowed.

Luc called out, "Bonjour, Reaper."

"Bonjour, Prince Luc," the Reaper replied as he straightened up and donned his cap. Huge, he was, seven or eight feet tall, and he was dressed in coarse-spun garb, as would a crofter be.

Luc reined to a halt next to the large man and dismounted, and Maurice followed suit, and both knight and guide began changing saddles to remounts.

"What news, my lord?" asked the Reaper.

"Ill word, I'm afraid, Moissonneur."

"Ill word?"

"Oui. It seems the witch Hradian has come into possession of a token to set free the wizard Orbane from his imprisonment."

"That is ill news indeed," said the Reaper.

"If so," replied Luc, "we will need all the aid we can summon."

"My lord, I will come when the time is right."

Luc frowned at this odd turn of phrase, yet he said, "We will welcome you," and both he and Maurice mounted up.

Luc then saluted the Reaper, and the huge man bowed in acknowledgment and watched as the two galloped away.

Then the Reaper sat down with his back to the great oak and positioned his huge scythe across his knees and smiled unto himself.

Warnings

After Laurent and Édouard galloped away, the Ice Sprite they had enlisted flashed from his icicle to the frozen mere where many of his kindred played, and he relayed the message to all. They in turn spread throughout the Winterwood, alerting their kindred as to the dreadful news. And as they went from icicle to frozen stream to ice-clad trees and boulders, unlike their winged kindred, they did not seem to cross through the intervening space at all; instead they were here, and then they were there. Hence, the word spread much more swiftly throughout this realm than through the other Forests of the Season, for it seemed as if an Ice Sprite could cross enormous distances in the blink of an eye.

And winged Sprites briefly came from the Springwood and Autumnwood and Summerwood, and they paused just long enough to tell of the plans for dealing with the crows ere fleeing back to their more hospitable domains.

And as in the other realms, the Ice Sprites spread the word from hamlet to hunter, from cottage to fortress, from snowy vale to icy mountaintop, and to all beings wherever they found them, as long as ice was at hand.

And they, too, alerted the Root Dwellers, and they spied upon the crows massed along a section of the starwise border, waiting for winged Sprites to come flying through.

And the Root Dwellers harvested long, slender thorns, and they plotted and planned among themselves.

And while that was in progress, Ice Sprites went through the twilight borders along particular sectors of the Winterwood, to cross into other frozen realms, and they alerted their kindred, and the reindeer herders, and the seal hunters, and the woodsmen hewing trees, and other such hardy beings, and these folk, too, were dismayed to hear of the appalling news. Yet they clenched their jaws and straightened their backs and promised they would be ready.

And as the Ice Sprites bore the warning onward they also sought Raseri the Dragon and Rondalo the Elf, but this day it was in vain.

Conundrums

Down into a fog-laden vale plunged Roél and Dévereau. Their passage caused swirls in the clinging vapor, as of ghosts flying through the mist. But soon up a long slope they surged, and back into the sunlight of the Springwood they ran, the air among newly leafed-out foliage bearing the scent of the forest, fresh and full of promise. Yet old were these trees, some of them, their roots reaching deep, their great girths moss-covered, their branches spread wide and interlacing with others overhead. Oak there was, proud and majestic, and groves of birch, silver and white; maple and elm stood tall, with dogwood and wild cherry blossoms filling the air with their delicate scents. And down among the roots running across the soil, crocuses bloomed, as did small mossy flowers, yellow and lavender and white. Even though much of the woodland seemed aged, here and there stood new growth—thickets of saplings and lone seedlings and solitary treelets, all reaching upward in the search for light, their hues more vivid than those of their ancient kindred. Birds flitted among the verdant leaves, their songs claiming territory and calling for mates. The hum of bees sounded as they moved from blossom to blossom, and elsewhere beetles clambered along greening vines and stems. Overhead, scampering limb-runners chattered, and down among the grass and thatch, voles and other small living things rustled.

And streams burbled and splashed among stones, as if singing and dancing on their way to some collective goal. Bright and dark and twilight were these woods, and full of wakened life, and Roél, though he had lived herein for some four years in all, was filled with the marvel of this splendid place.

But unlike other times and other days, he did not stop to revel in the glory, but pressed his mount onward toward the distant goal.

Now and then across Roél's vision a winged Sprite would flash, much like a hummingbird in its swiftness, bearing the warning through some part of the realm. And occasionally, Root Dwellers and other such elfin folk would try to keep pace with them, but swift were the steeds and their riders, and shortly the small beings would be left far behind.

Even though their mission was urgent, of necessity Roél and Dévereau paused to relieve the horses, to water them and feed them a bit of grain and allow them some respite. And at these stops, they would change tack to fresher mounts and shortly take up the ride again, the horses pounding through the soft loam and the detritus of the forest floor.

One of these halts occurred nigh the noontide in the hamlet of Auberville, where the Sprite-borne warning had already come, and an assembly of folk looked unto the chevalier for answers. While the horses rested, Roél replied to their queries as best he could, but at last he and Dévereau mounted up to push on. Yet ere leaving, Roél wheeled his horse toward the gathering and said, "At this time, we are doing all we can to meet the threat of Orbane. Yet whether or no he gets free, in but a few days men will arrive to begin training those who are able-bodied, for there might come a time when battle cannot be avoided, and we must be ready. Thereafter, if the call to assemble is sounded, all fighters will then report to wherever the muster is to be held. Even so, some must remain behind, not only to protect the realm, but also to provide for the oldsters and youngsters and the sick and lame and enfeebled, for, though you might be eager to join the fight, we cannot abandon those herein who will need your aid."

And with that, Roél and Dévereau spurred away.

Across flowered glades hammered the mounts, spring melt trickling from the shadowy feet of trees, where snow yet huddled out of the rays of the sun.

And the sun itself slid through the sky and across and down as the day crept toward the eve. And as the orb set and dusk drew down on the land, Dévereau called out, "But a league or so and we'll be at the manse."

"Oui, Dévereau, I know," answered Roél, for he was quite familiar with the route between Springwood Manor and the Castle of the Seasons, having travelled it a number of times. Yet he was glad of Dévereau's company, for the flaxen-haired youth was of good spirit. Besides, should they meet up with trouble along the way, the youth, a member of the Springwood warband, was quite handy with a bow.

And as they galloped down a dark gallery of trees, in the near distance ahead something small and white stood upon the way.

"Rein back, Dévereau, rein back," called Roél. "We know not what this might be."

"Think you it is a trick of the witch?" called the youth, even as he and Roél slowed their mounts to a walk, the horses breathing heavily, lather running down their flanks.

"I know not," answered Roél, and he drew Coeur d'Acier, its silvery blade rune-marked.

Dévereau strung his bow and nocked an arrow, and slowly they pressed forward, both scanning the surround for waiting foe, yet in the light of dusk they saw none.

Now Roél gazed ahead at the creature in the trail. "Dévereau, methinks 'tis a goat."

"Indeed, Sieur, but something or someone small lies on the ground at its feet."

"I see," said Roél, frowning, then urging his mount onward. "Perhaps a new kid or a small child. Even so, keep a sharp eye."

And as they neared, they could see it was a youngster, a femme lying facedown. When they came unto her, Roél sheathed his sword and reined to a stop and leapt from his horse. The goat bleated and sidled but did not flee, and Roél turned the child over and cradled her head and shoulders. She was breathing but unconscious and looked to be no more than eight or nine summers old.

"Dévereau, your wineskin," snapped Roél as he supported the child's small frame, and he reached with his free hand toward his companion.

Dévereau untied the small leather bag from his cantle, and leapt down and uncapped the skin and handed it to Roél. Carefully, Roél dribbled a small amount in between the child's slightly parted lips. She lightly coughed and then swallowed, and opened a dark eye and whispered "More, please, Sieur."

"Oui, ma petite goaterd," said Roél, and he gave her a second sip.

She opened her other eye and said, "More please, Sieur."

As Roél tipped the skin to her lips, she grasped it with both hands and gulped and gulped and gulped.

"Non, child!" protested Roél, but with surprising strength she wrenched the wineskin from his grip and drained it. Then she looked up at Roél and cackled.

And of a sudden she was free from his embrace, and a dark shimmering came over her as she stood.

Roél sprang back and ripped free his blade from its scabbard, even as Dévereau snatched up his bow and nocked an arrow and drew.

And before them stood a black-haired, black-eyed toothless crone dressed in a black-limned ebon robe, and from somewhere, nowhere, everywhere came the sound of looms weaving.

Roél called out, "Dévereau, hold! Loose not!" and then he

sheathed his sword and knelt before the hag and said, "My lady Urd."

Behind him, Dévereau pointed his bow down and away and relaxed his draw, then he, too, fell to his knees in obeisance.

"Heh! Had you fooled, eh?" said Urd, even as she turned toward the goat and made a small gesture, and it vanished.

"Oui, my lady Doom," said Roél, yet kneeling before her. "Given the straits we find ourselves in, have you come with a message?"

"Of course, of course," snapped Urd. "Why else would I be here?"

"Only the Fates would know," answered Roél, a tiny smile playing at the corners of his mouth.

Urd gaped a gummy grin and said, "Given to bons mots, are we?"

"I rather thought you would like such," said Roél.

Urd hooted in glee and said, "And I thought no one could fathom even a trifle when it concerns the characters of my sisters and me."

"My lady Doom, I remember the pleasure you took in small joys when last we met."

"Hmm . . . Got to be careful around the likes of you, my lad, else I might let something unwarranted slip. Can't be too caught up in tomfooleries, especially not given the events to come." Urd's smile vanished, and her face took on an aspect even more careworn than her aged features would suggest.

"Events to come," said Roél. "That's why you are here."

"As always," said Urd. "By the rules we follow, 'tis only in times of a future need that we might appear, and even then not always."

"But I thought all was written," protested Dévereau.

Urd shook her head. "Although we have *seen*, still no event is permanently set until I finally bind it into the Tapestry of Time."

"How so?" asked the youth.

"My elder sister Skuld sees the future and weaves those scenes into the tapestry; Verdandi sees the present, and changes the weavings to reflect alterations in the events; and I finally bind all incidents into permanency. But heed me, Dévereau, Roél, great deeds are needed to change what Skuld and Verdandi weave and what I prepare to affix, but once I do the final binding, nought will recall any event whatsoever so that one might change the final outcome."

"And what you and your sisters have seen is dreadful?" asked Roél.

"Indeed."

"Then, my Lady Who Fixes the Past, tell me what I must do."

"Heh. You know the rules, Roél. First you must answer a riddle, and then I will give you advice."

Roél sighed and said, "Say on, Lady Doom, say on."

Urd took a deep breath, and the clack and thud of shuttles and battens swelled:

> *"They stood there as if long dead,*
> *Their children buried alive,*
> *And someone well might wonder:*
> *Did any of them survive?*
>
> *Parents awoke at my passing;*
> *New vigor seemed to flow;*
> *Some children then did rise up,*
> *Most all with a healthy glow.*
>
> *Now my riddle is done;*
> *I've given you sufficient hint.*
> *Tell me, Roél, who am I,*
> *And what is this grand event."*

The sound of looms abated, and Roél's heart fell. Dévereau started to speak, yet with a gesture Urd silenced him and said, "This is for Roél alone to answer here in the Springwood."

Here in the Springwood? Is that another hint? Roél frowned in deep thought. *What is it vis-à-vis this demesne that might give a clue to the answer?* He looked about in the twilight to see burgeoning trees and flowers and new leaves, and sprouts pressing upward. It was a woodland of eternal—

"Spring, my lady Doom, bringing with it resurrection and life anew. The ones standing as if long dead are the trees and shrubs and grasses and other such in their winter sleep. And the buried children are seeds in the ground. And when spring comes they quit their slumber, vigor flows, and seeds sprout. And so, my lady Urd, I say the answer to your riddle is the coming of spring and the awakening of life."

Fretting, he looked up at her, and Urd said, "Exactly so, Roél. It is spring and rebirth, indeed."

Dévereau shook his head. "And here I thought it had to do with parents grieving over children trapped in a collapsed mine or cave and the ones who came to dig them out."

"Heh!" crowed Urd. "Fooled you, eh?"

"Oui, Lady Doom."

"That'll teach you to stop and think ere speaking, laddie."

"Lady Urd," said Roél, "have you a rede now to give us?"

"Impatient, are we?"

"Somewhat, my lady Doom, yet I am at your behest."

Urd nodded and cackled, her toothless smile wide, and once again the clack of shuttles and thud of battens intensified.

> " 'Pon the precipice will ye be held,
> *As surely as can be,*
> *Yet can ye but touch the deadly arcane,*
> *The least shall set ye free.*"

And as the sound of weaving fell, Roél frowned but remained silent, yet Dévereau said, "But, Lady Doom, I, for one, do not understand. Will you not tell us more?"

"Non, I will not," replied the black-eyed crone. "But this I can tell you for nought: If you do not solve this rede, Roél, then all as we now know it to be will come to a horrible end."

And after laying that terrible responsibility upon Roél, again the clack and thud intensified, and then vanished as did Lady Urd.

Manors

Just after dusk, Laurent and Édouard spurred up a wide, snow-laden pathway along the face of a high bluff, and as they crested the rise, they came into the lights of a great mansion—Winterwood Manor—the walls of which were fashioned of massive dark timbers cut square, and its roof was steeply pitched. A full three storeys high, with many chimneys scattered along its considerable length, the manse spanned the entire width of the flat. All along its breadth the windows were protected with heavy-planked shutters, most of them closed as if for a blow. Even so, enough were open so that warm and yellow lanternlight shone out onto a stone courtyard cleared of snow. Atop the lofty river bluff it sat like a great aerie, not only for surveying the wide vale below but also the white world beyond.

With remounts trailing behind, the knight and his guide crossed the flat and came unto the courtyard and clattered upon the stone of the broad forecourt, where lit lanterns illuminated their way, and warmly dressed men were on hand to greet them.

Reining to a halt, from his sweat-lathered horse Laurent somewhat stiffly dismounted, and to the men who took the steeds in hand he said, "Rub them down well, and feed them extra rations, for they did run most gallantly."

"Oui, Sieur," said one of the men, while another asked, "Is it true the word Ice Sprites brought? Does the witch Hradian really have the means to set Orbane free?"

"Sadly, so," said Laurent.

"Enough," commanded one of the men, tall and spare and somber. "We must let Sieur Laurent and Édouard warm themselves and have a meal. There will be plenty of time to learn exactly what is afoot."

The men touched their caps in obeisance and led the horses away, as Arnot, the steward of Winterwood, escorted Laurent and Édouard 'neath a sheltering portico to the great double doors, and they passed along a short corridor to come to a broad welcoming hall. And there assembled were a somber gathering of members of the mansion household—maids, servants, footmen, seamstresses, bakers, kitchen- and waitstaff, laundresses, gamekeepers, and others—men and women deeply concerned, though they managed smiles in welcome and bowed or curtseyed accordingly.

Ere Arnot could shoo them away, Laurent stepped across the heavy-planked floor to a wide marble circle inset in the wood, within which was a great hexagonal silver inlay depicting a delicate snowflake. Laurent looked at the anxious faces and said, "The message the Sprites have brought is true: the witch Hradian does indeed have a key to the Castle of Shadows. We do not know if she has the means or the knowledge to use it, but if she does, then without doubt she will set Orbane free."

Some in the hall gasped, while others' faces grew grim. A few shed tears.

Laurent went on: "Regardless, we must needs prepare for such an eventuality, hence able-bodied men throughout the Forests of the Seasons must stand ready, for surely Orbane will raise his own forces to become master of the whole of Faery.

"All is not bleak, for even now the word is spreading across the realms, and others will answer the call. We will have allies, and powerful ones at that, one of whom is your very own prince who will be here in but a few days.

"So, let me ask that you go about your business in the knowledge that we will meet the challenge. Dark times might be coming, but brighter times lie beyond."

Then Laurent smiled and said, "Now, I wonder, could Édouard and I have a warm meal, with a soothing hot bath afterward?"

For a moment none said ought, but then a redheaded woman snapped, "Well, you heard Sieur Laurent. To my kitchen, *tout de suite!*"

As the staff bustled away, Laurent turned to Arnot and said, "Steward, I would have you join Édouard and me, for I bear messages from Prince Borel, and I would have you know all that has come to pass. Much will be afoot in the coming days, and we must make ready."

Outside a soft snow began to fall, as if the Winterwood paid no heed to these matters of men.

. . .

In the dining chamber of Autumnwood Manor, Luc set down his glass of wine and turned to Zacharie, steward of the realm. "The princess will be here within a few days. She and the warband will start their journey as soon as the ceremonies are concluded at the faire. In the meanwhile, we need send falcons to the other manors and King Valeray's castle as well, reporting our safe arrival." Luc frowned and added, "And I would also tell them of Moissonneur's strange reply."

"Strange reply? The Reaper?" asked Zacharie, a tall, gaunt man with dark hair and pale blue eyes.

"Oui," said Luc. "When I told him we would need all the aid we could summon, he said, 'My lord, I will come when the time is right.' It was as if he would be waiting for some unknown event ere joining us. Do you know what it might be?"

"Non," replied Zacharie, "but Princess Liaze might."

"Or even King Valeray," said Maurice, 'round a mouthful of roast duck.

"What know you of him?" asked Luc.

"The Reaper, you mean?" said Zacharie, and at Luc's nod, the steward went on: "Very little, I'm afraid. It seems he has always been under that oak, waiting for someone to need grain from the field below. It is only then he leaves the tree and takes that great scythe of his and with a few strokes—*swish, swash*—the yield is ready to be sheaved."

"And otherwise he never goes away from the oak?"

"Non, my lord, at least not to my knowledge."

"Then what does he eat and drink, and how does he obtain it?"

Zacharie turned up his hands. "I know not, my lord."

"Did he participate in the last war against Orbane?"

"I think not, my lord," said Zacharie. "Some say there is an old Keltoi legend that the Reaper waits for some event, just as you have surmised."

"Hmm . . ." mused Luc. Then he took a deep breath and dug into the green beans.

· · ·

In the bathing house of Summerwood Manor, with their bellies full, Blaise and Jérôme and Regar luxuriated in hot water, soaking the soreness of the long, swift ride from their bones. On the tub's edge sat tiny Flic, with Buzzer adoze on a soft towel nearby. At hand stood grey-haired Lanval, steward of this demesne. Also close by sat a young man at a small table, with quill and inkpot and parchment ready. "And what would you have in this message, Sieur Blaise?" asked Lanval.

"Ah," replied the knight. "We need to tell all the others just what it is that Lady Verdandi said, for perhaps they can unravel the riddle. Now let me see, how does it go? Ah, oui:

· · ·

" 'Grim are the dark days looming ahead
Now that the die is cast.
Fight for the living, weep for the dead;
Those who are first must come last.

Summon them not ere the final day
For his limit to be found.
Great is his power all order to slay,
Yet even his might has a bound.' "

The steward nodded at the young man, and the youth began scribbling, pausing now and again for clarification from Blaise.

Flic frowned and asked, "I say, will all of that writing fit on a falcon-borne message, or will the bird have to walk all the way under the load?"

The men laughed, and Lanval said, "Fear not for the falcon, Sieur Flic, for the message will be transcribed in diminutive script on the thin strip of tissue the birds customarily bear in their message capsules."

"Are all four missives to be the same?" asked the youth.

"Oui, Randin," said Blaise. "—Oh, and add that we arrived safely."

"Won't they deduce that from the mere fact that you dispatched a message?" asked Flic.

"Oh, right," said Blaise. "Scratch that, Randin."

"You might add," said Regar, "that Flic, Fleurette, Buzzer, and I are pushing on for the halls of the Fairy King."

"When?" asked the youth.

"On the morrow," said Regar. Then he looked at Flic. "Right?"

"Oui," replied the Sprite. "We cannot delay in something such as this. I'll get Buzzer to dance out a course for us."

Regar frowned. "Dance out a course?"

"Oui," said Flic. "You see, Buzzer can fly the most direct

line to anywhere she has been. All we need to do is describe the type of flowers there, and some of the terrain. And she will do a honeybee dance to tell me the direction we must go. It will surely be shorter than the one Borel, Buzzer, and I followed when we were on the quest to rescue Lady Michelle."

Blaise glanced at Buzzer and said, "Honeybee dance? But she is not a honeybee."

"Non, she is not," said Flic, "but I taught her the dance and she adopted it immediately."

"There is a story here for the telling," said Regar. "But I must say that I don't know any of the kinds of flowers that grow in my father's domain."

Flic grinned. "You forget, my prince, that both Buzzer and I have been there ere now."

. . .

In the Springwood, as Roél dried off, he said, "I wonder if any of the others ran afoul of the Three Sisters?"

Vidal frowned and said, "Sieur Roél, I would not character-ize coming across any of the Fates as 'running afoul' of them."

Roél smiled at the dignified, silver-haired steward. "Think you they might take offense?"

"Who knows?" asked Vidal, casting his eyes skyward.

Roél laughed, then sobered. "Still, I wonder."

"If others did indeed receive redes from the Ladies Wyrd and Lot and Doom, then surely things are dire," said Vidal.

Roél frowned. "Hmm . . . Isn't it true that they only appear when one or more of Valeray's get are present? If so, then why did Lady Doom appear to Dévereau and me?"

Vidal shook his head. "Non, Valeray's get are not necessary for the Fates to show themselves, for they aided Lady Camille, and she was alone."

"Oui, I had forgotten about Camille, but every other time— Look, they did appear before Céleste and me on our quest to rescue Avélaine, and they did manifest in front of Camille and Alain and the staff of Summerwood Manor along with the Dwarves of the *Nordavind* on what was then Troll Isle, as well as at several other gatherings where many were present. And so, setting aside the early part of Camille's quest, in all of those cases, the get of Valeray were on hand." Roél paused, his gaze lost in thought. Finally he said, "I wonder why this might be different?"

Vidal shrugged. "None knows the ways of the Fates, Sieur Roél. Certainly not I."

Roél sighed and laid the towel aside and slipped into a silken robe. "Regardless, if the others think to send messages, we will soon know whether or not any other Sister appeared."

Vidal nodded. "Come the dawn, falcons will fly, and then we shall see."

Roél yawned and stepped through the doorway and toward the bed. "Even if none else received a cryptic message, at least the Sprite-borne warnings are spreading and the muster has begun."

Vidal nodded and stepped to the chamber door, where he took up a glass-chimneyed candle to see his way to his own rooms. "Let us pray to Mithras that one of them has found Raseri and Rondalo, and that they have intercepted the witch so that it won't come to another war with Orbane."

"Indeed," said Roél, yawning again as he crawled into the canopied bed.

As the knight pulled the covers about himself, Vidal said, "*Bonne nuit, Sieur, et bon repos*, for tomorrow promises to be demanding."

Roél did not reply, for he was quite sound asleep.

Vidal withdrew and softly closed the door and went into the darkness beyond.

A Murder of Crows

The sun had long set, followed by the moon, and in the darkness of the Springwood and the Summerwood, as well as the Autumnwood and the Winterwood, from within the embraces of the roots of the trees along a key portion of the starwise bounds of each forest, small beings emerged in the night and stealthily climbed upward. And they had with them razor-sharp shards of flint and obsidian, and slender barbs and nooses and other such weaponry, all of a size for the Root Dwellers, and all silent when compared to brute-force smashing weapons, such as hammers and mauls. Out along the limbs the tiny people crept, searching, seeking, hunting for crows, and death came mutely among the birds.

And from deeper within the Springwood and Summerwood and Autumnwood, more Sprites came with long thorns in hand and silently glided toward the trees.

And from Valeray's demesne, Sprites drifted on wings through the twilight bound, needles and scarfpins and thorns in hand, to join in the murder of crows.

And they settled to the roosts of given trees and at a specified signal, they stabbed through the eyes and into the brains of the ebon birds. Even though slain, the crows fell to the ground and flopped and fluttered for long moments, yet other dark birds asleep in adjacent trees did not note the passing of their kindred. And when all fell quiet once more, the troops of tiny warriors moved to the next set of full roosts.

In the Winterwood it was Ice Sprites who popped from frozen pond to icicle to ice-laden limbs, seeking blackbirds who perched on ice, and there the winter Sprites reached forth with their tiny fingers to oh-so-lightly touch the birds at the places where they grasped the clad branch; and the Sprites froze them to death, while the Root Dwellers of that forest slew the ones who sat on ice-free roosts.

When morning came in these four domains, the floor of each woodland along those portions of the starwise margins was littered with dead birds, like black leaves fallen to ground.

24

Leave-taking

At dawn the day after Luc, Roél, Laurent, and Blaise and their guides had ridden away, Michelle and the Winterwood retainers as well as Avélaine and half of the Springwood warband prepared to set out for their respective manors. At Sieur Émile's manse, Avélaine would pick up a small escort of men and ride on to her home in Port Mizon, there where her husband Vicomte Chevell readied a battlefleet with the intent of once and for all clearing out the corsair stronghold on the island fortress of Brados. Just how a release of Orbane from the Castle of Shadows might affect this seafaring mission, none could say, for Orbane was not noted for conflicts upon the brine, but the warring of armies on land instead.

Regardless, Michelle would be at Winterwood Manor by morrow eve to await the arrival of Borel, while Avélaine's return to her port city would take a seven-day altogether.

Borel embraced Michelle and said, "I'll be on my way the very moment the closing ceremonies are done; the Wolves and I will press through the night, so look for me the morning following the eve we get quit of this faire."

Lady Simone kissed Avélaine and said, "Take care, my daughter, for there is more than just you to worry about. I would not have my future grandchild placed in jeopardy."

Sieur Émile gently embraced Avélaine. "Avi, heed your

mother, for in war, who knows what might come. Thank Mithras you live by the sea and should be fairly safe, for the war will be fought aland. Even so, the battles might come close, so be ready to hie to a safer place."

"Oh, la," said Avélaine. "I think this Orbane, even if he does get free, will be put down by you and the king and his men, to say nought of Rollie and Blaise and Laurent."

"And Luc," said Liaze, gazing toward the duskward bound beyond which lay her realm.

"Mais oui," said Avélaine. "I did not mean to leave him out, nor Borel and Alain. All will do magnificently, of that I am certain."

A tall, dark-haired man approached and said, "Lady Michelle, we are ready."

"Oui, Armsmaster Jules," replied Michelle to the warband leader.

"We are ready as well," said stocky, redheaded Anton, captain of the Springwood warband.

Quick embraces were exchanged all 'round, and Valeray, Saissa and their get, as well as Camille and Duran, stepped back, along with Simone and Émile. The men and the two ladies mounted up, and, with a sliding of massive bars and the creaking of hinges, the gates of the castle were opened. With waves and calls of *au revoir*, across the flagstone clattered the horses and out into the land beyond, and as faire-goers watched, away trotted the war bands, one group heading dawnwise, the other starwise.

And as the two ladies and their escorts rode away on their separate paths, through the early morning light on glittering wings came Sprites to report to the king.

. . .

It was midmorning when Michelle and Jules and the warband crossed over into the Winterwood. Foxes looked up from their feasting, and scattered away into the snow-laden 'scape.

Michelle marveled at the litter of crows, yet she and the others paused not, but pressed on toward a number of small fires glimmering not far ahead, around which tiny folk clustered.

. . .

Past the crow-slaughter at the starwise bound of the Springwood rode Avélaine and her entourage. And they came among small beings, the wee Root Dwellers, where birds roasting on spits filled the air with a meaty aroma. These diminutive fey folk, some unclothed, others not, many now adorned with black feathers, bowed and curtseyed gracefully as the sparse cavalcade fared by. As always, Avélaine marveled at the sight of them, with their quite exotic elfin features—long tipped ears and tilted eyes, eyes usually filled with mischievous gaiety. And she listened to their tiny, piping voices, sometimes mistaken for bird twitters by those who did not know better. Some doffed crudely stitched hats, revealing nearly bald heads, while others sported hair to the waist, or even to the anklebone. And as they bowed and curtseyed to Avélaine, she nodded and smiled in return, giving them their due. And through the long gauntlet of Root Dwellers, some yet bearing the weapons used in the slaughter, rode the lady and her escort, while spitted crows roasted above flames.

When the warband had passed out of earshot, Captain Anton turned to Avélaine and said, "Remind me, m'lady, never to make enemies of the wee ones, else I am a dead bird." Then he roared with laughter, as did all his men, Avélaine joining in.

. . .

And so as the sun rode up and across the sky and started its slow descent, in the Winterwood and the Springwood, warbands of men escorted ladies toward home, while elsewhere in Faery and riding across the sky a figure, streaming danglers and tatters like ephemeral shadows, flew swiftly toward her goal.

Pilgrimage

Leaving Crapaud behind to ward the cote, up and up above the swamp did Hradian fly, her besom firmly grasped as she straddled the long, thick shaft. No sidesaddle rider she, for it gave her no pleasure to do so, and instead she fully reveled in the joy of flight, riding as she did.

High up above the foetid morass she soared, above the miasma of rot and stench, and away sunward she darted, the Black Wall of the World her aim, though it lay far, far away.

Across the world of Faery did Hradian soar through the dark, the starry skies witness to her flight. O'er the swamp she flew, and leagues fell away behind her. Finally a twilight wall she crossed, and out from the realm of her mire. And still she flew onward as the night wheeled above, until came the faint light of dawn.

Still onward she pressed through twilight bound after bound, morning now lighting the way. And she soared o'er dark mountains and rivers and steads and cities, villages and forests and lakes, and barren wastes of ice or sand or rock all passing 'neath her broom. And yet to these she but barely paid attention, for she had flown since childhood, and all was as familiar as treading the same road over and over again. And so she little noted the clouds like foreign castles and great châteaus rising all 'round, nor other strange shapes these billows of the sky took on—shaggy animals, long dragons, boars, horses, cattle, and droll faces of women and men. Nor did she see *damiers* and échiquiers below in the patterns of sown fields over which she passed, nor the glitter of lakes like diamonds, nor the sails of ships like gull wings as above an arm of a distant sea she went, the fishermen plying their skills below.

And still through looming walls of twilight she flew, Faery borders, one after another, so many she lost count as the sun slid up the sky and across and down. Yet Hradian pressed on, her flight draining her of energy, for it took much out of her to maintain the spell. And besides, she had flown very far the past three days—all the way to and from Valeray's demesne, and now, with but a short rest, onward to the Black Wall.

But at last, as the sinking sun touched the distant horizon, Hradian began to circle down, for in the distance ahead and looming up into the sky an ebon barrier stood; it seemed a black beyond black, so dark it was. Yet even though it was within easy flight, she had not the vigor to broach it this eve, for flying into the Great Darkness required almost as much arcane power as did her flight to come unto this place. Instead she spiralled down toward a small town below, where she would spend the night, resting and regaining her strength.

Down coiled Hradian and down, to finally come alight upon a knoll, the village a short walk beyond. She cast a glamour upon herself, and a young man with a stave in hand and pack on his back headed downslope through the dusk and toward the only hostel in the hamlet.

26

Bee Dance

After an overnight stay at Summerwood Manor, early the following morn Blaise and Regar and Flic and Fleurette and Buzzer took breakfast in one of the white gazebos sprinkled across the broad estate. The two men downed eggs and rashers and toast and butter and jams and good strong hot tea, while the Sprites and the bee alternated between honey and preserves, though both Flic and Fleurette also ate tiny bits of toast dipped in the sweets. The day was cloudless, the sky blue, and alongside the gazebo a clear and slow-flowing stream meandered, passing under the branches of a large willow overhanging the lucid water. A small cluster of black swans awkwardly waddled down the bank and entered the drift, where it seemed elegance overtook them as they coursed away downcurrent on an errand of their own.

As he watched the graceful dark birds, "The messenger falcons flew at dawn," said Blaise. "Mayhap soon we'll know whether others met up with one or more of the Fates."

"If so," said Fleurette, "we can expect more redes to confound us."

"Non," said Regar, "for you and Flic and Buzzer and I will be away by then."

"Then you're leaving for the halls of the Fairy King ere any falcons arrive?" asked Blaise.

Regar turned and looked past the manse and toward the stables beyond, where four horses were being readied for travel. "Oui, for as Flic said yester, our mission cannot wait."

"Even so," said Flic, "I could tarry here for part of the day and learn the contents of whatever missives might come from one of the other demesnes."

Fleurette shook her head. "Oh, Flic, you know Buzzer will not fly a course unless you are along. Besides, neither Regar nor I can speak Bee, and should we need to change direction, well, we'd be at a loss. Still, I could wait for messages to arrive and catch up with you later."

As Flic's face fell at the thought of leaving Fleurette behind, Regar said, "Non, Wee Flower, I think we should all go, for who knows whether or no falcons will ever come? There is this as well: with you starting out to find us a half day or more behind, you could easily stray from whatever line Buzzer takes, and even a small error can lead to a wide miss; non, Fleurette, I would not have you flitting about seeking us in a woodland, especially one where the witch's crows are at large."

"But most are massed at the starwise border," said Fleurette.

Regar shook his head. "Even so, we know not what lies before us. Mayhap there are more along the way we will travel."

Fleurette glanced at the silver épée at Flic's side and said, "I could carry a thorn. Too, given the nature of our kindred Sprites, mayhap by now no crows remain anywhere within the four forests."

"That we do not know," said Flic, peering toward distant trees and the clear skies above. Then he added, "Regar is correct. We should all go together."

A silence fell among them, and they continued to break their fast. And soon the horses were led across the sward toward the gazebo. One was fitted with a small rack, several modest bags of provisions affixed thereon. Of the other three horses, two were completely unladen, while one was fully equipped with tack, saddlebags included.

Followed by Buzzer, Flic flew up and landed on one of the bags and said to the hostler, "I say, have you enough honey packed away in these? Buzzer will require quite a bit, you know; we don't want to have to stop along the way to gather nectar because we've run out."

"Three full jars, wee sieur." The stableman held his hands in such a way to indicate the size.

"Perhaps it is enough," said Flic, frowning, for as yet he did not know just how far hence the halls of the Fairy King lay. He looked at Buzzer and then flew back to the gazebo. "Prince Regar, are we ready to leave?"

Regar downed the last of his tea and stood. "As soon as you point the way."

"Follow me," said Flic, and he flew to a large flat of flagstone on the path bordering a flowerbed nearby, Buzzer and Fleurette following awing, Blaise and Regar afoot. As soon as the Sprites and bee alighted, Flic said, "Now let me see, nigh the entrance to the halls of the King Under the Hill, there are white phlox and purple thistle and tiny bluebells. Oh, and yellow poppies, but only in spring." He frowned. "I wonder what season it is there?"

"It was summer in Valeray's demesne," said Fleurette, "and I believe his realm properly follows the march of the sun."

"Oh, then," said Flic, "tiger lilies instead, but only near streams."

Flic sank to his knees and it appeared he was speaking to the bee, yet what he said, only Fleurette seemed to have a glimmering. Buzzer began a peculiar wiggling and buzzing dance, Flic paying rapt attention. Back and forth in a straight line the bee wriggled, pausing now and again to thrum her wings. And then Buzzer began dancing in a different direction, and again and again she buzzed and wriggled and paused. Once more and again and several times thereafter she changed the course of the dance, each on a separate tack. Finally, she stopped, and Flic shook his head and growled.

"What is it?" asked Blaise.

Flic sighed. "Buzzer knows of a number of places with all four things, some closer than others, but most of them quite far. Now let me think, is there anything more? —Oh, of course, the large dolmen and the light that streams out. But wait, that only happens at night, when Buzzer is quite asleep." He pondered a bit more, and then said, "Aha! I have it. It's where we spent a fortnight waiting for Prince Borel to emerge; Buzzer knows him as Slowfoot Who Does Not Fly."

Again Flic conversed with the bee, and Buzzer took up the dance once more, now wriggling and buzzing and pausing, this time in a single direction.

"Good," said Flic, looking up at Regar. "She has it. Yon is our way." Flic pointed, aiming more or less in the direction the bee had danced: a bit to sun of duskwise, or as some would name it, more or less west-southwest. "There are a few marges of twilight to cross. Still, it is much shorter than the twisty path that Prince Borel and I took to get there, for we went many other places ere aiming for the halls of the King Under the Hill."

Regar smiled and said, "Well then, let us hie." He turned to Blaise and the two men embraced and pounded one another on the back, and Regar said, "I will do my best to rally my Fairy King grandsire to bring his armies to join in the battle against Orbane, should the wizard get free."

Blaise nodded and said, "If Orbane does escape, then, just as we sent the warning throughout the lands, so too shall we send word as to where to assemble."

"Well and good," said Regar. "And even if my grandsire disapproves and refuses to join, certainly I will be there."

"And I," said Flic, flashing his tiny silver épée on high. "Buzzer, too, for we are mighty with our stingers."

"And I," said Fleurette, "even if I have to fight with nought but a thorn."

"Oh, Fleurette," said Flic, "I think it too dangerous for—"

"Nonsense, Flic," snapped Fleurette. "Where you go, so go I."

Regar turned to Blaise and said sotto voce, "Methinks it will be a very long journey if these two continue to argue over who should and should not join the fight."

Blaise laughed and said, "Methinks you are right, Prince."

Regar slapped the tricorn on his helm and mounted the saddled steed.

Flic and Fleurette, yet squabbling, flew up to stand in the prow of the three-cornered hat, and with a whispered word to Buzzer, the bee flew up and 'round and took a bearing on the sun, then shot off on a direct line a bit to sun of duskwise.

"May Mithras hold you in his hand," said Blaise.

"You as well, my friend," replied Regar. And he spurred away following the beeline, with remounts and the pack animal in tow.

Across the sward they cantered, veering to go out one of the gates in the long wall surrounding the immediate estate. Then they hewed back to the line Buzzer flew, and toward the far wooded rise of the wide vale they angled.

Blaise watched until they at last disappeared among the boles of the green-leafed forest. Then he turned and headed back toward the manor, for there was much planning to do to make ready for an oncoming war.

27

Redes

From Springwood Manor at dawn, four messenger falcons took flight; they were conveying missives to the other three manors of the Forests of the Seasons as well as to Valeray's castle. Likewise did four falcons fly from Summerwood Manor, and four each from the Autumnwood and Winterwood. The message capsules held tidings of arrivals, with three sets bearing reports of meetings with the Three Sisters and of the redes they spoke, and one set—those from the Autumnwood—speaking of the Reaper's odd words. Not long thereafter—ere midmorn had come—the skies above the various manors and o'er the Castle of the Seasons were filled with the *skree*s of arriving raptors turning on wings to come unto the mews, and shortly thereafter falconers came running with message capsules to be opened by stewards and king alike.

In the manors, stewards read the words and then took the messages to the knights, while in the castle, the king summoned queen and prince and princess alike, as well as Sieur Émile and Lady Simone.

"Hmm . . ." mused Valeray as he passed the messages about, "If Skuld and Verdandi and Urd are involved, then dire events lie before us."

"Yet," said Camille, "if Raseri is found in time to intercept Hradian, then mayhap all can be avoided."

Saissa sighed. "I would not hold hope for such, Camille, for it would appear from the words of the redes that Raseri will not be found."

"I agree," said Céleste. "Look at this one from Blaise. He tells that Lady Lot said:

> *"Grim are the dark days looming ahead*
> *Now that the die is cast.*
> *Fight for the living, weep for the dead.*

"That certainly sounds to me as if war with Orbane is inevitable. I mean, Verdandi says 'the die is cast,' and so what else would we interpret it to mean?"

A pall fell upon the gathering, and Borel said, "Then should we not leave now, return to our demesnes and prepare?"

"What could you do that Laurent isn't already doing?" asked Simone.

Borel growled in frustration and said, "At least I would be doing *something* rather than standing about doing nought."

"I would go, too, Brother," said Alain, "yet surely Blaise is taking all necessary steps, and I could add little."

"Your very presence would keep the men's spirits up," said Camille.

"List," said Liaze, "by riding in haste after the faire is done, we will be at our manors the very next day, all but Camille and Duran and their escort, for of needs they must go at a pace the young prince can withstand. And though I would rather be at my manor with Luc, lending moral support if nought else, there's little we can do."

Alain turned to Valeray. "Sire, can we not forgo the final ceremonies here at the faire?"

Valeray frowned and looked at Saissa, and she said, "I think it important we show we are steadfast and let things go on as usual, rather than rushing off as if panic-stricken."

"Yet, Maman," said Alain, "if we do nought, then won't the people think we dillydally in the face of danger?"

"Ah, but we are not doing nought, for already the call has gone out for recruits. Too, the Sprites are flying and bearing the news, and Luc, Roél, Laurent, and Blaise are even now at the manors making ready for a possible war."

Saissa turned to Valeray, and he added, "Surely Orbane, even if set free this very day, cannot assemble his armies of old in less than several fortnights at best. Non, my sons and daughters, it is as your mother says: we need to show our loyal subjects that we are calm and in control, hence all should be present at the closing mark."

Again Borel growled in frustration, while Alain took in a deep breath and blew it out. Céleste and Liaze sighed in resigned acceptance, and thus was the matter once again decided.

"Still, there is something we can do," said Camille, "and that is to try to puzzle out the meanings of these redes. If we succeed, then it should gain us considerable advantage, else the Sisters would not have told them to Laurent, Blaise, and Roél."

Sieur Émile turned to Valeray. "Why those three? I thought only your get received messages from the Fates. So why have they spoken to my sons, rather than to your children?"

Valeray turned up his hands in puzzlement, but Saissa said, "The Three Sisters have appeared before others, large gatherings for one, so choosing your sons seems no odd event."

"Yet," said Camille, "in every case where they did so, one or more of your children were present, Lady Saissa."

"You were alone when they appeared to you, Camille," said Valeray.

"Oui, but I came upon them along the shores of the River of Time, where it is said they dwell. —Oh, no, not quite true, for Skuld in her guise of Lady Sorcière, the Lady of the Mere, came to me ere I set out on the quest to find Alain."

"Yet that was on the estate of Summerwood Manor," said Alain. "Mayhap that's why she appeared."

"Argh!" growled Borel. "Who knows the ways of the Fates? Not I, my friends, not I."

A silence fell among them, and then Liaze peered at Luc's message now in hand and said, "What I'd like to know is the significance of the Reaper's words. 'My Lord, I will come when the time is right.' That's what he said to Luc." Liaze turned to Valeray. "Papa, do you know ought of what this means, and do these words carry special import?"

Valeray shrugged. "All I know is in the last war with Orbane, there were reports Moissonneur seemed to be waiting for some special event, yet what that might have been, or this time might be, I cannot say, and he has never spoken ought of it."

"Hmph," grunted Borel. "Mayhap the next time I gut and spit conies for him I'll ask. —But for me, it's what Skuld said in the Winterwood that gives me pause.

> *"Swift are the children of his namesake,*
> *That which a child does bear.*

"Those words have sent something skittering about in my mind, yet I cannot catch hold of it."

Borel glanced at Céleste and she turned up a hand and shrugged. Then she said, "Urd's rede to my Roél is the most mysterious of all, I think:

> *"Yet can ye but touch the deadly arcane,*
> *The least shall set ye free.*

"I wonder just what that might mean."

None had an answer for Céleste.

"You know the most dreadful things said by the three Fates?" asked Liaze. "It was their parting words."

Liaze turned to Borel and he looked at the message he held. "Skuld said to Laurent, 'If you do not give this message to the one for whom it is intended, then all will be lost forever.' "

Liaze then looked at Alain and he peered at his missive. "Verdandi told Blaise, 'Heed my rede, all of it, and make certain you do not send word prematurely, else the world will be fallen to ruin.' "

Liaze then looked at Céleste, and she glanced at her message. "Urd said, 'If you do not solve this rede, Roél, then all as we now know it to be will come to a horrible end.' "

"Oh my," said Simone, and she peered 'round the table from face to face to see nought but grim visages looking back.

28

Dragonflight

In the light of a waxing crescent moon, Ziv popped from icicle to frozen pond to ice-clad limb to—

What's this?

The Ice Sprite sensed in the distance afar a great frozen mass, more than he had ever felt before.

'Tis a long jump, but—

Of a sudden he was there. How far he had flashed, he had no notion, and he found himself in a vast conglomeration of ice. *Ah, a glacier.* He cast about with his Ice-Sprite perception. Its mass was nearly beyond his comprehension. *Oh, my, we've none this size in the Winterwood.* Ziv peered out through the frozen surface; there were mountains all 'round.

Ziv was far from his home and well into his mission of spreading the warning to all who could understand his unspoken language: the shaman of the snow-dwellers; the sages of the reindeer herders; the wise women of the seal- and whale-hunters; the ice-talkers of the high-mountain dwellers; others. Too, he looked for Raseri, for Rondalo, for Lady Chemine. Yet he thought they wouldn't be found in the icy reaches where Sprites of his kind travelled.

But even as he rejected his chances, he saw a great winged shape slide across the arc of the sinking moon and toward one of the peaks. Could it be the Drake he sought? Dark and ruddy it seemed, with splashes of ebon blackness glittering here and there among its deep crimson scales. Its vast leathery wings were stretched out wide as it turned through the air as if to come to a landing on that particular mountain crest.

Ziv threw his senses toward the apex, seeking ice thereon.

.   .   .

"Ha!" roared Raseri as he glided toward the rocky pinnacle. "That was a pleasure, eh?"

Rondalo lifted an eyebrow. "Pleasure? My friend, your ideas of pleasure are somewhat strange. Exciting, oui, but pleasure?" He shifted his spear onto his back by its sling. "Methinks in the future, should we encounter another Giant, 'twould be best not to set his hair on fire."

The Dragon laughed. "Did you see how clumsily he cast boulders at us?"

"Had he better aim," said the Elf, "we would now be in his cook pot."

"Where is your sense of adventure, Rondalo?"

"Adventure is one thing; foolhardiness another."

"Pah," snorted Raseri as he spiralled down toward the snowy crag. "What about the time you set an entire aerie of Great Eagles 'pon us? I suppose that was adventure and not folly."

"But you yourself agreed we needed a tail feather."

"Oui, but I was going to politely ask, rather than jerk one out and run."

Both Rondalo and Raseri roared in laughter, and the Drake came to a landing atop the crest, where the Elf dismounted.

From the worst of enemies to the best of friends these two had come, thanks to Camille some five years past.

Tall and lean and fair-haired, Rondalo cast back his cloak and unlaced the front of his breeks. As he relieved himself he said, "I think we ought to be on hand when Vicomte Chevell sails. We can help him rid Faery of the corsairs of Brados."

"Hmph!" snorted Raseri. "You and I alone could rid the seas of that menace."

"Oui, but taking the fortress—either by stealth or with siege engines—is a straightforward though perilous task for many men afoot, a more suitable job for Chevell's marines than one Dragon and a lone lancer."

"Forget not your bow, Rondalo." Raseri then raised a forefoot and flexed its dark, saberlike claws. "I think I could gut that bastion of theirs."

Rondalo began relacing his leathers. "Mayhap you could, though they say the stone is two or three strides thick. Still, here is my thought: we can destroy more corsairs at sea much quicker than Chevell's entire fleet, and that, my friend, is a better charge for you and me to take on."

Yet flexing his claws, Raseri growled, but said nought.

Rondalo adjusted his cloak and said, "I think it's time we were— Ho, what's this?"

Within a patch of clear ice wedged in a crevice a tiny figure gestured wildly.

"An Ice Sprite," said Rondalo. "Raseri, can you speak his tongue?"

"Elf, I am a Dragon," replied Raseri as he slithered 'round to peer into the crevice. "I have the gift of all tongues."

Raseri made a gesture.

The Sprite replied.

Raseri made more gestures.

Again the Sprite responded, this time with a long series of gesticulations.

Raseri bellowed in rage, flame shooting out. The Sprite quailed at this blast of fire, but remained in the icy crevice.

"What is it?" asked Rondalo.

"Ready your bow, Rondalo, we must go, and now," spat the Dragon. As the Elf strung the weapon, Raseri made another series of motions to the Sprite, and it replied with a single gesture and vanished.

Using the elbow of Raseri's right foreleg as a mounting block, Rondalo leapt to his perch at the base of the Drake's neck. A double row of great barbels, soft and flexible, ran from Raseri's head to his shoulders. Rondalo grasped the pair before him and said, "Ready."

With a roar, the Dragon sprang into the air.

Aloft, Rondalo called out, "What said the Sprite?"

Raseri growled and said, "The witch Hradian has obtained a key to the Castle of Shadows, and even now might be on her way to the Black Wall of the World. King Valeray asks us to intercept her ere she can set Orbane free. That's where we are headed."

High across Faery did the Dragon soar, over the glacier and icy bleak mountains below and beyond a shadowlight border to come into a realm of lush jungle, with widely scattered clusters of leaf-thatched huts in clearings virtually the only thing to break the endless sea of green. Across this verdant ocean he flew to pass through another twilight marge.

O'er a land of rivers he passed, dotted here and there with lakes, to come to another tenebrous bound.

Cultivated fields passed beneath, and both Rondalo and Raseri travelled in grim silence, but for the beat of the Dragon's tireless wings. Villages they sped over and tiny campfires, these latter seemingly nought but sparks, so high were the Drake and Elf.

The crescent moon sank below the horizon, yet onward they flew, now under stars alone. They passed a marge to come into a storm-laden sky, and Raseri soared up and up until he was above the rage, and lightning flashed below, the roar of thunder to follow.

Through looming walls of twilight they flew, Faery borders, eight, nine, more.

Yet Raseri's wings never seemed to slow. . . .

. . . And the night aged. . . .

. . . And the dawnwise sky began to brighten.

Finally, Raseri said, "Just one more twilight wall, Rondalo, and then we'll be in the realm at the far side of which there looms the Black Wall."

"What if the witch is not there?"

"Then we wait."

"What if she's gone beyond and into the Great Darkness?"

"I will fly therein, and if we find her, we will slay her. If not, then we will set ward on the wall, and slay her when she comes nigh."

"Can you see in the Great Darkness?"

"It is the one place where even the sight of Dragons is muted somewhat. Still, if she is within, she will be on a course toward the Castle of Shadows, and *that* course I know."

Rondalo unslung his bow, and on toward the nearing twilight border the Dragon flew as the sun broached the rim of the world.

29

Prospect

After an overnight stay at Sieur Émile's manse in the Springwood, Avélaine set out with a small escort of her father's retainers for the coastal city of Port Mizon in King Avélar's realm, for she was going home to her husband—*My handsome and daring Vicomte Chevell.*

The group rode at haste, remounts in tow, for Avélaine was now anxious to return; with the bodeful incidents of the last few days—the witch Hradian's spying and her trickery to freely obtain the key to the Castle of Shadows to set loose the wizard Orbane—and with the threat of war looming, Avélaine on her journey from the Castle of the Seasons had come to realize just how hazardous a place Faery could be. And with her newfound comprehension, she felt the urgency to return to her truelove Chevell. It would not be erelong before he set out to lead the king's fleet to destroy the corsairs of Brados.

It was yet early morn when she and her escort came upon Springwood Manor, and there she paused to find her brother Roél to bid him au revoir and to caution him to take care. She found the manse in a state of activity as the staff bustled here and there, preparing for the arrival of raw recruits to be trained in the art of combat and war. Too, the smiths and bow masters were hard at work to make weaponry for various members of the warband and the houseguard to take to various villages in the Springwood, where they would call the nearby men together and prepare them for battle as well.

Roél broke off from his planning and came running downstairs to the welcoming hall to greet Avélaine. "Avi, the king sent a falcon and said you were on your way. It is good to see you. Will you stay this eve?"

"No, Rollie. I must get back to my Chevell, for I've come to realize just how dreadfully dire many things have become. And of a sudden I grasp that this sea venture my love embarks upon, instead of being the lark he would make of it, is hazardous in the extreme. And if war is to be visited upon Faery, then I would be at his side in the time we have left. Oh, Rollie, I'm afraid I thought with the death of the Changeling Lord and our escape from his realm, that the rest of Faery would always be charming, with wee people popping out from under bushes, and Sprites flying here and there, and Elves and Fairies and other such being nought but good."

"Avi, Faery is indeed a marvelous place, but a perilous one as well. Yet I hope you never lose your sense of wonder at the splendid things herein. Even so, you are right: Chevell's mission is a hazardous one, and you do need to be with him ere he sets sail. Still, can you not at least stay for a meal?"

"Non. As soon as the horses are watered and given some grain, we are off for the sunwise border."

"Take care where you cross, little sister, else you just might fall in the ocean."

She laughed. "I well know the place, brother of mine, to make entry into King Avélar's realm. Unlike you, I'll cross at leisure, rather than while running for my life; hence do I plan to stay out of the rolling waters of that sea where you and Céleste nigh went for a swim, yet, thanks to the Fates, you did not."

Now it was Roél who laughed, but then he sobered. "Speaking of the Fates, little sister, I met one on the way here."

"You did?"

"Oui. And so did Laurent and Blaise. Did you not get the messages we sent?"

"Non. I was already on the way."

"Ah, well then, let me tell you what they said. . . ."

. . .

". . . and so you see, their redes are quite puzzling. Have you any glimmer of what they might mean? —Other than the obvious, that is?"

Avélaine shook her head. "Non, Rollie. But, oh, what terrible words they spoke."

Roél sighed and nodded in agreement. "The coming days might be grim, Avi, and here you are with child; you must needs take care of yourself."

"I know, Rollie, I know."

A grizzled retainer came into the manor and stood nigh and waited to be recognized. Avélaine turned to him. "Oui, Malon?"

"The horses, they be ready, Vicomtesse."

Avélaine nodded, and, following Malon, she and Roél walked out to the forecourt. Another retainer led a horse to her.

Avélaine took Roél by the hands and said, "You are the one to take care, Rollie, for if it comes to the worst of it, you will be in battle."

Roél shrugged, and then he fiercely embraced his sister and kissed her on the forehead, and she kissed him on the cheek. She mounted up and, with a bright smile, wheeled about and rode away, finally letting tears spill down her cheeks.

Roél watched her go, his vision blurred by tears unshed, for well he knew that perhaps this would be the last time they would see one another. And when she and her band disappeared into the surrounding woodland, Roél turned on his heel and ran back into the manor, where men were making ready for war.

. . .

Lady Michelle sat at breakfast with Sieur Laurent. She looked across the table and said, "It seems you have things well underway."

"Oui, yet there is much to do—training, equipping, forging, fletching, and the like. All the other manors are doing likewise. Yet I feel we are at somewhat of a disadvantage, for I know nought of this foe and his manner of battle, and I think that my brothers are just as ignorant of his means as am I. Perhaps even Luc has no knowledge of this wizard and his method of waging war. Tell me, my lady, what can you say of Orbane? What is his aim?"

Michelle turned up a hand. "I know only that of which my father has spoken, for I was not yet born when last Orbane inflicted his evil upon Faery. Still, he and his armies of Goblins and Bogles and Trolls came close to conquering all." Michelle fell silent for a moment, but then added, "—Oh, as to his aim, this I do know: Camille says the Fates told her if Orbane gets loose, he would pollute the River of Time, yet what that might mean, I cannot say."

"River of Time?"

"Oui. It seems that somewhere in Faery, time flows in a silvery river, and along this flow is where the Three Sisters fashion the Tapestry of Time: Skuld weaving what she sees of the future; Verdandi fixing present events into the weft and warp of the fabric; Urd binding all forever into the past."

"Hmm . . ." Laurent paused for a sip of tea, and then said, "Where is this river?"

"That I do not know."

"Then where does it empty into the ocean?"

"Again, I do not know, yet Camille speculates it flows out of Faery to spread over the mortal world, for time itself does not seem to touch Faery, though some say it originates herein."

"And so, polluting the River of Time would harm the mortal world?"

"If Camille is right, then I suppose it would."

Laurent clenched a fist. "We must not let that happen."

A sad smile passed over Michelle's face, and she nodded but said nought.

Laurent frowned and said, "The riddles of the Fates said nought about any River of Time."

"But they did speak of conflict," said Michelle, who had heard of the redes upon reaching her manse. "And I fear for the lives of all the young men should war come."

Laurent pushed out a hand of negation. "My lady, we will not strip the Winterwood of all vigorous young men, for some must stay to defend the realm, as well as to care for those who need tending."

There came a polite cough, and Michelle turned to see the steward of the Winterwood—a dark-haired, light-blue-eyed, slender man—standing at the entrance to the overlook chamber.

"Arnot?"

"Princess, an Ice Sprite has brought word that Raseri and Rondalo were located late yesternight, and even now they are on their way to the Black Wall of the World."

Michelle cried, "Wonderful!" and clapped her hands. "We must get word to the king, as well as to the other manors."

"I will send falcons, my lady."

"Oh, do so immediately, Arnot."

Arnot inclined his head and then hurried away.

Michelle turned to Laurent. "How utterly splendid. Perhaps it won't come to war after all."

"We cannot be certain of that, my lady, even though this is indeed good news."

. . .

In midmorn, a hawkmaster rushed down from the falcon-tower mews, a message capsule in hand. He hurried to the yard where King Valeray and Sieur Émile and the warband were looking over the first group of recruits.

"A message, my lord, from the Winterwood."

Valeray opened the capsule and drew out the tissue-thin scroll. Moments later he whooped. Sieur Émile and the others looked at him. " 'Tis marvelous news: Raseri and Rondalo are on their way to the Black Wall of the World to intercept Hradian."

Sieur Émile smiled, but then grew somber. "Let us hope they get there in time."

"Indeed," said Valeray. "Now I must take these good tidings to the others."

Valeray found Céleste and Saissa and Borel in the grass court getting ready to set out to pass among the faire-goers, for with the arrival of men to undergo training, uneasy was the mood. Upon hearing this, Saissa insisted that she and others go among the folks and reassure them, for as she said, "They should enjoy themselves while they can."

Upon hearing the falcon-borne message, Saissa asked, "When were they found?"

"Yesternight, late," said Valeray.

"Then, by now they might have reached the Black Wall. We can but hope for their success."

"May Mithras watch over them," said Céleste as she looked past Borel to see three-summers-old Duran running across the sward, his toy horse Asphodel in hand.

30

Darkness

Dawn came to the village that lay a league or two from the Black Wall of the World, and a young man bearing a knapsack and a walking stave came down to the common room of the inn where he ate a hasty meal. He then paid his fare and set out ere the sun broached the horizon.

Up the hill past the hamlet he hied, and over the crest, and just beyond he threw off the glamour concealing him . . . and Hradian mounted her besom and sped toward the ebony darkness looming into the sky.

With one hand she clutched the amulet that would set her master free, and she gloated over her victory in obtaining it in the manner she had, and she reveled over the vengeance she would exact from Valeray and all his get for the deaths of her sisters.

On toward the Black Wall she hurtled, and her heart began to pound, for beyond that towering shade a dreadful darkness lay, and had it not been for her sister Iniquí she would not have known the way to the Castle of Shadows, and to get lost in the blackness would spell her doom. Only incredible fortune would allow someone astray therein to find his way back unto Faery. Yet Iniquí, unearthing ancient scrolls and tomes and a grimoire or two—perhaps one of them even Orbane's—had studied the darkness and the castle within, and she not only had found a description of the key—the amulet—she had also found the way to and from the dreadful prison, a straight course, oui, but one at an angle to the wall itself: down and leftward was the way. This sinister and sinking path she had shown to her sisters, and now Hradian was the only one left of the four acolytes—*But I will make those murderers pay, and dearly. Oh, but the revenge my master will visit upon them will be so very sweet. And I will be the one to loose him upon them as well as upon the entire world.*

Just before Hradian reached the blackness, she took a sight on the sun, whose limb just then rose o'er the rim of the world, and she arced leftward and downward.

Oh, Sister Iniquí, let me pray to the gods of Enfer that the way to the castle remains true, and it has not drifted from its place in the Great Darkness beyond.

And, gritting her teeth and trembling, into the blackness she plunged.

She could see nought beyond the tip of her broom in the darkness nigh absolute. Yet on she hurtled, the strain of keeping her flying spell active causing beads of sweat to gather on her brow and runnel down her face. For the Great Darkness seemed to sap magical energies, and not long could even the most powerful of warlocks or witches or wizards withstand the depletion. And as to the darkness itself, it stretched away in all directions—sinister, dextral, forward, hindward, upward, downward—the blackness extending outward forever, its limit unreachable, no matter the course but one.

And within this Great Darkness floated a castle, supported by nought, a castle it is said of many dimensions, but Iniquí's scrolls and tomes and grimoires did not tell how this was known. Oh, they did speak of a Keltoi tale-teller who told of it in a riddle, yet how such a place had come to be—a Castle of Shadows in the Great Darkness beyond the Black Wall of the World—none could say. And it was a terrible prison—

inescapable, it was claimed. Yet e'en could one win his way free, then what? Unless he knew the course, the single way to escape the darkness, and the means to follow it, he would be lost forever. Might as well remain in the castle, instead.

Ah, but I have the key, and I know how to use it. Quite simple it is, yet in its simplicity lies its secret. Oh, how Orbane will reward me, for I alone will set him free.

On she hurtled in a straight line, down and leftward from the wall. And but for her beating heart and the sapping of her spell, she had no way of measuring how long the flight.

. . . And on she went. . . .

. . . and on.

But then in the distance ahead—*A faint glow! Oh, Iniquí, the gods of Enfer have smiled upon me, and I have found the way.*

On she flew, the glow nearing, and now she could see the stone bridge. Out it jutted from the dark castle for no more than fifty strides, where it abruptly ended, as if shorn off from another half standing elsewhere far away. Along its low stone walls stood ever-burning torches, barely casting a glow, the light itself seemingly sucked away by the ebon surround.

Weary, Hradian alit upon the stone of the bridge, and above her loomed the massive bulk of the castle, great dark blocks milled from rock and assembled into walls and turrets and buttresses and roofing. Massive and strong it seemed, unbreachable.

Hradian looked up at the dark stone faintly glinting in the torchlight. *What's this? There was but a single tower when Iniquí led us here, yet now it is of a size to host a multitude. Did my master somehow change it to what it has become? Ah, faugh, it is of no import. Instead, I must set my master free.*

Clutching the amulet, Hradian strode forward, toward a gaping archway, its opening filled with shadowlight, much like that of the twilight walls. And as she reached it, she paused. *Iniquí, if you are wrong about this key, and if my vision of its use was in error, then I, too, shall be imprisoned forever. If that happens, then when I am dead, I will hunt down your ghost and rend it to shreds.*

And with that bitter vow, into the shadowlight of the entryway she trod.

Into a great throne chamber she entered: hundreds of strides it was to the fore and hundreds to left and right, and the ceiling was far above. Wide stairways to either side led up to balconies, with archways into corridors leading off to quarters beyond. Likewise, archways on this level also led into corridors, down which, presumably, other rooms lay. Ever-lit lanterns illuminated all.

But Hradian did not see these stairways and balconies and arches and corridors, for in the center of the chamber stood a dais, and upon that block of stone sat a throne, and in the throne lounged a person, and his eyes widened in astonishment at the sight of Hradian striding toward him. He stood, his crimson cloak swirling about his somber garb. Tall and dark he was and slender, his hair black as midnight, his eyes of the same color as well. His face was long and saturnine, his nose narrow and hooked, hawklike. His fingers were lengthy and tapered, as if made for grasping. His mouth seemed to be one that would naturally curve into a sardonic sneer. Cruelly handsome he was, yet for the nonce his face registered shock at the appearance of a woman nearing.

Hradian came and abased herself at the foot of the dais. "My lord."

"Hradian, is it you?"

Yet on her hands and knees, Hradian looked up and simpered. "Oui, my lord."

"They have imprisoned you as well?"

"Non, my lord. Instead, I have come to set you free."

"Ah, you fool, you have come to your doom; this place is inescapable."

"Non, my lord, if my studies are true, it is not, for you see I—"

Rage flashed over Orbane's features. "Silence!" he shouted.

Hradian flinched and jerked her face toward the floor and curled in upon herself and trembled at his wrath.

Orbane seethed. "Do you not know that I, with all my power, have tried and yet failed innumerable times?"

"Yes, my lord. That I know, and yet . . ."

"And yet?" he demanded.

Hradian cast a sideways glance upward. "My lord, may I rise?"

With a gesture, Orbane allowed her to her feet.

"And now, my lord, may I show you something?"

Orbane sighed. "Very well."

"Please, my lord, take my hand."

Orbane stepped down from the dais and held out a hand, the look on his face one of exasperation. Hradian took his fingers in hers and led him toward the archway to the bridge. And as they neared—"This won't work, Hradian, we'll simply—"

Of a sudden they were standing beyond the archway and out on the torchlit span.

Orbane gasped in surprise. Then he turned to Hradian and swept her up with a joyous whoop and whirled her about. But then with a moan he laid her to the pave of the bridge and pushed her skirt up and away from her legs, and shoved down his pants and dropped atop her, forcing himself within. And amid grunts and groans and shrieks of joy, he swived her there on the stone.

. . .

Panting, his member yet erect, he looked about. "Where are your sisters? I would reward them as well."

"Dead. Slain by the get of Valeray. Oh, Master, I would have my revenge. You must kill them for me."

"Rhensibé, Nefasí, and Iniquí all dead?"

"Oui, my lord. Murdered by the children of he who stole two of your very own clay amulets, the seals that were used by the Firsts to cast you herein, hence Valeray is the one the most responsible for your imprisonment."

Orbane clenched a fist, and rage flashed across his features. "Then I shall—" Of a sudden he paused, and a look of cunning replaced that of wrath. "No, not kill him or his get. Instead, I have something even more fitting in mind. Take me to them, Hradian. Your revenge and mine will be sweet."

"My lord, I am wearied by my journey here. Can we not retire to the quarters within and once again—"

"Non, for I would go and go now. I have seen enough of that place."

"Very well, my lord."

Hradian took up her besom and straddled it. Orbane straddled it right behind. He embraced her, his hands upon her breasts, his fingers kneading and tweaking. "Now, Hradian. Let us go."

With moans of desire, Hradian mumbled arcane words, and up and away they flew: sinister, upward, at an angle from the castle, coursing along the only line leading toward Faery.

. . .

With the sun now risen, Raseri neared the Black Wall. "See you any sign of the witch?"

"Non," replied Rondalo. "The skies are clear for as far as my sight reaches."

"Then set an arrow to your bow, for I plan on entering the Great Darkness and flying the track to the Castle of Shadows. If she is within, I will burn her to a crisp, yet on the off chance I miss, you can feather her through and through."

As Rondalo nocked a shaft to string, with Raseri's great wings churning, through the Black Wall they went.

"Mithras, but I cannot see," cried Rondalo. "My bow will be useless."

"That is of little matter, for I see dimly," replied Raseri. "Even so, should she escape back into Faery, well then your bow will serve, that is if I give you a chance, for I intend to rend her to shreds."

And on into the darkness they flew, sinister and downward at an angle and on the line toward their goal.

. . .

Flying with two was even more draining upon Hradian's power. And yet she persevered, as Orbane's hands caressed her body, for he knew lust would increase her efficacy, raise her energy. And he ran his questing fingers here and there, teasing, touching, and now and then she gasped as if on the verge.

But then ahead in the darkness, black on black a darker form loomed, and Hradian jerked her besom to the left even as a great gout of flame shot past. She shrilled in terror, and Orbane shouted in alarm.

And then the massive shape was beyond her.

"Faster!" shrieked Orbane. " 'Tis a Dragon in this endless void."

Driven by fear, Hradian urged her besom to greater speed, yet she could hear the whoosh of immense wings overhauling. And from hindward came a cry, "Raseri, I saw them by your flame. I am ready."

" 'Tis Raseri and Rondalo, my lord," shouted Hradian, "friends of the whore Camille, Valeray's daughter-in-law. I have spied upon them. Can you not throw a spell to ward off the Drake?"

"I need more power than the Great Darkness will yield," cried Orbane. "Get me to Faery and then—"

But Hradian heard the Drake take in a great breath, and she jerked rightward, even as more flame shot past. And something whistled by in the black.

With her hair now singed and the twigs of her besom smoldering, Hradian goaded more speed from her broom. Yet the sound of wings grew louder, and Hradian dived just as great long claws went raking past and a huge tail lashed above.

Once more the Dragon hurtled by, and Hradian flew up and back on the track, and before her the massive form wheeled and again turned toward her. This time Hradian waited until the last moment, and she jerked the broom upward as flame shot below her, and again something whistled in the darkness, and there came a meaty *thuck!* and Orbane groaned.

"My leg. There's an arrow through my leg." With a cry of rage to offset the pain, he snapped the shaft in twain, throwing away one piece and wrenching out the other to cast it away as well.

Once more the thunder of wings drew nigh, but in that very moment Hradian and Orbane burst through the Black Wall and into the light of Faery.

And right behind came Raseri and Rondalo, and even as the Dragon took in a breath to burn wizard and witch to cinders, and Rondalo drew to the full for a shot that could not miss, Orbane twisted about and gestured at the Drake and shouted arcane words, and a roaring, whirling, ebon wind enveloped Elf and Dragon alike and bore them off through the Black Wall of the World and into the Great Darkness beyond.

31

Omens

L isane bolted upright in her bed.

What wakened me?

She peered out through the window of her chamber. Beyond willow branches dangling down and gently swaying in the breeze, she could see Thale cropping grass, his lustrous horn gleaming in the early morning light.

Lisane slipped out from under the covers and padded to her small kitchen, where she set a kettle on to boil above the tiny hearth fire.

Something dreadful is afoot, I can feel it. I must see what I can see. First I'll lay out the square—four and four—for it is the most stable of all, and speaks of the here and now.

She opened a small cedarwood box, and removed a taroc deck wrapped in blue silk cloth. She spread the silk upon the oaken plank that served as her table, then took up the taroc deck and began to shuffle, all the while concentrating upon the question as to what the day might bring. She dealt out cards, sixteen in all, four across and four down, their faces hidden. Then one by one she began turning them up: first the upper left corner, the Hierophant *droit;* then the upper right, the Naïf, also droit; then the lower right, the Lovers, this card, too, facing her; and finally, still moving deasil, the lower left, the Sun, droit.

Oh, my, four of the major arcana, and all upright, all fac-

ing me, all droit. The Hierophant: at times she represents me. The Naïf: perhaps someone I know, or perhaps not. Lovers: two paths; a time for choice, the outcome of which is vital. Too, it could mean— Ah, but wait, the Sun: happiness, joy. This is an odd configuration. Let me see the other cards.

Swiftly Lisane turned the remaining cards over.

Oh, Mithras, so many swords. Conflict. And yet—

In that moment the kettle began to whistle, and Lisane stepped to the fire and took the vessel from the hook and poured steaming water over the waiting leaves in the teapot.

When she returned to the table and looked at the layout, of a sudden she said, "I see. I am to get visitors today, on an urgent mission and peril follows. Oh, my, what's this? One of them will steal the heart of the Hierophant. Is it my heart the arrangement speaks of?"

Lisane shook her head to try to clear it of these fey thoughts.

Perhaps I'd better try the wheel.

She took up the cards and once again began to shuffle, this time concentrating upon seeking events to come near and afar. Cutting the deck thrice, she began laying out a pattern upon the blue silk. When she was done, a great circular array of cards lay, rings within rings, concentric, the cards facing *opposé*, away from the center; or inward, droit, toward.

Once again there are so many swords, so very many swords, here about the center. It could mean great conflict, and even combat, fighting, bloodshed. It can also mean confrontation, a great physical effort, a testing of wit, any number of things: conflicts of the heart and mind and body and spirit and soul; conflicts from within and without.

Long did Lisane study the pattern. Finally she took a deep breath and closed her eyes, then circled her left hand widdershins above the wheel of cards, followed by her right hand, circling deasil. She then opened her eyes and said, "This is what I see." And, to increase her focus, she began speaking aloud the meanings of the cards and their relation to one another, and as she spoke, she touched each card: her right hand for those upright, *droit*—facing inward—and her left hand for those reversed, *opposé, inverse*—facing out.

"Here nigh the beginning sits the Tower, reversed. I can but think the card bespeaks of the inevitable breakdown of present circumstance. But flanking are the upright three of swords on one side and the upright four of swords on the other. Taken together they mean separation, isolation, and disaster. Immediately at hand is the three of cups, *opposé*, signalling a reversal of circumstance, and what was good now causes pain. It is directly followed by the nine of swords, and *droit* it means despair, anxiety, misery. This is either what has been or signifies what is happening now.

"Here is the two of cups upright, flanked by the Hierophant and the Naïf; it indicates harmony between two souls." Liaze frowned and thought of the previous four-by-four spread. "Does this represent me and someone I've yet to meet? Its position in the layout might signify that."

Finally, Lisane shrugged. "I cannot say, yet these cards flanking, this one *droit*, the six of cups, signifies friends, while in this ring the three of cups reversed speaks of a test or tests, the double-edged nature of intuition, and since it is *opposé*, my intuition, or mayhap my first thought, may be wrong."

And on Lisane spoke aloud, touching cards, explaining unto herself, as she moved 'round the layout, coming ever closer to the center. "Here are the four Chevaliers—of cups, wands, pentacles, and of swords—and they all are arrayed against the Magician, and he is at the center of things. Oh my, we have Justice inverse, as is the Wheel of Fortune: together they seem to spell doom." Lisane paused, her brow furrowing. "This trouble seems centered on the Magician, and the nearby Priestess, who, in this pattern, appears to be but an acolyte of the Mage.

"But in opposition are the four knights. —Oh, and here we see the Hermit, who is flanked by the threes of wands and pentacles. Three Hermits also aiding? Whatever might that mean? It is a strange configuration. Yet there is something familiar about this spread, and it spells great disaster. Where and when did I last see—?"

Of a sudden, Lisane gasped. "Ah, I remember: it was when Orbane and his armies marched across Faery. Although this arrangement is not the same, there is a great likeness. Can it be that Orbane is somehow involved with whatever jolted me awake?"

Lisane frowned. "But he is imprisoned and cannot get free, and so I think this must be a spurious reading. Perhaps I'd better try again."

She reached toward the layout to take up the cards, but hesitated. "What if it's not spurious? Perhaps I'd better continue."

Again she began touching each card. "If Orbane somehow again threatens Faery, there seems to be hope, given the Chariot as well as the Star. Yet by their positions, it is such a slim hope."

On she spoke, reading the wheels—the rings within rings within rings—but at last she reached the center of the circles. Even so, she was not finished, for four cards were yet to come.

Lisane looked at the remainder of the deck, the cards not yet dealt, and said, "Now for the four primes, first the two which speak of things to be nigh the end.

"Cardinal *premier*," said Lisane, and she turned up a card and laid it directly before her, just below the wheel; the card pointed toward the center. Even so, she sucked in air between clenched teeth, saying, "Devil, upright: a terrible omen, for it means ravage, violence, vehemence. It could be a dweller without, someone not permitted within." Lisane glanced at the Magician in the center of the array. "Can it be Orbane?"

Lisane took a deep breath and dealt the second card. "Cardinal *deux*," and this time she laid it directly opposite and just above the wheel. "Death, reversed. This can mean death just escaped, partial change, or transformation. Even so, it can also suggest great destruction as well, and coupled with the Devil upright, I deem it signals a disaster none can avoid."

Lisane turned up another card and placed it just outside the left of the wheel. "Cardinal *trois*, Judgment, droit. Follow guidance to forge ahead. Yet, with the array laid out as it is, the guidance is most obscure. And here it is adjacent to the Naïf, which would indicate one must think wisely and make the right choice. Ah, me, I wonder whether the destruction can be avoided if the choice is wrong and the guidance remains unresolved."

Lisane took a deep breath and drew the last card and set it down outside the wheel to the right. "Cardinal *quatre*, the World upright. Triumph, but whose? The Devil or those who oppose? The Magician or the Knights? Yet with this King of Swords in the pattern, that could mean victory or defeat for the Knights, depending with whom the King is allied."

She studied the layout a bit longer, and then said, "Spurious or no, you are quite a puzzle."

. . .

It was just after dawn when a large bee buzzed down the length of the main street in the village of Ardon, followed by a man ahorse, galloping, with three steeds in tow: one was fitted with a small rack, several modest bags of provisions affixed thereon, and two were completely unladen. Down the main street they thundered, people rushing aside to get out of the way. And in a moment they were gone, leaving a wondering populace behind.

"Do you think this has anything to do with the message the Sprites brought?" asked one.

"Mayhap it was a kingsman on a mission dire," said another.

"He wasn't wearing a tabard, like most kingsmen do. Instead, sporting a tricorn, he was, and on a metal helm, no less."

Two beautiful and buxom, dark-haired, blue-eyed sisters who lived at the far edge of the village watched as the horseman galloped away.

"Oh, Romy, I do believe it was a knight errant, for I saw armor 'neath his cloak."

"You are right, Vivette: armor indeed he wore. I wonder why he did not stop to dally?"

"Mayhap the other knight errants did not tell him of us."

Romy sighed. "Perhaps none told him of the manner of our . . . hmm . . . entertainment."

"His loss," said Vivette, plucking flowers to weave into her very long hair.

Romy, plucking flowers as well, sighed and said, "Ours too."

. . .

Nigh the noontide, Regar and Flic and Fleurette passed through a twilight border to come into a dismal mire, bogland left and right of the road, with cypresses and black willows and dark, gnarled oaks twisting up out from the quag, some trees alive, others quite dead. And from these latter, long strands of lifeless gray moss hung adrip from withered branches, as if the parasite had sucked every last bit of sustenance from the limbs, hence, not only murdering the host, but killing itself as well. 'Round the roots and boles of the trees and past sodden hummocks, scum-laden water receded deep into the dimness beyond, the yellow-green surface faintly undulating, as if some vast creature slowly breathed in the turgid muck below. Ocherous reeds grew in clumps and clusters, and here and there rotting logs covered with pallid toadstools and brownish ooze jutted out at shallow angles from the dark sludge, the swamp slowly ingesting slain trees. Mounded above the fen, the road itself twisted onward, into the shadowy morass ahead.

Within these miserable environs Regar stopped to change mounts, and he paid little heed to the surroundings, as he moved the black to the end of the line and switched the saddle to the bay.

But Flic nervously eyed the bog as from within there came soft ploppings and slitherings. What made these sounds, Flic could not see.

"Why are you uneasy?" asked Fleurette.

"Because this reminds me of the swamp that Lord Borel and I passed through on our way to rescue Lady Michelle. If it is anything like that one, we best be on our way, for there could be an invisible monster living herein."

"It's not invisible monsters we should worry about," said Fleurette, pointing, "but those."

Gnats and bloodsuckers and biting flies came swarming out from the bog, drawn by the odor of lathered horses.

But just as they reached the road, Regar jerked the cinch tight and leapt into the saddle, and with a "Yah!" away from the oncoming cloud he cantered, the road more or less following the line of the bee.

Slowly the way ascended, and the mire to either side diminished. Walking, trotting, cantering, varying the gaits to preserve the horses, by midafternoon Regar's small group broke free of the swamp to come into low rolling hills. They paused by a clear-running stream to water the horses and to give them some grain and to feed Buzzer some honey.

Shortly, though, once again they took up the trek, and the sun slowly slid down the sky. As eve drew on, Buzzer flew back to the tricorn and landed. Flic said, "Time to find a good place to camp, for with night coming, Buzzer will soon be asleep."

"How about under that great willow up ahead and off to the left," said Fleurette.

"If it has a stream, well and good," said Regar.

And so they rode toward the massive tree, the willow fully

a hundred feet tall, its long swaying branches hanging down all 'round, highlighted by the red light of the setting sun. Beyond the dangling branches they could see the massive girth of the bole, perhaps fifteen or twenty human strides across, and some three times that around.

"Oh, look!" cried Fleurette. "A door and windows. Oh, my, what a place of wonder."

There was indeed a door into the trunk, and it of a pale yellow hue; two windows on either side looked out on the world. Willow-bark shutters, standing wide, graced both windows and the door.

Regar stopped just outside the long limbs, and dismounted. Even as he did so, the door opened, and therein stood a lithe, redheaded woman. Her face was narrow, her eyes emerald green and aslant, her skin alabaster, tinged with gold.

"Bon soir," she said. "I have been expecting you."

Regar stepped 'round from the opposite side of the horse to greet her, and at one and the same time, both he and she drew in sharp breaths.

Never had he seen someone so beautiful.

Never had she seen someone so handsome.

"Demoiselle," he said, bowing, "I am Regar."

"Prince Regar," added Flic.

The demoiselle didn't even seem to hear the Sprite, so entranced was she by the man. "Sieur," she said, curtseying, "many know me as the Lady of the Bower, yet my name is Lisane."

"Oh, look, a Unicorn, " breathed Fleurette, awe in her voice, for even in Faery, they were rare.

At the far side of the clearing a splendid white creature stood. Horselike, it was, but smaller and with cloven hooves and a pearlescent horn jutting from its forehead, a thin spiral groove running up from its base to its very sharp tip. Of a sudden it snorted and retreated into the forest beyond.

Momentarily, Lisane's face fell, but she managed a smile and said, " 'Tis Thale. He senses . . ." Lisane did not finish the spoken thought, yet she knew that Thale had read her heart at that very moment. Then Lisane brightened and said, "Sprites. I have not seen Sprites for many a day."

"Then, my lady, you do not know?" asked Regar.

"Know what?"

.   .   .

"So *that's* what the cards meant," said Lisane. "It wasn't a spurious reading after all."

"Spurious reading?" asked Fleurette.

"I am a seer," said Lisane. "I divine the future through taroc."

"Ah," said Regar, "so that's what you meant when you said you were expecting us."

A blush rose to Lisane's cheeks, and she cast her gaze down and aside. "Oui, Prince Regar. I saw you in the cards."

Regar swirled his cup and studiously watched the motion of the tea, for every time he looked at Lisane she took his breath away.

Fleurette nudged Flic and quietly giggled. Flic frowned at her in puzzlement and shrugged as if to say, *What?*

They were gathered in Lisane's tiny kitchen: Regar and Lisane sitting in the only two chairs; Flic and Fleurette seated atop the plank table; Buzzer quite asleep on Regar's tricorn set off to one side.

"Then, my lady," said Regar, "can you divine the meaning of Lady Verdandi's rede?"

"It seems to mean that war is on the way."

"Then you think Orbane is free?"

Lisane took a deep breath and slowly let it out. "This morn I was jolted awake by something unknown. Mayhap it was Orbane's escape. The cards would seem to say so."

"The cards again?" said Fleurette.

Lisane nodded. "Let me show you what I saw. . . ."

. . .

... Regar frowned. "And I am this Naïf and you the Hierophant?"

Again Lisane blushed. "Oui."

"What about us?" asked Flic, standing and peering at the wheels of cards.

Fleurette elbowed Flic. "We're not important."

Lisane shook her head. "Ah, do not be too quick to judge, Fleurette, for the six of cups signifies friends, and that's where I think you are. Still, that might not be, yet the cards do not see all."

"Even so, they seem to spell doom," said Regar.

"Things are dire, that I admit," said Lisane. "Yet the taroc speaks not to what *will* be, but rather what *might* be, and then only if the reader has interpreted wisely and true, and only if the acts portrayed are not contravened by actions unshown."

They sat in silence for long moments, but then Regar said, "Do you believe the four Knights in opposition to the Magician are Luc, Roél, Blaise, and Laurent?"

Lisane shrugged. "Mayhap, but then again the knights might simply indicate armies in opposition to those of the Mage, if indeed armies become involved."

"Well, it's all quite beyond me," said Flic, stretching and yawning. "Oh, my, but I must sleep."

"I'll fix a pillow by the hearth," said Lisane.

Fleurette smiled and said, "There is no need. We can find a place up in the branches of your tree."

"It is certainly no bother, Fleurette. Besides, I think it safer inside."

Regar stood. "I will sleep out beneath the fronds of your willow, my lady."

Lisane seemed as if she had something to say, yet she remained silent.

. . .

As mid of night approached, and the waxing crescent moon sank low, Regar lay awake, his face toward the stars wheeling above and glinting down through the long strands of willow. Yet he saw not the leaves nor the celestial display, for his mind was filled with the features of Lisane, his heart quite stolen away.

He heard a soft step, and turned to see Lisane, the moonlight shining through her filmy negligee.

With his pulse pounding in his ears, Regar raised up on his elbows. "My lady, I—"

She knelt and put a finger to his lips. "My prince, I did not tell all I saw in the cards, for early this morn, long ere you arrived, I dealt out what might happen this day, and it seems it has come true."

"My lady?"

Lisane took him by the hands and raised him up. "Come with me. I will show you." And she led him into her bower.

Putrescence

With the twigs of her besom smoking and threatening to burst into flame, down Hradian spiralled toward the town, while the wizard Orbane laughed in glee and crowed, "Not only have I escaped the Great Darkness, I sent a fearsome enemy into that dreadful void."

"My lord," gasped Hradian, "I am too weary to go onward, and my broom needs new willow twigs, else it will fly like nought more than a stick."

"Very well, Acolyte, come to rest in the village, for I would have food and drink and entertainment. Too, I would have you stanch my leg."

They came to ground in the center of the hamlet, and faces peered out through the windows of the inn, stark with mouths agape. Shocked villagers cried out in fear and rushed into homes and slammed shut the doors, though should the wizard or witch want in, there was nought could be done to stop them.

Limping slightly, Orbane strode toward the hostel, where a white-lettered but otherwise black sign proclaimed the place to be *Le Mur Noir*. Hradian followed, though she paused a moment to dunk the glowing end of her besom into the horse trough to extinguish the smoldering twigs. She caught up with her master as he stepped across the porch, the door opening at his gesture. The innkeeper quailed to see the wizard and witch enter his small establishment. He started to bolt but, with whispered word and a casual wave, Orbane arrested his flight. And Hradian ground her teeth in envy, for this was a spell she could not master. Oh, her three sisters could do so, and they had laughed at her pitiful attempts, but the spell was simply beyond her grasp. Even so, she was much better with herbal magery than they, and in turn she had laughed at them.

"Food and drink, fool," Orbane snarled at the innkeeper, "for I have had neither lately."

Hradian frowned. "My lord?"

Orbane snorted. "One of the foulnesses of that loathsome castle, Acolyte: neither food nor drink are provided or needed. One cannot enjoy a good meal or a fine vintage, or the simple pleasure of emptying one's bladder or bowels."

Orbane again gestured at the innkeeper. The man jerked about and faced the wizard, and then slumped as he was released.

"M-my lord," he stuttered, "I have b-but simple fare: a joint of beef, a flagon of ale, a loaf of bread is all I can provide."

"Away, and bring it," commanded Orbane, and he stepped into the common room.

Patrons therein blenched as wizard and witch entered. Orbane looked 'round, then gestured. "Out!" he commanded, but then, even as they stood to go, Orbane's eyes lit up and he said, "Non, wait. *Hommes* out, *femmes* remain."

The women sat down as the men left, some bolting, others reluctant and in tears yet helpless to do ought else.

Orbane drew down his trousers. "Acolyte, deal with my leg."

Hradian unslung her rucksack and rummaged about within. She withdrew packets of herbs and simples and bandages. Even as she treated his wound, there where the arrow had pierced, she could not help but to glance in anticipation at his now-erect member.

And when the treatment was done, in between bites of beef and bread and gulps of ale, Orbane swived every femme in the place, some several times.

And Hradian laughed to see his joyous diversion, and shrieked in pleasure at her own.

Then Orbane left the inn and began swaggering from house to house.

. . .

At dawn the next morning, the innkeeper delivered a bundle of willow twigs to Hradian. She shed the charred withes from her besom, and bound new unto the shaft. The moment it was ready, she and Orbane took flight, leaving behind a stricken village in which every woman wept.

Through many twilight bounds they flew and over the lands below as the sun crept up and across the sky and down, and, as the eve drew upon them, Hradian guided her broom o'er the stench of her vast swamp.

They lit upon the flet of her cottage, and Crapaud plaintively croaked upon his mistress's return, but seemingly took no note of Orbane.

"Oui, oui, all right, you may feed at will," snapped Hradian.

Crapaud waddled to the edge and fell into the mire.

Orbane surveyed the immensity of the bog and drew in a deep breath and took in the odor. "Mayhap it will do." And he gestured down at the undulant surface and up rose a thin tendril of a thick, yellow-green gaseous vapor, motes swirling within. Orbane reached out and touched the miasma with a single finger and lifted it to his nostrils and inhaled. He turned to Hradian and smiled. "You have chosen well, Acolyte. It is virulent, this Sickness lying at the bottom of your swamp. It will be more than enough to accomplish the deed, and then shall I rule. But to begin with, I must reawaken the hatred in my allies of old, and reassemble my armies."

Hradian nodded but said, "Yet first, my lord, we must visit revenge upon Valeray and his—"

"Silence!" roared Orbane.

Hradian fell to her knees and pressed her hands to her mouth and peered down at his feet.

Orbane gritted his teeth in rage. "You presume to tell me what I must do?"

"Non, Master. It's just that Valeray and his get are allied with the Three Sisters, and—"

"What? Skuld, Verdandi, and Urd?"

"Oui, my lord. The Sisters aid them at every turn."

"Why did you not tell me this before?" demanded Orbane.

Hradian pressed her forehead against the flet and mumbled, "Because I am a fool."

"Where are they now, this Valeray and his children?"

"My lord, let me look in my dark mirror, and then will I say."

"Very well. Arise and do my bidding."

"Oui, Master."

Hradian backed away on hands and knees and then stood. She stepped into the cote and took up her bowl and filled it with water and in moments peered into ebon depths.

. . .

The next morning again she gazed into the arcane mirror, and then she and Orbane took to flight, on their way to avenge the deaths of the three acolytes and to remove the principal allies of the Fates, but most of all to take revenge for the imprisonment of Orbane.

Mizon

Three and a half days after setting out from the Castle of the Seasons, Avélaine and her escort rode into Port Mizon. They had ridden in haste, remounts in tow, the journey taking but half the usual time. Rather than going to her estate, Avélaine headed for the docks. Stopping on a hill above, she saw Vicomte Chevell at the central pier poring over plans and speaking with a number of men. And beyond and anchored in the bay were perhaps a dozen large ships and numerous smaller ones.

"*Merci*, Malon, I'll walk from here; my legs need the stretch after so much time in the saddle," said Avélaine as she dismounted. "Take the men on to the manor and find food and drink and quarters for a good rest. You and they deserve a day or two with nought to do ere heading back to my father's manse."

The grizzled retainer frowned. "But, Lady Avélaine, how will you—?"

"Fear not, the vicomte will see me home."

Malon touched a hand to his brow, then wheeled his horse, as did his men, and, trailing remounts, they trotted away.

Down the slope headed Avélaine, yet ere she reached the bottom, one of the men with the vicomte said something to him and pointed. Chevell turned and shaded his eyes, and then broke into a lope toward her, and she ran down the hill toward him.

He caught her up and whirled her 'round, and rained her face with kisses. "Oh, Avélaine, I missed you so."

And after another kiss, this one long and breathtaking, she replied, "I missed you too, my love."

He set her to her feet and said, "My eyes are hungry to look at you," and he held her at arm's length. "Avélaine, you are so beautiful. Are you weary from the journey?"

Avélaine laughed. "Do I look that haggard?"

"Non, my sweet. Did I not say you are beautiful?"

"You did, and I am somewhat tired, for the ride here was long."

"Is the faire already— But wait, I thought this was the day it would close, yet you are here instead."

Avélaine looked into the clear blue eyes of the somewhat stocky sea captain. "Indeed, the faire will be over as of this eve, but Valeray sent me away three days past, Love, and I'm glad he did."

"Three days? But that means you must have raced all the way."

"Oui. But for one night in my father's manse, all we did was ride and camp and ride and camp until we got here. I am looking forward to a night in my own bed."

Chevell frowned. "Why did the king send you away?"

"Oh, Love, it was not in anger. But with Hradian having gotten the key to the Castle of Shadows, they thought it best."

"Ah, I see. The Sprites brought word of the witch's deed, yet they also brought word that Raseri and Rondalo are on the way to intercept her."

"Oh, my, I had not heard that," said Avélaine. "What wonderful news."

"Wonderful if they stop her," said Chevell, brushing a stray lock of his red hair from his brow.

Avélaine smiled at the gesture—*So like him*—then sobered and said, "If Raseri and Rondalo do not manage to intervene, then Valeray and his get are in special peril, for Hradian will seek vengeance for the deaths of her sisters, and Orbane, if he gets free, will want revenge for his imprisonment, a thing for which Valeray is most responsible, for 'twas he who stole the seals that locked the wizard away. And so, that's one reason they sent me away."

"One reason? There is another?"

Avélaine smiled and said, "They did not want our unborn to share this jeopardy."

"Our unborn—? Avélaine, is it true?"

"Oui, my love. I am with child."

Chevell shouted in joy and took her up to swing her about, but then gasped and set her down gently. "Oh, chérie, you rode at a gallop all the way here, and now I am manhandling you. Will it hurt the—?"

Avélaine laughed. "Non, non, my captain. As I once heard someone else say, at this point I am just a little pregnant."

Chevell roared in laughter. "Who?"

"I believe it was Camille when we got back from the realm of the Changelings. Oh, chéri, you should see the child she and Alain have. Such a sweet little boy. I hope we are as fortunate."

Chevell shook his head. "Boy or girl, it matters not, for we will love the child. And how could it not be sweet, coming from someone such as you."

Laughing, hand in hand they walked down toward the central pier.

"There is one more reason I am here early," said Avélaine.

"Oh, and what is that?"

"I came to realize that this endeavor you are about to undertake is not the lark you make it out to be. My love, you are sailing into perilous waters, and I would have every spare moment of your time ere you embark."

Chevell did not reply, other than to squeeze her hand. Had

he looked at her he would have seen eyes brimming with un-shed tears.

She took a deep breath and slowly exhaled. "Speaking of your mission, how goes the fleet?"

Chevell made a wide, sweeping gesture toward the bay. "We have twelve ships of the line, with another five or six due to arrive any day now. Some we are fitting with new ballistas and the latest in fireballs. Some only need refurbishing. Some need new rigging, others new canvas, still others nought but fresh paint and a cleansing of barnacles. When we are finished we will have the finest armada in all of Faery. And all the captains are eager, for all would see the corsairs eliminated forever. And up in the hills, King Avélar's own warmaster is training a battalion of marines in ship-to-ship tactics and in grappling and boarding and fighting in close quarters and in conquering a fort."

Chevell frowned and then added, "Yet, if Orbane gets free, he might take a hand in this battle, for in the last war, he tried to recruit the corsairs unto his side. This time he might succeed."

Avélaine stopped in her tracks, and swung Chevell toward her. "Oh, chéri, if that happens, what will it mean?"

"There's nought to say it will happen, but if it does, then things will be dire. 'Tis all the more reason we should set sail, and soon, and destroy the corsairs ere he can seduce them."

Avélaine hugged him fiercely, and he gently returned her embrace.

Blow

Alain laughed and turned Prince Duran upside down, the lad squealing in delight, and Scruff flew about, chirping in joy. Yet Alain's conversation was anything but playful. "Not since yesternight and this morning, eh?"

"Non," replied Camille, adjusting the small tiara and inspecting herself in the mirror. "Just those two times."

Alain lifted the boy up and set him upon a shoulder. "Why is it, I wonder, we males do not sense it, this sinister spying? And if not Hradian, then who?"

"That I know not, my love," said Camille, smoothing the front of her wide-sweeping gown. "But there is this to consider: if it is Hradian, then Raseri and Rondalo have yet to deal with her." She turned to Alain. "Ready?"

Alain looked up at Duran. "Are we ready, Little Prince?"

"Asphodel," said the lad.

"Oh, my, that's right. It would not be complete without your Fairy horse."

Alain set Duran down, and the boy scrambled across the chamber and took up the toy. "Now we are ready, Papa."

Scruff flew to Camille's shoulder and lit, and out into the hallway all went and down the stairs, Duran holding onto Alain's hand and jumping two-footed from step to step with a minor boost from his sire. As they reached the great welcoming hall,

Borel stood and said, "At last we can close this faire, and the sooner done with that, then the quicker we can get out of this finery and get on with the business of making ready for war."

Both he and Alain were dressed in silks and satins, Borel in his customary white and pale blue, signifying the Winterwood, and Alain in his green and gold, signifying the Summerwood. Likewise was Duran in green and gold, as was Camille, and under her gown she wore gold pantaloons for riding ahorse in the rade.

Borel looked about impatiently. "Now where are our dear sisters and mother and father?"

Alain pushed out a hand. "Forbear, brother, forbear. They'll be here anon."

Even as he said it, sweeping down the grand staircase came Liaze in russet and yellow and Céleste in pale pink and white.

Almost immediately they were followed by Saissa and Valeray, both in dark crimson and black.

. . .

In the late afternoon sunlight, across the Springwood hurtled Hradian and Orbane astride the witch's besom, and as they came to the starwise border, Hradian looked down to see the corpses of slain birds amid a litter of black feathers. "My crows, my beautiful crows. What has happened here?"

"Your crows?"

"My lord, I set them to watch the borders to stop the flight of Sprites to slow the spreading of the alarm. And now they are all dead, my beautiful, beautiful crows."

Seething, Orbane sucked air through clenched teeth. "Since you failed in that small matter, Acolyte, we can assume that the word is spreading even now. All the more reason to hurry and assemble my armies before these fools can assemble theirs. Faster, Acolyte, faster."

Hradian urged her broom to greater speed, and through the twilight bound they plunged.

.   .   .

Out through the gate and over the bridge rode the royal party, Wolves to the fore and aflank and aft. Through the grounds of the faire they went, the crowd cheering, though rather thinly, and many faces were filled with concern. The news had spread like wildfire of Hradian's obtaining a means to possibly free Orbane, and the appearance of men arriving at the castle to be trained for war had all citizenry on edge. Many had left the faire-grounds and even then were on their way to their homes: some in Valeray's demesne, others in one or another of the four Forests of the Seasons, and still others from farther away.

The baggage trains of the princes and princesses had departed yester, and Princess Michelle and the Vicomtesse Avélaine had gone two days ere then, each party trailing remounts no less, for they were in a hurry.

And yet King Valeray and Queen Saissa and their get, as well as Princess Camille and wee Prince Duran, had remained, and this had had a calming effect on many a taut nerve.

Still, at the stables stood other horses, ready to bear Borel and Liaze and Céleste in haste to their own manors. Only Prince Alain and Princess Camille would ride at a more leisurely pace, and that was because of wee Prince Duran, who would slow the stride of that particular cavalcade. Even so, they would press forward as fast as they could, for if the Wizard Orbane were indeed to be set free, then the presence of prince and princess in their demesnes would strengthen trembling hearts.

And so, as the sun sank through the sky, through the dilute crowd of well-wishers rode the procession and toward the arena where the faire would come to an end.

A fanfare of trumpets sounded the entry of the royal party into the amphitheater, and 'round the perimeter rode the procession, people cheering to see them pass by, especially Prince Duran, seated before his father on a high-stepping black.

To the royal box rode all, and there they dismounted, and

pages led the horses away as into the seats King Valeray and his family ascended. At a gesture from Borel, the Wolves plopped down upon the ground off to one side.

And as Valeray stood to give the ceremonial closing speech, Borel smiled as Duran "clip-clopped" his toy along the forward rail.

Of a sudden, Borel's eyes widened. "Mithras!" he exclaimed, turning to Alain. "But I now know what at least a part of Skuld's rede means, though I don't understand the full of it."

In that same moment, Scruff leapt into the shoulder pocket of Camille's gown and frantically tugged on her hair, and Wolves sprang to their feet, and a Sprite came hurtling through the air and across the arena, shrilling, "It's not a crow, not a crow!"

Camille glanced up to see a black bird lazily circling o'erhead—

—and then it wasn't a bird, but a witch and someone else astride a broom.

"Orbane!" cried Valeray.

"Hradian!" shouted Alain, even as Camille reached for Duran.

Arcane words rent the air, and amid gleeful laughter from above, a great, roaring, whirling black wind descended upon the royal box and bore them all away.

Pack

The black wind roared; posts and rails and the boards of the arena stands hurtled through the shrieking air and smashed into whatever stood in the way—ripping, rending, bashing, killing—people and horses and ought else. Dust and dirt and wood shavings and rocks and straw hurled 'round and blinded all, and men and women and animals screamed and fled, some running straight to their doom. And all the while unheard laughter rang down from above.

And then the wind lifted up and away, and wreckage and dirt and stones fell, and straw and wood shavings fluttered down . . . and the air cleared, revealing the devastation wrought: men and women and children lay wounded or slain; horses lay dead or dying; nought remained of the arena but shattered wood and rent cloth and other such flinders.

But in the center of all stood Slate and the pack, for the great Wolf had led the others to the safety of the eye of the spin, where they stood their ground and snarled at the witch and wizard above.

"The Wolves, my lord," shrieked Hradian, "kill the Wolves." Even as she called for their deaths, Hradian reached for the thong about her throat, where hung the last of the clay amulets known as the Seals of Orbane—terrible talismans filled with arcane power. With it she could easily slaughter the animals.

But Orbane snarled, "Pah! They are of no import whatsoever, for the Fates and Wolves truck not with one another."

"But they are the ones who tore Rhensibé asunder."

"Silence! Would you have me discipline you?"

Hradian cowered, a mewl of fear escaping her lips.

"Away, Acolyte," commanded Orbane. "I have removed those with whom the Fates ally themselves. Now little stands in my path. Away, I say, to rally my own armies."

With one last venomous glance at the pack below, Hradian's hand fell away from her throat, and she spun the besom about, and toward the dawnwise bound she and Orbane sped.

. . .

Slate and the pack watched the bitch two-legs and the other one vanish. Not-birds they were, yet still they flew. Once before the Wolves had seen the same bird-not-bird bitch two-legs, there at the little stone den near the long bad place in the territory of snow. That, too, was a time when a terrible black wind bore their master away.

Slate turned to the others and chuffed, and then he and the pack trotted past the broken-legged and maimed horses and those that were not-alive, past the two-legs that were hurt, some of those not-alive, too, while other two-legs wandered among the sharp odor of mark-water, and the strong smell of mark-pile, and the intense reek of life-water. Through the wrack they passed and among the two-legs now rushing toward the not-alive and hurt ones, many two-legs running out from the big stone den.

And when they were free of the place of the two-legs in the field, and had rounded the big stone den, Slate broke into a lope, with Dark, Render, Shank, Trot, Loll, and Blue-eye following. Starwise they ran, toward where they knew lay the territory of snow, for the last time the black wind had carried their master away, they had waited at his big den, and he had finally come home with his own bitch two-legs. And the master had begun to teach his bitch a limited form of True-People-speak, for the two-legs had no tails and could not move their ears; still she had much left to learn. And even though her understanding was stunted, he would tell her of the terrible black wind taking the master away.

Through the warm-days woodland the pack sped, and ere the sun had set they came to the twilight border, and they slowed not a step but plunged on through.

Foxes scattered before them, and Slate paused a moment to snap up the remains of a dead crow, mostly rent of feathers, thanks to the canine brethren. All others in the pack lingered a moment to take up stripped birds of their own. And with a snap and a crunch and a swallow, they were swiftly on their way once more.

Through the snow they hammered, white clots flying from paws, and they came to a swift-running stream, ice lining the banks though the center flowed free. They took a moment to lap water, and with thirsts quenched, away they sped.

On they ran and on, tireless in their pace, and the waxing half-moon high above slowly sank duskwise through the star-laden wheeling sky.

Some Sprites watched them run, and some raced alongside the Wolves, popping from icicle to clad limb to covered rock to frozen pond, while others flashed on ahead to bear mute word to the manor of the presence of the pack in the wood.

· · ·

"M'lady," said Arnot.

Michelle looked up from her book. "Oui?"

"M'lady, the Sprites tell that the Wolves are on their way."

"Ah, good. Then my Borel will soon be home."

Arnot shook his head. "The prince is not with them."

Michelle frowned. "Not with them? But why would he send them on alone? —Oh, my, are you then telling me Borel comes without the pack's protection?"

"Princess, the Sprites say that Borel has not entered the Winterwood."

"Non Borel; just Wolves?"

"Oui."

Michelle set her book aside and stood. She bowed her head and frowned a moment in thought, and then looked up and said, "Have a falcon ready to fly on the wings of dawn, Arnot, for I would know what is afoot."

"Mayhap, my lady, a falcon will come from the castle ere midmorn and let us know."

"Perhaps . . . yet I would not wait, for the pack would not leave him without cause."

"Mayhap, my lady, it is as you first said: the prince sent them on ahead."

Michelle slowly nodded and said, " 'Tis unlikely." Of a sudden, anxiety filled her eyes. "—Oh, Arnot, I feel something is amiss, yet what it might be escapes me."

A silence fell between them, but then Arnot said, "The only time I've known the prince to be without his Wolves is when he and they went beyond the blight to the cottage of the witch, and she reft him away and into imprisonment by using one of the Seals of Orbane."

Michelle blanched. "But surely that cannot be the case."

Arnot shrugged. "I would think not, for if Hradian yet lives, she should be far from here. Even so, we cannot be certain."

Michelle sat down, but immediately stood again. "Oh, I wish we had word of Raseri and Rondalo's mission; surely they've killed the witch by now."

"If they caught up to her," said Arnot.

Michelle sighed and said, "Given where the Sprites saw them, how long ere the pack arrives?"

Arnot pursed his lips. "Nigh dawn, give or take a candlemark."

"Have the Sprites bring word when the pack passes the

blighted section. And then find me, for I shall speak with Slate and the others the moment they reach the manor. In the meanwhile, have a page come to me, for I would send a message to the scribe to post by falcon at dawn."

"Oui, m'lady."

After Arnot was gone, Michelle sat down at a nearby escritoire and composed a short query:

The Wolves have come alone. What is afoot? —Chelle

Moments later, a page appeared at the door.

"Burton, take this to the scribe and have him pen it small enough for a falcon-borne message to King Valeray. But do not have him send it to the mews as of yet, for I would first speak with the Wolves."

"The Wolves, m'lady? But they're not here."

"They are on the way, Burton. Now take that to the scribe."

"Oui, m'lady."

As the lad rushed away, Michelle tried to return to her reading, but in moments she placed a ribbon between the pages to mark her place and then set the book aside.

. . .

On raced Slate and the pack, and soon they passed the small stone den where the bird-not-bird bitch two-legs had once lived, the den smelling of old char.

They plunged into the tangle of the long-bad place, the trees twisted and stunted, some shattered, the branches hard and bare and clawlike. And the pack felt the faint itch of the same itch felt when the bird-not-bird bitch two-legs made the master go away on the wind.

As they emerged from the long-bad place, a nearby Sprite looked out from a plane of ice and then vanished. But Slate ignored the tiny being, except to note it had gone.

On ran the pack, and as the dawnwise light began to glimmer, they raced up the long slope and onto the flat where the master's great den sat. And there to greet them stood the master's two-legs bitch and others of the master's two-legs pack.

. . .

Michelle knelt and ruffled Slate's fur, the huge Wolf deigning to be so petted. The remainder of the pack gathered about and waited their turns, some fawning, though Slate stood quite still.

After she had greeted each Wolf, Michelle signed to the waiting attendants, and they brought buckets of water for the pack to drink. And when all had slaked their thirst, Michelle struck a posture, and then another, and rumbled as best she could, followed by a short whine. Then she murmured to Arnot, "I've asked Slate, where's Borel?"

With pricked ears and cocked head Slate replied: *Where master?*

Michelle looked away and raised her nose to the wind, answering: *Not here.*

Slate raised his nose and looked the same direction and whined: *Not here?*

Michelle took on another posture and then shifted: *Not here. Where Borel?*

Slate emitted a low rumble of disappointment and anger.

Michelle: *Where Borel?*

Slate gave a whine of uncertainty.

Michelle growled low: *Tell.*

Slate: *Bird-not-bird bitch two-legs.*

Michelle gave a whine of confusion.

Slate repeated: *Bird-not-bird bitch two-legs.*

Michelle: *Whine.*

Slate snorted and flopped down and looked at Dark and rumbled, for his own bitch and her delicate True-People-speak seemed more able to talk with the master's bitch two-legs.

Dark struck a single posture: *Bitch.*

Michelle replied with a chuff of understanding.

Again Dark struck a single posture: head low, tail down, eyes fixed straight ahead.

Michelle frowned, for the posture could mean "bad" or "danger" or "immediate threat" or any number of allied things, depending upon what came before or after. Nevertheless, with her heart sinking, she replied: *Chuff.*

Dark: *Two-legs.*

Michelle: *Chuff.*

Dark: *Bird.*

Michelle: *Chuff.*

Dark: *Not-bird.*

Michelle: *Whine.*

Michelle turned to Arnot. "They have told me they do not know where Borel is, and now are trying to tell me something having to do with a bird and peril and a female."

Arnot shrugged and then looked at the others standing nigh. "Any suggestions?"

Men looked at one another, yet none had ought to say.

Michelle turned back to Dark and whined in puzzlement.

Dark: *Not.*

Michelle again frowned, for this could mean "no" or "not" or "stop" or the like, again depending on context. Michelle replied with a *chuff.*

Dark: *Not-bird.*

"Ah," said Michelle, enlightened, followed by *Chuff.*

Dark raised her nose high.

Michelle sighed, for that posture could mean "air" or "wind" or "odor on the wind" or "scent" or other similarities. *Chuff.*

And then Dark struck many poses, putting it all together: *Bird-not-bird danger bitch two-legs. Master gone. Bad wind.*

With a cry of dismay, Michelle fell to her knees and buried her face in her hands and wept.

Seers

It was not yet midmorn when, in the skies above the manors of the Forests of the Seasons, falcons from Valeray's domain announced their presence and spiralled down to the mews. Waiting attendants detached message capsules and bolted away, while others fetched fresh mice for the raptors.

In the Springwood, Steward Vidal, his face somber, came onto the training grounds, where Roél looked over the arriving recruits. "My lord," said Vidal, distress in his voice, "we have received terrible news." He handed the message to the knight.

Roél frowned and read and blanched. Shaken, he turned to the captain of the houseguard. "Theon, I leave you in charge until Armsmaster Anton returns. See to the men." And without another word he spun on his heel and ran toward the manor, Vidal following apace.

To his quarters hurried Roél, and therein he unracked his armor and—

"My lord," asked Vidal, "what is it you plan to do?"

"Find Céleste and the others," replied the knight.

"But you do not know where to search."

"I will ride through all of Faery if necessary," spat Roél.

. . .

Some distance away in the Autumnwood Manor, Luc looked at tall and gaunt Zacharie. "It matters not, Steward, for no matter

216 / Dennis L. McKiernan

where Orbane has cast them with his black wind, I will find them."

"But, my lord," said Zacharie, "Faery is said to be an endless place, hence setting out with no knowledge whatsoever will lead to nothing at all."

. . .

In Summerwood Manor, Blaise glared at grey-haired Lanval. "Then what do you suggest I do?"

"My lord, nearby is the Lady of the Mere, and she at times gives aid."

"And just who is this Lady of the Mere?"

"A seer, my lord. A seer."

. . .

In the armory of Winterwood Manor Laurent set down his helm and looked at Michelle. "A seer?"

Michelle nodded. "Or so the Steward Arnot tells me."

Arnot inclined his head. "Vadun lives starwise from here, a day's journey beyond the blight."

"And he will be able to tell us where this black wind of Orbane's has taken them?"

Arnot frowned. "He is a dream seer, hence might or might not be able to aid."

Michelle said, " 'Tis better than setting out and searching at random."

. . .

Roél sighed and reracked his armor. "You are right, Vidal. But where can we find a seer?"

"I know of four: the Lady of the Mere in the Summerwood; Seer Malgan in the Autumnwood; Vadun, a *voyant de rêves* in the Winterwood; and Lisane, the Lady of the Bower, yet I am not certain where she lives."

"And there is none in the Springwood?"

"None I know of."

"Are there any in Valeray's domain?"

Vidal shrugged and turned up his hands.

"Then we must send falcons to the other manors and bid them to seek out these seers and discover what they can of where Orbane has had our family borne off to."

. . .

"Ah, me," said Luc, "my first impulse was to ride out and seek Liaze, yet it seems a hopeless cause without further knowledge. Send for Seer Malgan; mayhap he can give us aid. In the meanwhile, there is a war to plan, yet once my father takes command of the army—"

"But, my lord, will he not need you to lead the Autumnwood battalion?"

Luc sighed. "Truelove versus the good of the many, a terrible choice to make."

. . .

Blaise looked at Lanval. "Where do I find this Lady of the Mere?"

Lanval slowly shook his head. "She only appears at dawn, and she does not come at just anyone's beck, and things must be quite dire, else she appears not."

Blaise spread his arms wide and gestured about. "The king, queen, princes, and princesses ripped away on a black wind. What is more dreadful than that?"

"Orbane," replied Lanval gravely. "The wizard is a good deal more terrible, for he threatens all of Faery and not just King Valeray and Queen Saissa and their get and Princess Camille and wee Prince Duran."

Blaise slammed a fist into palm. "Bloody Orbane!" He turned to the steward and said, "Oh, Lanval, 'tis the wont of knights to ride to the rescue, and yet for the moment I and my brothers and Prince Luc cannot. And even did we know where they were, still we are faced with an ill choice, for there is Orbane and his armies we must defeat."

"My lord, I suggest you remain at the manor and see to the

planning of the war. On morrow's dawn I will go to the mere; mayhap she will come at my call."

. . .

Michelle gazed out a window slit at the snow. "With Orbane on the loose it means that Raseri and Rondalo did not succeed."

Arnot nodded and said, "Oui, my lady, they did not, yet mayhap they are still on the hunt. 'Tis another thing a seer might be able to answer."

Michelle sighed. "Very well, then, Arnot, have Armsmaster Jules ride in haste to Vadun and pose him our questions. Mayhap in spite of the fact that this mage is a voyant de rêves he can shed light on Raseri and Rondalo and on where Orbane's black wind took my Borel and the others; to his Troll holes or the dungeons of one of his many castles, I imagine, and none knows where they all are. In the meanwhile, send messages to the remaining manors and have them also seek the aid of seers."

"Oui, m'lady," replied the steward.

When Arnot was gone, Michelle said, "And you, sieur knight, have a war to plan."

"As you command," said Laurent, and he, too, stepped away from the chamber.

Michelle looked long out through the slit at the black and white forest touched with subtle shades of grey. Finally, she took a deep breath and turned and strode from the armory.

Once Borel came to rescue me, and then his Wolves saved us both. It is time I returned the favor to my love, and once again the pack will aid.

Down the hall she trod, pausing long enough to take up a warm cloak. Then she stepped through a doorway and into the wintry 'scape beyond. At the edge of the woods she found the pack at rest, and she singled out Dark. Michelle struck postures and voiced growls Borel had said she might one day need:

Michelle: *I want learn all Wolfspeak.*

Dark: *Master's bitch want all True-People-speak?*
Michelle: *All.*

Dark looked at Slate, and he raised his head and rumbled his unconcern and then laid his chin back on his paws.

And so, slowly and laboriously, with many mistakes and many repeats, as well as many long work-arounds until the new word was understood, in spite of the fact that this two-legs had no tail and could not move her ears or raise any hackles, the bitch Dark began teaching Master's bitch the words of the True People.

37

Changeling

Nigh the noontide on the second day after the black wind had hurled her cursed enemies away to their doom, Hradian spiralled down toward a dark tower looming up from amid a cluster of stone buildings clutched among massifs and crags in dark mountains high. A long and steep roadway twisted up from the foothills below to disappear within an archway marking a passage through the wall surrounding the structures entire.

"We are here, my lord," said Hradian.

"I am not blind, Acolyte," growled Orbane as he peered downward. The lesser buildings, their roofs all connected, surrounded the broad, square-based, tall edifice. But there gaped an opening among the buildings, revealing a small plaza before the entrance to the tower. "That courtyard is where we'll alight."

"Oui, my lord," replied Hradian, and she headed toward the square. As she descended, Hradian added, "There are no Changelings about, Lord Orbane. The place looks abandoned."

"Bah, Acolyte. This is the seat of power in this realm. There will be someone to greet us."

Down into a deserted stone courtyard they settled, and before them at the foot of the tower an enshadowed opening yawned. Dismounting, Orbane said, "Come, Acolyte, let us see just who is the new Changeling Lord." And toward the entry he strode, Hradian scuttling after.

Into a long empty corridor they went and toward the far end, where stood a massive door flung wide. They passed a swath of something lying dark upon the hallway floor, something that might have once been a thick, oozing puddle, now long dried. Orbane paused and peered at it. "Grume," he sneered, "the remains of a Changeling," and then strode onward, the blackness crackling underfoot.

Hradian stepped wide of the patch that had once been a shape-shifting being and scurried after her master.

Through the doorway they went, turning rightward and toward the distant throne chamber, where long past Orbane had faced Morgrif, then the Lord of the Changelings. But Morgrif had refused to hew to Orbane's cause, for there was nought of significance the Changeling Lord would have gained in such a venture. And so Orbane had gone away enraged, for Changelings would have greatly enhanced his armies, shapeshifters that they were.

To either side open doorways showed room after room furnished with tables and chairs and cabinets and lounges and other such. In none were the fireplaces lit, and a layer of fine dust coated all.

They passed a chamber where on the wall a huge celestial astrolabe slowly turned, the large disks of the golden sun and silver moon and the smaller disks of the five wandering stars—red, blue, yellow, green, and white—all crept in great circular paths. Black and silver was the lunar disk, echoing the current gibbous state of the waxing moon. But on they strode, did Orbane and Hradian, not pausing to marvel at this splendid device.

Past more doorways they went, and as they came to a cross corridor, "*Hsst!*" murmured Orbane, signaling for silence.

From leftward, drifting along this passage, came the cadent sounds of chanting, rising and falling in pitch.

Orbane smiled. "Acolyte, I think we hear the whinings of the new Lord of the Changelings."

Leftward he stepped, and Hradian gasped, "My lord, be wary."

Orbane stopped and slowly turned and glared at her, and she fell to her knees and groveled.

Then he laughed, and took up the pace again, leaving Hradian to scramble after.

Down the passage ahead, an archway glowed, and, as Orbane approached, the sound of chanting grew.

At last the wizard and witch came to the entry, and it led into a grand room bare of furniture, with a great, round skylight centered overhead: the main source of illumination in the chamber, though candles also cast a glow. The marble floor was dark with long-dried puddles: the mingled remains of many slain Changelings. And on the floor as well lay a bundle of black rags wrapped about a desiccated corpse. Yet these things did not interest Orbane, for there with his back to the door, at the center of the chamber in the midst of a circle engraved in the floor with five black candles ringed 'round, each joined by five straight lines forming an enclosed pentagonal shape, a manlike being stood with his arms upraised, and he chanted, as if invoking some great spell.

In that moment there came an anguished cry from Hradian, and a clatter as she dropped her broom. Past Orbane she darted and across the dried puddles of dead Changelings and to the corpse on the floor. "Nefasí!" she shrieked as she dropped to her knees next to her long-dead sister.

In the pentagram the being whirled about, his chant cut short, and a dark shimmering came over him and of a sudden he was no longer there but instead stood as a massive Ogre.

Eighteen feet tall, the monster roared and raised huge taloned hands to attack, but with a casual gesture, Orbane stopped the Ogre in its tracks, the creature unable to move.

To one side Hradian wailed, and she clutched the corpse in her arms and rocked back and forth in seeming agony. And she kissed the parchmentlike lips, skin sluffing to the floor in response.

Again Orbane made a gesture, and silence fell within the room, though Hradian yet rocked and howled, but no sound whatsoever seeped beyond the tight, encircling bounds of Orbane's spell.

Once more Orbane turned to the Ogre. "I will set you free, but only if you shift back to your lesser self." He twitched a finger and added, "Do you agree? You may nod."

Slowly and with effort the Ogre nodded, and Orbane said, "I warn you," and then he made another gesture.

The Ogre's tense muscles slumped, and its hands dropped to its side, and a darkness shimmered over the gigantic form, and a manlike being stood where the Ogre had been. Dressed in black, slender he was and tall and dark-haired, and his fingers were long and tapered. His eyes were deep gray and his features hawklike, much like those of the former Changeling Lord slain, or even of Orbane himself.

"That's better," said Orbane. "Now give me your name."

The man glanced from Orbane to Hradian and then back again. "Effroi."

"Terror, you say?" Orbane laughed. "Well, *Effroi*, I am Orbane."

"Orbane!" blurted Effroi, his dark eyes wide in astonishment. "But he is, I mean, you are, that is, in the Castle of Shadows—"

"I was, but am no longer, Effroi."

Orbane then looked at the circle and the black candles and the pentagon. "What is it you were trying to do?"

For a moment it seemed as if Effroi would not speak, but at last he said, "I was trying to recover the cloak of my sire."

Orbane smiled unto himself. "Morgrif was your sire, then." His words were not a question.

"Oui," said Effroi.

"And this cloak?"

Again Effroi hesitated before answering. Finally he said, "It contains the power of the Changeling Lord."

"Ah, I see. And who has it now?"

"The Queen of the Changelings."

"Your mère, I take it?"

"Oui. She will not yield it to me, the rightful heir."

"And you want this cloak because . . . ?"

"With it I can fetch mortal virgins and keep my people strong."

Orbane smiled. "Ah, and these mortal virgins, you plow them yourself and sow your seed?"

Effroi jerked a nod.

"Why not merely take the cloak from the queen?"

"Her magic is too powerful, and she insists that we woo these mortal women instead of taking what is rightfully ours in our traditional manner."

Orbane nodded. "By force, you mean." Again his words were not a question.

Effroi nodded once more.

"As it should be," said Orbane. "Tell me, have you tried to fetch the cloak by way of a spell before?"

Effroi sighed. "Oui, but I have failed each time. Did I not say her magic is strong?"

A small flash of ire crossed Orbane's face, but he managed to quell his rage at being questioned. "I heard you the first time . . . boy."

Effroi looked at Orbane. "My lord, they say your magic, too, is mighty. Think you that you can overcome the power of the Queen of the Changelings?"

Again rage briefly flashed upon Orbane's features, but he said, "Effroi, do the Changelings once commanded by your sire now acknowledge you as their liege?"

"Oui."

"Then, my lord," said Orbane, "I have a proposition to make, one that will restore the cloak to you and give you all the mortal virgins you desire. And all it requires is that you and your minions join me in a minor venture."

Effroi's face lighted with the expectation of promises fulfilled. "Say on, my lord, say on."

.   .   .

"They start their march on the morrow, Acolyte, and gather strength of numbers as they go. All I had to do was promise Effroi I would retrieve his father's cloak and give it to him. The fool! As if I would actually yield up that splendid mantle. Why, with it I will be able to instantly transport myself to wherever it is I desire. Black it is, and limned in scarlet—how fitting that I shall be the one to own it."

Hradian did not respond. Instead she ground her teeth in frustration, for what she had sought, the corpse of her sister had not had. There had been no thong about Nefasí's neck with a clay amulet dangling. Instead, it seems she had not had any of the Seals of Orbane, or if she had, they had not been on her person when she had been slain by that whore Céleste. Yet gritting her teeth, Hradian bore down on her besom to urge more speed from it, as toward the Isle of Brados they raced and the corsair stronghold thereon.

38

Under the Hill

"There it is, at the top of that tall mound," cried Flic as Regar crested a hill and stopped, the horses lathered and blowing.

Across the expanse of green rolling downs, Regar could see a great grassy mound on which sat a dolmen, with three upright, twice-man-tall megaliths equidistant from one another and a great flat capstone atop.

Two days earlier in the dawn they had left Lisane's great willow tree abode. She had wept, and Regar had embraced her dearly, his own eyes filled with sadness. Yet both knew he could not remain, for momentous events were afoot. And so, following Buzzer, Regar had ridden away, Lisane's sweet kiss yet lingering on his lips. "*Au revoir*, Lady of the Bower," had cried Flic. "I am certain we shall see you again." And off they had galloped, and, even as they went apace, Fleurette had drawn in a gasp of wonder, and quickly she wiped away her own tears of parting, for trotting across the sward had come a Unicorn to comfort weeping Lisane.

But that had been two days past, and they had ridden far and had crossed many a twilight marge. And not but a few moments ago they had emerged from the final crepuscular bound to come into these verdant downs.

"Oh, Flic," said Fleurette, peering at the dolmen, "should

we go near? As you once said, the Fey Lord Gwynn is quite capricious and might give us some onerous task to perform."

"Fear not, my sweetling, for the sun is o'erhead and the passage will not open until the eventide, by which time we can be at a distance, and Gwynn will not know we are nigh."

"You name him Gwynn?" asked Regar.

"Oui," said Flic.

"My grandmother called him Auberon, for that was the name he gave her."

"Ah, he is known by many names, depending on who is speaking, Gwynn and Auberon being just two."

"His queen has many names as well," said Fleurette, "Mab, Titania, and Gloriana being but three."

"My grandmother called her Gloriana," said Regar.

"By any name, she is the Fairy Queen, just as he is the Fey King."

"Well and good," said Regar, "but let us tarry no longer."

Regar spurred his mount and galloped down the far side of the hill, the remounts and the pack horse in tow. Across the swale below and then up to the dolmen they went, where Buzzer awaited atop the capstone, her task as guide now done.

"My lord," said Flic, "you'll have to wait until the coming of dusk, for none can enter ere then. It's shut, you see."

But as Regar dismounted, the moment his foot touched the sod, a great hole yawned open 'neath the dolmen, revealing stairs and a wagon ramp leading down and in, a dim glow seeping upward.

"Oh, my!" exclaimed Flic. "I wonder what—?"

"Perhaps it's my blood," said Regar.

Flic frowned. "Your blood?"

"Oh, love," said Fleurette, "he *is*, after all, the grandson of the Fairy King."

"Ah," said Flic, enlightened.

Regar stepped under the capstone and looked into the gape. "You tell me that time strides at a different pace therein?"

Flic nodded, though on the tricorn as he was, the Prince could not see his assent. At an elbow from Fleurette, Flic added, "Oui, my lord. When last Buzzer and I were here with Prince Borel and he had gone within, we waited for him for a full fortnight, and yet to him but a few candlemarks had passed ere he emerged once more."

Regar stepped back out from under and looked about, and both Sprites flew to alight upon the edge of the capstone.

"Tell me, my tiny comrades, can you keep the horses from running away?"

"Oh, yes," replied Flic.

Fleurette giggled and added, "We oft play tricks on crofters' steeds, and the farmers find them far afield."

"How so, Little Flower?" asked Regar.

"Well, they are trained, you see, and so we merely light in the animal's ear and command them with a gee and a haw and a hup and a whoa, and they go where we wish."

Regar broke into laughter, and then he began unlading the cargo from the pack horse and removing the tack from the one he had ridden and the tethered halters from the remounts. After he had rubbed them down, he said, "There's good grazing at hand, and I see a stream in the distance. So while you'll watch over the steeds, I will go see my grandsire."

"Ah, good," said Flic. "That way you can tell the Fey Lord that we are down by the stream and tending a task, and he won't think of something for us to do."

"But please, Prince Regar," said Fleurette, "leave a honey jar open for us to sup upon should you be a long while returning."

"Mais oui," said Regar, fetching out one of the small stone crocks and uncapping it and setting it in the shade of the dolmen.

"Speaking of dining, my prince," said Flic, "remember to eat no food and drink no wine nor take any other form of refreshment from them . . . not even water. For if you do, 'tis said that you might forget all."

Fleurette frowned and said, "I'm not certain of that, my love."

"Oh?"

"Oui. He has the blood of the Fairy King in his veins."

"Ah, I see," said Flic. He turned to Regar and said, "But still if I were you I'd be cautious."

"I'll keep that in mind," said Regar. Then he looked from Flic to Fleurette to Buzzer. "Well, now, there's nothing for it but for me to go." And he stepped under the capstone and down into the gaping hole.

"May the Fates watch over you," called Flic. But in that very moment, the hole closed behind the prince, leaving nought but green sod in its place.

. . .

Down the steps alongside the wagon ramp went Regar, a soft silvery light throughout showing the way. Both the stairs and road swept downward in a wide and shallow spiral as into the hollow hills he went. Finally, around a last turn, Regar came to the bottom, where to one side stables marched away—magnificent steeds therein—and opposite the stables and up three steps was a long corridor leading toward brighter light. And Regar could hear music beyond.

Into the passageway he went, and yet to his gaze along one wall loomed what appeared to be a stone archway, though it seemed to be there and then not there, as if somehow illusory in nature. As he drew nigh he gazed through a solid wall of stone—or was it altogether absent?—and within a long chamber beyond, he espied what looked to be endless rows of glittering weaponry, as if to arm a legion or more. Even so, he could not tell if it was real or merely the semblance of something real.

*Perhaps if I had what Flic calls Fey sight, I would then know.
—But wait! Mayhap with the blood of the Fey Lord flowing in
my veins, I am seeing something mortals cannot, though not
as well as perhaps the Fey.*

Shaking his head in puzzlement, Regar pressed on, and he
came unto a great banquet hall, and therein lithe males and
lissome females gracefully danced. And they all were of exotic
beauty, with faces long and narrow and ears tipped and eyes
aslant, their forms most pleasing. Fey, they were, of a size to be
human, but no humans these. Instead they were Fairykind or
Elvenkind, Regar could not tell which.

And as Regar crossed the threshold, some of these Fey folk
turned to see this person who had come uninvited into the hall,
while others simply continued their elegant dance and paid
him little or no heed.

Yet from the throne on which he sat, a redheaded male
looked to see Regar enter, and his green eyes flew wide in
astonishment, and he peered overhead as if seeing through
the stone above. Then he gazed back at Regar and frowned in
perplexity.

A corridor opened up among the dancers, and Regar walked
through and to the foot of the dais, where he bowed low and
said, "Your Highness," for Regar's grandmother had described
this homme, and he could be none other than the King Under
the Hill.

To the right of the Fey Lord sat a femme of incredible loveli-
ness, her hair raven-black, her eyes sapphire blue, her flawless
skin tinged with just a hint of gold, a tint held by all the Folk
within the hall, a bit more so than Regar's own hue.

Again Regar bowed and said, "My lady."

Both King Auberon and Queen Gloriana inclined their heads
in acknowledgment, and the High Lord signalled for silence,
and the music stopped, as did the dancers. When quiet fell, he
smiled and said, "I am surprised for 'tis yet daylight without,

and still you entered. Only those of great power might do so. I would have your name, Stranger."

"I am Regar, of the Wyldwood, son of Lady Mirabelle and grandson of Lady Alisette, both of the Wyldwood as well."

At these words, the Fey Lord's eyes again flew wide, this time in understanding, but the queen's eyes narrowed, in understanding as well.

Auberon turned to his queen and said, "Do not hold him responsible for my misdeeds."

A cold stare was her only response.

The king then turned back to Regar. "Now I realize how you could enter even though daylight graces the land above."

"It is my blood, then?" said Regar.

"Indeed."

"*Quart-sang,*" spat Gloriana.

Auberon glowered at her and then took a deep breath and turned toward his court and in a loud voice proclaimed, "I present to you Prince Regar, of the seed of my loins."

A surprised whisper muttered through the assembly, and, in spite of the queen's icy mien, the lords and ladies bowed and curtseyed, many smiling, and some of the ladies cast covetous gazes upon the handsome prince.

"Take care they do not steal your heart away," murmured the king.

"Fear not, my lord," said Regar, "for it belongs to another."

At these words a gleam came into Gloriana's eye, and she called out, "Let us have wine to welcome our guest."

Regar sighed and said, "I do apologize, my lady, but my mission is urgent and to partake of food and drink must wait, for time passes upon Faery above, and I would not be late to the war."

The king frowned. "War?"

A stillness fell upon the court.

"Pah!" snapped the queen. "What have we to do with the

petty squabbles of *your* kind? Nought, I say, nought. Nought whatsoever. Let you mongrels and humans slay one another until you are all dead. Perhaps then the mortal world will return to what it should be, to what it was before any of you came."

Regar was stunned by the accusative bitterness of her words and the murmurs of agreement rippling through the court. Nevertheless, he said, "My lord, my lady, have you not heard?"

"Heard what?" demanded the queen.

"Oh, my lady, if war does come, it is not only humankind and the mortal world in peril, but the whole of Faery, too."

A gasp of horror now replaced the murmurs, and the Fey Lord said, "Your meaning?"

Regar sighed, then took a deep breath and plunged on: "A sevenday past, the witch Hradian, by cunning and guile, stole a key to the Castle of Shadows. She intends—"

Regar's words were drowned out by shouts of alarm and denial. The Fey Lord's face blanched, and the queen looked at Regar agape.

Auberon held his hands up for silence, but it was a long while coming. When the uproar had run its course, Regar continued: "She intends to set Orbane free. Yet there is hope, for Sprites search for Raseri and Rondalo, and they might be able to intercept her. But, if the Drake and Elf are not found, and if the witch succeeds, then I am sent by King Valeray to urge you to arms, for surely the wizard will raise his armies of old and once again seek to master the whole of Faery."

Auberon turned to Gloriana, but ere he could speak, she called out, "My mirror! I must look in my mirror." And she sprang to her feet and rushed away.

The Fey Lord motioned to Regar and commanded, "Follow."

Through long corridors they went, to finally come unto the queen's chamber, and as they entered, Regar saw her standing before a tall silver mirror, her head bowed in deep concentration. Regar and Auberon stepped forward to flank the queen, her reflection between their two.

Of a sudden the image wavered, and slowly another formed. It showed a tall, dark, hawk-faced homme who was speaking to a sly-eyed femme dressed in black, with trim and danglers hanging down like shadows streaming away.

Gloriana gasped and clutched Auberon's arm, her face pale, nearly white. "Our son, our son. 'Tis our son."

But even as the likenesses formed, the man glanced up and 'round, and then he made a gesture, and the mirror went dark.

Auberon, his features grim, looked at Regar and said, "It is Orbane, and he is free."

39

Visions

"Princess?"

Michelle turned to see Steward Arnot standing in the snow.

"Oui?"

"My lady, Vadun is here. He came with Armsmaster Jules."

"Ah, then, I'll be right there."

As Arnot trudged away, Michelle signaled the pack *au revoir*, though what they interpreted was *I go*, for what the princess and the Wolves said to one another, though understandable, had slightly different meanings, such as Michelle's posture for *femme* was taken as *bitch* by the pack, and vice versa.

Regardless, for the past three days not only had Michelle been intensely acquiring Wolfspeak, she had also learned from the pack some of the human words and silent hand-signals Borel had taught them all. In the beginning it had been painfully slow, but as her Wolfspeak vocabulary had grown, it had gone much faster. At times the entire pack had been involved; even Slate had deigned to speak with her.

As Michelle bade the Wolves "au revoir," Slate turned to Dark and said: *Master's bitch two-legs cub-smart.* Tears brimmed in Michelle's eyes, and yet she had a great smile on her face, for never had any praise from her former human tutors made her as proud as Slate's casual aside to Dark.

. . .

Chelle hurried through the corridors to come to the blue room, where Jules and Arnot and Laurent waited with the guest. And as she entered, the princess paused, for Vadun was not like anyone Chelle had ever seen before: small, he was, child sized, and seemed to be dressed in nought but leaves and twigs. His hair, while clean, was unruly and long, reaching unto his waist, and though it was brown it had a greenish tint shimmering among the strands. His tilted eyes were green as well, though pale and translucent, as of the most delicate of jade. His face was narrow and his form slender, and his arms and legs lean. His smooth light brown skin seemed to match that of a young tree sprout, and his feet were shod in bark shoes. It was almost as if some small woodland being akin to a bush or a tree had somehow come to animate life. That such a creature lived in a realm of ice and snow was a mystery, one that Michelle, for reasons unknown, felt she had no right to delve into.

And as the princess entered the chamber, Vadun stood and bowed and said, "My lady." His voice was soft, almost a whisper, as of a zephyr gently stirring foliage.

Michelle inclined her head and replied, "Voyant Vadun."

She took a comfortable chair and gestured to the others to be seated as well, and Vadun returned to the cushioned footstool that fitted his size.

"Princess," said the small being, "Armsmaster Jules has told me the terrible news, yet unless someone in your household has had a dream bearing upon the calamity, I know not how I can help."

Even as Michelle's heart sank, Jules said, "He suggested I bring him here, my lady, just in case someone has had such a rêve."

At the armsmaster's words, Vadun smiled, showing rather catlike teeth.

Michelle turned up her hands. "I know of no one who has said so."

"Princess," said Arnot, "recall that you and Borel were dream-linked during your imprisonment."

"Oui. We were."

Arnot turned to Vadun. "Shouldn't that help?"

"Perhaps," murmured the dream seer. "What were the circumstances?"

With her hope rising, quickly Michelle explained.

Vadun sighed and said, "I see. Yet that was an enchanted sleep, and the fact that you could meet one another in your dreams is quite rare, even when one is enspelled, and rarer still in normal sleep, though great love or loyalty aids."

As Michelle's heart fell again, Laurent said, "I do not seem to recall any of my dreams, yet that doesn't mean someone else might not have dreamt of Prince Borel or any of the others. We could ask everyone here."

Vadun again smiled, his features gentle in spite of the sharpness of his teeth. "Sieur Laurent, though it would help, one need not recall a dream for me to . . . *See*."

"What mean you?"

"Just that I merely need to be in contact, one at a time, with each member of the household."

"What do you need?" asked Michelle.

"A quiet and peaceful room, preferably smaller than this, darkened and lit by a single candle. It should be furnished with a couch or such in which the member of staff can be at ease, and a comfortable chair for me at the head of the dreamer's divan. I would also like some mint tea or other such to be brewing and fill the chamber with a pleasant scent."

Michelle looked at Arnot. "The green room?"

He nodded. "A good choice, my lady."

Michelle then turned to Vadun. "Forgive my manners, Voyant Vadun, but have you eaten? And surely you need rest from your travels."

"I would appreciate a meal, my lady, but I need no rest, for the sooner started the sooner we might know."

Arnot said, "Your pardon, Dreamseer, but what would you have to eat?"

"Some tea would be nice as well as . . . might you have a vole?"

Arnot frowned. "Vole? Mean you a mouse?"

"Oui. A mouse will do. Preferably alive."

Inwardly, Michelle shuddered. *How can such a rather plantlike being as is Vadun eat a live mouse!* She looked at him and smiled, one that he returned, his catlike teeth showing.

. . .

Passing among a gaggle of waiting, nervous women, some tittering, Michelle paused a moment to caution them to quietness, and then stepped down the hall to the green room, for she would be the first person Vadun would examine. Into the candlelit chamber she stepped and softly closed the door behind. The odor of chamomile subtly filled the room.

The voyant de rêves welcomed her with a smile, and he gestured to the couch. When she was fully reclined, he took his seat, the chair with piled cushions to raise him up on a level with the head of the divan.

"Now, my lady," he murmured, "I ask you to clear your mind of as many thoughts as you can and to concentrate only on Prince Borel."

"That will be rather easy," whispered Michelle. She took a deep breath and thought of her truelove, with his silver-sheened hair, his ice-blue eyes, his handsome face, his ready wit and infectious smile, his caressing hands, his lean body, his—

Michelle felt a gentle touch upon her brow, yet she managed to maintain her thoughts of Borel and his ways.

"Oh, my, what strength of feelings," Vadun softly said. "And what troubled dreams of recent, yet pleasant ones as well: of Wolves and speaking to them, of ordinary things, but also of unknown and unseen dangers, of the prince and loving and of making love—"

Suddenly, Vadun broke contact.

Embarrassed over this last, Michelle said, "I did not mean to—"

"Oh, Princess, all beings have somewhat . . . lustful dreams."

"But then why did you break contact. Did you see Borel? Did you find him?"

"Non, Princess, you have not dreamt a dream that can aid us in the search for the prince. Yet, do I understand it correctly? You can speak with his Wolves?"

"Oui, though I am still learning."

"Ah, good. Wolves are closer to nature, and extremely loyal to the pack, and, to their way of thinking, Prince Borel is one of them. Too, they dream. I would like to see if any have dreamt of your prince, their master."

"You can do that? Be a voyant to their dreams?"

"Oui."

"What of the members of my staff?"

"My lady, if the Wolves yield nought, then we shall return to the staff."

"Where would you have me bring the pack?"

Vadun shook his head. "Non, my lady, I will go to them, for they need to be in a place they find comfortable in order for me to see into their dreams."

"Then follow me, Vadun."

.   .   .

In the Summerwood, this time Blaise, instead of Lanval, went to see the Lady of the Mere, but she did not appear at his beck. And, upon his return, he found that no falcons had come bearing messages of what other seers might have learned.

.   .   .

In the Autumnwood, Luc, fresh from the training grounds, had just sat down to his lunch as rawboned Rémy, armsmaster at Autumnwood Manor, escorted a man into the chamber. "My lord," said Rémy as they came forward, "I present Seer Malgan."

Luc saw before him a reed-thin, sallow-faced homme with lank, straw-colored hair, his hands tucked across and within the sleeves of his red satin buttoned gown, a man who twitched away from unseen companions and yet whispered to them as he approached. As he came to stand nigh Luc, he bowed, and then glared left and right as if bidding others to show the prince courtesy as well.

When the seer straightened up, Luc asked, "Can you aid us to find Liaze and the others?"

"My lord," replied Malgan, his voice high-pitched. He paused a moment and cocked his head as if listening to an un-heard voice. "I will need something . . . intimate of Princess Liaze's—an oft-worn adornment, a lock of her hair, something in close contact with her personage." Of a sudden he looked to his right. "What? What? Of course, of course." He turned back to Luc and added, "A precious gem of sorts: amulet, ring, or the like. In fact, a gemstone would be best if you've not a lock of her hair."

As Malgan muttered to someone aside, Luc cocked an eye at Rémy and slowly shook his head in disbelief that this scare-crow of a madman could help them. "A gemstone, you say." His words were not a question.

Malgan looked back at Luc. "Indeed, and the more precious the better."

Luc stood and pulled a bell cord. Then he turned to Rémy and Malgan and said, "Won't you join me at lunch?"

Malgan dithered over his choices, standing at the sideboard and taking up first one chunk of bread and then returning it for another, repeating this several times, not only over the choice of bread, but also of plates and cups and pats of butter and amount of tea and cuts of meat and selection of vegetables and pieces of fruit, all the while whispering to invisible beings.

As the Seer took a seat, then changed it for another, a page appeared.

Luc looked up at the lad. "Breton, fetch Zoé and tell her that we need an item from among Liaze's jewelry, something set with a precious stone—ring, pendant, earring, necklace, or the like—something that is dear to Liaze, something oft in intimate contact with her." Even as he instructed the boy, an ephemeral thought skittered 'round the edges of Luc's mind, but ere he could capture it—

Malgan peered down at the floor and hissed, "Yes, yes, I know." Then he looked at the youth. "Tell her, tell this Zoé person, to take it to the forge."

"The forge, my lord?" asked the page.

"The forge, the forge, boy," said Malgan, looking to his left where sat an empty chair at the table, one he had pulled out as if to sit in but then had chosen another.

The page looked at Luc, and he shrugged and nodded.

As the lad rushed away, Malgan glanced at Rémy. "There is an anvil within, I take it."

"Oui," said Rémy, frowning.

"And tools? —Hammers and such?"

"Oui."

"Good," said Malgan. Then he peered across the table and said apparently to no one, "I told you so."

· · ·

Zoé had brought several pieces to the smithy. She held a pearl pendant up to her ear. "This one, my lord, is one of her favorites."

"Here, here, put them all on the anvil," said Malgan.

Zoé placed on the large bronze anvil the pearl earring and a ruby-set ring and a diamond on a silvery chain, as well as a fire opal set in a golden torque.

Malgan then muttered and whispered and pushed the jewelry about and finally said, "Yes, yes, I know: the diamond."

He took up a bronze hammer and, with a single blow, smashed the gem into powder.

Zoé shrieked and snatched away the remaining jewelry and protectively clutched it to her breast and turned her back to the seer, using her body to shield it from him. But Malgan did not seem to notice. Instead he peered at the resulting glitter casting its myriad glints unto the eye, and then turned to Luc and said, "My lord, all I see, all we see, is a vast darkness."

.   .   .

Vadun and Michelle found the Wolves in a nearby snow-laden pine-tree glade, and Michelle introduced the voyant to them.

What she believed she said was: *This person is here to help find Borel.*

What they read in her postures and growls was: *Two-legs here help find master.*

After they had surrounded Vadun and had snuffled and had taken in his scent and found it to be friendly and unafraid, though a bit plantlike and smelling somewhat of an eaten mouse, Slate pronounced him acceptable.

Vadun said, "Are they comfortable herein?"

"Oui."

"Then please tell them that I will be touching them one by one."

Michelle said: *This person will touch each of you.*

Wolves interpreted: *Two-legs touch one all.*

Vadun then said, "Princess, as I touch each one, ask them to envision Borel."

Michelle nodded, and when Vadun placed a gentle hand on Slate's head, Michelle said: *See Borel.*

Slate stepped away from Vadun and turned his head this way and that and lifted his nose in the air. Finally, he said to Michelle: *Master not here.*

Michelle sighed in exasperation. "I am having trouble asking them to envison Borel. Let me see if I can think of another way to put it."

Finally, she said to Slate: *Borel not here.*

Slate: *Chuff.*

Michelle: *Do not move, but see Borel.*

Slate whined in puzzlement.

Michelle turned to Dark: *Dark. Do not move, but see Borel.*

Dark whined in puzzlement, but then said: *No move, hunt master?*

"Yes!" exclaimed Michelle. Then she turned to Slate: *Do not move, but seek Borel. Do not move, but smell.*

Slate: *Chuff.*

And the great Wolf stood still and slowly inhaled scents and tried to find the master, and Vadun laid a light hand upon Slate's head.

"Non, my lady, he has not dreamt of Borel," said the voyant.

"Dark. Here," said Michelle, and the bitch Wolf came to stand beside the princess.

Michelle: *Do not move, but seek Borel. Do not move, but smell.*

Vadun placed a hand upon this Wolf's head, and then he shook his own.

Down through the pack they went in hierarchical order: after Slate and Dark came Render, then Shank, Trot, and Loll.

And as Michelle's heart sank with each failure, at last they came to Blue-eye. Again Michelle repeated her command, and as Blue-eye stood still and took in the scent on the wind, Vadun said, "Ah, yes."

Michelle gasped. "What? What is it, Vadun?"

Vadun's voice took on a low growl, and as if in a trance he began to move and posture, and Michelle interpreted.

Then Vadun shook himself as if becoming aware of his surroundings. "What did I say?"

"I know what you said in Wolfspeak, but I do not understand."

"Tell me."

"Well, literally you said: No moon. No stars. No smell. No see. Hear Borel in all big dark."

Vadun frowned. "I do not understand either."

. . .

In the middle of the night, in Winterwood Manor, Michelle started up from a restless sleep, as did Luc in the Autumnwood.

Each knew with certainty just where their loved one was—be it in the "big dark" as told by Blue-eye through Vadun, or in "a vast darkness" as glitters of shattered-gem light and invisible companions had told Malgan.

40

Imprisoned

"No matter how many times you try it, my lord, you'll not get out," said Rondalo.

The tall and slender Elf lounged on the throne, one leg over the padded arm of the chair, and watched as again Valeray stepped through the shadowlight-filled archway and vanished. Moments later, the king trudged out from a corridor above and paced down the stairs to return to the vast chamber.

Raseri raised up his head, and Duran, astride the Dragon, squealed in delight and held fast to the barbels as he was lifted into the air. Standing below, Alain caught his breath and remained ready to catch the youngster should Duran lose his grip.

Some three days and a night past, as near as they could reckon, Valeray and Saissa and their get, as well as Camille and Duran, had awakened in this place, borne here by Orbane's black wind. When Camille had come to, she had looked straight into the sapphire gaze of the tilted eyes of Rondalo as he chafed her wrists in concern. His narrow face was framed in a halo of fair hair, and, upon her rousing, his features flooded with gentle affection. Blood rushed to her face, for the Elf had for a while travelled across Faery with her in her long search for Alain, and she at one time, overcome with loneliness, had kissed him with passion, and then had fled away in confusion, wondering if she could love two men at the same time. But that was nigh four summers ago and not now. Yet flustered, she had heard a soft sigh nearby, and had turned to see Alain lying unconscious, with Duran seeming asleep at his side. And she had scrambled up and tended them, while Rondalo took care of others. And even as Camille alternated between Alain and Duran, she heard a soft peep as Scruff came awake in her shoulder pocket. Soon all were roused, and for the next three days, they had sought a means of escape, all to no avail.

Valeray shook his head. "This time I started by stepping through the twilight archway in the topmost tower, and it brought me to the one down the lower hallway yon. Then I crossed this chamber and went out through that one, and back to the topmost tower I came. Ah, fie! I keep thinking that there should be some combination of exits and entries that might set us free, for oft there are complex sequences a thief must master ere a treasure can be won . . . in this case, our freedom."

Sitting on the dais next to Rondalo, Borel said, "Once when Flic and I were in the Endless Sands, I explained to him how such a place might be so named, and this prison in which we find ourselves seems to be but a variation on that theme."

Rondalo swung his leg from the arm of the chair and turned toward Borel. "How so?"

Borel looked at the Elf. "I told him to think of that vast desert as simply a room with two doorways, and when one exits out through one, he simply comes in the other, and, of course, the reverse as well. In the Endless Sands the twilight bounds could be thought of as the 'doorways.' I also mentioned that the Castle of Shadows might be constructed the same way."

"And that's why you believe we are now entrapped in the Castle of Shadows and not somewhere else?" asked Raseri.

"Oui," replied Borel.

As Raseri lowered his head and Alain fetched Duran down, Valeray sighed and said, "I believe you are right, Borel, for what

246 / Dennis L. McKiernan

better vengeance could Orbane inflict than to hurl us all into the place where he himself was cast and held captive these many seasons."

Alain nodded in agreement. "Oui, Papa, Orbane would do such, for you and Lord Rulon—Chelle's sire—were the chief architects in bringing him to ruin. Yet I imagine that Hradian would rather have seen us slain in repayment for the deaths of her sisters than simply to be trapped herein."

"I agree," called down Saissa, as she and Liaze and Céleste and Camille traversed a balcony above to descend the long set of stairs. Scruff, riding on Camille's shoulder, took to wing and flew about the chamber, the tiny sparrow chirping all the while.

Rondalo and Borel stood as the women reached the floor of the vast hall and passed around Raseri, the Drake inclining his head in acknowledgement.

"My lady Saissa, your seat of state," said Rondalo, sweeping a hand toward the chair on the dais.

"Pishposh, Rondalo, I will sit on a step."

As the women took seat along the treads of the dais, and Scruff glided down to alight upon the back of the throne, Valeray looked 'round and said, "Inmates all and—" Valeray's words chopped to a halt. But then he put a hand to his forehead. "Oh, my, I just realized *this* is why the Fates spoke to Sieur Émile's sons and not us."

Céleste frowned. "Your meaning, Papa?"

"We are trapped herein and can do nought, while Laurent, Blaise, and Roél are free, as well as Luc. The Three Sisters knew it all along."

"And yet they did not warn you?" said Rondalo.

Valeray slowly shook his head. "Perhaps there was nought anyone could do to prevent it."

Rondalo blew out a sharp puff of air and glanced at Camille. "Even so . . ."

"What's done is done," said Valeray, sighing.

"Then," said Céleste, "if we are truly trapped in the Castle of Shadows, we can only hope Roél and Laurent and Blaise and Luc recover the key and set us loose."

Raseri growled and glared toward the entrance and asked, "And just who will bring the key to yon portal?"

Céleste turned to the Drake. "I do not understand, Raseri."

"I am one of the few to know the way through the Great Darkness to come to the Castle of Shadows."

"There is no one else?"

"I did not say that, Princess. But if someone *is* to come, they must be able to fly."

"Fly?" said Liaze.

"Oui, for the Castle of Shadows floats free in the Great Darkness. There is no road to the gates—only dark emptiness—a place where any rescuer, flyer or not, can become lost forever."

"Raseri," said Camille, "if you have seen the Castle of Shadows by flying through the dark, does it have this shape? If so, then we will truly know where we are."

Raseri shook his head. "Even though I have seen the Castle of Shadows, still I cannot say this is it."

"Why so?"

"When last I saw the Castle, it was but a single square-based tower, fit to hold one person—Orbane." Raseri looked at Borel and said, "In the manner of your explanation of the Endless Sands, two doorways it had, one on each side, and a shorn-off bridge leading away from each."

"But this is not a single tower," said Céleste.

"Non, it is not," said Raseri.

"Then mayhap we are not in the Castle of Shadows," said Liaze.

"Perhaps not, but then again perhaps so," said Raseri, "for there are legends." The Drake looked at Rondalo.

The Elf nodded and said, "My mother, Chemine, spoke of the lore and told some of it to me. She said the gods made the castle such that it would change to accommodate whoever was to be kept within." Rondalo gestured wide. "Look about you. Behold this vast throne room—a hall to hold Raseri, *n'est-ce pas?*"

Liaze shrugged, but said nought.

"Is there ought else of the legends of the Castle of Shadows?" asked Camille.

"Oui, and they seem to confirm that we are indeed imprisoned in it, for we need neither food nor drink, and we cannot escape."

Valeray looked about the chamber. "We need a way to break out."

"Think you we have not tried?" growled Raseri. He flexed his great black saberlike claws. "These walls resist my efforts to rend them asunder, and flame mars them not."

At these words, Camille fell into pondering, chasing an elusive thought skittering just beyond reach on the edge of her mind.

"I wonder if something the Fates said in one of their redes spoken to the three brothers tells ought of our fate," said Alain, watching Duran clip-clopping his toy horse across the floor.

"Perhaps," said Borel, also watching the wee prince down on his hands and knees with the toy. "For in the very moment that Orbane and Hradian appeared, I had solved at least a part of the rede Skuld gave to Laurent."

"Which part?" asked Liaze.

Borel frowned and then intoned:

> *"Swift are the get of his namesake,*
> *That which a child does bear."*

Liaze shook her head. "And its meaning is . . . ?"

Borel pointed at Duran. "The colts of Asphodel—the Fairy

King's horse—the namesake of that which the child does bear."

Camille, who was yet in deep thought, seemed not to hear Borel's solution, but all the others looked at the young prince and his white horse with its tiny silver bells ajingle.

"Mais oui," said Alain, "you told us of that marvelous steed. And now that you say it, I think I know what the very next part of the rede means:

> "Ask the one who rides the one
> To send seven children there."

In that moment Camille broke from her pondering and exclaimed, "Aha! Now I know what it is I was chasing. Rondalo, you said that legend has it that the gods fashioned the Castle of Shadows such that it would change to accommodate whoever was to be kept within, oui?"

Rondalo nodded.

Camille then stood and turned to Raseri and curtseyed. "My Lord Dragon, your bedchamber upstairs is ready."

"My bedchamber? Upstairs? What is this banter of yours?" Raseri gestured at the steps to the archways above and the corridors beyond. "The stairwell is too narrow, the passages too constricted. This is the only chamber large enough to contain me."

"Then you have not tried?"

"Non."

"Heed me, my dear Raseri, we must all of us here think beyond the bounds of our expectations, for, if the legends are factual, and this is truly the Castle of Shadows in the Great Darkness beyond the Black Wall of the World, we can prove it by you going to your chambers above."

"But there are no chambers for me above."

"Perhaps if you believe there are, then they will indeed be

there. After all, the Castle of Shadows *is* said to be enchanted to accommodate its prisoners."

Raseri looked at Rondalo, and the Elf turned up his hands and shrugged, but Scruff gave a loud chirp as if to say "Try."

Rising up and wheeling about, the great Dragon headed for the stairs, and even as he did so, they swiftly started to expand, as did the balcony and archways and the corridors beyond.

Camille then turned to Valeray and said, "Given the legends are true, surely this confirms we are trapped in a prison we have not the means to escape."

At these words, Saissa began to silently weep, and Valeray took her in his embrace, while Duran in his innocence laughed gaily as he galloped Asphodel away.

41

Corsairs

"Ah, there it is," said Orbane.

In the distance ahead lay a rocky upjut of an island in the clear waters of the sparkling sea. Even from the height Hradian flew, as they neared they could see that its craggy interior was filled with scrub and twisted trees, though here and there groves of tall pines stood. Some five miles across it was and thrice that around, and the shoreline itself was nought more than a rocky shingle, sand absent for the most part. Massive blocks of stone reared up here and there along the perimeter, but mostly long cliffs of sheer rock rising up from the sea beringed the entire isle. On the far side loomed a fortress of gray stone, sitting atop a low rise jutting out from the fall of the land. On beyond and farther down, another half mile or so, stood a town, curving about a modest bay. Rover ships were moored in the dark waters of the cove, with the arc of the island shouldering up all 'round. Hradian and Orbane could see folk in the streets of the port, and the docks were busy. Farther on, out on the brine, vessels fared away from the bay, while others approached. They were three-masted dhows for the most part, with lateen sails a vivid red to strike fear in the hearts of their victims, for they were corsairs, and this was the Isle of Brados.

As to the fortress itself, roughly square it was, an outer wall running 'round o'er the rough ground, some ten feet high and three hundred feet to a side and five feet thick at the top, wider at the base. A road ran down through a series of switchbacks to the town below.

Between the outer bulwark ringing 'round and the main bastion lay nought but open space, the land completely barren of growth; 'twas a killing ground should invaders come.

Centered within this outer wall and killing ground, the dark citadel stood: also built in a square some two hundred feet to a side, a massive wall stood some fifty feet high to the banquette with towers and turrets along its length and a great courtyard within. And at the very midpoint of the quadrangle stood a tall slender structure, mayhap some seventy feet high, window slits up its length, arrow slits up its sides as well.

And as Hradian and Orbane spiralled down, from somewhere below there came the clanging of an alarm gong, and, on the fortress walls, horns blew, and men pointed upward at the besom-riding pair.

"Acolyte, land on the balcony ringing 'round the top of the tower."

"Oui, my lord."

But as they approached, armed and armored men rushed out, crossbows and cutlasses at the ready. Yet with a whispered word and a simple gesture, Orbane halted them in their tracks, and they stood like statues, no longer able to move.

As warders in the courtyard below and upon the fortress walls called out in alarm, Hradian came to rest among the men frozen in place, and Orbane moved past them and into the chamber beyond, his acolyte following.

They came into a large room, with windows all 'round overlooking not only the fortress itself and the nearby surrounding terrain, but also the town below and the dark bay beyond.

In the center of the chamber sat a large round table, a scatter of charts thereon, and at the far edge stood a swarthy and bearded man, also frozen in place.

"My lord," hissed Hradian. She pointed at an open trapdoor, revealing a spiral stair leading downward. "More come."

But Orbane paid her no heed, and instead stepped to the man and made a small gesture, releasing him from the spell.

As the man raised a forearm in a protective flinch, louder came curses and running footsteps of ascending brigands, and Hradian darted to the trapdoor and slammed it to and shot the bolt, barring the corsairs from entry.

"You have seen but a mere iota of my power," said Orbane.

The man, in spite of his fright, lowered his arm and glared. "And you are?"

"I am Orbane."

Once again fear filled the man's features; even so, he found his voice. "You escaped?"

"I did."

"What is it you want?"

"I want to see your commander, for I have an alliance to propose, one that will gain you incalculable riches."

A hint of greed flashed through the eyes of the man. "I am Burque, Captain of Captains."

A hammering rattled the trapdoor, and voices called out, "Burque, open the way. We'll deal with these interlopers."

Orbane sneered at these words. "You command these rabble, Captain?"

"Oui. But, my lord, I ask you to harm them not, for they only seek to come to my aid."

"Ah, loyalty, eh?"

"Oui, for unlike the days of Caralos, under my command they prosper."

"Caralos?"

"The former Captain of Captains, slain here in this tower by an unknown hand during a fireship raid."

"By an unknown hand, eh? Was it not you?"

"Nay, my lord, though oft I contemplated it. Instead it was

someone who stole a valuable map ere it could be delivered to the one who commissioned its theft."

"Well, Burque, ally with me and you will not have to stoop to petty thievery, but instead prosper beyond your wildest dreams."

"And what would this alliance demand of me?"

"Just that you transport an army of mine from Port Cíent to a distant shore."

"A distant shore?"

Orbane nodded. "Another port."

Burque frowned and said, "You want to loot the town?"

"Not just the town, but the whole of Faery and all the riches within. And you will share in the wealth."

"But to dream of conquering the whole of Faery is folly," said Burque.

Rage flashed in Orbane's gaze, rage quickly quelled. "The army you will transport will be but a minuscule part of the whole, I merely need you to put them ashore at the nearest place where they can join me."

Boom! Boom! There came a great pounding on the trapdoor, as if the men below were using a ram.

"My lord!" shrilled Hradian, desperation in her eyes.

Orbane sighed in exasperation and gestured at the entry, and a dead silence fell. Then he turned to Burque. "Well?"

"This army of yours we are to transport from Port Cíent, are they assembled? If so, it will take me a good six moons to gather most of the fleet together."

"Nonsense," snapped Orbane. "Simply take me to where there are seagulls, and I will send messages to all."

"You can do that, my lord?"

Again ire at being questioned crossed Orbane's face, but he held himself in check. "The gulls, Captain, the gulls, and I will have your fleet at Port Cíent in less than a fortnight."

"And this army we are to transport, how many in all? For that will determine the number of ships."

"Mayhap two thousand or so," said Orbane.

"Your pardon, my lord, but a mere two thousand does not seem to be much of an army to me."

Orbane smiled. "If they were just men, then I would agree. But this is an army of Changelings."

"Changelings!" blurted Burque. "I am not certain my men will put up with Changelings on their ships."

"Are you not the Captain of Captains?" seethed Orbane.

"I am, but—"

"Let me put it this way, my Captain of Captains, if you do not transport them, then they will find a way to come unto Brados, and when they arrive they will destroy all that is here. They are Changelings, and you have no defenses that will stop them from the air and sea and land and under the land. So, you can either move my army for me and win your riches, or not do so and see your fiefdom utterly destroyed and your fleet at the bottom of the sea."

. . .

Three days later, with the agreement struck and the message-bearing gulls long gone, Hradian and Orbane left Brados. The Captain of Captains was glad to be well quit of them, for Orbane had ruined many a woman in the town, and Hradian many a man.

. . .

Another day went by, and in the harbor at Port Mizon, a seagull landed upon a dhow, one of the ships captured of recent by a ship of King Avélar's fleet. The gull, a capsule attached to a leg, did not seem afraid of men, and in fact sought one out. Within a candlemark the missive was in the hands of Vicomte Chevell.

"It is in the old corsair cipher," said Chevell, peering at the runes. "One I well know." He reached for a quill and parchment.

Within but moments he had the message decoded. He paled and said, "Oh, my," and then turned to an aide. "Fetch me a horse."

As the lad ran away, "A horse, Captain?" asked Armond, former second in command on Chevell's *Sea Eagle* but now a captain of his own vessel—the *Hawk*.

"Oui. I must see the king. It seems Orbane is loose."

"Orbane loose?"

Chevell nodded. "And that's not all. The corsairs are sailing to Port Cíent to board an army of Changelings and deliver them here."

Distant Drums

Messenger falcons flew back and forth among the Forests of the Seasons as well as to and fro the king's demesne, and, given the seers' visions and Michelle's and Luc's conjectures, all decided the most likely place for Valeray and Saissa and the princes and princesses was that they were somewhere in the Great Darkness beyond the Black Wall of the World. And from the legends concerning that void, the only safe place to be therein was the Castle of Shadows, else one could be lost forever, mayhap even falling endlessly through the impenetrable dark. And so they concluded there was nought to be done but to find Hradian and retrieve the key, and then to seek someone who knew the way to that inescapable gaol and hope against hope that is where the prisoners would be found. They also decided the best chance of running down Hradian lay with Raseri and Rondalo, about whom they had heard nought whatsoever since the Ice Sprite had found them.

Some five days after the seers had given their visions, Prince Roél and Armsmaster Anton strode among the men at wooden swordplay on the training grounds at Springwood Manor, and they corrected feints, and showed the way of parries and ripostes, and demonstrated shield bashes, and other such one-on-one combat tactics, giving praise where praise was due, and correction where it was warranted. Elsewhere in the Springwood, in scattered villages, where men from the towns and nearby steads had gathered, experienced warriors of the manor warband also conducted lessons in the art of killing foe while preventing them from doing the same. Likewise, in the Summerwood, Autumnwood, and Winterwood, and in Valeray's realm, men were training at arms as well, for Luc and Laurent and Blaise and Émile and the war bands under their command were hard at work preparing, should war become necessary.

In the Springwood, Roél finally called a halt to the duels, and he stood on a small platform and looked out over the men— some three hundred altogether—as they gathered 'round.

And he raised his voice so that all could hear: " 'Tis not likely any of us will have the luxury of fighting a single foe, for in war all is chaos and madness, with enemy before and aflank and behind, and mêlée is the rule. And so—"

A distant horn cry interrupted Roél's words.

He frowned and looked toward the far woods.

Again sounded the horn, and bursting out from among the trees came a rider, a remount in tow. Across the sward galloped the stranger, and he wore the tabard of a king, but just which king it was—

" 'Tis Avélar's man," said Anton.

"Oui, I see it is," replied Roél.

Once more sounded the horn, and, with the men parting before him, up to the stand galloped the youth. He leapt from his steed and called, "A message from Vicomte Chevell." He unlooped the canister strap over his head and from 'round his shoulder and handed the container to Roél.

Roél popped the cylinder open and took the parchment from within and unrolled it. " 'Tis in Avélaine's hand." A moment later—"Merde! Orbane is free."

A murmur of consternation whispered through the men. Anton glared at them, and the mutter quelled.

Roél looked at the armsmaster and said, "It seems Raseri

and Rondalo did not intercept the witch ere she let the wizard loose. We can only hope they succeed in running Orbane and Hradian down and killing them."

Roél then read the remainder of the message and sighed. "It seems the corsairs are to ferry an army of Changelings to Port Mizon. Chevell intends for the king's fleet to intercept them at sea and thwart Orbane's scheme."

As Roél fell silent, "My lord," said the courier, "I am to say that this same message has been sent to your brothers and Prince Luc, but that you are to send the message on by falcon to your sire, for those swift fliers can reach him ere we could by riding."

Roél nodded and called an aide to him. "Take this to the scribe and have him set down a copy in his finest hand to go by falcon to Sieur Émile." Roél glanced at the sun. "And haste! For there is yet enough of the day for the falcon to reach the Castle of the Seasons."

"Oui, my lord," said the lad, and off he sped.

.   .   .

In the Winterwood, Michelle ran through the snow, the Wolf-pack ranging among the trees, her guardians on the run. She had begun training each day, for, in spite of Steward Arnot's protestations, she was determined to go on the campaign against Orbane should war come to Faery.

"But, Princess, war is no place for a lady."

"Nonsense, Arnot. Ever have there been women warriors. Besides, what better scouts to have than a pack of Wolves?"

"Sprites, my lady. Sprites."

"Sprites cannot withstand the chill."

"Ice Sprites can."

"Oui, but the campaign mayhap will go from summer to winter to spring to fall, depending upon which borders we cross. Neither the Ice Sprites nor the winged ones can follow in places, but the Wolves and I suffer not those limitations."

260 / Dennis L. McKiernan

The debate had gone on, yet Michelle had been adamant, and finally Arnot yielded. And so she had practiced with her bow, and had run with the Wolves, and every day had become more fluent in their speech.

Laurent could see the worth of having Wolves to reconnoiter, for he knew the value of good scouts. Even so, he would not have Michelle endangering herself. But she pointed out that no one else could speak their tongue; she also maintained she could remain somewhat at a distance while the Wolves did the work of reconnaissance. In the end Laurent threw up his hands and gave way as well.

And so she ran with the grey hunters in daylight and moonlight as well as the twilight of dusk and dawn. And she told them what she planned.

They agreed, for they would have Borel back at the side of his cub-smart two-legs bitch.

It was at the end of one of these runs, when Michelle heard the sound of a clarion. Wolves pricked up their ears and gazed sunwise.

Slate: *Two-legs call. Tall four-legs run.*

Michelle: *How many four-legs?*

Slate: *Two.*

Michelle had learned that the Wolves had their own numbering method, six levels in all: *one, two, four, more, small herd, big herd.*

Michelle: *We run.*

And she and the pack began trotting toward the manor.

. . .

After she had read the message, Michelle turned to Arnot and Laurent and Jules and said, "Well then, it seems there will be a war after all."

The men nodded solemnly, including the courier from Chevell.

"Let us get the word to all the men throughout the Winterwood. Too, we need alert the Sprites in other realms to be on the watch for Orbane's army on the march, for we will need to intercept his force, wherever it is bound. Also, we need to make certain that our allies in other realms know of this, and to rally under Valeray's flag when we choose a place to rendezvous."

"That will be difficult, my lady," said Armsmaster Jules.

"How so?"

"The twilight borders of Faery are tricky, to say the least. And wherever it is that it *seems* Orbane has decided to march, he can simply change his crossing point a minor amount and be headed somewhere else entirely."

"Then the Sprites must be at their best to keep us informed," said Michelle.

She glanced at Laurent, and he said, "This fighting in Faery is not like anything I have e'er done before, and so I depend upon you to get me and the army to the battle, for 'tis in combat that I know how and what to do."

Michelle nodded and said, "Arnot, Laurent, Jules, here is what I propose: have all armsmasters meet with Luc, for he is of Faery, while Sieur Émile and his sons are not. Hence, Luc should be more familiar with the 'trickiness' of the twilight borders as well as to the shifts in direction Orbane might employ. He and the armsmasters must come up with a plan not only for organizing the Sprites and finding our way, but also for tracking Orbane and his army so that we might intercept them. And when we do, it must be at a place to take advantage of the terrain, whether it be the high ground or an ambush or by meeting them in a narrow lieu, or anywhere we have the edge." Michelle paused a moment in thought. "Too, Arnot, see that my sire gets Chevell's message as well."

Even as Arnot said "Oui," the courier said, "My lady, Prince Roél was to inform Sieur Émile."

"Indeed," replied Michelle, "yet if that courier is delayed or worse . . ." Michelle paused, then turned to Arnot. "In fact, send falcons with Chevell's words to all manors as well as the castle, for who knows what Orbane might have done?"

"As you will, my lady," said Arnot, and then he and the men withdrew.

She sighed and peered into the flames of the hearthfire, yet she did not attend to ought there. Instead her mind turned toward the future and wondered what it would bring.

. . .

That night, in between snatches of restless sleep, Michelle tossed and turned and tried to get comfortable, yet it seemed she could not. Finally, she arose from her bed and padded to a window and threw wide the shutters. In the cold bracing wind, she peered out on the bright 'scape, the full moon above shining down. And running through her sleepless mind was the question she'd been gnawing upon all eve: *Who knows what Orbane might have done?*

And where are Raseri and Rondalo? Why haven't they— Oh, Mithras, what if Orbane caused a dread wind to carry the Drake and Elf away? Mayhap that's why we've not heard from them, and surely we should have by now. Are they, too, trapped in the Great Darkness beyond the Black Wall of the World?

Michelle did not sleep again that night.

43

Throngs

Under dark, brooding skies sped Hradian, to come in among snow-laden mountains, their grim jagged crags and rearing massifs looming all 'round. The peaks marched away beyond seeing toward starwise and dawnwise and duskwise bounds, and seldom did outside folk come this way, and then only if they were desperate, for this was the *Chaine Maléfique*, and herein did dreadful Trolls live. Yet Hradian felt no fear of these monsters, for, along with other dire folk, they were her allies. Besides, Orbane was with her, and he could easily keep them at bay.

Deeper into the bleak mountains she flew, until at last she espied her goal. Then down she spiralled and down, down toward a large gape of a cavern below, the opening yawning wide. She came to ground at the entrance, where she and Orbane dismounted. And standing just inside the mouth hulked an enormous being. Hideous, he was, and massive, some nine foot tall or so. And all about him was a terrible miasma, a rotting stench, like a burst-open animal lying days dead in a hot summer sun. He was dressed in greasy hides, and he had yellow eyes and green-scummed tusks that showed as he bared his teeth at the appearance of this twain.

As Hradian and Orbane started for the entrance, *"Stanna!"* demanded the Troll in a guttural growl.

Orbane paid him no heed and strode on. *"Stoppa!"* roared the huge creature.

Still Orbane trod forward, and the Troll stepped in front of the wizard.

Orbane muttered a word and made a gesture, and the monster stood rooted in place.

"Acolyte, I lend you a meager portion of my might; you may destroy this creature for trying to bar my way."

"My lord, is that—?" Hradian's words chopped short as she realized she was about to ask him if it were "wise." Instead, she pushed an upturned clawlike hand out toward the chest of the Troll and, with nearly orgasmic power pulsing through her, as if she were squeezing something, she slowly closed her fingers.

The Troll groaned but once, its face turning gray, and then it crashed down at her feet, dead ere it hit the stone.

On into the cavern strode Orbane, with a floating globe of arcane light preceding him and Hradian scurrying after. Twisting and turning, they followed the way as it wrenched deeper into the darkness. But at last they came to a torchlit hall, a number of Trolls therein, the stench nearly unbearable. And on an upraised dais and in a massive chair of stone sat one larger than the rest.

"Bolock!" called Orbane.

The Troll's yellow eyes flew wide in astonishment. "Lord Orbane?"

Orbane laughed. "Indeed, my old ally. And I have come to tell you that this time we will not fail."

Bolock turned to the other Trolls and snarled, "Down, fools! Can you not see Lord Orbane has returned?"

As Trolls groveled on the stone cavern floor, Orbane stepped to the dais.

Bolock grinned, his great tusks a dingy green in the yellow torchlight, and he said, "But I thought you were trapped in the—"

"I was, but I escaped."

Behind Orbane, Hradian's shoulders sagged, for it was she who had got her lord free, and yet he gave her no credit. Still, she understood that if the minions thought he had escaped on his own, then they would think him even greater than anyone could imagine. Nevertheless, she desired the praise that would come with recognition.

"I have a new plan, Bolock," said Orbane, "one that your throng will share in, and the rewards you and your like will reap will be unimaginable. . . ."

. . .

Over the next fortnight, Hradian ferried Orbane thither and yon throughout portions of Faery, where he exhorted his allies of old to gather from far and near. They went to the great grasslands to enlist the Serpentines and their scaled, cloven-hoofed steeds; to the hills to gather up the Goblins; to the swamps to command the Bogles to heed the call; and to other domains as well. Most immediately joined Orbane's cause; some delayed their decisions; still others refused him outright, those who were powerful enough to tell him no. The congress of Wyverns were among those who rejected Orbane's demand, their flames smoldering as a warning to the wizard that if he tried to use his powers they would incinerate him; although Orbane could have immobilized them, still he would not make enemies of these powerful creatures, and so he left in a rage of frustration.

Orbane did not approach some beings, for he knew they would not ally themselves with him, such as Lord Dread, who was the leader of the Wild Hunt. Neither did Orbane speak to such creatures as the Pooka, or Corpse-candles, or the Spriggans, and other such. For although some of those were deadly, still he needed an army for his plan, and they simply would not do, for some were wild, others stubborn, some cowardly, and still others independent with agendas of their own, hence would not yield to his command.

And after each meeting, as the witch flew the wizard toward the next goal, Orbane laughed at what fools these dolts were, expecting he would reward them. "No, no, Acolyte, my plan will rain chaos not only over all of Faery, but the mortal world as well. And as both the wise and the unwise alike flounder about in such madness, I will become master of all."

And so, from many parts of Faery, long marches began, dreadful allies all heading for a rendezvous with their lord and master. Bearing flails and cudgels and barbed spears and other such brutish weaponry, they came. And in the beginning, each croft and hamlet and village and town they encountered they pillaged and raped and slaughtered and burned. In their wake they left nought but ruins, and men slain and women murdered and half-eaten corpses of children torn asunder. Soon every dwelling or *ville* they came to they found abandoned, the inhabitants run away to hide in the hills or the forest or in other surround. Even so, the deserted steads and towns did not survive.

And in the temperate lands, from the screening foliage of nearby woodland trees and bushes and from the concealing stalks of field grasses, tiny beings followed the dreadful progress and noted the lines of the march, and soon wee Sprites went winging toward distant goals, while in the frozen realms, Ice Sprites watched long moments and then flashed away.

44

Geas

When her silver mirror went black, Gloriana staggered and fell weak, nearly swooning, and Auberon scooped her up in his arms and bore her to her bed, all the while calling for her ladies-in-waiting. He knelt at the bedside and took her hand in his and chafed her wrist and whispered to her, but what he said, Regar knew not. First one and then another and then two more Fairy maidens came rushing in. "My king," said the first, "we will attend her now." After a hesitant moment, Auberon kissed the queen's fingers and stood and motioned to Regar, and together they stepped from the room.

"I'm afraid it came as a great shock to her, to us both," said Auberon as they walked down the corridor. "We each thought him safe, locked away as he was, in the Castle of Shadows."

"My lord," said Regar as they entered another chamber, "the Wizard Orbane is your son?"

Glumly, Auberon nodded. "Blood of my loins, as is your mother."

"And yet you raised your armies against him in the last war."

"Oui. He had to be stopped, and without my aid it could not have been done . . . or rather, it could not have been done in time. I and the others delayed him until a solution could be found. Little did we know that two thieves would provide the key to defeating my son."

"Two thieves?"

"Valeray and Roulan."

"Valeray? Of Le Coeur de les Saisons?"

At Auberon's nod, Regar said, "But he is now a king."

"Oui, and Roulan is now a duke. 'Twas their rewards for the part they played in the war, for they are the ones who stole the amulets that brought Orbane down. My son's own magic did him in, just as foreseen by Lisane."

"Lisane? You know Lisane?"

"Oui. A lovely Elfmaiden she is."

Regar's eyes flew wide in startlement. "Elfmaiden? Lisane is an Elf?"

Auberon frowned. "You know Lisane?"

Regar's gaze softened. "She is my truelove."

"And yet you did not recognize her as an Elf?"

"I have not had dealings with Elves," said Regar.

Auberon laughed. "Ah, my petit-fils, did you not see her faint golden hue, much the same as yours?"

"But my own mère had a hint of *d'or* about her, and so I thought it but natural."

Auberon smiled and said, " 'Tis the glimmer of both Fairies and Elves, for we are much the same."

The intimate room they had entered was lit with soft light. A sofa and two comfortable chairs centered about a low table formed a conversation pit, and on a sideboard sat glasses and a crystal decanter filled with a deep ruby-red wine. At Auberon's gesture, Regar took one of the chairs, while the Fairy King poured a bit of the liquid into each of two goblets. He handed one to Regar and kept the other for himself and sat in the chair opposite.

Flic said I was to take neither food nor drink, for—

"Fear not, Grandson," said Auberon, with a smile. "I have not magicked the liqueur. Besides, I am not certain it would work against you, Fairy-blooded as you are. You may safely drink."

Regar hesitated but a fraction, and then took a sip. A warm glow slid down his throat and into his chest.

"It is made from bluebells and blackberries," said Auberon, sipping his own. "An old family recipe, very old. Someday I'll tell you how 'tis done."

An amiable silence fell between them, one that could not last, for dreadful events were afoot. Finally Regar said, "Well then, Grand-père, your only son, my mother's half-brother, my own *demi-oncle*, is now loose, and once again there will be war. Will you aid this time? Raise your armies and oppose your own son?"

Auberon sighed. "Oui, I must, for to do otherwise leads to chaos."

Regar nodded. "And will you and your good Fairies oppose him with your magic?"

"We cannot," said Auberon.

"You cannot?"

"Non. Gloriana has laid an unbreakable geas upon us all, herself included, and, by her fiat, neither Fairy magic nor Elven magic can be used to oppose her son."

"What of his armies? Can you use your numinous powers against them?"

Auberon's shoulders sagged. "Not while they protect Orbane. The queen's love for her only child has tied our hands, and our magic cannot oppose him . . . nor aid him, for that matter. No Fey magic whatsoever can be used."

"But you can fight his armies with sword and spear and such?"

"Oui, though we cannot bring them to bear against Orbane himself. As I said, the queen has tied our hands."

Regar frowned in puzzlement. "But, if Elven magic cannot be used against Orbane, then how is it in times gone that Lisane, an Elfmaiden, was able to see his downfall? And of recent she has read the taroc and again sees looming a great struggle, though this time not how it will end."

"Her magic is not in direct opposition, for it only speaks of possible outcomes and not sureties."

"I see," said Regar. They sat in silence for a moment, but then Regar took a deep breath. "My lord, would you stop someone who is neither Elf nor Fairy from taking your son's life?"

A tear slowly slid down Auberon's face, and he tried to speak, but could not. He looked at Regar in agony, and finally turned his face away.

"You would not oppose?"

At last Auberon found his voice enough to choke out, "I would not."

He would let others slay his son, though they can be neither Fairies nor Elves. And given the geas of Gloriana, I wonder if I, with Auberon's blood flowing in my veins, though dilute, can raise my sword or loose an arrow against their only son, my oncle, evil though he is. And if not I, then who, I wonder, will dare do the deed and reap the wrath of the Fairy Queen?

45

Compass

"My lady?" A lithe handmaiden bearing a glass-chimneyed candle crossed the chamber to come to the side of the bed.

Michelle struggled up from the tangle of blankets. "Oui, Amelie."

"My lady, Steward Anton and Sieur Laurent stand at the door."

Michelle swung her feet out from under the covers and caught up her robe. "Light candles, Amelie, and give me a moment, then let them in."

Shock registered on Amelie's face. "Into your boudoir, my lady?"

"Oui, Amelie, into my boudoir."

The princess stepped into her private bathing chamber and relieved herself, then splashed water upon her face to drive out the last dregs of sleep and took up a towel and blotted dry. When she stepped back into the bedchamber, Amelie stood by the door, and, at a signal from Michelle, the demure handmaiden, with blood rising to her face, summoned the two men in.

"Princess," said Anton, bowing, Laurent at his side bowing as well.

"We would not have disturbed you," said the steward, "but the Ice Sprites bring ill news."

"Ill news?"

"Oui. It seems a great army of Trolls is on the march."

"Where?"

"In the Chaine Maléfique."

Michelle nodded, for the Baleful Range was well entwined within the lore of Faery. "Whence are they bound?"

"Ah, my lady, that we cannot say, for with the twilight marges, a minor shift in where they cross could lead them somewhere altogether different."

"The Sprites say they move dawnwise through the mountains," said Laurent.

"Even so," said Anton, "we know not their goal, nor the best way to intercept them, should we wish our army to do so."

"No doubt they go to rendezvous with Orbane," said Laurent. He clenched his jaw in frustration, and then spat, "By damn, I am discovering fighting a war in Faery is nearly impossible, not knowing where anything goes. I say this: give me a good map and knowledge of the terrain, and the particulars on the numbers and composition of the enemy, and a well-trained army to lead, and I can take on any foe. Yet even though we have Winterwood fighters at our beck and good scouts as well, we have no maps of any consequence to even know where to go. Bah! Faery! Herein things are all entangled in a maze of twilight borders, where a trivial adjustment can throw one leagues upon leagues away from where one would like to be."

"We must depend upon the Sprites to guide us, Laurent," said Michelle softly. "Still, our aim is not to engage a Troll army, but to keep Orbane from realizing whatever goal he has in mind."

"Stop his armies and we stop him," replied Laurent.

"Perhaps," said Anton. "Even so, Princess Michelle is correct: we must not go haring off to engage a Troll brigade. Instead we must try to find Orbane and do him in."

"There is an old adage," said Michelle, "one my father often cited: cut off the head of the snake, and the body dies."

"I agree, my lady," said Laurent, "yet how do we find this particular snake?"

Michelle turned up her hands. "The Trolls will lead us to him, yet they are not the whole of Orbane's might, for, as reported by Chevell, the Changelings are allied with the wizard, too, and together they will be formidable."

"Forget not the Redcaps and the Bogles," said Anton. "In the last war they sided with Orbane as well."

As Michelle nodded, Laurent said, "I suppose we'll have to wait for more Sprites to report movements of others of Orbane's allies, then perhaps we can deduce where the muster will be. Still, I detest waiting until the whole of the enemy is assembled, for in numbers they gain strength."

"Oui," said Anton.

Laurent then added, "Had we our own armies gathered— those of the Forests of the Seasons, as well the one at the Castle of the Seasons—we could take on Orbane's separate legions one at a time, rather than when they are all together. Given the reports of the previous war with the wizard, I'm afraid we'll be rather thin to face the whole of his might."

"What of our allies from other realms?" asked Anton. "Surely they will add to our strength can we link up with them."

"The Sprites will guide them to us," said Michelle, "just as soon as we know where we need be."

Clearly agitated, Laurent blew out a great breath of air. "Damn the gods for making such a puzzle place as is Faery."

"Mithras!" exclaimed Amelie, who had been standing quietly by the door. "Oh, Sieur Laurent, do not tempt the gods to take retribution."

Laurent sighed and his shoulders slumped, but he said nought.

Michelle stood a moment in thought. "Anton, at dawn send

falcons to the others, and tell them what the Ice Sprites have seen. Say unto them that until we know where Orbane is, we simply must wait."

Michelle then turned to Laurent. "Sieur, we are all of us frustrated by unfolding events and our inability to head things off, yet have faith, for surely evil will not win in the end. Now I say let us regain our beds and try to get some sleep."

"Oui, my lady," said Laurent, and he and Anton bowed and withdrew.

Amelie extinguished all candles but one at the bedside and the one in her hand and then withdrew as well. Michelle blew out the remaining light and took to her bower, yet she did not sleep again that night.

.   .   .

By midmorning, falcons spiralled down from the skies above the other manors and the castle. And in those realms, Luc, Blaise, Roél, and Émile read the grim news.

It was on the practice field in the Autumnwood where warriors drilled at spears that Luc sat with Rémy in the stands and mulled over the falcon-brought message. And the armsmaster said, "Lady Michelle is right: we need a way of finding where Orbane doffs his cloak, for he is the head of the snake, a head we must lop off."

The prince nodded. "Finding Orbane is—" Of a sudden, Luc's voice jerked to a halt, and the elusive thought that had been skating on the fringes of his mind for nigh on a fortnight suddenly burst clear. He slapped himself in the forehead and leapt to his feet. "Rémy, Rémy, what an utter fool am I. We have no way of directly finding Orbane, but Hradian is another matter altogether." Luc spun on his heel and headed for the manor, the armsmaster hard after.

"My lord?"

"Ah, Rémy, we need to fetch the seer back here, madman though he is."

"Malgan, my lord?"

"Oui, Malgan and all his invisible companions."

"But, my lord, why?"

"I think I have something that will tell us where she is."

"My lord?"

"Come with me, Rémy, and pray that I didn't lose it, or that some servant hasn't cast it away."

They rushed into the manse and up the stairs and into the prince's quarters and to the large closet-chamber therein, Luc calling out, "Daimbert, Daimbert, where are you?"

The valet stepped out from the adjoining bathing room and looked about in puzzlement, for he did not see the prince. "Oui, my lord? Oui?"

Luc stuck his head from the closet. "Daimbert, hurry, I need to find my red waistcoat."

The valet bustled to the chamber and inside, where rack upon rack of fine garments hung. "Which red waistcoat, my lord?"

"The one I took with me to the faire. Surely it came back with the baggage train."

"Mais oui, my lord," said Daimbert. He stepped past several racks and to one with many different waistcoats. He fetched a red satin vest from among them and held it out. "Here it is, my prince."

Luc reached into the right-hand pocket and frowned, and then into the left-hand one. "Nothing! Daimbert, where is the vial I had in one of the pockets?"

"Vial, my lord?"

Luc's face fell, and he glanced at Rémy, despair in the prince's eyes. "Oui. A small vial, about so big." Luc gapped his right thumb and forefinger some three inches apart. "It had residue of an ocherous hue."

"Ah, my lord, I remember it now." Daimbert turned and stepped to a chest of drawers. "I did not know what it was, but even so, I put it here." He turned and in his hand was the vial Alain had found at the faire at the side of Luc's pavilion.

"Oui!" Luc carefully took the small container from the valet. "Rémy, if Alain was right, this held a potion crafted by Hradian. If so, it might lead us to her, and the key to the Castle of Shadows. Not only that, but where Hradian is, I'll wager we'll also find Orbane."

Now Rémy's eyes lit up. "Indeed, Prince."

"Fly like the wind, Rémy, and fetch Malgan, for I would have him use this to point the way."

. . .

In late afternoon of the following day, Rémy and a string of remounts returned with Malgan, the seer somewhat disgruntled at having to ride in haste, for his horsemanship was not the best, and, at the pace set and the sharp veerings through the woodland, he had nearly fallen from the saddle several times.

Even so, amid his twitchings and flinchings and mutterings and hissings, and his asides to his invisible coterie, he said, "This vial indeed was used to change someone into someone else, and the ocherous residue seems still to hold the essence of someone, for among many other things, it has merde and urine and *salive* and *sueur* and—" Of a sudden, Malgan snarled to the vacant air on his left: "Of course I know what it is! Be still!" Then he turned back to the prince and said, "And *humidité du vagin*; and all of these are from the same femme."

Luc grinned at Rémy. "As I hoped." Then he turned back to the seer. "*Très bon*, Malgan. Now tell me, will it point the way to this woman."

"Point the way? Oh, no."

"You mean you cannot find her?"

Malgan snapped his head 'round leftward and shouted, "No! Stay out of this!" Then he said to Luc, "Oh, I can tell you where she is at this moment, though to do so I will have to destroy the vial. If you want it to point the—I said I would handle this!—if you want to point the way, Prince Luc, you will have to fetch Mage Caldor."

Luc frowned. "Caldor?"

"The one Prince Alain calls a charlatan," said Rémy.

"Oh no," said Malgan, "he is not a charlatan." Malgan turned aside toward an invisible companion, if indeed there was one standing where Malgan looked, and asked, "What, what? Ah, I see." He turned back to Luc. "Prince Alain calls Caldor a charlatan because Caldor could not lift the curse laid upon him by one of the Seals of Orbane—Yes, I know! I know! Now be quiet! I am the one telling this!—but none of us could lift that dreadful curse, for Orbane's magic was simply too strong."

"Well, charlatan or no, Malgan, think you this Mage Caldor can use this vial to aid us in finding the woman whose residue of fluids reside herein?"

"Oui, I do, we do. He might be able to fashion a compass that will point to this femme. Otherwise I'll—All right! All right! I'm getting to it!—otherwise I can only tell you where she is at the moment I break it."

Luc sighed and turned to the armsmaster. "Rémy, where is this Caldor to be found?"

"In the Springwood, my lord."

"Then send a falcon to Roél, and have him get Caldor here as swift as he can."

"Oh, no. Oh, no, we are not going," hissed Malgan to someone unseen. "Yes, you are right: we did nearly fall off several times. No more fast rides. No more."

. . .

The following day a falcon came to Luc from Roél with the message that Garron, a member of the Springwood warband, had been dispatched with a string of remounts to locate Mage Caldor and hie him to Autumnwood Manor.

In the afternoon of that same day, winged Sprites came flying to Springwood, Summerwood, and Autumnwood Manors bearing the news that armies of Goblins were on the march from their holes in the hills—Redcaps and Dunters and Skrikers alike. Too, vast numbers of Bogles as well as Long-Armed Wights were moving 'cross land from swamp to swamp, and the Serpentines were riding in bands out from their grasslands. Also, Trolls had emerged from their icy mountains and were tramping across more temperate realms, and the Changelings were moving toward Port Cíent. And these dread forces were slaughtering and burning as they went. Surely they were all headed for a rendezvous with Orbane. But where? None but the marchers knew.

For that day and the next, falcons flew back and forth as well as to the Castle of the Seasons, and Sieur Émile ordered the gathering of the five armies under his overall command.

They would start out a three-day hence and rendezvous in the Autumnwood, for there the food was plentiful, the harvest ever for the taking.

· · ·

In Port Mizon, Chevell embraced Avélaine, and they kissed one another. He then stepped into a tender, and a crew rowed him out to his flagship—the *Sea Eagle*. As its anchor was hoisted, sails were lofted and bellied in the wind, and slowly, majestically, the craft got underway on the outflowing tide. And as the *Eagle* sailed from the bay, Chevell on the fantail turned to wave Avélaine au revoir; she to wave him good-bye as well. Then into the waters beyond went the *Eagle*, where awaited the king's fleet—eighteen ships of the line, each with a full crew as well as seventy-five marines aboard. Too, two swift sloops and a fast schooner sailed with the fleet—to act as scouts and escorts, to relay messages up and down the line, and to act as rescue vessels and take up any men in the water should a craft be sunk. And as the *Eagle* sailed from the bay, each of the other ships lofted canvas to match her pace. Three points to larboard of sunwise they fared, on a heading for Port Cíent, for somewhere between here and there they hoped to intercept the corsair fleet and the Changeling army thereon.

Long were the craft in sight from the headland where Avélaine had gotten to, but finally the last sail disappeared o'er the horizon. It was then and only then that Avélaine let the tears flow.

.   .   .

On the day after, two men and a string of lathered remounts galloped across the sward before Autumnwood Manor and came to a halt in the forecourt. As stableboys led the blowing horses away, the men stepped toward the entrance, where armed and armored members of the houseguard stood ward. A page, sitting on a side bench, leapt to his feet and waited as the men approached.

"Your business?" asked one of the guards.

"We are here at the request of Prince Luc."

"Your names, Sieur?"

"I am Garron of the warband of Springwood Manor, and"— he motioned toward the other man—"this is Mage Caldor."

"Oh, my," blurted the page, "the prince is expecting you. I will tell him you are here," and off he dashed.

"Sieur Garron, Mage Caldor, this way, please," said the warder, and he led the men through the entrance and down a short corridor to the welcoming hall within, and from there to an intimate chamber, with comfortable chairs and a writing desk. "There is a washroom with a pissoir through that door, where you may refresh yourselves," said the guard. "I believe Prince Luc will be along shortly. Need you ought, I will be at your beck." He stepped out into the hallway and closed the door behind.

Moments later, Luc strode in. He nodded to Garron, for they knew one another from the campaign some four years past in the realm of the Changelings. Luc introduced himself to Caldor, the mage a tall, bald man in rune-marked blue robes. Even as Caldor bowed, Malgan entered the room, the seer hissing to unseen companions and instructing them to be polite. The moment Caldor straightened and saw Malgan, a supercilious sneer filled his face.

"I did not know *he* would be here," said Caldor.

"Seer Malgan recommends you highly," said Luc.

Caldor's eyebrows raised in surprise.

"Malgan tells me you are just the mage I need to accomplish a critical task."

"Oh?" Now Caldor frowned at the seer.

"Shut up! Shut up!" muttered Malgan to someone unseen on his left. "You may not tell him he is an ass."

Garron coughed to cover a snort of a laugh, and Luc sighed.

"Never mind him," said Caldor, haughty disdain in his tone. "Just what is this task you would have me do?"

"I have a vial that contains the essences of a certain femme— salive, humidité du vagin, urine, sueur, and merde."

"Don't forget the drops of *sang* and *larme*," hissed Malgan.

"There are blood and teardrops in there as well?" asked Luc.

"Oui, my lord. Did I not say?" Malgan whipped to the left and whispered, "See what you made me do! I missed telling him." Then he turned back to the prince and said, "I think they were tears of pain, as if brought about by someone deliberately hurting themselves to cause tears to fall."

"Ah, oui, that makes sense, given the femme."

"My lord," said Caldor, drawing himself up to his full height, "I am not some common hedge witch; prince or no, I do not stoop to spells for fetching or finding femmes whom hommes lust after, no matter who they are."

Luc burst into laughter. "Oh, no, Caldor. I do not lust after this femme. Just the opposite: I would run her down and slay her."

"And just who is this woman you wish me to help you kill?"

"She is Hradian the Witch. And heed me, Caldor: where she is, so, too, I deem, will be Orbane, and I would slay them both."

Caldor gasped in fear. "You want me to help you against Orbane? Oh, non, non. I will not oppose him, for to do so would mean my doom, for spells cast against him rebound, and the caster is slain by his own power."

Seer Malgan also sucked air in through clenched teeth, for, until that very moment, he knew not Luc's aim.

"I do not ask you to help me slay Orbane, Mage Caldor, nor even to aid me to kill the witch. Instead, I would have you make for me a thing that will lead me to Hradian."

"I have not the skill," said Caldor.

"He lies, he lies," hissed Malgan, to someone down at his feet. "Can you not see he lies?"

Luc's eyes narrowed in perilous threat.

Caldor's shoulders slumped, and he sighed and admitted, "Oui, Malgan is correct. I do have the skill to make you what you desire. —But I will not accompany you on your quest."

"Non, non," muttered Malgan to the unseen host surrounding him, "we won't go either. Oui, oui, I promise."

Luc shook his head in mild disdain, and Garron growled in sheer contempt. And Luc said, "All I ask is that you give me what I need. And as for running down Hradian and thereby Orbane, neither of you need take part."

Caldor nodded, and Malgan whispered aside, "See, I told you."

Then Caldor said, "Let me see this vial for myself. And I will need a place to work, as well as the aid of someone with a fine hand at shaping glass and fashioning settings for gems, preferably someone who can work silver or gold—a jeweler or the like."

. . .

Three days later, with Steward Zacharie and Jeweler Minot and Armsmaster Rémy standing by, Mage Caldor presented Luc with a small gold disk-shaped case no larger than the palm of his hand. When its lid was opened, Luc saw inside and under glass a silver, arrow-shaped needle that pivoted on a silver axle, each pointed end of which rode within a tiny diamond hub, one in the golden base and one embedded in the glass lens. The arrowhead itself was ocherous in color, as if some of the residue within the vial had been affixed thereon. And no matter which way Luc turned himself or rotated the case, the needle pointed a bit to dawn of starwise.

"It will always point at the witch," said Caldor, "and will take you to her by the most direct route."

"You mean the shortest?"

"Oui."

"Does it in some fashion tell how far away she is?"

"Non. It only gives direction, not distance."

"Can you make one of these to find Princess Liaze?"

Caldor frowned. "Have you her vital fluids—sueur, sang, larme, the rest?"

Luc's features fell. "Non."

"Then I cannot," said Caldor.

Luc sighed and said in resignation, "I was afraid it would be so." He looked at Rémy and said, "Still, we can now run down the witch, as well as the wizard if he is with her."

"Beware, Prince Luc," warned Caldor, "for though it points to Hradian, the compass might lead you across a twilight bound into quicksand or lava or an ocean or into other dire ends, for the needle knows only which direction she lies and not what is along the way."

"Even so," said Luc, "it is a marvelous device, Mage Caldor." The prince turned to the jeweler and smiled and said, "Thank you, Minot." The craftsman returned the smile and bowed, and Luc inclined his head in acknowledgment.

"My lord," said Zacharie, "although the armies are even now on the way and will learn of this device as soon as they arrive, I would send falcons to the other stewards so they, too, will know the legion now has a means to find Hradian and most likely Orbane. For 'tis good news, and will strengthen the hearts of those of us who must remain behind."

Luc nodded. "By all means, Zacharie, let it be so."

.   .   .

Two days later, Blaise and the legion of the Summerwood was the first to arrive, followed close on by Émile and the command of the Castle of the Seasons. Then came Laurent's Winterwood force, with Lady Michelle and a Wolfpack leading. And two days after that, Roél and the Springwood warriors arrived.

At last they were all together: five battalions assembled under the leadership of Sieur Émile.

And on that same day, Sprites came winging from the sunwise bound with word that several throngs of Goblins and Bogles had come together in a great swamp, and, given the directions that other of Orbane's allies fared and their likely courses, it seemed they were on the way toward that same goal. Soon, mayhap, Orbane would have his horde ready to march, yet as to where he would ultimately lead his vast swarm, only the Fates and he knew.

46

Uncertain Trek

Émile peered at the unwàvering, silver needle. "Dawnwise of starwise—east of north? But won't that just lead us back into Valeray's demesne?"

"Not likely, Papa," said Roél. "There is only a limited segment of the starwise borders in each of the four forests that leads into Le Coeur de les Saisons. The rest of the starwise bound will take us elsewhere."

"Several elsewheres," amended Luc.

Émile shook his head and pointed sunwise. "But the Sprites came from that southern—er, sunwise—bound to bring us news of the great swamp where Orbane's allies muster. Shouldn't that be the direction we march?"

"This arcane compass gives us the most direct route to Hradian," said Luc, "and where she is we are likely to find Orbane."

"And the key to the Castle of Shadows," added Michelle.

"If she yet has it," said Blaise.

"But the Sprites can lead us to them as well," said Laurent.

"But not by the shortest route," said Roél.

"Argh!" growled Laurent. "Faery and its blasted twilight borders."

Émile looked at Luc. "Trust you this Caldor, this mage who will not fare with us into battle? We go by his word alone if we follow this device of his."

Luc stood a moment in thought. Finally, he said, "Malgan vouched for him, and Minot worked beside him and said Caldor seemed to know what he was doing."

Émile frowned. "Malgan?"

Michelle said, "One of the seers whose visions of darkness led us to believe our loved ones are perhaps trapped in the Castle of Shadows."

"And you trust him?"

Luc sighed and said, "In spite of the fact that he twitches and flinches and talks to invisible beings . . . oui, I trust him."

Émile pursed his lips. "And this Minot . . . ?"

"The jeweler who fashioned the compass."

"Hah!" snorted Laurent. "A cowardly mage, a jittery babbler, and a ring-maker?"

Luc's eyes narrowed, and his lips grew thin, and he looked directly at Laurent. "Oui, Sieur. Coward, babbler, and craftsman: I trust them all."

Laurent bristled, but Roél said, "Stand down, Brother. As for me, mage, seer, and craftsman, those three I know not. But I do know Prince Luc, and him I do trust. And if he says to follow the needle, then I for one am with him."

"As am I," said Michelle softly.

Luc held up a hand of caution. "If we do follow the needle, Caldor gave me a warning: it only shows the most direct route to Hradian and not the safest. We will need have Sprites with us so that at every bound we come to we know what is on the other side ere we cross, such that we fall not into an ocean as once did Roél, nor that we pass into a realm of fire, or come to other such dire ends."

"Oh, my," said Blaise. He gestured starwise. "One way the most direct, hence the quickest." He then pointed sunwise. "The other way perhaps safer, yet slower."

"Céleste and I did not exactly fall into an ocean, Luc," said Roél. "Yet I take your meaning. Boundaries can indeed be perilous, and crossing them blindly is best avoided."

Sieur Émile shook his head. "As for Sprites, I brought along Peti and Trit, but if we do indeed come to an ocean or a land of fire or other such, are we not then thwarted?"

"Oui, at least for a while," said Michelle. "But can we cross at another place, the compass will show us the shortest way from there."

"But, if I correctly understand these strange borders, that could be even farther away from our beginning, were we to take the sunwise route and follow the Sprites to the swamp."

"Here then is the dilemma," said Luc. "One way is sure and mayhap roundabout, while the other is uncertain and direct."

"I would have your advice," said Émile, looking about the table.

"I say we follow the compass—the quickest way—and hope for the best," said Blaise. "For if Orbane marches toward his goal, then too late is the same as never."

Laurent looked from Roél to Blaise to Luc to Michelle, and lastly to his sire. "Though I trust not this coward Caldor, still, if the compass will do as he has said, then I say Blaise is right, Père: let us take the direct way."

"I agree," said Michelle.

"So do I," said Roél.

Émile looked at Luc.

"I trust Caldor, for Malgan did vouch for him," said the prince.

Émile sat in thought for long moments. At length he said, "I cannot dispute the point Blaise made, for indeed too late is the same as never. But if we are wrong, then Mithras have mercy 'pon Faery."

. . .

And so they prepared to march on the course set by a silver needle. Even so, Luc added this advice: "Sieur Émile, I ween you should send Sprites to our allies, and have those armies follow them unto the swamp. Should they arrive ere we get there, have them wait unless they have no choice but to engage in battle, for 'tis better that we meet Orbane's throng with a unified strategy than to fight him piecemeal."

Émile nodded and said, "So shall it be." And Sprites were sent winging, though the courses they would lead the allies on were certain to be indirect.

Two days later, fully stocked for a lengthy campaign, long trains of mules and asses laden with supplies, the Legion of Seasons set out, following the route chosen by a silver needle pivoting on a silver axle hubbed in diamonds and encased in a glass-lensed golden box. A bit to dawn of starwise they went, Michelle in the lead riding point, the arcane compass in her hand. Out before her ranged a pack of Wolves, now and then taking guidance from their master's bitch. Riding on a tricorn Michelle wore were two tiny Sprites: Peti and Trit, who had come with Émile from *Le Coeur*. These two would report what lay across the twilight borders as they came to them.

There had been much controversy over Michelle taking the lead, for with Sprites at their beck, who needed Wolves? Yet Chelle maintained that the Wolves with their better hearing and ability to scent were needed on point, for they could sense things the Sprites could not. Sieur Émile conceded that she was right, after which Michelle added, "And since I am the only one who knows Wolfspeak . . ."

Thus, she rode on point.

Yet Armsmaster Jules would not let her ride out front alone, so he assigned to her an escort: Galion, a giant of a man and a fierce member of the Winterwood warband who four years past had performed exceptionally in the campaign against the Changelings.

A distance behind Chelle rode the vanguard, Roél in the lead, and behind them rode the bulk of the legion, first the Battalion of the Castle of Seasons, followed in order by the Springwood, Summerwood, Autumnwood, and Winterwood battalions, with elements of the supply train scattered throughout. Some three thousand men and five thousand animals in all, the army stretched out nigh some three leagues from front to rear as through the Autumnwood they travelled.

Nigh sunset two days later, they came to the starwise border, and the silver needle yet pointed steadily a bit dawnwise. Émile turned to Vardon, armsmaster of the Castle of the Seasons, and said, "Let us hope we do not pass back into Le Coeur, else all this march has been a waste."

While Michelle and the Wolfpack and Galion waited—Michelle with her bow strung and an arrow nocked; Galion with his mace in hand; and all those behind bearing arms as well—Peti and Trit flew through the bound. In but moments they came flying back. "It's a grassy prairie," said Trit, "with nothing in sight but rolling plains."

Michelle looked left and right and noted a laden cherry tree and an apple tree dangling fruit. She pointed them out to Trit and said, "Fly back and inform the vanguard precisely where to cross, then catch up."

"Oui, Princess."

As Trit shot away and Peti settled on the tricorn, Michelle gave a short bark, and the Wolves got to their feet and loped through, Michelle and Galion following. Into the twilight they went, the way growing darker and then ebon and then lighter, and, when they emerged, Michelle glanced at the setting sun, for more oft than not bearings shift 'round when passing through a marge, sometimes greatly, other times less, and once in a while not at all. On this occasion, although they had angled into the shadowlight heading a bit to dawn of starwise, they emerged heading due duskwise. Michelle flipped open the top of the arcane compass and saw the needle now pointed due duskwise as well.

They camped that eve on the broad plains, and for the next two days, both filled with drenching rain, they crossed the sea of grass, where antlered herds of shaggy yet deerlike animals fled before them.

Midmorn of the following sunny day, they passed into a mountain vale, with swift, icy streams leaping and cascading down stony slopes from snowy heights, where wild goats and large-horned sheep watched from among rocky crags as the army passed below.

And in this land of steep slopes, they acquired three hundred more fighters, swelling their ranks to three thousand three hundred.

One more day saw them crossing long, rolling dunes while a cold wind blew and filled the air with fine grit, and nought else moved across the land.

The next day they slogged through marshy lowlands, tall reeds swish-swashing as they went and blocking any line of sight for all but the Sprites, and then only when they were airborne. Gnats and biting flies and mosquitoes swarmed about them, and leeches feasted upon the unprotected legs of the horses and mules and asses, while red-winged ebon-bodied birds cawed and hurtled through the air just above the tops of the reeds, feasting upon the insects stirred up by the passage.

And thus did the army progress, where at every twilight marge they came to Trit and Peti would cross first to scout the way and make certain that no visible calamity awaited the march on the opposite side. And always would Chelle take a new bearing and follow the line of the needle.

The morning of the tenth day of the march, with their numbers now nigh four thousand, found them trekking through a realm of nought but blue flowers and flights of small yellow butterflies. And as Chelle opened the lid of the compass to take another bearing, she discovered the needle inching across the dial: leftward it gradually swung, starwise. She watched as it continued to edge along, and finally she raised a hand to call a halt. And she and Galion waited for Roél and the vanguard to catch up.

Roél spurred his horse forward and came alongside. "Is ought amiss?"

"The needle, it creeps," said Chelle, passing the compass to him.

Roél peered at the arcane device, then he looked at Chelle and said, "I deem the witch is on the move."

"As do I," said Chelle, nodding. "Think you Orbane's throngs are on the march as well?"

Roél shrugged and again peered at the contrivance. Peti flew down from the prow of Michelle's tricorn and perched on Roél's wrist and watched the needle's gradual progress. Finally she said, "Last night was the dark of the moon, an ill omen at best. Perhaps it was what Orbane was waiting for, there in the swamp, wherever it might be."

Again Roél shrugged, but of a sudden said, "Whoa!" and Peti gasped.

"What?" asked Michelle.

"The needle: it just whipped from northeast to south—er, starwise of dawnwise to sunwise." He handed the compass back to her, and Peti again took up her perch beside Trit in the prow of the tricorn.

Chelle looked at the needle and frowned. "Mayhap she just crossed a border."

"Ah," said Roél, nodding, "that must be it."

"It continues to gradually swing," said Chelle, "only now it creeps opposite."

By this time, Sieur Émile and Blaise rode up.

"Why are we stopped?" asked Émile.

"The witch is on the move," said Michelle, gesturing at the device.

"On the move?"

"Oui. And mayhap Orbane's army as well." Michelle handed the compass to Blaise, who glanced at it and then passed it on across to Émile, the latter taking it gingerly, as if it were a poisonous snake.

Émile watched as the needle crawled from sunwise toward duskwise. "Merde! I *knew* we should have followed Sprites instead of this—this *thing*!"

"Non, Papa," said Blaise. "The needle shows us the most direct route to the witch, and so, no matter what, we are closer to Orbane than we would have been had we gone the other way."

"But only if the witch is with the wizard," said Roél.

"I for one believe she is," said Michelle.

"So does Luc," said Blaise, glancing back along the line of horses and mules and asses to see the prince galloping toward them, Laurent farther back also riding this way.

Émile took another look at the pointer and sighed. "We'll simply have to wait until the needle stops ere we take up the trek again."

"But what if Hradian has gone away from Orbane?" asked Laurent.

"She could just as easily be going to him," said Blaise.

"What if she has gone away for a day or two or three or more to do some foul deed or other, then plans on going back?" countered Laurent.

"If so," replied Blaise glumly, "then we'll be chasing a wild goose o'er all of Faery."

"Merde! Merde, merde, merde!" spat Émile, glaring down at the device.

"Sieur," said Michelle softly, "I deem you had the right of it the first time: we simply must wait."

. . .

The army came to a complete stop, and all day Michelle and the others kept track of the needle as, at a snail's pace, it gradually inched 'round the dial, and time after time it instantly jerked across the face to take up a new bearing and then began to creep again.

Émile paced and ground his teeth and cursed the decision to

follow that cowardly mage's thing, a thing perhaps somehow gone awry.

Roél and Blaise and Laurent and Luc occasionally rode along the line of warriors and spoke with the warband leaders and the men, for nothing is so unsettling to an army as to be kept in the dark.

Trit and Peti played tag with the butterflies, while Slate and the Wolves slept, all but Trot, who stood on watch.

And Michelle kept an eye on the inconstant needle and prayed to Mithras that by using the compass they had not made a dreadful mistake.

47

Dark of the Moon

Flying all silk, the single-masted scout ship *Tern*, a swift sloop, ran toward the fleet from the fore, then came about along the windward side of the *Sea Eagle* and deliberately luffed a sail to match the slower speed of the larger ship. Her captain called out through his voice horn, "My Lord Chevell, a point to the fore and just beyond the larboard horizon the corsairs run in a line on a beam reach."

"How many?" called Chevell through his own megaphone.

"Two dozen, my lord: all two-masted dhows."

"And their course?"

"Some three points to dusk of starwise."

Chevell turned to his first officer. "Lieutenant Jourdan, run up the signals: all ships to come about, and to the starboard, away from the corsair line, for I would not have the foe know we are in these waters."

"Our course, my lord?" asked the small, dark-haired man.

"Three points to dusk of starwise. And have the line fall in behind the *Eagle*. We will run parallel to and out of sight of these brigands until I have relayed the battle plan to all commanders."

"Oui, my lord."

Chevelle looked at Delon, captain of the marines in the fleet. "They are on a direct course for Port Mizon, and have six more ships than we, as well as Changelings aboard."

The tall redhead shrugged and tapped the hilt of his sword and said, "Changelings to behead and turn into slime."

Chevell then took up his voice horn and called down to the sloop. "Captain Benoit, run along our line and make certain that all captains understand my orders: to come about to the starboard and fall in a line behind the *Eagle*. Too, have Captain Armond and the *Hawk* take the midmost position in the file."

"Oui, my lord. Is there ought else?"

"As soon as you have relayed the signal to the fleet to come about, have the *Sandpiper* and the *Gull* as well as your ship stand ready to dispatch the battle plan. —Now, go."

The *Tern* cinched up the luffed sail and ran up her own signal flags to echo those now flying on the *Eagle*, then came about and hauled to the windward of the remaining ships, pausing at each to relay Chevell's orders.

And with each ship in Avélar's fleet wearing around the wind, soon all had fallen in behind the *Eagle*, now heading in the direction of Port Mizon.

Two candlemarks or so later, the remaining scout ships—the sloop *Sandpiper* and the schooner *Gull*—came back into view from their duskwise and sunwise runs, and slowly they overtook the fleet, and shortly thereafter were ready to dispatch the battle plan.

"We have two advantages," said Chevell to Marine Captain Delon, "one, they know not we are here, and, two, 'tis the dark of the moon and the night will be black."

"A night attack, then?"

"Not quite, Captain. Instead, I plan to ambush the foe, to run toward the enemy in the predawn marks and come upon them just as dawn twilight fills the sky." Chevell unrolled a chart, and he placed twenty-four markers in a line upon it. "Here is the enemy fleet, with six more ships than we have. —And here is our force somewhat ahead and to their larboard." Chevell then placed eighteen markers in a parallel line on the left and to the fore of the enemy. "Now, Captain, just as will we, in the night the foe will be running with fore and aft lanterns to maintain their line."

"But if we run with lanterns," said Captain Delon, "they will see us— Ah, wait, you plan to course upon them unlighted, oui?"

Chevell smiled. "Just so, Captain, just so. —You see, on command, we will extinguish all our own fore and aft lanterns and swing starboard, and, with a following wind, we bear down upon them"—Chevell began moving the markers—"the last ship in our line taking on the last ship in their line, and our next to last taking their next to last, and so on. As we come into range in the dark, we will loose fire upon them, and slice behind their sterns, raking their decks with our own broadside fire as we pass through their line, like so, and then swing 'round to their starboard wales and grapple, and your marines will board the foe. If we have planned it just right, that should occur in the twilight of the oncoming dawn."

"But, my lord," said Lieutenant Jourdan, "if each one of our eighteen takes on eighteen of theirs"—he pointed to the leading corsair markers—"that leaves six of the enemy ships unengaged."

"Oui, Lieutenant, but those six ships are the six to the fore, and given their maneuverability and rate they sail, it will take them a full candlemark ere they can wear 'round and come at us, and by that time we should be ready for them."

"Ah, clever, my lord," said Delon. "Now I see why we take on the eighteen from the rear rather than from the front: 'tis to keep those six out of the fray for as long as possible."

Chevell nodded. But then the marine captain frowned. "My lord, the plan depends upon bearing down swiftly upon them, yet what if the wind shifts?"

" 'Tis unlikely, Captain, for this is the season of the steady trades, and we are to the windward of them."

"My lord," said Jourdan, grinning, "they ought to call you the Fox of the Sea."

Chevell laughed, but quickly sobered. " 'Twill not be an easy task, yet I ween we can catch them by surprise. Even so, they are not to be taken lightly, for not only are they able seamen skilled with cutlasses, but aboard their ships is an army of Changelings as well."

. . .

The *Tern*, *Sandpiper*, and the *Gull* swiftly relayed the battle plan unto all captains, and the three scout ships waited until darkness, and, taking turns, kept track of the enemy fleet. In the meanwhile, Chevell calculated: he knew that the sun would broach the horizon five and a half candlemarks after mid of night; yet enough dawnlight to see and be seen would occur a full candlemark ere then, and so he added that into his figures; too, he took into account the lead the king's fleet had over the corsairs, as well as the distance between the parallel courses of the two fleets—some twenty-two nautical miles. And given the wind speed and the rate at which the slowest ship in the king's fleet could close upon the foe, he reckoned that just after the midnight mark, they would have to turn on the intercept course. He relayed these figures to the other vessels, and he commanded his captains to set their sails so that all would come upon the foe simultaneously, or at least that was the plan; hence the slowest ship would run full out, while the others would reef their sails enough to match that pace.

And they hove on.

And the scouts brought word that the foe, as was their wont, yet sailed in a straight line, all benefiting from the wind on the beam.

And the constant trades blew.

And the ships of friend and foe alike sliced through the waters, one fleet knowing the other was there, one fleet sailing in ignorance.

Finally, a half candlemark after mid of night under the dark of the moon, Chevell gave the signal.

And ships turned on an intercept course, and then extinguished their bow and stern lanterns.

Risky was the plan, for close-sailing in a fleet in darkness could lead to collisions, yet Chevell had planned for that, for he kept a hooded lantern on the larboard and starboard of each ship, with orders to extinguish them the moment the top lookouts spotted the fore and aft lanterns of the foe.

And, so through the darkness did they sail, keeping their own line by the dim glimmers of hooded lights abeam.

Some two candlemarks after turning on the intercept course, the lanterns of the foe came into view of the lookouts, and the hooded lanterns of the king's fleet were extinguished. And moments later, the enemy's lights became visible to the men adeck.

Captains now counted the enemy ships, and struck courses on their own, each aiming his ship on an intercept heading to take on the foe assigned.

"Remember, men," said Captain Delon to his contingent of marines, "cut off the head of a Changeling, and he turns to slime. It is something about their shape-shifting nature that causes such to be."

And as Captain Delon instructed his immediate command, his lieutenants did the same on the other ships, all the marines well-trained in grappling and boarding and combat.

And the sailors aboard each ship stood ready at the ballistas, fireballs loaded on the racks, others in crates at hand, strikers and torches at the ready to be ignited.

And, at a closing angle, the king's fleet hove toward the foe in the darkness, guided by the enemy's own lanterns.

"Steady as she goes, helmsman," whispered Chevell.

"Oui, my lord," came the murmured response.

Sssshhhssh . . . Hulls sliced through the brine.

On they drew and on. . . .

But at last . . .

Some ships reached their goal slightly before others, yet all corsairs were taken by surprise, as "Loose fire," came the command, and strikers struck and torches ignited to light fireballs in turn. *Thnn!* sang ballistas, and flaming balls hurtled across the waves, the larboard ballistas to rake the foe to the fore, the starboard ones to hurl into the foe aft. Great lateen sails burst into furious flame, and *clk-clk-clk-* . . . *!* clattered ratchets as ballista bows were drawn and new fireballs laded. *Thnn!* more blazing missiles hurtled through the air to splash on masts and decks and upon awakening enemy, burning, flaming, destroying. Amid screams of men ablaze, the foe cranked up their own fire weapons, yet, for the most part, they could not bring them to bear, for the ships of the king's fleet were now directly astern each of their target ships and raking the corsair decks with their broadsides.

And then sailors haled the yards about and the attacking fleet swung 'round, bringing the king's ships' larboards to corsairs' starboard beams. Grapnel hooks flew to *chnk!* into enemy wales, and marines and sailors hauled to bring the hulls together. Even so, Changelings shifted shape, and in the firelight, hideous were their forms—beastly animals, unnatural creatures, dire flying things, and other such monstrosities. Arrows flew 'gainst these dreadful beings, wounding some, missing others, while some Changelings took to flight and dropped fire down upon the king's ships and men.

Sails burst into flame, as did marines and sailors alike, but still the king's men continued raking the enemy decks with missiles and fire and death.

Thdd! grappled hulls banged together, and, with swords in hand, marines and sailors yelled and swarmed onto enemy ships, to be met by dreadful Changelings as well as corsairs wielding blades of their own.

Fierce was the fighting, and on some vessels the enemy prevailed and swarmed onto the king's ships, and the decks ran red with blood and dark with slime and other colors of slaughter.

The *Hawk* went down in flames, burning even as she sank.

On the *Eagle*, Chevell and his men leapt over the wales to the dhow and engaged the corsairs and Changelings, for Delon's marines could not do it alone.

And amidst battle cries and screams and fire and death, the war at sea raged on. . . .

And the sky lightened as day crept upon the brine, unheeding of the butchery below.

But finally, the crew and marines of the *Eagle* prevailed, the corsair ship nought but a wreck, her sails burnt, her crew dead, the Changelings now nought but dark puddles of sludge.

But even as Chevell reboarded his craft, "Captain!" shouted Lieutenant Jourdan, "On the starboard beam!"

Chevell looked, and bearing down upon the *Eagle* came a dhow under full sail, and at her helm stood a monstrous Ogre, his features twisted in rage; and the crew of the oncoming corsair screamed in terror and some tried to intervene; they feared neither ship would survive such a collision; but the Ogre batted them aside, for he intended to ram.

"Loose fire!" commanded Chevell, and his men scrambled to obey. Yet the ballistas were slack, uncocked, for on that side of the ship their last raking fire had been loosed as they had clove between their own target ship and the one trailing after.

Clk-clk-clk- . . . *!* rattled the ratchets, yet ere a single fireball was loaded and loosed, with a horrendous crash the prow of the corsair slammed into the *Eagle*, and the hulls of both ships splintered and shivered, and water began pouring in.

"*Rraww!*" roared the great Ogre, and he ran forward and leapt onto the *Eagle*'s deck. Eighteen feet tall he was, and massive, and with mighty blows he smashed down masts, and slaughtered men, and rent marines asunder. Arrows flew, and the Ogre snarled in pain at these barbs, yet they slew him not. Chevell ran behind the hideous monster, and he clove his sword into the creature's heel and severed a tendon. The Ogre bellowed in agony, and swung 'round and smote Chevell, knocking him aside, and all went black for the vicomte.

And still the water poured in, and locked in a deadly embrace, the *Eagle* and the corsair went down into the brine, and the dhow yet tightly grappled to the *Eagle* sank with them both. The Ogre, unable to swim, shrieked in fear, and, in spite of flailing about in the waters, drowned, taking men under with him as he sank.

. . .

When Chevell came to he found he was entangled in the rigging of a broken spar, the *Eagle*'s flag affixed thereon. Painfully, he worked himself loose, and when he was free and clinging to the shattered mast, he looked about, only to see a corsair ship bearing down upon him.

48

Flotsam

Orbane kicked Crapaud aside and snarled, "Where are the Changelings?"

"I do not know, my lord," quavered Hradian, keeping her eyes downcast.

Orbane stalked to the edge of the flet and peered into the turgid waters. "Last night was the dark of the moon, Acolyte; they should have been here by now."

"Indeed, my lord."

Orbane frowned and looked dawnwise, toward the light of the just-risen sun. "I wonder . . . ?"

Hradian remained silent, afraid anything she might say would spur his wrath.

"Mayhap the corsairs have betrayed me," hissed Orbane. "—Acolyte, ride your besom along the intended line of march and see what delays them."

"How far should I go, my lord?"

Orbane rounded upon Hradian and bellowed, "Till you find them, fool! To Port Mizon or across the sea and all the way to Port Cíent, if necessary!"

Hradian scrambled hindward and snatched up her broom and moments later flew up above the swamp and away.

Still trembling, through one border and then another she arrowed. And in but three candlemarks she came to Port Mizon, and as of yet she had seen no army of Changelings making their way across land.

And so, out over the ocean she hurtled, now on a course for Port Cíent, three points to dawn of sunwise.

. . .

And farther out in the sea, Vicomte Chevell clung to the spar and watched as the corsair clove the water on a course directly for the flotsam of combat, directly on a course for him. And he gritted his teeth and looked about for a weapon he could use, should they take him aboard the dhow. But he saw nought but bits of wreckage that had floated up from the *Eagle* as she and two corsairs had gone to the bottom, along with her crew and those of the foe and the Changelings led by the Ogre.

Nothing. No weapon in sight. But I think it matters not, for they'll merely spend an arrow or two and do me in.

And so Chevell waited and watched as his doom drew nigh.

And the ship, she wore around the wind, as if coming to tie up to a buoy. Her lateen sails fell slack as she nosed into the trades, and her headway dropped off until she moved no more.

And then someone peered over the rail and a voice called out, "My lord, might I give you a lift?"

'Twas Armond, captain of the *Hawk*, that ship, too, now resting on the bottom.

Even as a line came snaking through the air to splash into the water at Chevell's side, tears sprang into his eyes, and he managed to croak, "Indeed, Captain, though I find a swim now and again pleasant, I would enjoy the ride."

Armond laughed as Chevell took up the line, and the crew made ready to reel the vicomte in, but then Chevell cried out, "Wait!" And he paused a moment to retrieve the flag of the *Eagle* yet attached to the shivered mast. When he had it well in hand, he called out, "Heave ho," and the crew drew him in and up and onto the deck of the corsair dhow.

Dripping, he clasped Armond's hand and said, "I thought you gone down with the *Hawk*."

"Non, my lord, I and my crew and my complement of marines simply took on this corsair, and though the *Hawk* sank, still I had a ship to command. I call her the *Hawk II*."

"Nicely done, Armond. Indeed, nicely done."

"My lord, I now turn over the command of this vessel to you."

"Oh, non, Armond, it is your ship, and I am merely a passenger."

Armond inclined his head in acknowledgment, and then gave orders to get underway, and the great long sails were haled about to pick up the wind and the dhow began to move.

"What of the battle, Captain?" asked Chevell.

"It yet goes on, my lord, and I plan to rejoin it, for I have taken up more than enough men from the waters to sail into combat again."

"Indeed, and I am one of those taken up," said the vicomte. "Just give me a blade and some dry clothes, and I will be glad to join in."

. . .

They sailed on a course to intercept a corsair fleeing from the fight, and, by subterfuge and acting as would fellow pirates, they drew alongside the dhow, her decks and rigging showing signs of fire, and her crew appearing shorthanded. *"Ahoy, lá!"* called Chevell, using the tongue of the corsairs, for the vicomte had been one of their own long past.

"Quem são você!" replied the enemy captain.

"He wants to know who we are," murmured Chevell, and he called out, *"A Lâmina Vermelha!"*

"What did you tell him?" asked Armond, even as they drew closer to the enemy dhow.

"I said we were the *Red Blade*, the name of my old ship."

The corsair captain then shouted, *"Eu sei de nenhuma Lâmina Vermelha."*

" 'I know of no *Red Blade*,' " translated Chevell.

By then the *Hawk II* was close enough, and, at a sharp command from Armond, grappling hooks sailed through the air and thunked into the wales of the corsair, and arrows slashed across the space between, felling foe even as marines haled the two ships hull to hull.

The fight was short, for not only were the corsairs surprised, but they were disheartened as well, for they had suffered great losses ere the *Hawk II* had come upon them.

They quickly surrendered, did the corsairs, and were taken prisoner.

Then Chevell took command of this ship and flew the flag of the *Eagle* from the standard at the taffrail.

Half of the crew of the *Hawk II* stepped onto the deck of the *New Eagle*, and together they struck a course for the few ships yet engaged in battle on the sunwise horizon. Yet by the time they got there, the enemy had been done in, their ships burning furiously as they went down.

And so, a ragtag group of nine ships, two of them dhows—all with decks aslime with the remains of Changelings, masts and sails showing char and burn—took on survivors picked up by the *Tern* and the *Sandpiper* and the *Gull* and finally set sail for Port Mizon, their holds full of human prisoners, their battle this day done.

And as they cut through the waters, Chevell looked up to see a crow soaring high above, the ebon bird to turn on the wind and fly toward Port Mizon as well. Chevell frowned and wondered just what a crow might be doing this far from land, but soon the bird was out of sight and he questioned it no more.

· · ·

Nigh sundown, Hradian came flying back to the swamp, and she lit upon the flet of her cote and trembled to tell Orbane the news. Yet she had no choice.

"Well?" he demanded.

Hradian fell to her knees upon the floor and buried her face in her hands and pressed her forehead to the wood. "My lord, the corsair fleet is gone, sunk, and nought is left of it but bits of wreckage floating upon the waters."

"*What?*"

"My lord," mumbled Hradian, "all I saw in addition to the flotsam were a few of King Avélar's ships escorting two captured dhows and heading toward Port Mizon; all ships were scarred by fire, and their crews were sparse. I deem there was a great battle, and the corsairs and Changelings are no more."

Rage suffused Orbane's face, and he looked about for someone to punish, and though throngs of Goblins and Bogles and Trolls were camped thither and yon in the great swamp, Hradian was the only being at hand, and so he stepped forward to where she lay trembling. . . .

.   .   .

In the plains of blue flowers and yellow butterflies, Michelle waited long moments ere speaking, but finally she said, "The needle, it has stopped moving."

Sieur Émile looked up from his evening ration of jerky and tack. "Stopped, you say? Well and good. What be our new course, Princess?"

"The very same as the old course," said Michelle, frowning. " 'Tis the very same."

Gathering Storm

As warders watched the silver needle throughout the night, it remained fixed dawnwise. And when the encampment roused in the morn, dawnwise the needle continued to hew. And so, off they set, four thousand strong, riding and tramping toward the just-risen sun. And as they marched, one of the distant outriders assigned to the right flank came galloping toward the vanguard and sounded a horn. Roél spurred his mount forth to meet him, and, following Wolves, Michelle and Galion on point slowed their pace and watched.

And the outrider and Roél met a short distance away from the main body.

"My lord, good news," said Bayard, pointing back the way he had come, "a force of fifty knights leads an army of two thousand. They follow Sprites, and their leader is a chevalier named Léon, and he says they are from the realm of Château Bleu."

"Ah, Léon. I know him, Bayard." Roél glanced back along the train. "He is Prince Luc's steward when Luc is in the Autumnwood. —Come, let us take this good news to Sieur Émile, and then to Prince Luc."

"There is more good news, my lord," said the outrider.

"More?"

"Oui. Léon's Sprites tell me that when we cross the next border, we will be in the realm where lies the swamp we seek."

. . .

"Acolyte!" called Orbane. "Up from your bed. I need you to lend me your power."

"My power, my lord?" said Hradian, struggling up from her cot, wincing because of her bruises. "But it is so minuscule compared to yours."

A twist of rage flashed across Orbane's face at being even obliquely questioned. Still, he reveled in the fact that she had rightly seen in comparison to him she was all but insignificant. "Nevertheless, Acolyte, I would have it, for this day I will cover the sky with darkness, and, when that is in place, then on the morrow I will raise the putrescence, and then we march."

. . .

Regar looked at Auberon, the Fairy Lord yet somber. "My lord, though the queen is indisposed, and your son is free, although we cannot use Fairy magic or Elven magic 'gainst him, still we must needs raise your army, else the whole of Faery and the mortal world will likely be lost to him."

Auberon sighed and nodded, and stepped to a bell cord and tugged it. Moments later a page appeared.

"Fanir, bring me my horn, for I would summon the army."

As the page darted away, Regar looked at his grandfather in puzzlement. "My lord, a horn?"

"Oui."

"But will it be heard?"

Auberon smiled. "Indeed, though only by the Fey."

"But we are underground . . . under the hills."

"Even so, mon petit-fils, it will be heard."

Regar shook his head and sighed. "There is much for me to learn about my kind, quart-sang—quarter-blood—though I am."

In that moment the page returned, and in his grasp was a silver trump. He gave it over to Auberon.

"How long will it take for the army to muster?" asked Regar.

"They will be here within the day," said Auberon. Then the Fairy King raised the clarion to his lips and sounded a call, and the cry rang throughout the hollow hills and beyond.

. . .

Even as Roél and the outrider galloped back toward the long column, Peti and Trit gasped.

"What is it?" asked Michelle.

"The Fey Lord has summoned his army," said Trit.

"Fey L—the Fairy King?"

"Oui," replied Peti.

"And you know this how?"

"He has sounded his horn."

"But I heard nought," said Galion.

" 'Tis not meant for your ears," said Trit.

Galion grunted but made no other comment, yet Michelle said, "If the Fey Lord is mustering his legions, it means Prince Regar has succeeded in his mission." She glanced hindward at the vanguard, where Roél and the outrider had gotten to. "You must fly back and tell Sieur Émile. It might change his battle plans to know the Fairy Army will come."

. . .

Gesturing at the sky and shouting out arcane words, Orbane stood on the flet, Hradian beside him, and directly high above a cloud began to form—a dark cloud, an ominous cloud, a great tower of blackness slowly building up and up. And soon lightning began to flash within its bowels and thunder boomed, yet no rain came flashing down. And still Orbane called to the sky, and the monstrous dark began to spread, even as it continued to grow upward.

And Hradian sagged under the drain on her vigor. "Crapaud," she managed to croak, and the bloated creature waddled to her side. "Crapaud," she whispered as she touched him on his forehead, "lend me your power."

And the great toad belched but once and then fell somnolent.

. . .

Angling in from sunwise and following Sprites, the Château
Bleu contingent slowly merged with that from the Forests
of the Seasons and others. And Léon, sighting the crimson
and gold flag of the Autumnwood, gave over command to the
château armsmaster and then spurred his horse toward the
banner.

"My Lord," said Léon as he fell in alongside Prince Luc, "I
turn over to you *le Bataillon du Château Bleu*."

"Non, Léon," replied Luc, " 'tis yours to retain, for I am
in command of the Autumnwood battalion. It is Sieur Émile
in charge of this legion, and, just as are all the others, your
force will be at his disposal. He is seasoned in war, and he and
his sons—Roél, Blaise, and Laurent—have been in many cam-
paigns. And so, the Battalion of the Blue Château is yours to
command under his leadership. Now come, let us ride forward
to meet him."

Luc heeled his horse into a canter, and with Léon coursing
alongside, ahead to the van they went, where they dropped into
a walk aflank of Sieur Émile.

After the introductions had been made, Émile broke into a
broad smile. "You bring fifty chevaliers? Mithras, but that is
splendid news. I was beginning to wonder if we could prevail
with the few we have."

"Forget not, Sire," said Roél, "there might be more on the
way. And certainly the Fairy King will bring his fey knights to
our side."

And on they rode, and they were joined by Laurent and
Blaise, as well as Petain and Georges, two of the commanders
they had acquired on the march. And they spoke of strategy
and tactics, and of the best way to use the windfall of a half-
hundred chevaliers, Léon giving and taking in the discussion
among his battle peers.

. . .

They crossed the twilight marge in midafternoon, to come under dark and ominous skies. And the silver needle and the Sprites who had been in this region before agreed that the great swamp lay a point to sun of duskwise, hence in that direction did they fare.

The land itself was of rolling hills, dotted here and there with small groves and thickets, while rough grass and wild weed covered the rest. In the distance starwise, low mountains loomed and streams flowed down from the heights.

Accompanied by the Wolves, Michelle yet rode on point, now escorted not only by Galion but also by two of the knights of Château Bleu. Sprites ranged out before them, now and then flitting back to say what lay ahead. And as they went onward, the cast above, dark as it was, grew even blacker, and lightning raged and thunder roared, and light stuttered within the ebon gloom above, and dimness lay over all.

In late afternoon they approached a long rise in the land that went up and up to a broad ridge, running down from the distant mountains to starwise to stretch horizontal for a way, only to drop off sharply into hills leftward. And waiting on the near side of the crest of the ridge, as foretold by the Sprites, were another two thousand men. A man named Bailen led them, and he rode forth to meet with Sieur Émile.

"Just beyond that rise," said Bailen, lifting his voice to be heard above the roar of thunder, "the land gently falls for a league or so to come to a broad plain, and another league on lies the swamp. Except for my hidden warders, I have kept my men on this side of the slope so as not to alert Orbane as to our numbers. —Would you care to see, my lord?"

"Indeed," replied Émile. "For much needs to be planned."

And so he and Bailen rode upslope and dismounted just this side of the crest. They walked to the top, and, under black, roiling skies, Émile took in the view. The ridge slowly fell away and into a shallow, ever-widening valley. Off to the right the land rose steeply; to the left it turned into rolling hills, where the ridge itself dropped sharply to join them. But in between and at the bottom of the league-long slope lay the broad plain. And some two leagues away from where Émile took in the view stood the beginnings of the mire.

The swamp was vast and fed by streams and rivers flowing down from the mountains to starwise and the hills sunwise; the morass stretched out for as far as the eye could see.

"How is the land on the plain? Soft, treacherous, or does it provide good footing?"

"My lord, I do not know, for I got here but this morn, and I would not give our presence away to the foe."

"What say the Sprites?"

"My lord, they are not of a size to gauge the pack of the soil, for to them even soft loam seems good footing."

"I and my Wolves can go in the night," said Michelle softly.

Émile turned to see the princess had come up to take a look as well.

"My lady," said Émile, "I would not have you—"

"We have been through this argument before, Sieur, and again I say, there is none better to take on this task."

"Oui, but—"

"Sieur, I insist."

Émile took a deep breath and slowly let it out. "Then I will send Galion to—"

"Sieur, non! Where one person and seven Wolves can go in stealth, two-and-seven more than doubles the risk. My pack will not be seen, and I have been training with them, whereas Galion has not."

"But, Princess—"

"Sieur Émile!"

Again Émile took a deep breath, and slowly let it out. Finally he said, "No unnecessary risks."

"No unnecessary risks," agreed Michelle.

. . .

Splatting through the swamp, the Serpentine scout rode at a gallop, his scaled steed running flat out. The vertical pupils of the rider's viperous eyes were open to the full, and his way in the dismal mire was lighted by the nearly continuous barrage of lightning above.

At last he came to where he could see the witch's cote standing on stilts and surrounded by a quag of turgid water, and he called out for her to attend.

Hradian barely heard the cry, for, just moments before, Orbane had completed his spell casting. The dark pall above was now more than sufficient to carry out his plan. And so he let her enthrallment lapse, and she in turn released Crapaud. She was drained of nearly all energy, and she lay in a collapsed heap, sweat streaming from her body.

"See what he wants, Acolyte," demanded Orbane.

Hradian crawled to the edge of the flet, and she croaked out, "Speak," her voice but barely above a whisper.

"My lord and master Orbane, there is an army of some eight or ten thousand humans just beyond the dawnwise brim of the swamp."

"My lord," whispered Hradian, "he says—"

"I heard what he said, Fool!" raged Orbane. Then he shouted out, "Humans? Only humans? No others?"

"Some Sprites, my lord."

"Ah, good," murmured Orbane. "Then my sire is not with them. I heard his horn this morning, but it will take a while for the Fey to assemble, and by the time that is done, I will have succeeded. Yet these pests of humans now think to beleaguer me. Bah! Without my father they will easily fall. And I must keep them from delaying the lifting up of the putrescence." Then he shouted to the Serpentine scout, "Bring Bolok to me! Now!"

. . .

Given the dark of the overcast, night came on uncertain feet. Yet at the point when the blackness was complete but for the lightning above, Michelle and Slate and Dark and Render, Shank, Trot, Loll, and Blue-eye slipped up the rise and over and down and headed toward the plain below. The Sprite Trit rode in the prow of her tricorn.

Down they went and down, the Wolves raising their muzzles and taking in the air, taking in scent, and by the stutter of lightning they could see the way ahead.

They came to the edge of the flat, and there Michelle paused, and under the violent coruscations of the churning skies they could see the dark beginnings of the vast swamp to the fore.

"Oh, my," said Trit in dismay, in between thunderous booms. "What a dreadful place that is."

"Dreadful? Why so?"

"Princess, at the bottom of every swamp lies great sickness, a sickness whose very vapors can cause the ague and boils and other such horrible manifestations of its terrible strength, and even a short exposure to this ghastly effluence is deadly to Sprites and lethal to humans if either remain too long in its grasp."

"What of its effects upon Goblins and Bogles and Trolls and other such beings?"

"Oh, my lady, it harms them not, for Goblins and Trolls are akin to Bogles, who themselves live in swamps."

"And the Serpentines?"

"The Serpentines and their mounts are more snake than people and steeds, and such corruption harms them not."

"Well then, Trit, if we can choose our battleground, let it be on this plain and not in the midst of the mire."

"But only if the soil is firm," said Trit, "or so Sieur Émile said."

"Let us test it," said Michelle, and she gave a soft growl, and Slate led the Wolves onto the plain, Michelle following after and probing with a slender, sharp staff.

. . .

Among the roars of thunder, "Bolok, you are the *cham* of my armies," said Orbane, looking down at the great Troll standing waist-deep in the water at the edge of the flet. "I would have you lead them against these humans. By no means let the humans enter the swamp until my spell casting is done. Then it won't matter."

"Humans?"

"Oui. There is an army of them on the dawnwise marge of the swamp. Ten thousand or so."

Bolok laughed. "Ten thousand? Why, my Trolls alone could slaughter them all."

"Non, Bolok, for I need make certain that you protect me on my way to the goal. Hence you will use all under my command to do this ragtag army in."

"All, my lord? All forty thousand?"

"Oui, all forty thousand. And heed me, more are on the way; if they arrive in time, then throw them into the battle as well, for you must keep the ragtags from disturbing me as I maintain the darkness above and cast the second great spell."

"As you will, my lord," said Bolok.

"Then go, and go now, and destroy them all or, at a minimum, keep them at bay."

Bolok laughed and turned and waded through the scum-laden waters to round up the throngs and give them their orders.

. . .

In the hollow hills, Regar and Auberon waited as the Fey army came together, Fairies riding from all directions upon their splendid mounts. They wore silver-chased bronze armor polished to a high sheen, and their weapons were bows and arrows as well as long spears, pointed at both ends, one tip for lancing, the other for stabbing down upon a foe. Girted at their waists were finely honed sabers, and strapped to their thighs were keen long-knives.

"My lord," said Regar, "are we not ready to ride?"

"Nearly," said Auberon.

Regar stopped his pacing. "Do you know where we should go?"

"When we looked through the queen's silver mirror, I recognized a witch named Hradian, and behind her and my son I could see what appeared to be a swamp, and that's where the witch has an abode. Too, I believe I know the goal of my son, and there is a pass he must fare through to get from the swamp to his target. It is in that pass where we'll make our stand."

"Well and good," said Regar. "I will be glad when this day is come to an end and the army is ready to hie, for I am in haste to ride."

"As am I," said the Fairy King, "and this day is nearly done."

"Hai!" exclaimed Regar, eager to be off, for somewhere Blaise and the others were waiting, yet what Regar had temporarily forgotten was that time steps at a different pace in the Halls of the Fairy King.

.   .   .

Michelle looked across the assembly of leaders, and raised her voice to be heard. And in a lull in the thunderous skies she said, "Until you are nigh upon the swamp itself, the plain is firm, Sieur Émile."

"Good. Did you"—Émile waited as the heavens roared—"or the Wolves see or sense any foe?"

"Non. All was quiet but for the storm above, though there yet falls no rain."

"I have not seen skies like this ere now," said Roél.

The others chimed their agreement.

All commanders and armsmasters and warband leaders were gathered to plan the morrow, assuming they could draw Orbane's forces out onto the plain.

After giving her report, Michelle withdrew, for with no

316 / DENNIS L. MCKIERNAN

scouting to be done, or at least no scouting that she and the Wolves might accomplish, she felt her role would be that of one of the archers. Laurent would tell her where to be in the fight to come.

And even as the planners sat in council, Chelle and the Wolves went back to the crest of the slope, and they watched as lightning flared to illuminate the land below. Finally, Michelle turned to go back into the encampment, yet a flow of movement caught the corner of her eye. At the next lightning flare she saw a great blot of darkness moving down the starwise slopes toward the swamp. Again lightning stuttered across the sky, and this time she could see that it was a great throng of Goblins, perhaps as many as ten or twelve thousand. And then the leading edge of the swarm reached the swamp and slowly the mire engulfed them.

She and another of the warders standing atop the ridge took this news to Sieur Émile and his commanders. Émile sighed and said, "It's just more we have to face."

"Pah!" snorted Laurent. "Goblins? We'll make short shrift of them."

Luc looked at the eldest of Émile's get and slowly shook his head.

And the planning went on, and they argued on how best to draw Orbane's forces out.

Little did they know that even then Bolok and an army forty thousand strong, soon to be fifty thousand, force-marched for the edge of the swamp to do battle with them.

Clash

During the flashes in the night the allied warders discerned movement against the black wall of swamp lying some two leagues away, yet what this stirring might portend, they could not clearly see. They notified Sieur Émile, and he in turn sounded the alert and called the brigade commanders to him. And as the army stood armed and armored and ready, they met to consider what to do. And none did note when Michelle and the Wolves slipped away from the encampment, not even the sentries on duty, so stealthy were she and the pack. Nor did they note when Michelle and the Wolves returned, slipping unseen through the line. They made their way to the war council and reported what they had seen, and the commanders, after a moment of disconcertment that she had done such a foolhardy thing, then did pay close heed.

"I drew nigh enough to see by the lightning that Goblins and Bogles and Trolls and Serpentines are gathering on the edge of the mire. Thousands upon thousands of them; I did not get an accurate count."

"Did it seem they were preparing to mount an attack in the dark?" asked Bailen.

"I think not," said Michelle, "for many lay down to rest or to sleep."

"Nevertheless," said Émile, "we must make ready should they come."

"I and my Wolves will take a forward station," said Michelle, "and should the foe—"

An uproar drowned out her words.

"Non, I forbid it!" snapped Émile. "Going as you did was foolish enough, but I'll not—"

"My lord, who else?" asked Michelle. "Who else has the skills to slip unheard and unseen through the darkness but me? And who other than the members of my pack can scent danger as it comes?"

Laurent shook his head and spat a low oath, but Luc said, "Send the Wolves, Princess, but you stay nigh the top of the ridge, and should the foe begin movement this way have the pack bring word, and we will meet them on the downside of the slope and attack from the high ground."

Michelle's eyes narrowed, but she then gave thought, and finally she said, "Well and good."

. . .

After a sleepless night, dawn came late under the dark roiling sky with its lightning and thunder and churn. But when the glimmer of dim day finally made its overdue appearance, arrayed in a long arc out on the plain before the way into the swamp stood Orbane's throng.

"My lord," said Armsmaster Vardon, "it appears we are outnumbered five or six to one."

"Oui," replied Émile, though at the moment the count of the enemy did not overly concern him. Instead, he surveyed their deployment, noting the disposition of the foe, and strategy and tactics tumbled through his mind.

Finally, he said, "I need an accurate estimate of the numbers and kinds of the foe. And call for the brigade commanders to join me, for I would confer with them."

. . .

Orbane swallowed a vial of the potion Hradian had made at his instructions. It was an elixir of protection she had concocted once long ago for her and her sisters and Orbane. It was the time they had, as a test, denuded a small realm of all plant and animal life, much to the dismay of an impervious rocklike creature high on a mountainside.

Hradian, too, drank a vial of the elixir, for this was the day when Orbane would raise the putrescence.

Under the dark and raging skies they stood on the flet of Hradian's cote, and Orbane peered into the turgid murk below.

"Lend me your power, Acolyte," he demanded.

"Oui, my lord," said Hradian, even as she in turn added Crapaud's power to her own.

And Orbane began to whisper and gesture down at the slime-laden waters, and a thin tendril of bilious vapor rose up through the ooze and the water and began to blossom, spreading outward, gaining in volume, the tendril becoming a cord and then a rope and then more, and the swamp water whirled and gurgled, turbulent eddies spinning away. Faster and faster spewed the yellow-green gaseous upsurge, vomiting forth from the swamp under-bottom. And it began spreading wide as it bellowed out. And the leaves on nearby trees drooped, and hummocky grasses sagged. And Orbane continued his sibilant whispering, as from a churning vortex the putrescence erupted.

.   .   .

"Why do they not attack?" asked Laurent.

"I deem they wait for us to make the first move," replied Luc. "Likely they plan a trap."

Standing beside Luc, Émile nodded and said, "Note how they are arrayed: Goblins with Goblins, Bogles with Bogles, Trolls with Trolls, and mounted Serpentines on the right flank."

" 'Tis their cavalry, Sieur Émile, these Serpentines," said Léon.

"Mithras," said Blaise, "but there must be two hundred Trolls there in the center of the line."

The commanders stood on the ridge and surveyed the enemy

standing two leagues away. They were joined this day by Michelle, for as Émile had said, "I will not have you running off willy-nilly without my express command." And so, disgruntled, she sat to one side listening, with Slate and the others flopped down nearby.

"How many heavy crossbows have we altogether?" asked Bailen, adding, "I have in my brigade twenty."

Émile frowned and said, "I have a total of twenty-five."

Petain glanced at Georges and said, "Between us, we have ten."

"That adds up to fifty-five heavy crossbows," said Roél, "not enough to slay two hundred Trolls in one volley. Of course, can they get off four shots apiece, and if each is a kill then it is more than enough. Yet that is an unlikely scenario, given the time it takes to cock and reload and loose, and the Trolls will not be standing still."

Léon glanced at Luc and said, "Then, after the first barrage, I think it's up to my knights to deal with the Trolls, even as the heavy crossbows are made ready for a second volley."

"Whoa, now," said Blaise, "that means your fifty knights will be outnumbered by the Trolls at a minimum some three to one, at least until more are brought down by the crossbows."

"I realize that," said Léon grimly.

"But what of the Serpentines?" asked Georges. "Aren't the knights more useful in bringing them down?"

"Oui," said Sieur Émile, "they would be, yet I think our own cavalry can deal with the Serpentines."

"You have a plan?" asked Georges.

Émile gestured at the plain. "The reason the Serpentines are on their right flank is because the starwise land on their left is steep and not given to a charge. Hence, they are stationed where they are to attack from the flat."

Georges nodded.

"Too," continued Émile, now squatting in the dirt and drawing with his dagger, "I ween the Serpentines think to round our left flank and come at us from the rear, trapping us between themselves the Trolls and Goblins and the Bogles, much like catching us between their hammer and the army's anvil."

Émile looked up and smiled. "But two can play at that game."

"How so?" asked Bailen.

"Heed," said Émile, "they are arrayed in a cupping arc, like so"—he drew a long curve—"in the hope of surrounding us when we attack the center, for well do they know we will try to deal with the Trolls first. But if we march out in a long, diagonal line, a phalanx, like so"—Émile drew a slanting line in the soil—"and if we more or less conceal our cavalry behind the end farthest away from them"—now he drew a slash at the near end of the line—"then the Serpentines will have to ride down the phalanx to round our flank, thusly, and then—"

"And then we hit the Serpentines in their own flank with our concealed cavalry," blurted Blaise.

"Brilliant," murmured Luc.

"Indeed," said Léon. "For by taking their cavalry in the flank with ours head on, they cannot easily bring their lances to bear upon our charge."

"Ah, but how do we manage to conceal our own cavalry?" asked Petain. "I mean, we are coming downslope in full view. Will they not see this ruse?"

"Three things," said Émile, raising a hand, three fingers upraised. "*Un*"—he ticked down one finger—"it is dark under these dismal skies, and vision is hampered not only by the murk but also by bright flashes of lightning." Émile ticked down a second finger. "*Deux*: our knights and heavy crossbowmen will be on the lead, the phalanx to follow, and while the attention is on them." Émile ticked down the last finger. "*Trois*: our cavalry will have ridden on this side of the ridge to the gap on the left, where they will dismount and walk their horses through and conceal themselves behind yon nearby hill"—all eyes swung to the left of the plain, where stood the hilly land—"and when the final phalanx marches past, again they will walk the horses, and, by this ruse, to seem to be but more foot soldiers as they slip in behind."

"Ah," said Bailen. "And who will lead the cavalry?"

Émile looked at Laurent, and then said, "Luc."

Laurent started to protest, but it died on his lips ere spoken, for Bailen then asked, "And who will lead the chevaliers 'gainst the Trolls?"

"Laurent."

Even as Laurent clenched a fist and grinned, "But aren't Luc and Laurent needed to lead their own battalions?" asked Léon.

"Non. Luc's battalion will be led by Armsmaster Dévereau, and Laurent's by Armsmaster Jules."

"And what of me and Roél?" asked Blaise.

"You both will join Laurent and the knights against the Trolls, and Armsmasters Bertran and Anton respectively will lead your battalions." Émile looked down at the battle plan scratched in the dirt. "You see, except for delegating our champion of champions to lead the cavalry and eliminate the Serpentines, our knights are more valuable in dealing with the Trolls than in any other role, and all of the armsmasters are well suited to command."

Émile turned to Luc. "And you, my boy, when the Serpentines are done in, we will turn the tables on them, for you will bring the cavalry about and trap the enemy between your hammer and our anvil."

Luc smiled and inclined his head in assent.

"Now to the archers," said Émile, and Michelle stood and watched Émile draw, "this is how we will proceed. . . ."

. . .

Thus went the planning through the early morn, in the midst of which Émile paused and looked again at the enemy. "Hmm . . .

I wonder. We are outnumbered some six to one. Mayhap this is the time to rally the Firsts to our side."

"Non, Papa," said Blaise, his eyes lighting up with sudden understanding, "I think this is not the time."

"Your meaning?"

"Lady Lot's rede," said Blaise, "the one she gave me, I think I understand it."

"Lady Lot?" asked Bailen. "Verdandi? She gave you a rede?"

"Oui," said Blaise.

> "Grim are the dark days looming ahead
> Now that the die is cast.
> Fight for the living, weep for the dead;
> Those who are first must come last.
>
> Summon them not ere the final day
> For his limit to be found.
> Great is his power all order to slay,
> Yet even his might has a bound."

Blaise looked down at the waiting enemy. "I just now realized that the key is in the line 'Those who are first must come last.' And who else could that mean but the Firsts? Too, I think this is not the 'final day' spoken of in Verdandi's conundrum, and so we should not summon them except à extremité."

"We don't know how to summon them anyway," said Laurent.

"But we do," came a tiny voice.

Émile and the others skewed about. It was the Sprite Peti, now sitting on Michelle's shoulder.

"Demoiselle?" said Émile.

Peti took to wing and flew in among the men, where she alighted on Sieur Émile's arm. "The other Sprites tell me that the Firsts are nearly assembled, and they but await the word as to where to go. Yet they also heed Lady Verdandi's rede, and will not come ere what they judge to be the so-called 'final day.' I believe Blaise is right: Verdandi's rede can mean none else but the Firsts, and this is not the day to summon them."

"And when that day comes . . . ?" asked Laurent.

"Then we Sprites will fetch them."

. . .

Orbane continued to hiss sibilant words, and Hradian sagged under the strain. Crapaud sat somnolent, and whether he felt the drain is not known. And as lightning shattered across the black sky and thunder boomed, the vapor yet spewed up from the swamp bottom in a bilious cloud roaring forth from the vortex and continuing to expand; and it oozed across the mire and among the trees and grasses. Some ten feet deep the vapor lay, a sickly yellow-green, and things wilted where it flowed. Yet these were swamp creatures and plants, and somewhat immune to the putrescence, and mayhap they would not die, nor, perhaps, would the swamp creatures living among them.

And the morning went on, while at the far dawnwise bound of the morass, two armies made ready to do battle, one greatly outnumbering the other: the throng commanded by Cham Bolok, a towering Troll; the army commanded by Sieur Émile, a human. Each had his plan: one was committed to a victory by sheer numbers; the other was committed to winning by guile.

. . .

As a line of riders came over the crest of the ridge Bolok grunted and then shouted, "Look alive, you slugs, they come at last." But then he frowned. "What's this? Just one— Ah, no, here come more."

He watched as to his left a group came tramping over the top and then marched down the long slope, spearmen all, their shields locked together, or so it seemed. And then another group came, and another after that, and then more. Bolok had never before seen a phalanx, much less as many as these. Their deployment puzzled him, for he had expected the humans to attack head on, perhaps in a wedge, but down the slope they came on a long diagonal. *Bah! It matters not, for still my plan will work.*

"Stand fast, you slime," he bellowed. Then he looked to his right, beyond Bogles and beyond Goblins, to where stood his Serpentines at the end of the long rightward arc of the throng, and he gestured for them to mount up. They would simply ride down the angle of these pitiful humans and round their flank and come at them from behind. And in that moment he would signal his own forces to charge the enemy and crush them in between.

As lightning flashed and thunder roared in the dark skies overhead, Bolok watched as the enemy horsemen out front— a paltry fifty or so—rode toward his two hundred Trolls. *The fools!*

. . .

And in the bowels of the swamp, at Orbane's command, up from the under-bottom of the morass roared the *Sickness*, a dreadful miasma, spewing outward through the vast bog, fettered only by Orbane's control.

. . .

Down the angle the Serpentines hammered, the riders sissing cries as onward they plunged, with long, cruelly barbed spears in their grasp. Hairless were their steeds, scaled instead, a glittering green in the lightning, with pale undersides and long, lashing, whiplike tails, the mounts an impossible crossbreed of serpent and horse. And they blew and grunted with effort, and the ground shook under their pounding cloven hooves as down the phalanx they galloped.

And in the lead Hsthir gloated, his long forked tongue flicking out and in, *tasting* the scent of the humans they would spit on their spears. And tonight the clutch would feed, yet not on fire-ruined meat as the stupid Trolls were wont to do, but on raw gobbets of flesh swallowed whole, as was only proper.

And reveling upon the feast yet to come, Hsthir heeled his spikes into the plated flanks of his soth to urge it even to greater speed, though it was already running at full gallop.

. . .

Bolok watched as the fifty or so enemy riders neared. But then— *What's this?*—they reined to a halt. It was as if they were waiting for something to occur. *Can this be some sort of trickery?* And under roiling black skies, Bolok grasped his great horn and stepped forward, ready to call the charge as soon as the Serpentines rounded their flank, and his gaze swept the field, seeking, seeking. . . .

. . .

Hsthir and the Serpentines neared the last of the phalanx, and he cried out the command for the clutch to—

. . .

Running full tilt, Luc and the cavalry smashed headlong into the Serpentines' flank, lances piercing, their horses bowling over the scaled steeds of the foe. The Serpentines could not bring their own spears to bear, and Luc and the cavalry drove on through, leaving nought but devastation in their wake. They spun their horses about and charged back into the disarrayed enemy, and some men, their pikes gone—embedded in fallen snake people—drew their sabers and laid about, hacking, hewing, slashing, while others hurtled back through, lances skewering foe.

And from somewhere within the phalanx, a horn sounded, and the riders facing the Trolls parted, and concealed behind them had been the heavy crossbowmen, and they released a deadly volley into the massed enemy, bringing down some fifty of the hulking brutes, Bolok out front being the first one slain.

And then with a shout from Laurent, he and Blaise and Roél and fifty others lowered their lances and charged.

And at the horn cry as well, the shields of the phalanx warriors were unlocked, and through the now-opened lines stepped the archers, Michelle among them, and they loosed a great flight of arrows, the shafts to arc down among the foe, slaying Goblin and Bogle alike.

Yet the enemy answered in kind, their arrows sissing through the air in return, but the archers had stepped back behind the first row of the phalanx and once again the shields overlapped. And Michelle stood directly behind Galion, his shield to cover them both.

"Yahh!" cried Laurent as he smashed in among the Trolls, his lance stabbing one in the throat, to lodge in the creature's spine, and the weapon wrenched from Laurent's grasp as the slain Troll fell. To Laurent's right, Roél's spear was lost to another of the foe, but Roél hewed about with Coeur d'Acier, the silver-flashed rune-bound steel blade keen and devastating.

Blaise yet held his pike, and stabbed and stabbed as he hammered on through, but then a Troll smashed down the knight's horse, and Blaise crashed to the soil, stunned.

The Troll loomed above him and raised his great club to crash it down upon Blaise, but then the monster jerked back, his arms falling to his side, and he looked down in astonishment at the point of the heavy crossbow bolt now jutting forth from his chest. And with a sigh he fell sideways, dead ere striking dirt. And Blaise scrambled to his feet and caught up a freerunning mount and reentered the fray.

On the left flank of the phalanx, surviving Serpentines in full disarray fled from Luc's cavalry, and the prince and his men now turned and spurred toward the enemy's right flank. A few of the Goblins there spun 'round and bolted back into the mire, and others, seeing them flee, ran into the bog as well. Yet some stood their ground and loosed arrows at the oncoming men, some to fatally strike, others to wound, and still others to miss altogether.

In the main body of the allies, again the shields unlocked, and again archers loosed, and arrows flew and enemy fell, and arrows flew in return, some to bring down men, most to bounce harmlessly from the again-overlapping defense.

In the center, one of the Trolls bashed through the knights to reach Bolok's corpse, and he took up the horn and blew a blast even as a crossbow bolt slew him. With ululating yells, the elements of the foe charged, and the phalanx closed ranks, the spearmen ready to meet the onrushing foe.

Luc's cavalry rounded behind the masses of the throng, and they smashed into the unprotected rear of the enemy, and some Goblins threw down their weapons and fled, though most turned to give battle.

Luc fought his way toward the mêlée taking place among the Trolls and knights, even as the Bogles and the Long-Armed Wights and the throng's greater numbers managed to smash open the phalanx. . . .

. . . and the battlefield turned into chaos.

The Goblins rushed in among the men with dreadful effect: Skrikers shrieked out long, wordless death cries as they hacked with axes; Dunters clacked grinding noisemakers even as they laid about with clubs; Redcaps shrilled and stabbed with pike-staffs. And the Bogles and Long-Armed Wights smashed and slashed with their flails and scythes, and slew man after man.

But the men with their spears and swords and shields and greater discipline managed to form squares and deal devastating death in return.

Next to Galion, who watched for arrows and fended with his shield, Michelle stood on the battlefield, surrounded by seven Wolves, and she calmly nocked and drew and aimed and loosed, choosing Bogles and Wights as targets.

The foe veered away from Slate and the pack, all but the

most foolhardy, and those that attacked paid with their lives, their throats torn away by fangs.

And still knights and Trolls and men with heavy cross-bows fought in their own private battle, for should the Trolls come in among the army proper, then their effect would be overwhelming.

Elsewhere the battle raged on, and the cavalry swept through the enemy again and again, and, even though outnumbered, the humans slowly gained the upper hand, though at dreadful cost.

But then, oozing outward from the swamp came a bilious yellow-green vapor. And slowly it began to envelop the battle.

Slate lifted his muzzle and then postured before Michelle: *Bad smell bad. Go!*

Michelle frowned and looked at him: *Go?*

Slate: *Go!*

Of a sudden, Trit landed upon Michelle's shoulder. "Princess! The *Sickness*—from the swamp it comes. You must flee. Now!"

Michelle looked at the oncoming miasma. It did not seem to affect the throng, but men began retching, and horses nigh foundered, and Michelle gasped as a nauseating whiff filled her nostrils. Sprites flew thither and yon, crying out to the allies; and some of the wee beings fell to the ground, overcome by the dreadful vapor.

And from the slopes above the plain, there came a horn cry, as Émile sounded the retreat, for the Sprites had borne the alarm to him as well.

Hacking and wheezing, some vomiting, taking up their wounded and leaving their dead behind, the men began to with-draw, snatching up fallen Sprites as they fled. Yet the throng did not pursue, for they had had enough of battle.

And in the heart of the swamp under black, roiling skies riven by flares of lightning, Orbane released Hradian, and she fell to the flet beside Crapaud. And Orbane looked about at the lovely putrescence and laughed, for his spell was complete: he had raised the *Sickness*, the great contamination, and now nothing and no one could stand in his way, and he would be ruler of all.

51

March

Under the flare of lightning and the judder of thunder raging in the black skies above, from the ridge Émile and the others watched as the miasmic cloud spread out over the battlefield. They could see little within the bilious depths, yet now and again they glimpsed shadowy movement therein, which showed that Goblins and Bogles and Trolls yet lived. And then the yellow-green vapor began to withdraw back into the swamp, and when the field was finally clear of its dreadful presence, the ground was bare of all plant and animal life, and no corpses of horses or men or even foe remained, nor did any of the surviving throng. All bodies were gone, though some weaponry yet remained.

"They've dragged our dead away," spat Laurent.

"For what purpose?" asked Blaise.

Léon sighed and shook his head. "Goblins and such savor human flesh, and Trolls love the meat of horses."

"You mean they've taken them for food?"

Laurent spat an oath, and Léon nodded but said, "Either that, or the terrible cloud has destroyed all."

"It is the *Sickness*," said Peti.

"*Sickness?*" asked Émile.

"Oui . . . the dreadful contamination that lies in the under-bottom of each and every swamp. Somehow Orbane has raised it up."

"The Goblins and Bogles and Trolls seemed unaffected by it," said Luc, "but it nearly did us in. It is a great pollution—a dreadful weapon."

At these words, a murmur of agreement muttered among the men, but for Michelle it triggered an elusive thought along the margins of her mind. Of a sudden she snared it and said, "I think Orbane does not intend it as a battlefield weapon."

Émile turned to her. "Non?"

"Non."

"Then what other use could he possibly have for such a dreadful thing?"

Michelle glanced from Luc to Émile to his sons, finally settling on Laurent. "Recall what I said that Camille had told me about the River of Time."

Laurent nodded. "That if Orbane ever got free, he would pollute it."

Michelle said, "And Luc has rightly named the cloud just that: a pollution."

"How does Camille know this thing?" asked Émile.

Laurent looked at Michelle, and she said, "The Fates are the ones who told her."

"Just what is this River of Time Orbane would despoil?" asked Blaise.

Michelle said, "As Camille tells it, it seems that somewhere in Faery, time flows in a silvery river, and along this flow is where the Three Sisters fashion the Tapestry of Time: Skuld weaving what she sees of the future; Verdandi fixing present events into the weft and warp of the fabric; Urd binding all forever into the past. Camille speculates the river flows out of Faery to spread over the mortal world, for time itself does not seem to touch Faery, though some say it originates herein."

"And just what would polluting the River of Time do to Faery?" asked Émile, "—or to the mortal world, for that matter?"

Michelle shrugged. "That I do not know, Sieur, yet if Time itself is despoiled in some manner, the result cannot be pleasant. Too, it seems to me that the greater harm, whatever it is, will occur to the mortal world."

"Why is that?" asked Blaise.

"Because, if Camille is right, Time spreads over the mortal world, while in Faery it is confined."

Roél slammed a fist into palm. "Confined or not, I say it is *enough* that Skuld, Verdandi, and Urd each tell that dreadful calamity will befall Faery, too."

"I agree with Roél," said Luc, "for we here cannot know what effect the contamination of that arcane river will bring— it is beyond our ken. Yet if Orbane is to use the *Sickness* to pollute Time's flow, he will have to move it from this swamp to wherever the river is."

Sieur Émile pursed his lips and then asked, "But where along the river would he go to do this deed?"

Luc frowned. "I do not think he would go somewhere *along* the course, Sieur Émile, but to the headwaters instead, for from there he could foul the river its entire length."

"Mais oui," said Émile, nodding. He turned to Michelle. "Just where is this river?"

Michelle turned up her hands.

"We know," said Peti.

"The Sprites know?"

"Oui. It is a place we avoid, for we would not suffer the ravages of Time."

"Ravages or no, Sieur Émile," said Léon, "we must needs somehow foil Orbane's plan."

"But our forces are devastated," said Bailen.

"Nevertheless," said Léon.

"First," said Luc, "we need to know if indeed the *Sickness* is at Orbane's beck. Then we need to know whether he will march or not. If he does march and the pollution goes with him, then we need to know if this river is indeed his goal. Lastly, we need to know whether or no we have the wherewithal to stop him."

"What is the count of our able-bodied?" asked Émile.

"The armsmasters are taking the tally now," said Léon.

Émile nodded then said, "Peti, the Sprites need fly above the swamp and keep track of the foe."

"Oh, my," said Peti, alarmed.

But Trit took her hand and said, "We will just have to fly at height, well above the corruption."

Peti nodded, then looked at Émile, and he said, "When and if they begin to move, we must know which route they take, and if it is toward this River of Time then we need to get ahead of them and plan an ambush or trap, or find some other means of thwarting Orbane."

"What about the dreadful miasma?" asked Bailen. "I mean, if Orbane does move the contamination, how do we counter that?"

Émile looked from face to face, but none knew the answer.

. . .

The tally of able-bodied came to just over four thousand. In addition, there were some six hundred wounded who had made it free of the battleground, and they were being attended by chirurgeons and healers. Some three thousand four hundred men had been lost in the battle—four of every ten men. Five Sprites had been felled by the bilious pall, half their total, though the men had managed to take up three of them during the retreat; even so, the loss of just two Sprites had been keenly felt by all. Of the fifty knights Léon had brought with him, thirty-five were yet hale. As to the enemy casualties, none knew the count.

. . .

"Those fools, those bloody fools," seethed Orbane. "More than half my Trolls and Bogles, and nearly all my Serpentines."

"Half the Goblins as well," said Hradian.

"Pah!" spat Orbane. "Who cares about the Goblins? They

are just fodder. 'Tis the Trolls and Bogles and Serpentines I count on to protect me on the march."

"Yet your throng gave good account of themselves, for they dragged nearly four thousand human corpses away from the battlefield to feast upon, and surely just as many men suffered wounds. I deem this ragtag army will flee the field, my master, and you will be free of these pests who would stand in your way. Compared to you, my puissant lord, they are less than fleas, than mites."

Orbane rounded on Hradian and glared into her eyes, and she fell to her knees and trembled before him. Then he threw her on her back and parted her legs and slid in between, and she began screaming in pleasure.

.   .   .

The following day the raging darkness above began moving, and shortly after, Dil, one of the Sprites, came winging into the encampment. "Sieur," he said to Émile, "the throng marches, the *Sickness* moves, they are faring through the hills a point to dusk of sunwise."

"Is that the way toward the River of Time?"

"Oui, Sieur, it is."

Émile jumped to his feet and summoned his bugler. "Sound the alert, for we march."

.   .   .

As planned, they left their wounded behind, along with a chirurgeon and three healers, with instructions for the lesser of the hurt to aid with the greater. Too, one of the Sprites remained with them to guide the mule-drawn wains through the shadow-light bounds on their way to a goodly sized distant town.

All in the force that went sunwise were mounted on horses, with mules and asses in the train. And in haste they travelled the first day, and soon they were beyond the marching throng and the *Sickness*, and then the allies turned on the course pointed out by the Sprites.

That evening they came to the twilight border, and when they passed through, they emerged under clear skies, where the blackness and lightning and thunder had been left behind. And here did they gain another six hundred men who were on their way to the mire, for that was where the rendezvous had been called. Yet they turned their march toward the goal set by Émile: the headwaters of the River of Time.

. . .

As Orbane moved across the land, once the *Sickness* had cleared the morass, where it flowed it destroyed all plants as well as the animals—those that did not flee—leaving nought but wither and sere behind.

The following day, Orbane and his throng reached the sunwise border, and here it was that once again the wizard commanded the witch to lend him her power. And he cast a great spell, and then ordered the march to continue, and when they went through the twilight bound, so, too, did the thundering skies above as well as the pollution below.

Hradian had known that shadowlight borders are tricky, and usually a storm or blowing air and rivers and other such oft did not flow across as would a traveler go but appear somewhere else altogether. And although birds in the air passed through twilight marges much the same as did people, the air itself did not; instead it blew elsewhere. In contrast, fish and other aquatic creatures seemed to remain within the stream and flow through wherever the water went—though that was not the case with boats. And so, when Orbane had cast his spell and had caused the *Sickness* and the black skies to pass through as he had wished—first starting the darkness across, then his throng, followed by himself and Hradian and the corruption, with the remainder of the darkness following after—it had taken great magic indeed, and Hradian could but marvel at his power.

Just on the opposite side, a battalion of Goblins joined them—Dunters all, it seems.

. . .

And so the army marched, as did the throng, and each took on new recruits as across the realms they went. But as to Orbane, nought but barren soil was left along the wide, wide track of the dreadful pall.

. . .

Under the hollow hills, at last Auberon pronounced all was ready, and Regar was given a fine horse and glittering armor, as well as a new bronze sword and a long-knife and a long lance pointed on both ends. But he kept his own bow and quiver, though the Fey Lord filled it with arrows he said would not miss.

And the Fairy army—three thousand strong—rode up and out from the mounds, with arms and armor flashing in the sunlight of early morn and small silver bells ringing ajingle upon the caparisons of magnificent, prancing steeds.

And then did Flic and Fleurette and Buzzer join Regar, and Flic said, "Oh, my prince, we thought you trapped, thought that you had eaten food or taken drink and would be caught for a millennia or more."

Regar looked at them in puzzlement. "Thought me trapped? I was under the hill for but a mere day."

"No, my lord," said Fleurette, "you have been under the mound for nearly two moons altogether."

"*Two moons?*"

"Just two days shy."

Alarmed, Regar turned to Auberon. "We must ride, my lord, else we will be too late."

Auberon lifted his silver horn and sounded a long cry. And the Fairy horses leapt forward, Auberon leading the way.

52

Gap

Some seven thousand strong the allies now marched, for they had collected additional warbands along the way. And as they tramped toward a distant goal, "Look ahead, my lord," said Léon to Luc.

"I see it," said the prince, "and surely so has Sieur Émile."

To the fore stood a craggy mountain range, and the Sprites led the army toward a gap in the chain.

"It seems quite narrow," said Léon.

"We are yet at a distance, Léon, and no doubt it will be wider when we get there."

Léon barked a laugh, even as he nodded in agreement.

They rode onward, and shortly there came a page to summon them to Émile's side. Forward they spurred, and soon they reached the vanguard, and within a quarter candlemark all the commanders had arrived.

"Should it be a suitable lieu, I deem we can make a stand in yon slot," said Émile, raising his voice so that all could hear.

"If we do so, my lord," said Captain Valodet, a newcomer and commander of four hundred horse, "we might not be able to flank them."

"Oui, Captain, we might not. Yet on the other hand, they might not be able to flank us either."

"My lord," said Petain, "the Sprites report that Orbane's

forces gain enormous strength as they march. Their numbers increase seemingly without bound."

Roél said, "Then mayhap that's all the more reason for us to make a stand in a narrow lieu where they cannot bring those numbers to bear."

Luc nodded in agreement with Roél. " 'Tis the best way for dealing with great numbers, yet what of the *Sickness*? How will we contend with that?"

Émile sighed and said, "The Sprites tell us that the throng marches out before the contamination, and so I deem we can do battle until the corruption comes upon us." He looked about and said, "It is not the way I would want it, yet it is the best we can do."

"Mayhap the Firsts can deal with it, as well as with Orbane," said Laurent.

Blaise shook his head. "If I understand what went before in the war with Orbane, the Firsts could not do more than delay him. And, given Lady Lot's rede, I think that making a stand in the slot is not the last gasp, not the final day."

Laurent growled. "Why do we depend upon the words of a soothsayer?"

"My boy," said Sieur Émile, "she is not a mere soothsayer. Lady Lot, Lady Verdandi, she is one of the Fates."

A silence fell among them as on toward the gap they fared, but then Michelle said, "It is the last quatrain that seems to provide some clue, yet what it might mean escapes my grasp."

"Refresh my memory," said Émile.

Michelle nodded and intoned:

> "Summon them not ere the final day
> For his limit to be found.
> Great is his power all order to slay,
> Yet even his might has a bound."

As Michelle fell silent, Luc said, "*'All order to slay,'* might that not refer to the corruption of the River of Time, mayhap throwing all things into chaos?"

"I think you have it," said Blaise.

They rode a bit farther, and Blaise added, "It seems to me that when the Firsts come to the battle at last, then the limit of Orbane's power will be reached."

"And . . . ?" asked Laurent.

Blaise looked at his older brother. " 'And,' you ask? Laurent, I do not know what will take place when he reaches the limit of his power. Yet this I do know: whatever it is that might happen, Lady Lot says we need it to occur."

They rode onward, for long moments, and finally Sieur Émile said, "Since none has come up with a better plan, tell all your warriors this: if the gap is suitable for making a stand, we shall do so. And if the pollution comes upon us, then will we make our retreat."

"What of our deployment?" asked Bailen.

Émile said, "Orbane is a day behind us. Hence, let us first look at the ground in the gap ere we make our plans."

. . .

The following day the skies grew black, lightning and thunder raging overhead. Even so, no rain fell, nor did the darkness bring cooling air with it.

"They will not be far behind," said Blaise, sitting on a rock and sharpening his blade.

"Non, they will not," said Luc, adjusting the tack on Deadly Nightshade, his well-trained horse of war.

A candlemark passed, and a horn sounded to the fore.

"They are sighted," said Laurent.

"Indeed," said Roél, buckling on Coeur d'Acier.

They mounted up, did these four knights, did these four horsemen—deadly in their power—on mounts white and roan and black and grey. And they rode up a small slope toward the opening of the gap, for with Léon's chevaliers following, they would be the first to meet the foe after the archers were done.

Up to the crest of the rise they went, and there they stopped. And they watched as across the plain below came Orbane's throng, the putrescence following after.

"Oh, Mithras," said Blaise, "there must be sixty, seventy thousand of them."

"More like ninety," said Léon, riding up alongside.

"They'll funnel down when they get to this gap," said Luc, "and we can deal with—what?—two or three thousand at a time?"

Émile, who had joined them, looked at the width of the pass. "I think even less; mayhap half that."

"Even so," said Luc, "with their numbers, they can afford for ten to fall for every one of us."

"Then mayhap you can use some help," sounded a familiar voice amid a jingle of silver bells.

Luc turned to see Prince Regar stop alongside, and downslope behind him came the Fairy army, Auberon in the lead.

53

Straits

Under roiling black skies streaked with lightning and reverberating with thunder, Auberon looked down at the oncoming throng and then beyond to the bilious cloud that followed, and he sucked air in between clenched teeth. "He has raised the *Sickness*."

Both Flic and Fleurette, sitting upon Regar's tricorn, gasped in alarm. Buzzer was quite asleep between them, under the dark skies.

"Oui, my lord," said Émile.

"Sickness? What is this so-called 'sickness'?" asked Regar. "Is it that low-lying yellow-green cloud I see?"

"Oui," said Blaise at the prince's side. "Note how it moves: it follows Orbane's horde."

"To what purpose?"

"With it, somehow, Orbane intends to pollute the River of Time."

Auberon sighed and looked at Regar. "It comes from the under-bottom of swamps, where it lies entrapped unless someone or something sets it free. It can cause great illnesses among living things, and will slay all that remains within its embrace too long."

"Even the Fey, grand-père?"

"Especially the Fey, *mon petit-fils*."

"Can you do nothing to stop it?" asked Luc. "Use Fairy magic or such?"

"Non. Gloriana's geas has seen to that."

"Gloriana?" asked Blaise.

"Orbane's mère," said Regar.

Blaise cocked an eyebrow, an unspoken question in his gaze.

"Auberon's consort," said Regar, quietly. "Orbane is their only child."

"Oh, my," said Blaise, but then fell silent.

As they watched the throng and the *Sickness* move across the plains and toward the gap where the allies stood, Auberon sank into thought. Finally he said, "But there is something I *can* do, and that is to cast a protection spell over all of us."

"All of us?" asked Émile.

"All of the allies," replied Auberon.

"Horses too?"

"Oui. Horses too."

"But what of the geas?" asked Regar.

"This spell is to give us temporary protection from some of the ills of the *Sickness*," replied Auberon, "hence is a healer's charm, and one, I think, that I will be able to cast, for it is not in direct opposition to Orbane."

"Will it negate the putrescence?" asked Émile, hope playing across his face.

"Not completely," replied Auberon. "It will protect us on the fringes of the contagion, but the deeper one goes into the miasma, the less effect it will have."

"Will it allow one of us to reach Orbane?" asked Regar.

Blaise swiftly glanced from Regar to Auberon to see the look of sad dismay that flickered across Auberon's face. But then Auberon's mien shifted to one of determination, and he said, "I don't know. Certainly it will not protect one of the Fey long enough to reach him, and you, my grandson, are one of the Fey. But as to a human doing so, that I cannot say."

"I will go," said Laurent.

And I, said Blaise and Roél together.

"But first," said Luc, pointing to the masses of Goblins and Bogles and Trolls and Serpentines, "we will have to win our way through that."

"You four?" asked Regar. "You four will go after Orbane?"

A rakish grin crossed Luc's face as he glanced at the three others. "We four."

We four! they responded.

"But as you say, Prince Luc," said Auberon, "first you have to win your way through an entire throng." The Fey Lord turned to Émile. "My archers will stand to the fore, for with each arrowcast, we will bring one of them down . . . until we run out of shafts, that is, for there are more of the foe than we bargained for."

"And I will stand with your archers," said Michelle, sitting ahorse to one side, with her Wolves gathered 'round.

"It will be perilous, my lady," said Auberon.

"Nevertheless," replied the princess.

Auberon looked to Émile for a countering word, but he merely shook his head and said, "I lost that argument long past, my lord. Besides, she will have seven Wolves and a warrior named Galion to protect her."

"Trained Wolves?"

"Oh no, my lord," replied Chelle. "It is Borel's pack. We work as a team."

Auberon smiled and said, "And where is your prince, my lady?"

"Trapped with the others in the Castle of Shadows," said Chelle, "or so it is we think."

Regar took in a sharp breath at this news, and both Flic and Fleurette burst into tears. "What others?" asked Regar.

"The entire royal family," said Chelle. "Valeray, Saissa, Borel, Liaze, Alain, Céleste, Camille, and Duran—all trapped, borne away on a black wind. Mayhap Raseri and Rondalo, too, for a black wind bore them away as well."

Auberon gestured at the roiling sky. "He was always master of the winds; the rage above declares it, if nought else."

"You've got to get them out," said Fleurette, choking back her tears.

Luc jerked a nod and said, "As soon as I retrieve the key to the castle and we find someone to fly it through the Great Darkness to set the prisoners free. Hradian has the amulet, and we deem she is marching at Orbane's side."

"This is ill news, and mayhap there is more," said Auberon, "but it will have to wait. I must needs cast a great spell, and then deploy my archers."

. . .

As they rode back down to the midst of the army, Regar glanced across at Luc and Roél, Blaise and Laurent. "My mother once told me of an old legend about four deadly horsemen: the fable tells that the rider on the white horse was Plague himself, while the one on red was War; the one on black—or was it grey? Ah, never mind—was Famine, while the one on grey was Death."

Blaise laughed and said, "Well, then, I must be War, for I ride a red horse. Whereas, Laurent on white is Plague. That leaves Luc on black to be Famine or Death and Roél to be vice versa, whichever it is the legend says. But as for me, I would pick Roél to be Death."

"And why is that, other than simple family pride."

"Because he has a special sword—Coeur d'Acier."

"Heart of Steel?" Regar frowned and declared, "But iron and steel are forbidden in Faery."

Blaise smiled. "Oui, I know, though I've been told there are a few exceptions—the arms and armor of the Dwarves of the ship *Nordavind* being one, and the weapons of King Arle and his riders being another, now that they've broken their curse, though they'll not take iron or steel into the Halls of the Fairy

Lord ever again. Yet did I not say Roél's sword is special? The steel, you see, is bound by arcane runes flashed in silver, hence I am told it does not twist the aethyr, whatever that might be. It was given to Roél by Sage Geron, who got it from a source he will not or perhaps cannot name. Regardless, with the sword Roél cut through the Changeling Lord's magical protection and took off his head, and thereby set Laurent and me free from an enchantment."

"It overcame a spell of protection?"

"Oui," said Blaise. "I think it's the steel that did it, or perhaps the runes."

"Mayhap both together," said Regar. " 'Tis a powerful weapon indeed."

"Then can we name Roél 'Death'?"

Regar laughed and said, "As you will, Blaise, as you will. But regardless of what you call one another, I hope that when you four go after Orbane, you are just as deadly as are your namesakes."

"So do I," replied Blaise, as Roél and Luc merely shook their heads and Laurent snorted and spurred forward to come alongside Auberon.

"A splendid high-stepper of a mount you have, my lord," said Laurent. "Are all Fairy horses such as he?"

"To a lesser degree," replied Auberon. He patted the white animal's neck. "Asphodel is quite special."

"Asphodel? Ah, then *that's* where Duran gets the name for his toy hor—" Of a sudden, Laurent's words jerked to a halt, and he frowned in puzzlement and then his face lit up in revelation.

"My lord, I do not know what all of this means, but Lady Wyrd gave me a rede."

"Skuld?"

"Oui, my lord, and I think it has to do with Asphodel."

"Asphodel? Say on, Laurent. Say on."

"The rede goes like this." Laurent paused in recollection and then intoned:

> *"Swift are the get of his namesake,*
> *That which a child does bear;*
> *Ask the one who rides the one*
> *To send seven children there.*
>
> *At the wall there is a need*
> *For seven to stand and wait,*
> *Yet when they are asked to run,*
> *They must fly at swiftest gait.*
>
> *The whole must face the one reviled*
> *Where all events begin:*
> *Parent and child and child of child*
> *Else shall dark evil win."*

Laurent paused and Auberon frowned and said, "I do not understand."

"My lord, Prince Duran, the child of Alain and Camille, has a toy horse named Asphodel. And so the first two lines of the rede refer to that: *Swift are the get of his namesake, that which a child does bear.* Thus the get of Asphodel are swift, or so I would surmise. Does he have any offspring?"

"Oui, he has sired seven colts."

Laurent clenched a fist and grinned in triumph. "Then list, the next lines say: *Ask the one who rides the one to send seven children there.* Hence, my lord, I ask, can you send the seven colts somewhere?"

"Oui, I only need to give the command. But where?"

"To the Black Wall of the World, my lord, for the next lines say: *At the wall there is a need for the seven to stand and wait.* Hence they are to go to the Black Wall of the World, for what other wall could it be? And when they get there they are to wait."

"Ah," said Auberon, then frowned. "But wait for what?"

"I don't know, my lord, but Lady Wyrd's words *must* mean something, else she would not have said them. She also said that if I did not give this message to the one for whom it is intended, then all will be lost forever. And you, my lord, are surely the one for whom it is intended."

Auberon slowly nodded. "Sieur, I do not know what is intended, yet if Skuld said those words, then indeed I must heed them."

Auberon raised his silver horn to his lips and blew a call, silent to the human ears, though Asphodel nickered and all the Fey glanced toward their lord.

And even as Laurent looked on, out from among the Fairy horses, seven trotted forth. White they were, each and every one, as was their sire, and they were caparisoned with gilt bridles and saddles, and silver bells sounded as they came, and each was laded with accoutrements to equip a warrior.

"Where are their riders?" asked Laurent.

"They haven't any," said Auberon. "Asphodel, by snorting and nickering, insisted they come unridden and bearing gear, and now, it seems by this rede, we know why."

"Perhaps he, too, speaks with Lady Wyrd," said Laurent.

Auberon laughed and said, "Mayhap."

Then the Fey lord dismounted and stepped to the colts, and they all looked at him intently, as if expecting a command. And Auberon uttered words in an arcane tongue, but what he said, Laurent could not tell, yet the seven colts whickered in return, and then galloped away, straight for the end of the pass toward which the throng marched.

Laurent wheeled his horse, Impérial, and galloped after, yet the colts were all the way down on the plains ere Laurent reached the crest of the outlet slope where he could see. He marveled at their fleetness as they hurtled ahead, passing wide of the oncoming horde and racing onward.

. . .

"Loose!" cried Auberon, and arrows flew into the ranks of the throng, each one bringing sissing death with it. And Goblins shrilled and fell slain, as did Bogles and Serpentines. Trolls, though, were felled by heavy crossbow bolts, manned by Sieur Émile's men.

Yet onward came the horde, stepping over their fallen and boiling into the narrow pass, and again and again the archers loosed their sleet of arrows, thousands of the enemy dying with each volley.

Goblin shafts flew in return, most to be caught on the pavises born by the shield men.

Michelle stood in the ranks of the archers, her own shafts nearly as deadly as those flown by the Fey, but the Fairy arrows were quite lethal, in spite of the fact that their magic had been negated by Gloriana's unbreakable spell, a spell cast long past.

And yet the throng came onward, into the teeth of death, and soon on both sides the shafts of the archers had been spent, and now the phalanx of spearmen stood in the way of the horde.

Thousands of Goblins, gibbering in fear, were pushed forward by those behind, and, shrieking in terror, they tried to turn and flee back into the ranks. But the press would not let them, and on they came, only to be spitted by lances, or slaughtered by the blades of the men and the Fey. And the ones behind stumbled through entrails and blood and severed limbs and over the corpses of their dead, only to be slaughtered in turn.

Yet not all were killed ere they got in strikes of their own, and allies fell before the wildly swung clubs and bludgeons and scimitars and tulwars, of which there were so very many.

And the throng battered the allies back and back, deeper into the gut of the pass.

Time and again the knights hammered into the horde, reaping death as their harvest. And leading these charges were four lethal horsemen on white and red and black and grey mounts. They were not Plague and War and Famine and Death, yet they were nigh as fatal.

But then the *Sickness* came, the fringes of the bilious cloud to envelop Fey and man and horse.

Yet on they battled, the Fairy Lord's spell protecting them. And deeper into the deadly miasma they fought, but first the Fey and then the men began to retch and the horses to groan.

Émile called for a retreat, and, leaving their dead behind and aiding their wounded, hindward the allies reeled as night came on.

And the throng stopped to rest.

And a league farther along the slot, so did the allies.

. . .

And the next day and the next, the battle went on, the throng driving into the allies again and again, each time driving them hindward. Yet at last the horde broke free of the pass, and the allies fell back to make one final stand on the banks of the River of Time.

54

Away

For two moons and two days—as near as they could gauge by their waking and sleeping patterns—Valeray and his family as well as Raseri and Rondalo tried all they could to escape the confines of the Castle of Shadows. After they had discovered the castle would mold itself to accommodate its prisoners, they had attempted to push it beyond its limits by imagining that they needed long hallways and huge chambers and pools and forests and gardens and flowerbeds and stables and riding paths and a place for a Dragon to romp. Yet it seemed the castle itself was the only judge of what they actually needed, and so, some things it molded for their use, while other things it did not.

Still, the prisoners tried breaking through the walls, or scratching their way out, there where they suspected it was weakened or thin, all to no avail. And Valeray continued to try combinations of exits through the shadowlight doorways and windows, but always the moment he passed through one portal he immediately entered through another, not having achieved any exit from the castle whatsoever. Scruff, too, flew into the twilight arches, yet he, too, simply hurtled in through another.

And though it seemed hopeless, neither Camille nor Céleste nor Liaze would allow the others to fall into ennui, for the sake of Duran if nought else. And so they played games—échecs being one of these, and none could best Raseri—and they told tales and made up rhymes and puzzles and tried to resolve the redes of the Fates. And Camille and Rondalo and Alain sang all the songs they could remember—sometimes as solos, other times as duets, and even as trios, though occasionally all joined in, even Raseri, the Dragon now and then voicing in a register so low it was only felt and not heard.

Yet not all time was spent in these activities, for oft they passed candlemarks away from one another, resting in thought and spirit. And now and then Alain and Camille made love, as did Valeray and Saissa, though each of the couples felt somewhat guilty that the others did not have such respite.

And thus they slept and waked and pondered and kept active for what they guessed to be two moons and two days, but they did neither eat nor drink nor eliminate, for it seems in the Castle of Shadows such things were completely unnecessary.

Musing over the redes the Fates had given, Camille descended the steps of the staircase leading down from the quarters above, and, just as she sat on the lowermost one, of a sudden one more thing fell into place. *Ah, so* that's *what the words mean, or at least I so do think. If I am right, I understand more than I did, though there yet remain mysteries.*

She heard footsteps on the treads above, and she turned to see Alain moving down. She smiled, and he returned it, and he sat at her side.

"I think I've solved another small part of a rede," said Camille.

"Oh? Which one?"

"The one Urd gave to Roél."

"Which part?"

"Where it says: ' 'Pon the precipice will ye be held.' "

"And . . . ?"

"Well, I think the precipice is—"

"Have you seen Duran?" Céleste called from the entrance to one of the lower halls.

Alain turned toward her. "No. Why?"

"Well, I can't find him, and it is our time to play hide and seek."

"Then I imagine that rascal is already hidden."

Céleste came on out into the great chamber. "But I've looked everywhere. Ah, Alain, I am worried. He seems to have disappeared."

"Mayhap he's with Raseri," said Camille. "You know how Duran likes to go for a ride."

"Non, Camille, I've been there and elsewhere, too, and he's simply not to be found."

Alain stood. "I'll help you look."

"I'll go as well," said Camille.

"Go where?" asked Liaze from above.

"Duran is hiding," said Alain.

Liaze smiled. "The little sneak. I'll help look."

Alain turned to Céleste. "You and Liaze search the rooms above, while Camille and I take this floor."

"All right."

As Céleste started up the stairs, Camille called after her, "Make certain that Raseri hasn't hatched some jest of his, for he can be sneaky as well."

Alain roared in laughter.

When Camille turned toward him and cocked an eye, Alain smiled and said, "I merely find it peculiar to think of such a whopping big Drake as being 'sneaky' at anything."

Camille made a moue and said, "Oh, Alain, you know what I mean," but Alain kept on grinning.

. . .

A candlemark later no one was smiling, and all were now involved in the search, even Scruff, the small sparrow swiftly flying from room to room. Yet of Duran there was no sign.

"Oh, Love, do you think this awful castle has done something with him?"

Desperation shone on Alain's face as they hurried down from a high turret. "I don't know, Camille."

Borel's face was grim and he said, "Mayhap the castle *has* done something *to* him."

"Oh, don't say that, Borel," protested Saissa, nearly in tears.

Echoing from somewhere else in the castle, they heard Raseri's roar of frustration at finding nought, followed by words from Rondalo, but what the Elf said, they could not hear.

Saissa stepped into a junction between corridors, and she looked this way and that. "Oh, my little Duran, where have you gotten to?"

Valeray and Liaze popped out from an adjoining hallway, and Valeray growled, "I swear, this wing is empty. He is not here."

Camille burst into tears, and Alain took her in his arms. After a long moment he said, "Love, go back to the great chamber, while we work our way down. If he is somehow running before us, he will have to pass through."

Wiping her cheeks, Camille nodded, and she disengaged herself from Alain's embrace. And as they divided and headed back up to the turrets, Camille stepped to the stairs to descend.

And when she came to the great hall, there was Duran on hands and knees clip-clopping his Asphodel across the floor.

With a shriek, Camille flew to him and scooped him up and rained kisses upon his face. "Oh, Duran, my baby Duran, where have you been? We've searched everywhere."

Duran scowled and declared, "I'm not a baby, Maman."

"Oh no, oh no, you're not a baby, but you'll always be *my* baby."

Duran frowned in puzzlement, trying to work his way through her contradiction. But ere he could do so—

"Alain! Alain! I found him," cried Camille, hoping her call would be heard in the far turrets away. And then she hugged Duran tightly and kissed his face once more, and he pursed his lips and kissed her in return.

As if reluctant to let him go, she slowly set him down to the floor. "But where have you been, Duran?"

"Out on the bridge, playing with Asphodel."

"Out on what bridge?"

Duran pointed toward the arch filled with shadowlight. "That one there."

Camille's eyes flew wide. "You went through the . . . through the door? There's a bridge beyond?"

"Oui, Maman. Come, I'll show you."

Duran took Camille by the hand and led her to the crepuscular arch, where . . .

. . . they stepped through and Camille found herself on a torchlit bridge with nought but a great black void all 'round.

Camille gasped and turned about, and there before her looming up into the blackness stood the castle, with its turrets and towers and ramparts dimly lit by the torches along the parapets of the bridge.

Once again she turned 'round, and some fifty or so paces away, the bridge came to an abrupt end, as if it had somehow been severed in two by the stroke of a monstrous great axe. Where the missing part of the span was, she could not tell nor did it matter.

With her mind racing, she lifted up Duran and spun him about, laughing gaily, and then she crowed, "Lady Urd said, 'The least shall set ye free,' and, oh, my Duran, I think she must have meant you."

"Meant what, Maman?"

"Meant that you were a key to this dreadful place."

"I'm not a key," protested Duran, frowning. "I'm a boy."

Camille laughed with joy and said, "Mais oui, my sweet, you are my precious boy. Come, let us go back in and tell the others."

But when Camille came to the archway, every time she stepped into the shadowlight she found herself and Duran back on the bridge.

"Oh, child, I can't get through."

"Put me down, Maman. I'll take you in."

Camille set Duran to his feet, and he reached up and took her hand and . . .

. . . led her inside.

"Alain!" Camille called out again, for clearly he had not heard her the first time, else he and the others would be here by now. "Alain! Papa, Maman! Borel, Liaze, Céleste! Raseri, Rondalo! To me! To me!" she shouted, her voice echoing throughout the great chamber.

Céleste poked her head across the railing of a balcony high above. "What is it, Cam—? Oh, I see, you've found him." She turned and called to someone behind, and soon Borel looked over the parapet.

Shortly, all were in the great chamber, including Scruff, and Duran was now in his father's arms. And Camille said, "Duran can get us free."

What? exclaimed several at once.

Camille retrieved the child from Alain and set him to his feet and said, "Take me to the bridge."

Duran reached up and took her hand, and led her out to the torchlit half-span.

"Now, my little prince, go and get your father."

Within moments, Alain stood on the bridge. "But why? How?" he asked Camille.

"I don't know how 'tis done, Love, yet perhaps Urd's rede explains all. She said, *'The least shall set ye free,'* and here we are, outside the prison."

Alain knelt and hugged his child and said, "Duran, you must bring everyone out here."

"Raseri, too?"

Alain nodded. "Raseri, too."

"Scruff?"

"Oh, indeed, Scruff."

"And Asphodel."

"Yes, Duran, especially Asphodel."

And one by one Duran set them all free of the castle, and Camille and Alain were giddy with joy. And they laughed as Duran duckwalked out leading Scruff by a wing, the tiny sparrow querulously chirping yet hopping along by the boy's side. Finally he led Raseri out, holding onto the tip of one of the Drake's saberlike claws. But then, before any could stop him, Duran darted back in to the castle, and Camille despaired, for none could go and fetch the child. But moments later, Duran came clip-clopping his Asphodel out.

As Camille caught the child up in her arms, Raseri said, "I deem I can bear half beyond the Black Wall of the World, and then return for the other half."

"Ladies first," said Rondalo.

And Céleste said, "Rondalo, give me your bow, for we know not what waits on the far side, and I am the best of us four."

The slim Elf nodded, and strung his bow and handed it and the quiver of arrows to her.

Camille called Scruff to her shoulder pocket, and then all the women mounted, Céleste with the bow sitting foremost, and Alain lifted Duran up to Camille, along with Asphodel.

The Drake then slithered to the end of the span and leapt outward into the darkness and plummeted down, all riders but Scruff and Duran gasping in fear. Raseri unfurled his mighty wings and soared upward again. Scruff then fell asleep, for all about was a darkness deeper than that of night.

And with his wings hammering through the blackness, Raseri flew along the single course that would take them to freedom.

"The last time I did this," he bellowed, "I nearly caught Hradian and Orbane. Mayhap the next I see them, the ending will be different."

And on he flew. . . .

. . . to finally burst through the Black Wall of the World and fly into the silver light of dawn.

And waiting below stood seven white steeds.

"Oh, my," exclaimed Camille, "now I understand."

"Understand what?" asked Saissa.

"Lady Skuld's rede, spoken to Laurent, as well as the one Verdandi told to Blaise. —Raseri, land next to the horses, for they are the get of Asphodel and are meant for us."

Raseri spiralled down, to come to ground nigh the steeds.

"Now go, Raseri, fetch the others, and hurry," said Camille, "for we are needed elsewhere."

Without questioning the princess, Raseri said, "Ward your eyes," and Camille covered Duran's and closed her own. And the Dragon took to flight, his mighty pinions driving down great blasts of air—dust and grit and grass flying 'round—as he winged his way upward. Then he shot back through the Black Wall of the World and vanished.

The horses came trotting, and Duran laughed in glee for here were some "real" Asphodels, and for the first time the women could see that arms and armor—swords, long-knives, lances, bows and arrows, along with breastplates and helms and greaves—were affixed to the saddles, along with garb to be worn. And they cast off the dresses in which they had been garbed ever since the closing ceremonies of the Faire and donned the apparel given, and it all fitted nicely, though how someone could have known just what sizes were needed was anyone's guess. Saying that but for the bow she knew little of combat, Camille gave her own armor to wee Duran, and lo! it diminished to fit the child. And then they knew Fairy magic was at hand.

As she strapped on a greave, Liaze asked, "You have solved both Skuld and Verdandi's redes?"

"I think so, or at least enough to know what we must do, for Urd's rede applies as well. Or at least a part of each does."

"And that is . . . ?" asked Saissa.

"We must mount these children of Asphodel, all of us, and ride to the headwaters of the River of Time, for that's where Orbane will go, for he intends to pollute it beyond all redemption."

Liaze's eyes flew wide. "Ah, oui. You are right, Camille."

Saissa frowned in puzzlement. Liaze noted her mère's bafflement and said, "Camille is right, for the one rede says:

> "Swift are the get of his namesake,
> That which a child does bear;
> Ask the one who rides the one
> To send seven children there.
>
> At the wall there is a need
> For seven to stand and wait,
> Yet when they are asked to run,
> They must fly at swiftest gait.
>
> The whole must face the one reviled
> Where all events begin:
> Parent and child and child of child
> Else shall dark evil win."

"Ah," said Saissa, enlightened. She gestured at the white horses, one nuzzling Duran, the young prince laughing, Scruff now chirping in joy and circling about. "And these are the seven children. And they are here at the Black Wall, for here is a need."

"A need for us to face the one reviled," said Céleste. "Orbane."

"And we must go where all events begin," said Camille, "and that is at the headwaters of the River of Time."

Saissa said in dismay, "But surely we need not take wee Duran."

"We have no choice, Maman," said Liaze, "for the words tell

us that *all* must go: *'Parent and child and child of child,'* and that includes Duran."

"But why?"

"For his limit to be found," said Camille.

"Limit? What limit? Whose limit?" asked Saissa.

And Camille intoned:

> *"Grim are the dark days looming ahead*
> *Now that the die is cast.*
> *Fight for the living, weep for the dead;*
> *Those who are first must come last.*
>
> *Summon them not ere the final day*
> *For his limit to be found.*
> *Great is his power all order to slay,*
> *Yet even his might has a bound."*

Camille looked at her son and added, "I deem we are needed along with the Firsts to somehow thwart Orbane."

"The Firsts?" asked Céleste. But then she said, "Oh, I see: *'Those who are first must come last,'* and that means the Firsts."

"But what of Urd?" asked Liaze. "I do not see how what she said applies."

"But for one thing, or perhaps two," replied Camille, "I am not certain either. Yet here's what she said to Roél:

> *" 'Pon the precipice will ye be held,*
> *As surely as can be,*
> *Yet can ye but touch the deadly arcane,*
> *The least shall set ye free."*

Camille looked at Liaze and Céleste and then Saissa, and each frowned in puzzlement. "And what parts of the rede do you think apply?" asked Céleste.

"I think *'the precipice'* means the linn where the River of Time begins." Camille now looked at Duran and said, "And perhaps *'The least shall set ye free,'* somehow might mean Duran."

Saissa sighed. "And that's why he must go."

"Oui, Maman," said Camille, grimly, "that's why he must go."

In that moment, Raseri hammered through the Black Wall of the World, and spiralled down to deposit Valeray, Borel, and Alain.

And when all had been explained, Borel said, "Then it's to the headwaters of the River of Time we all go."

"I will guide," said Raseri.

"But shouldn't we fly ahead?" asked Rondalo, still astride.

Borel laughed. "If these colts run as fast as does their sire, then it will be all you can do to keep up."

"Pah!" snorted Raseri. "Let us test your words."

And so all mounted up, Camille and Duran and Scruff together upon one of the colts, and just as the limb of the morning sun broke across the rim of the world, away they all flew, Raseri in the air above, Asphodel's colts galloping across the lands below.

Although they were headed for the linn of the River of Time, Camille fretted, deeply concerned: *Did we soon enough discover the way out of the Castle of Shadows, or—Oh, Mithras—are we already too late?*

Crucible

Beneath the black skies in the uncertain dawn, from a distant knoll on the valley floor Sieur Émile and his commanders watched by lightning flash the stirrings of the distant throng. It was the morning after the foe had hammered the allies out from the pass to come down into the wide valley, shortly after followed by the dreadful *Sickness*. Night had then fallen, and each of the combatants had stopped to rest. But now it was morning, and once again Émile and his leadership assessed what was to be done.

Émile sighed and turned to Auberon and asked, "Where lies this River of Time?"

The Fey Lord pointed to the far side of the vale. "Beyond yon crest, out from this dale and into the next, there's where the river flows."

Émile frowned. "But you have turned us starwise . . . along the course of this valley. Should we not instead ride up and over?"

Auberon shook his head. "Non, for we cannot find the river that way, and even if we could, we would then intercept the course downstream of the headwaters."

Laurent, his bandaged arm in a makeshift sling, said, "But where is the problem, my lord? Can we not simply turn upstream and follow the river back to the source?"

Auberon shook his head. "Non, Sieur Laurent, for only the Fates and mayhap ghosts can go against the flow of time, whereas we can only move with it. Try otherwise and the river itself will vanish, and we'll not reach the wellspring. Instead, we must go some four leagues or so up this valley ere crossing over, and then turn sunwise to come upon the beginning. It is in fact the only way to reach the River of Time, for it can only be found by coming upon the source. Oh, perhaps there is another way, but, if so, I know it not."

Luc said, "If that is how one must reach the river, by starting at the fount, then that's why you turned us starwise, and I take it that Orbane has to do the same."

Auberon nodded and said, "Oui, for there is no other way."

"Four leagues from here to there? That's all?" asked Roél. "Then Orbane is nigh upon realizing his goal."

Blaise turned to his father and said, "Sire, let us send for the Firsts, for surely this is the last gasp."

Émile looked to Auberon, and the Fey Lord sighed and said, "I agree. And though they will not arrive here soon, it is time they came."

Luc said, "Though we are sore beset and few, if we continue to fiercely battle with Orbane's throng, mayhap we can delay him until the Firsts get here."

Roél on the far side of Sieur Émile nodded in agreement and said, "Let us make Orbane fight for every inch of the way and hope the Firsts come ere we are fordone."

"We can do so," said Auberon, "yet I think not even with their aid shall we long stem Orbane's march."

"Then I will call for the Sprites to tell the Firsts to come," said Émile.

Auberon shook his head and reached for the silver clarion at his side. "By the time the Sprites can fetch them, they will most certainly be too late. Instead, I will summon them with my horn."

But as the Fey Lord started to raise the trump to his lips, there came a horn cry echoing down the valley, and the riders turned, and starwise up the dale there came marching an army of men.

"Who can that be?" asked Laurent.

Regar and a rider, accoutered in a blue tabard marked with a silver sunburst, came galloping up the slope of the knoll to skid to a halt next to Émile. "Sieur," said the sunburst-marked rider, "Duke Roulan sends his compliments. He says to tell you he brings four thousand men, of which sixty-five are knights."

"Roulan? Michelle's father?" asked Laurent.

"Oui," replied the rider. "She is with him now."

"Four thousand men; sixty-five chevaliers," said Luc. "I deem this betters our chance of delaying Orbane until the Firsts arrive."

Auberon nodded, and again raised his horn to his lips, and this time he sounded a call, though none there heard ought but a breath of air expelled.

"Now they will come," said the Fey Lord.

. . .

Away from the Black Wall of the World ran the seven Fairy steeds, silver bells sounding the way, a single rider upon each but for the one who bore a mother and child and a sparrow. Above flew Raseri the Drake, and astraddle the base of the Dragon's neck rode Rondalo, the Elven lord carrying his bow and lance.

O'er the hills and tors ran the mounts, the slopes and crags themselves no barriers to these chargers, and then straight into the woodlands they sped, slowing down not one whit, for the Fairy horses careened like swift zephyrs weaving among the boles of the trees.

Of a sudden, Raseri and Rondalo each cocked their heads attentively. "The Fairy Lord summons us," said the Elf.

"Indeed," replied Raseri, for both he and Rondalo were counted among the Firsts.

Above rivers and streams the Dragon flew, while below silver-shod hooves left nought but ripples ringing outward in their wake.

They came to a twilight border and plunged straight through, and Raseri groaned, for directly below were nought but the waves of a great wide sea. Yet, lo! the Fairy horses ran atop the water itself. And both Drake and Elf could hear the ringing laughter of little Duran below, as across the billows the steeds galloped without pause.

. . .

Armed with fresh arrows brought by Duke Roulan and quarrels for their large crossbows, the allies watched as the throng came boiling onward, and behind the foe flowed the *Sickness*, a vast cloud spread across the entire width of the valley, and it left nought but sterile and barren soil in its wake as it poured across the plant and animal life. Somewhere in the midst of this contamination marched Orbane, with Hradian at his side. And as the men and Fey looked on they saw that the ranks of the enemy had swollen, for in the night more Goblins and Serpentines had come, as well as Bogles and Trolls. And once again the allies were sorely outnumbered—seven to one at best; ten to one at worst.

Regar sighed and asked, "Is there no limit to the numbers of these foul creatures?"

"Were we in the mortal world," said Lord Roulan, "then I would say yea; yet here in Faery, I think the answer might be nay."

"What I don't understand," said Blaise, "is why doesn't Orbane simply use that terrible cloud to drive us away? I mean, why fight battles? Why have a throng at all?"

"Because he is wary," said Auberon. "For we might have some weapon or potion or device that would permit us to breach the miasma. He uses the throng to protect him on his march; to him they are nought but chaff. Even so, it swells his pride to have command over such beings."

The warriors stood waiting, while knights sat their horses, as did the cavalry. Once again the chevaliers were assigned the task of dealing with the Trolls, while the cavalry would take on the Serpentines.

Howling wordless yawls, the front ranks of the throng charged, yet the archers and crossbowmen stood ready, but they flew no shafts.

On came the Goblins and Bogles and Trolls, and the Serpentines swept wide, for it was their intent to attack the allies from the rear, and this time Luc's cavalry would not take them by surprise.

At last the Fey Lord cried, "Loose!" and arrows *sissed* through the air arching up and over and down, bringing death on keen points.

The skies flared, thunder boomed, and, sounding his horn, Luc started his cavalry at a walk; and with another horn cry he moved to a trot; another call, and they changed to a canter; and, with one final cry, they galloped full tilt, lances lowered, and charged toward the Serpentines, whose own cruelly barbed spears were lowered as they hurtled toward the men. And with horses belling, and Serpentine steeds hissing, and men yelling and Serpentines shrieking, as lightning detonated the very air they smashed into one another; and spears *thuck*ed into flesh and lances punched through scales; and the air was filled with the death cries of men, and the very last hisses of Serpentines.

While on the main battlefield crossbow quarrels now spitted Trolls and arrows felled Bogles, but then the two sides crashed together, and blood and grume flew wide as swords hacked flesh and cudgels smashed bone and flails ripped through armor and body alike.

And the greater numbers of the throng sought to surround the allies, yet swift warriors moved to interpose their shields and long spears before the flanking enemy.

And the knights charged into the Trolls again and again, and for once the chevaliers outnumbered the monstrous foe. Even so, knights were felled by the terrible beings, and both Laurent and Blaise were wounded in the mêlée, Laurent for the second time.

And standing with Galion at her side, and surrounded by Wolves, Michelle calmly loosed arrow after arrow, felling Bogle after Bogle. . . .

But then the *Sickness* flowed across the combatants, and the men and Fey withdrew, the knights and cavalry fighting a rearguard action, while the bulk of the warriors retreated, taking their wounded with them, but leaving their dead behind.

. . .

Long did the colts of Asphodel course upon the vast sea, while Raseri flew above. Through numerous twilight borders they went, passing from calm to roiling waters, from warm oceans to cold, from a sea as smooth as glass to one raging with storms. And as they ran and flew, the sun rode up into the sky. And somewhere during this passage, Duran fell quite asleep.

And then up ahead they sighted a sheer cliff, and when the racing mounts came to the vertical rise, up the face of the stone they ran, leaping from ledge to ledge, their gait so smooth even sleeping Duran did not waken.

Across a wide plain they sped, and then up the slopes of low mountains the Fairy horses coursed, and they leapt o'er vast chasms hidden by the jagged rocks.

Over the range they passed and through another twilight marge to race across a vast bog, the steeds running so lightly they left not a track therein.

And still the sun rode through the sky, rising toward the zenith.

. . .

Time after time the allies engaged the foe, and time after time they were driven away by the dreadful miasma.

And they retreated and retreated, but at last Auberon turned them up the slopes of the valley, for this was the place where Orbane would cross over to come unto the headwaters of the River of Time.

They fought a battle on the slope itself, attacking from the high ground, and they wrought devastation upon the enemy, yet devastation was also wrought upon them.

Finally, they withdrew to the vale through which the river itself flowed, and they marched down into the dale toward the linn over which Time plunged.

Those in the lead could see in the distance a cascade plummeting down a precipice, and a long, silvery ribbon of water—if indeed it were water and not Time itself—flowing away sunwise. Yet it seemed right at the falls the spill had no origin, either that or it sprang directly from a misty cloud hovering above, the silvery vapor glimmering as of a gleaming within.

"This is it," said Auberon. "Here is where all time originates. And it runs from the future through the present to the past. Where the river ends, none I know has said, though, as you tell me, Princess Camille believes it flows out from Faery to spread over the mortal world. It is also told that the Fates themselves live along the banks of this numinous stream, yet I myself cannot say. You see, we Fey avoid this place, for we would not suffer the ravages of time. We believe that's for mortals to do. Yet here we must make a stand, for Orbane has forced it to be. Would that we could win this day, but I think it's not in the cards to do so."

Regar looked at the falls and the river flowing out beyond, and he said, "Grand-père, Lisane, my own truelove, has read those very cards, and she says the outcome is in doubt, and so she thinks we have a chance."

"As do the Fates," said Blaise, "whose redes have given us hope."

"May their sight be such that they see victory for us," said Auberon.

And there near the precipice of the cascade in the valley of the River of Time, the allies arrayed themselves for one final stand.

. . .

The colts emerged through another bound and came to a fiery land, with the ground arumble and mountains spewing flame, but they dodged and darted through the peril, as Raseri above flew onward.

Past that land, across a great plain they ran, while the sun continued to edge toward the zenith. Another border they breached, and another and another, and Camille had lost all count, as over snow they raced and lakes and ponds and ice and through the streets of towns and cities and within tall, vine-laden trees so closely bunched as to seem impossible to pass, yet the colts somehow managed. And finally they came to a long and wide and vast barren track completely desolate of all life, and along that scar the colts did turn, Raseri above veering that way as well.

. . .

Again and again the throng hammered into the allies and pressed them back and back. But then from the slope on the foe's right flank, a white steed with a pearlescent horn charged into the enemy. And a small brown man with a tiny bow stood on a jumble of boulders and flew wee crookedy missile after crookedy missile into the ranks of the throng. They were Thale the Unicorn and Adragh the Pwca, and high on the slopes above, Lisane winged shafts into the mass. Tisp the Sprite flew overhead, and she called all the Sprites to her, for just as were Lisane and Thale and Adragh, Tisp herself was a First. She gave a command to the Sprites, and they flew into the surround and gathered thorns and burrs and dropped them down on the enemy. Even as they did this, down the slope strode a huge man bearing an enormous bronze battleaxe—'twas Big Jack bearing Lady Bronze; another First had come—and he waded in, swinging Lady Bronze, leaving a bloody swath in his wake. And darting among the Skrikers and Dunters and Long-Armed Wights veered wildcats with foot-tall, leather-clad, tattooed men astride; Lord Kelmont and the Lynx Riders had come with their fatal arrows dealing death, even as more of the Firsts arrived and joined the fight. Yet the throng pushed them back and back, and soon the battle reached the linn, where the knights had gathered to make a stand.

But in that moment there came riding on a lark a tiny Twig Man. "One side, one side," squeaked the inch-tall being, "I will stomp them to death."

"Thank Mithras, 'tis Jotun," cried Auberon, "come at last."

"But how can he be of any significant help?" shouted Laurent.

"Just watch," Auberon replied.

The Twig Man leapt free of the lark, and then he whispered a word. There came a great *whoosh*ing outpush of air, icy cold, as if all the heat, all the power, had been sucked from it. Laurent gasped, for looming up toward the lightning-filled black roiling sky itself stood a giant of a man. Fully two hundred feet or more he towered upward, and he was dressed all in green and had brown hair. The Giant looked down upon the shrieking foe and lifted a foot and stomped. The world seemed to shudder, there at the headwaters of the River of Time, and a hundred or more Goblins were squashed. And he lifted his foot again, and Lynx Riders darted out from the fray as Goblins and Bogles and Trolls fled screaming.

And in the midst of the *Sickness*, Orbane hissed in rage, for he knew the corruption would not affect Jotun, for it would but swirl ankle-high on the Giant. Yet there was a way to stop the colossal being, in fact a way to stop them all—all the Firsts, all the humans, all the Fey—though it meant his great plan would be slowed to a crawl. And he raised his voice and shouted an arcane word, and Jotun and Big Jack and Thale and Adragh and the rest of the Firsts were frozen in place, as were Auberon and Luc and Roél and the remaining allies. All humans, all Fey, all Firsts, all Wolves, as well as all members of the throng, all were frozen in place by Orbane's dread power. And down from the skies drifted Sprites, their wings outstretched in uncontrolled glides, like maple seeds whirling down.

And at the linn the knights and others stood and watched and waited, for they could not move, not even a finger.

And there upon the entire battlefield it was as if all were nought but game pieces upon a board played by the gods, and the whole stood still, waiting for the moves to come. And though the churning black skies above roared with the claps of riven air, still in the brief silences between the cracks of lightning and the booms of thunder, there came to the ear what seemed to be the faint sound of looms weaving.

Long moments passed, and dimly at first but then more clearly, two figures could be seen moving forward through the miasma.

Yet, from above there came a *skreigh!* while at the same time down the slopes of the vale seven white Fairy horses ran. To the linn they galloped, there among the unmoving men and Fey. And Valeray and Saissa, Céleste and Liaze, Camille and Duran and Scruff, and Borel and Alain, all leapt from their mounts, even as Raseri and Rondalo came to land nearby.

"Roél, *chéri*," cried Céleste, as did Liaze call out to Luc, and Borel rushed to Michelle, his love yet surrounded by Wolves, all of them unmoving.

"What is this?" muttered Valeray, as he stepped among the men.

And emerging from the miasma came Orbane, Hradian closely following. "How did they escape?" asked the witch, her hand touching the amulet at her throat, the silver token set with a blue gem, to see if it was still there.

And then she reached for the other token at her throat—

a clay seal on a leather thong—to send these fools back into prison. But in that moment Orbane said, "Acolyte, lend me your power."

"Yes, my lord," she replied, her hand falling away.

Back at the linn, Céleste's eyes widened, and she snatched at her bow, and nocked an arrow, for she had seen the pair. Yet ere she could draw and loose, Orbane, using borrowed power, spoke again the arcane word, and Valeray and the others, including Duran and wee Scruff, were frozen in place, as were Raseri and Rondalo and the colts of Asphodel.

And Orbane, sneering in triumph, strode forward to come unto them, Hradian following after.

Reckoning

Orbane strutted among those trapped at the linn, and he stopped before Auberon and smirked. "Well, Père, tried to stop me again, did you? You fool. Neither you nor your allies nor anyone else can prevent me from taking the throne you so haughtily denied to me, your very own son, your rightful heir. But I will not simply be the new Fey Lord to merely rule Under the Hill, for when I am done I will command not only all of Faery but the whole of the mortal world as well."

Standing motionless beside Auberon, Roél raged and tried with all of his will and heart and spirit and grit to raise his sword and cut down this arrogant being, but the prince could not twitch even the slightest of muscles. Although he could not move, still he could hear, and there came to his ears the faint sound of looms weaving, and of a sudden he realized that this very instant had been foretold, for had not Urd said—?

> " 'Pon the precipice will ye be held,
> As surely as can be,
> Yet can ye but touch the deadly arcane,
> The least shall set ye free."

Roél's mind raced. *Surely this is the precipice of that conundrum as well as the moment of time. Yet did she not also say,*

"If you do not solve this rede, Roél, then all as we now know it to be will come to a horrible end"? And here we are held on the linn where Time begins. But what did she mean, "touch the deadly arcane"?

Orbane widely gestured toward the cascade and the silvery flow beyond, and then back to his pustulant cloud. "See, Papa, what I bring? The corruption, the contagion, the *Sickness*, and with it I will pollute the River of Time. Then will it overflow its banks to run this way and that without reason, and orderly Time, heretofore so tightly confined in Faery, will be free to flow helter-skelter without bound and foster nought but Chaos itself. And as you know, Père, I am not only the Master of the Winds, but the Master of Chaos as well."

Roél now paid no heed to Orbane's crowing, but frantically sought a solution to Urd's rede. *Clearly this is the place and the time, but what is it I am to do? Oh, Mithras, help me understand.*

Orbane stepped to the precipice of the linn, and he cried out, "Now is my time come, for henceforth the whole of the two worlds will be mine to rule."

Roél tried to calm his mind, and even as he did so, the solution came unto him, yet he could not move any part of himself, much less his hand, and so he despaired.

Orbane turned toward the *Sickness*, and he gestured for it to come, yet it moved not. Again Orbane gestured, and his face grimaced and sweat beaded on his forehead with the effort, for he not only had to move the cloud, but he also had to control the black roiling skies, while at the same time holding motionless the allies and Raseri and Rondalo and the other Firsts and Valeray's kith and the colts of Asphodel, as well as his very own throng. And it was at this moment he realized that had he not included his horde in the spell, he would have more than enough power to move the contagion. Yet he could not release the throng without releasing the others. And Luc and Roél and

Blaise and Laurent and all the other knights at the linn had weapons in hand. And even though Orbane commanded the pustulation to come, the bilious cloud neither moved forward nor backward nor sideways.

"Acolyte, I need more of your power."

"My lord, without Crapaud, I have no more to give."

Hissing in ire, Orbane slightly relaxed his hold as well as his link to Hradian to focus a bit more of his own power into fetching the *Sickness*, and oh so slowly the corruption began to drift toward the linn.

Roél, yet straining to control his hand found he could now move a single digit, though barely. *Will it be enough?*

Forward flowed the cloud even as downward inched the index finger on Roél's right hand.

Orbane's face twisted with the effort of trying to hasten the pollution unto the linn.

Down crept Roél's finger, over the cross guard of his sword. . . .

"Ha!" said Orbane, relaxing, for now the pustulation drifted under its own power.

. . . and that was the moment Roél managed to touch the deadly arcane—the silver-flashed rune-marked blade of Coeur d'Acier, a steel sword in the heart of Faery in the hand of a spellbound man. And Roél felt the blade grow warm, yet he despaired, for he still could not move, and it seemed all were yet frozen in place. But then he heard wee Scruff peep. *The sparrow speaks! Perhaps he has been set free, yet how can he possibly be of any—*

Scruff struggled out from Camille's shoulder pocket, and he flew into Hradian's face, chirping angrily and clawing and pecking, and she fell back in startlement—

—and the rune-weakened link between wizard and witch was completely broken—

—Raseri roared—

376 / Dennis L. McKiernan

—darkness swept over Alain—

—Liaze and Valeray and Borel drew long-knives—

—Céleste pulled her nocked arrow to the full—

—Saissa scooped up Duran—

—and Camille shoved Orbane in the back, the wizard to plummet screaming down the cascade and plunge into the River of Time.

And Roél staggered, as if a grip of powers warring through him had suddenly been released, and Coeur d'Aciere instantly cooled to his touch.

Hradian frantically reached for the clay amulet at her throat, the last of the Seals of Orbane, but Scruff stabbed at her eyes, and the Bear stepped forth from the darkness and, with a terrible roar and a swipe of a paw, eviscerated the witch. A look of astonishment crossed her face, and then she fell dead. Yet tiny Scruff kept pecking away and did not stop until he had pierced her eyes.

And down in the current of the River of Time, Orbane screamed and began to rapidly age, his hair falling out, his eyes becoming dim, as the ravages of Time came upon him.

The throng was freed, yet so were the allies, and Jotun began to stomp. Raseri took to the air, his fire devastating, and Big Jack with Lady Bronze dealt death. Borel and Michelle and the Wolves entered the fray with fangs and sword and arrows.

And Roél and Luc and Blaise and Laurent and the other knights mounted horses and charged in with lance and sword, while lightning split the black skies above, and the heavens roared with rage.

And in Time's flow Orbane shrieked, "Mother, help me!" And the air on one bank shimmered as of a silver mirror, and stepping through the glisten came Gloriana.

Orbane reached out his arms toward her. "Aid me, Mother." Yet Gloriana wrung her hands and cried out in torment, for she could do nothing, her own unbreakable geas preventing her from doing ought. And she stood on the shore and wept, as upon the linn did Auberon weep.

And seemingly from nowhere and striding across the vale toward the river and Orbane came the huge man they called the Reaper, and he held in his hands his scythe. "My lord, I will come when the time is right," he had told Luc, and now the Reaper was here. On he strode, toward the bank opposite from Gloriana, and he paused not at the edge of the flow but walked out upon it instead.

In that moment, Orbane began chanting, and slowly the aging of his face and form began to reverse.

But the Reaper cast his hood over his own head, and with every pace he took, he changed: his coarse-spun cloak turning dark and darker and finally to black. The flesh on his hands became withered, and then his fingers and the forearms showing from his sleeves turned skeletal, and his face, what could be seen of it, became skull-like.

Along the shore, Gloriana raged at the Reaper, yet just as Death held no power over her, she was equally ineffective in dealing with mortality.

But Orbane now saw the Reaper coming, and he began canting a faster chant, yet with one sweep of his scythe, the Reaper took off Orbane's head . . . and something dark and wispy was caught on the blade, and it struggled as if to get free yet could not, and the grim being and his scythe and mayhap a black soul then vanished altogether. And in the stream Orbane's head and body rapidly decayed and fell into dust and were swept away in the currents of Time.

Seal

Yet the *Sickness* continued to drift toward the linn, and it drove away allies and Firsts alike, all but Jotun and Raseri, the Dragon with Rondalo astride, for Raseri flew well above the miasma, and the contagion only swirled about Jotun's feet. They continued to go after the throng now hiding in the putrescence, with Jotun stomping and Raseri breathing fire and Rondalo loosing arrows against the dim shapes within.

At the cascade, with Scruff flying about and chirping frantically, the Bear reared up and roared and looked about for more enemies to slay. But Camille cried, "Alain! Alain! We must flee the precipice; Orbane's *Sickness* yet comes."

The Bear swung 'round toward Camille. "Alain!" she called again, and a dark shimmering came over the Bear, and from the shadow the prince emerged.

"What?" he asked, even as Camille pulled at him to get him out of the path of the contagion.

"The *Sickness* comes. We must away." Camille pointed to those now fleeing up the slopes of the vale, some running, others riding.

"Duran?" asked Alain, looking frantically about.

"Gone with Saissa and Valeray," said Camille, "and you and I must ride." She gestured at two of the colts of Asphodel, both of whom waited nigh at hand.

The contagion continued its drift.

Camille called Scruff to her, and then she and Alain started to mount, but of a sudden, Alain called, "Wait!"

He stepped back to Hradian's corpse, and there he sought to retrieve Luc's amulet, yet its protection stung him, for only the rightful heirs or those to whom it was freely given could safely touch the gem-set silver talisman. But then Alain espied the clay amulet on its leather thong about Hradian's neck, and he realized it was one of the Seals of Orbane.

Quickly he snapped the thong and snatched up the clay token and called out, "Camille, ride. I will come, yet I think I have the means to deal with the corruption."

"What is it?"

"A Seal of Orbane."

"But it can only lay curses and do harm to others," cried Camille.

And now the fringes of the putrescence came upon the pair, and a wave of queasiness swept through them.

But still Alain persevered. *How to curse the cloud? Wind? Non, for then it would simply blow elsewhere and harm others. Rain? Non, for then it would but run off into the River of Time and pollute it still. What of Mithra's light? Perhaps there's a chance.*

Coughing, nauseated, for neither he nor Camille had been protected by the Fey Lord's spell, Alain gagged, and yet he managed to lift the seal toward the darkness above, and as he called out, "I curse the *Sickness* to suffer the light of the sun," he broke the clay amulet in two.

A rift in the raging sky opened, and a beam shone down upon him, and then the heavens parted, the black skies were riven open, and the lightning vanished, taking with it the roar of thunder as all the darkness fled. And the full of the vale was bathed in the bright light of the midday sun.

There came a thin wail from the *Sickness* as the corrup-

tion boiled away in the clean rays of light. And the wail became a scream, and the scream a roar, as of a raging forest fire,
yet no heat was emitted as the radiance utterly destroyed the
contagion. And then the roar suddenly dropped to a whisper
and then to nought as the miasma vanished. The throng was
again exposed, and once more the Firsts and the allies rushed
into battle, and Buzzer, now awake in the sunlight, joined the
fray, her bumblebee stings assisting Flic in stabbing whatever
enemy Regar fought. The Bear and Big Jack fought side by side,
and they, along with Jotun and Raseri and the four deadly horsemen, were particularly devastating, and soon the Goblins and
Bogles and Trolls were no more, but for a smattering that managed somehow to escape the field.

Under bright skies, Luc came riding back to the linn, and
he dismounted and took up the amulet that was rightfully his
from Hradian's eviscerated corpse.

And Liaze came unto Luc, and they stood on the precipice
hand in hand and looked out over the River of Time, and in the
distance along the shore they saw Auberon embracing Gloriana, the Fairy King and Queen holding one another and weeping, as the River of Time flowed on.

58

Restoration

The Fey Lord sounded his silver horn, and Asphodel trotted down from the linn to the banks of the River of Time. Auberon mounted, and he took Gloriana up on the Fairy horse before him, and they rode over the crest to an adjoining vale and fared starwise, and then turned back toward the valley in which the arcane river flowed, and they came in among the allies. And when Liaze asked Luc why the Fairy king and his queen hadn't ridden directly up from where they had been standing, Luc replied, "Auberon told us that one cannot go against the flow of time, hence he had to leave its presence to return to the fount."

Gloriana then passed among the wounded, and lo! with nought but a simple touch she healed each and everyone entirely of cuts and broken bones and bruises and such and of the effects of the *Sickness*, for her powers in this regard were remarkable. Yet she could do nought for the slain—they had passed beyond her ability to restore.

And Jotun, with his great wide hands, collected the allied dead. Many were the pyres, and Camille and Alain and Rondalo sang their souls to the stars, while comrades and warriors wept. Having announced their intent to wed, Regar and Lisane stood with Auberon and Gloriana during these rites. And though Gloriana did not wholly accept Regar into her heart, still she came to a polite but cold truce with the bastard prince.

Jotun then collected the slain of the throng—Hradian one of these—and all were burned without ceremony, Raseri providing the flame.

Allies looked on with mixed emotions as the corpse of the witch was consumed by fire, for it was she who was responsible for setting Orbane free. The humans and the Firsts watched with grim satisfaction, whereas the Fairies themselves looked on in misery, for had she not acted, Orbane would yet be alive, and they all remembered him as a beautiful child who had somehow turned to iniquity.

Yet Camille came unto the Fey Lord and his queen, and she spoke of the Keltoi and their silver tongues, bards who caught the ear of the gods themselves, and they in turn made Faery manifest. Camille posited that one of these bards had told of a Fairy child named Orbane and the things that came of that. Both Auberon and Gloriana took small solace in Camille's supposition, yet mayhap in time it would give them comfort to think that it was nought they had done to turn their only child toward wickedness.

And after the fires had burned away, all rested for two days, for the campaign had been hard, and humans and Fey were weary. It was during this time, as Michelle lay sleeping, Slate looked at her and then at Borel, sitting and watching the sunrise, and Slate said: *Master's bitch cub-smart. Walk stealthy. Talk good True-People-speak.*

Borel cocked his head to one side: *What?*

Slate: *Master's bitch talk good True-People-speak.*

Blue-eye: *Walk stealthy.*

Dark: *Run fast.*

Render: *Cub-smart. Learn fast.*

Shank: *Talk almost good master.*

Loll: *Bitch lead fight.*

Trot: *Pack protect.*

The next thing Michelle knew, Borel had picked her up and

was whirling her about and laughing, and then he stopped and kissed her gently. She knew not what caused this outburst of joy but she did not question it; instead, she reveled in his glee and returned his kiss with passion.

The next day each faction of the allies set out for their various homelands: the Fairy army heading for The Halls Under the Hills; the Firsts withdrawing to go to their individual lieus, Jotun winging away on a lark as a Twig Man, heading for his mountain pass; various human brigades, with Sprites leading them, faring for their own domains; and Valeray and his family starting for the Forests of the Seasons, with Regar and Lisane accompanying them, for Saissa had asked them to come.

Ere they set out, Michelle kissed her sire, Duke Roulan, and promised to come unto Roulan Vale soon. And the duke and King Valeray embraced one another, for they were thieving comrades of old. Luc clasped Léon and said that he and Liaze would be at the Blue Château in the Lake of the Rose ere the summer came 'round again. And Auberon hugged Regar and asked him to visit soon, for there was much he would tell his grandson. Auberon also told Valeray and his family to keep the colts of Asphodel until they reached their goals, and then to simply whisper *"pays natal"* in their ears and turn them loose, and they would find their way home. Still more fond farewells were passed among those there, and then all parted their ways. And so, among bugle cries and calls of "farewell" and "adieu" and those of "Mithras go with you," the allies parted and rode away on separate tracks.

. . .

Some six moons later, Valeray's family sat before the great fireplace at the Castle of Seasons. A chill was in the air, for early spring was on the land, and in the demesne of Le Coeur de les Saisons, as the name suggests, the seasons followed their natural courses, unlike in the immediately adjoining domains, forever locked in spring, summer, autumn, and winter.

And they mused over all that had occurred in the conflict with Orbane, for there were yet questions unresolved.

"We saw the Reaper under his oak on our way here," said Liaze.

"Moissonneur?" asked Valeray.

"Oui."

"Oh, my," said Camille, shivering, "I think I'll never look upon him quite the same way."

"I think none of us will, my dear," said Saissa.

"What did he look like?" asked Céleste, her eyes wide with remembered vision.

"His usual," replied Liaze, "a big redheaded man in homespun garb with a great scythe across his knees."

"What did he have to say for himself?" asked Borel.

"Just that Faery is the one place he can come and simply be himself," said Luc.

"Ah . . ." said Valeray, and they all fell to silence, each lost in his own thoughts, and the fire in the great hearth crackled and popped and was the only sound heard.

Finally, Valeray said, "I still do not understand how it was that Duran was able to set us free, for he had no special amulet, nor did he have any—"

"We can answer that," came a voice, amid the sound of looms weaving. And of a sudden the Three Sisters stood before the family. Urd cackled and turned to warm her hands before the blaze, while both Skuld and Verdandi faced the gathering.

Valeray and the men got to their feet and bowed, and Saissa and the ladies stood and curtseyed. Verdandi waved them back to their seats, and Skuld looked at Camille and said, "Your son Duran could get out because he yet has that which each of you has lost"—Skuld fixed Valeray with a darting glance—"some more than others." She turned back to Camille. "Oh, Duran will lose it, too, yet at this time of his life he is truly an innocent, hence the Castle of Shadows could not contain him. You see, it is the lack of innocence that confines one therein and makes escape impossible, unless an innocent leads you out. And when Duran grasped your hand, he could set you free. Lack of innocence kept Orbane imprisoned for many long seasons; and none could come and rescue him, for he had no one in his life who was blameless—certainly not him nor any of his acolytes."

"What of my amulet?" asked Luc. "It allowed a wicked person to lead Orbane to freedom."

"Your amulet, Prince Luc, confers an aura of innocence upon the wearer, but only to the semisentient Castle of Shadows does it seem so, for those who crafted the castle foresaw that one day such might be needed, though they didn't anticipate someone as vile as Hradian would let an even more wicked person out. Regardless, that's how Hradian set Orbane free."

"Oh my," said Camille, "and here, Lady Urd, I thought you might have meant Duran when you said in your rede 'the least shall set you free,' and at the time I thought it applied to that prison. But now I know it to have been meant for the linn at the River of Time and applied to my Scruff." She turned and looked at the wee bird perched on a stand at her side.

As Urd cackled, Skuld said, "*Your* Scruff, Camille? Do you forget who gave you the sparrow?"

"Oh, non, Lady Skuld. It was you in your guise of Lady Sorciére who did so."

Skuld nodded, as if to say, *Just so.*

Roél smiled and looked at Lady Doom.

"Well, young man," snapped Urd, "what have you to say for yourself, grinning at me like a village idiot sitting on a welcoming wall?"

Roél barked a short laugh and said, "It's just that when I was trying to resolve your rede, I thought that, in addition to Duran, Flic or Fleurette or even Buzzer could have been the 'least' who would set us free. It never occurred to me it might be Scruff, a sparrow."

The wee bird chirped somewhat querulously and cocked an eye toward Roél.

"Oh, Scruff, I did not mean to ruffle your feathers," said Roél, and then he laughed.

"Scruff is the reason we are here," said Verdandi.

"Scruff?" asked Camille, alarm in her voice. Tears came into Camille's eyes. "You said one day you would come to reclaim him."

"Oui," said Skuld. "You see, he was cursed by the Fairy Queen, and to break the curse he first had to perform three deeds of heroism ere he could be set free."

"Scruff is cursed?" blurted Céleste.

"Did you not hear what my older sister said?" snapped Urd. "Perhaps you need to clean out your ears."

"Oh, Madam," said Céleste, abashed, "I was just surprised."

"Heh!" cackled Urd, grinning a toothless smile.

"Three heroic deeds?" asked Camille.

"Oui," said Skuld. "Can you tell me what they were?"

Camille thought back. "He did fly for aid during the battle with Olot at the castle on Troll Island."

Skuld nodded, and Verdandi said, "Now called L'Île de Camille."

"Too, he is the one who caused Te'efoon and her daughter Dre'ela to plummet to their deaths during that same battle."

Skuld and Verdandi nodded

"The third one, of course, is when he flew into the face of Hradian and somehow set us free."

"Oui," said Skuld. "He broke the link between Hradian and Orbane, and that set some of you free."

"But, my lady," said Liaze, "it has been six moons since he accomplished the third and last deed; why have you waited so long to come and remove the curse?"

"Heh!" snapped Urd. "Such daring, or mayhap impudence. Question us, would ye?"

"Lady Urd, I meant no disrespect, but I do want to know."

"Because it is now spring," said Skuld, "and time for 'Scruff,' as you name him, to accomplish one more deed."

"And that would be . . . ?" asked Alain.

"The whole family is impudent," said Urd. "Heh! I like that."

"Orbane's *Sickness* left desolation in its wake," said Verdandi. "It is an abomination, a scar on the world. 'Scruff' will heal that."

"Scruff? My sparrow? Or rather, your sparrow, Lady Skuld," said Camille. "How can a wee bird do such a thing?"

Skuld said, "Take him up and cast him into the fire."

What? all blurted at once.

"They're all impudent, and hard of hearing," said Urd.

"You must cast him onto the fire," repeated Skuld.

Camille broke into tears and said, "I cannot."

"But you must, I have seen it."

Camille stood and stepped to Scruff's perch and, sobbing, managed to say, "Lady Skuld, you yourself told me the future is not fixed, that great deeds can change what you have seen. And Scruff has performed great deeds, hence his future must be changed. Surely we do not need to burn this wee bird." Camille's tears then came without stopping, and Alain embraced her, and the family gathered 'round and grimly faced the Fates themselves.

Urd looked on, her own black eyes glistening, as of tears unshed.

"But you must," said Skuld. "I have woven it into the Tapestry of Time."

"And I will weave it into present events," said Verdandi.

"But I will not bind it therein," said Urd, a tear streaking down one withered cheek.

"Oh, Urd," said Skuld, "if you do not, then—"

"Silence!" cried Verdandi. "We cannot reveal what will happen should an event remain unbound."

In that moment, Scruff cocked his head and looked at Camille and quietly peeped. Then he hopped into her hand and peeped again.

Camille, weeping, stepped to the fire, but she could not bring herself to cast the wee bird into the flames. Instead she raised him to her lips and kissed him. Scruff pecked her on the cheek, and then swiftly took to wing and arrowed into the blaze. The fire caught at him and roared up, and Scruff burst into flames and blazed brightly and fell into the furious conflagration. Camille turned away, for she could not face the death of her companion of these many seasons.

Alain, Borel, Roél, and Luc all clenched fists and glared at the Three Sisters, and Valeray spat an oath.

Of a sudden the fire died, as if all fuel had been spent, and in that moment, up from the glowing coals, a splendid bird arose. Large as an eagle it was, with scarlet and gold plumage, and it voiced a melodious cry. Saissa gasped, and Camille whirled around and there she saw a Phoenix.

"Oh, Scruff," Camille cried, "is it you, is it truly you?"

And the Phoenix bowed as if to say, *Oui, Camille, I am truly your Scruff.* Then the Phoenix stepped to Camille and permitted her to do what none other had been allowed: to touch him and stroke the velvety feathers upon his crown just as she had often stroked those of a wee sparrow.

"You will have to let him go," said Verdandi, "for we have much for him to do."

"Let him go?" said Camille. "Oh, Lady Verdandi, you misunderstand me. Scruff has always been free to go, for I would not imprison him whatsoever, in a cage or a manor or ought else. It has always been his choice as to stay or leave; he can come and go as he pleases."

"I imagine you will see him again," said Verdandi.

"I can guarantee it," said Skuld, "for, as I have oft said, I have seen it in the currents of Time."

Urd cackled and squinted at the men. "It seems you five were about to assail the three of us. Heh! I said you were impudent, but I didn't think you foolish."

With Urd cackling, the sound of looms swelled, and the Three Sisters vanished, taking the Phoenix with them.

Their hearts yet pounding, their spirits soaring from the wonder of it all, the family once again settled, yet a look of puzzlement came upon Michelle's face.

"What is it, chérie?" asked Borel.

"I was just wondering: what is it Scruff did, the Phoenix, I mean, that caused Gloriana to curse him?"

They looked at one another and shrugged, for none knew the answer. And then Roél said, "I wonder if Coeur d'Acier would have done us any good had we indeed taken on the Fates."

Borel burst out laughing, and soon the entire family joined him . . . that is, until Valeray asked, "Anyone for échecs?"

59

Renewal

Over the lands the *Sickness* had despoiled a wondrous bird flew and sang, and where he passed the world was healed, the scar being replaced by new growth and fertility. The animals who had succumbed he could not restore, yet others of their kind were fecund and soon offspring would once again run among the trees and undergrowth and fly through the air and fill the streams, for such is the character of nature.

One of the lands he flew over was a small desolate demesne, where lived a rock creature named Caillou, who was mayhap an entire mountain of stone. And when the Phoenix had sailed on, Caillou gave a great shout of joy, and rocks cascaded down, for at last the land Orbane and his five acolytes had destroyed in a dreadful experiment was once again whole and fertile.

And elsewhere in Faery and a season later, at a mound where sat a great dolmen, Regar and Lisane were wed, and in attendance were many, including Raseri the Dragon and Rondalo the Elf and Chemine, Rondalo's mother, and many of the other Firsts, a tiny Twig Man among them. Too, in the number present were all the princes and princesses of the Forest of the Seasons, and King Valeray and Queen Saissa, and Duke Roulan, and Vicomte Chevell and his wife and newborn child, Avélaine and Amélie. Also, Sieur Émile and Lady Simone and their sons Sieurs Laurent and Blaise attended, as well as Flic and Fleurette and Buzzer.

Regar's mother, Mirabelle, had come from the Wyldwood for the wedding, but Regar's grandmother, Alisette, had stayed away, saying, "I am yet in love with Auberon, and perhaps he is yet in love with me. It would tear my heart out to see him again. What it might do to him, I cannot say. And Gloriana? Well, 'tis better I stay away."

As for Gloriana, she seemed softer, more placid, since the death of her only son. A gentle sadness had settled over her, as if a great burden had been lifted. And she had come to see that neither Regar nor Mirabelle could be held responsible for the straying of Auberon. Even so, she was merely cordial to Mirabelle, but she did bless the newlywed pair.

As to what the Phoenix had done to cause Gloriana to curse the magnificent bird, she did not volunteer, nor did anyone dare to ask.

Both the wedding and the reception after were held outside in the open air, for none present wished time to hasten by if they were foolish enough to dine in the chambers below.

But then who's to say what might have happened had they eaten Fairy food and drunk Fairy wine in the Fey Lord's Halls Under the Hill? Perhaps nought whatsoever; but then again . . .

Fini

In a distant swamp somewhere in Faery, a huge bloated toad waddled to the edge of the flet and fell into the turgid water, and, with ungainly kicks, finally managed to slip under the slime-laden surface. But just ere doing so, he emitted a monstrous belching croak, announcing to each and every thing within considerable hearing that—great bulging eyes, long sticky tongue, and beautiful warts and all—Crapaud was free at last.

"Did they all live happily ever after?"

"Perhaps, yet then again perhaps not,
for who knows what next the Keltoi will tell?"

Afterword

Thus ends the fifth and final story in this series of Faery tales. Perhaps I shall return to this twilit land some day and travel once more through the shadowlight borders. What I might find there is unsure at best, but it is certain to be wondrous.

Before I go, I want to thank Philip I of Macedon for creating the Macedonian phalanx by using *sarissae*—counterbalanced pikes about eighteen feet long. I also thank his son Alexander the Great for his tactics in the Battle of Issus. In this story I used, in modified form, both that phalanx and those tactics in the Battle at the Swamp.

Too, I would thank Admiral Lord Nelson, whose brilliant but risky naval tactics in the Battle of Trafalgar I used, though again in modified form, in the sea battle of Vicomte Chevell and King Avélar's fleet against the corsairs of Brados Isle.

In any event I am ready to leave. But ere I vanish, some might ask: What of Faery? What has happened to it? Where is it now? Well, I assure you it still exists, side by side with the mortal world. It is still a place where curses are laid and glamours yet disguise, where red-sailed corsairs ply the seas, and Sirens sit on rocks and comb their hair and sing. And Pixies and Nixies and Hobs and Giants and other such still roam and tweak and hide in streams and practice other such tricky arts.

One can get there in the blink of an eye if one so desires; all it takes is imagination—one simply must let it soar.

What's that? How does one *physically* get there? Well, now, that's a bit more difficult, yet I am certain it can be done, though I myself have not quite managed to do so. Still, there *must* be portals that open in the silvery shadowlight of dusk and dawn. After all, it *used* to be thus, or so it is I've been told, hence surely it must be true. I think we merely need to keep searching to find that magical realm. After all, how could such a place *not* be?

—*Dennis L. McKiernan*
Tucson, Arizona, 2007

About the Author

I have spent a great deal of my life looking through twilights and dawns seeking—what? Ah yes, I remember—seeking signs of wonder, searching for pixies and fairies and other such, looking in tree hollows and under snow-laden bushes and behind waterfalls and across wooded, moonlit dells. I did not outgrow that curiosity, that search for the edge of Faery when I outgrew childhood—not when I was in the U.S. Air Force during the Korean War, nor in college, nor in graduate school, nor in the thirty-one years I spent in Research and Development at Bell Telephone Laboratories as an engineer and manager on ballistic missile defense systems and then telephone systems and in think-tank activities. In fact I am still at it, still searching for glimmers and glimpses of wonder in the twilights and the dawns. I am abetted in this curious behavior by Martha Lee, my helpmate, lover, and, as of this writing, my wife of over fifty years.